ACCLAIM FOR

MW00620732

WHOSE NAMES ARE UNKNOWN

Finalist, Pen USA Literary Award, 2005

"Originally written and slated for publication in 1939, this long-forgotten masterpiece was shelved by Random House when *The Grapes of Wrath* met with wide acclaim. Babb, a native of Oklahoma's arid panhandle and a volunteer with the Farm Security Administration in California, brings an insider's knowledge and immediacy to this authentically compelling narrative. A slightly less political, more female-oriented, companion piece to *The Grapes of Wrath*."—*Booklist*

"...those who have read both books say Babb's novel is a better read for today's market than *The Grapes of Wrath*—leaner, faster paced and full of details that give a more insightful look at a tragic time in American history."—Mike Conklin, *Chicago Tribune*

"One of the best novels I have ever read about the Oklahoma Panhandle farmers during the 1930s....quite possibly as good as, perhaps better than, *The Grapes of Wrath*."—*Tulsa World*

"With characters less contrived than Steinbeck's, Babb has given us a sad and rugged novel about a sad and rugged people, the Okies. Each writer, Steinbeck and Babb, deserves to be read. The publication of *Whose Names Are Unknown* rights a decades old literary wrong."—*Salt Lake Tribune*

"Babb is a skillful artist who identified wholeheartedly with the ordeal of the dispossessed during the 1930s. The recovery of her novel is a miraculous gift that will play an important part in future reconsiderations of mid-century U.S. literature."—Alan M. Wald, author of *Exiles from a Future Time*

AN OWL ON EVERY POST

New Edition with Foreword by William Kennedy, 2013

"An unsung masterpiece—I was completely blown away. It offers an unforgettable picture of life as seen through the eyes of a sensitive, courageous young girl growing up on the drought-ravaged Great Plains."—Arnold Rampersad

"The lyricism of Sanora Babb's writing defines the luminous and transcendent landscape of this extraordinary memoir. ... On a par stylistically and thematically with Willa Cather's My Antonia, this is a classic that deserves to be rediscovered and cherished for years to come."—Linda P. Miller

"Sanora Babb, with quiet humor, and a great all-encompassing love for a land and her people, has created a warm hearth indeed in this book. I hold my hands out to it to be warmed."—Ray Bradbury

"Thought-provoking description of the mystery, wonder and poetry of growing up in a pioneering environment. A vivid restoration of an important phase of American history."—Ralph Ellison

"Babb's engaging memoir recalls a childhood spent on the harsh and wild Colorado frontier during the early 1900s."—*Publishers Weekly*

"Masterly. Hers is a small song, and not grand opera. But hearing it is a significant and salutary experience."—*London Times*

"The author has achieved a small miracle with this book for she has turned hunger, poverty, loneliness and depression into incomparable beauty by the magic of her writing."—*Pretoria News* (South Africa)

"Style and wit are rare and precious, and difficult to bring alive in autobiography. Sanora Babb's *An Owl on Every Post* combines these qualities and reading it is a significant experience."—*Advertiser* (Australia)

ON THE DIRTY PLATE TRAIL:
Remembering the Dust Bowl Refugee Camps
Edited with Introduction by Douglas Wixson

Finalist, National Council on Public History Book Award, 2008

"[Babb's] field notes, journalistic reports, and short stories, drawn mainly from her experiences at the FSA camps, along with photographs taken by her sister, Dorothy Babb, make up the core of the book. These photographs and the journalistic pieces, especially, are real gems. Sanora wrote empathetically yet unsentimentally about the farm workers' plight...Dorothy's pictures capture the lives of the workers with a directness that, unlike the more famous photographs by Dorothea Lange and Russell Lee, never seems designed to manipulate the viewer."—*The Chronicles of Oklahoma*

CRY OF THE TINAMOU

"Sanora Babb is a writer of great skill and humanity. A spirit of wise humor and compassion invests her stories, which deal with human struggle and endurance. . . .[She is] a clear-eyed observer of human behavior, a lyric poet of great sensitivity, and a gentle satirist of human folly. . . . Grounded firmly in place and social circumstance, her writing speaks to timeless concerns. Babb is a consummate artist of the short-story form."—Douglas Wixson, author of *Worker-Writer in America*

THE LOST
TRAVELER

SANORA BABB

Introduction by Douglas Wixson

THE LOST TRAVELER

MUSE INK PRESS

© 1958 by Sanora Babb. Originally published by Reynal & Company. UNM Press edition published 1995 by arrangement with the author. Introduction © 1995 by the University of New Mexico Press. All rights reserved. Published 2013 with permission from UNM Press. For information write Muse Ink Press, 1465 E. Putnam Avenue, Suite 529, Old Greenwich, Connecticut 06870.

The poem "Aspiration" is by Dorothy Babb.

Library of Congress Cataloging-in-Publication Data for the Print Edition
Babb, Sanora.
The lost traveler / Sanora Babb ; introduction by Douglas Wixson.
p. cm.
ISBN 0-8263-1568-2 (pa)
1. Depressions—Kansas—History—20th century—Fiction.
I. Title.
PS3552.A17L67 1995
813'. 54—dc20
95-7569 CIP

Printed in the United States of America

ISBN 978-0-9859915-1-7

www.sanorababb.com

TO

My Mother
and
My Father

INTRODUCTION

In the little world in which children have their existence,
whosoever brings them up, there is nothing so finely
perceived and so finely felt, as injustice.

—Charles Dickens, *Great Expectations*

WHEN SANORA Babb wrote her earliest essay, "How to Handle Men," she doubtlessly had her father in mind. At age eleven she had discovered a topic, family relationships, that furnished literary material for a long and distinguished life of writing. She had made it her purpose very early on to "figure out what had really happened to them all," even if it took a lifetime to do it.[1] First published in 1958, when Babb was fifty-one, *The Lost Traveler* returns to the essay's proposal, restating it in a semi-autobiographical narrative portraying family relationships in the form of a *roman d'initiation*.[2] It is a literary work of verve and intelligence that submits painful personal recollection to fair-minded scrutiny without sacrificing the youthful energy and emotional power of the source material. Babb's narrative broadens gender questions posed by an eleven-year old daughter into a novelized inquiry of kinship roles and family commitments.

Product of a long apprenticeship in the craft of writing, *The Lost Traveler* is an empathetic act of literary vindication by means of which the daughter-author (Babb) reaches a mature understanding of the difficult circumstances that led her parents to their condemnable actions long ago. The text's complex and balanced accounting penetrates the dark recesses of relationships that invisible family loyalties often obscure.[3] *The Lost Traveler* has lost nothing of its power and relevance in the intervening years since its original publication. Babb's novel offers a model of transparent clarity and simplicity, a counterexample to modernist skepticism regarding the communicability of language.

The title is drawn from the poem, "For the Sexes: The Gates of Paradise," in William Blake's "Prophetic Books." The concluding line of the poem reads: "The lost Traveller's Dream under the Hill." The two following passages likewise are relevant, underscoring principal themes of Babb's novel:

> *Mutual Forgiveness of each Vice,*
> *Such are the Gates of Paradise.*

> *Wife, Sister, Daughter, to the Tomb,*
> *Weaving to Dreams the Sexual strife*
> *And weeping over the Web of Life.*[4]

The first theme has to do with the redemptive power of language. The second has to do with the power of family loyalties, the invisible dimensions of commitment, devotion, and loyalty that figure most importantly in the accounting system of family relations, a point I shall return to presently.[5] In this, her first published novel, Babb uses kinship as structural framework to disclose and confirm personal identity within the network of family relationships. In doing so she avoids the self-absorbed tendencies of confessional literature, the laying bare of family secrets for their sensational value; nor does she yield to sentimentality or self-pity. The harsh circumstances of her early years are met with resolve, resilience, and humor. The tone is wondering and amused; memory, observation, and invention mix in nearly equal proportions. The lyrical, sometimes over-written style of her early short stories is pared down into a crisper, "simpler," more direct style—a "deceptively simple" style, wrote a reviewer of *The Lost Traveler*. It is an accomplishment involving painstaking revision. Seven times Babb revised the manuscript, submitting it to the critical eye of her Random House editor, Saxe Cummings. *Ars longa, vita brevis.*

Sanora Babb knew very early in her life that she wanted to write. The conditions for success could scarcely have been less favorable. Her father, Walter Babb, a baker when small-town bakeries were dying out, played semi-professional baseball in Kansas City and gambled. The Babbs moved restlessly from the hardscrabble communities of Redrock and Forgan, Oklahoma to a dugout home in eastern Colorado's drylands, and after several more moves, to Garden City, Kansas, the setting of this novel. Babb possessed the wisdom and heart to forge from early hardship and penury a compassion for others and an affectionate, devout curiosity towards a perplexing but beautiful nature. A sense of mystery and wonder coupled with shrewd, open-eyed observation, I believe, best characterizes her writing. Like William Blake, she is a deeply sacramental writer without a formal religious creed.

The sense of wonder and amusement obviously derive from an uncommon personal sensibility; in practical ways journalism trained her powers of observation. Babb was sixteen when the *Garden City Herald* hired her to perform office tasks. The editor assigned her to write a column on cooking, an area in which she had little experience. In desperation she reprinted magazine recipes. Experience served her better in the next assignment which was to interview farmers. A farm magazine called *Opportunity* published her articles. Determined to become a writer, Babb read hungrily the pocket-sized Little Blue Book editions of literary classics and history published by E. Haldeman-Julius in Girard, Kansas, on the press that had belonged to J. A. Wayland's famous Socialist newspaper, *Appeal to Reason*. Thousands of Little Blue Book titles were available by mail and in drugstores at five cents a copy. She and her sister Dorothy were eager patrons of the Garden City library, purchasing their own books from a Chicago mail-order distributor. Writers like Jack Conroy, Meridel Le Sueur, Babb, and other isolated midwesterners shared a virtual reading room together as youths in widely scattered towns and farms. Their interests merged—in literature, writing, and politics—despite their isolation. They knew one another, in most cases, only through letters.

One of Babb's earliest literary publications, a poem entitled, "To L——," appeared in Ben Hagglund's little magazine *Northern Light* in 1927. Hagglund published his magazine on an ancient hand-set press, earning his living fashioning brooms in his basement and as a casual harvest-hand. Through publication in little magazines with titles like *Northern Light, Morada, Pegasus, Prism, Haldeman-Julius Quarterly,* and magazines of wide circulation like H. L. Mencken's *American Mercury,* the midwestern literary radicals found their way into print despite their isolation and independence of literary cliques and institutions. The Depression spawned little magazines throughout the mid-west; most died after several issues. Babb's first short story appeared in José Garcia Villa's magazine *Clay* in 1932, edited in Albuquerque, New Mexico. Villa purported to "present only honest writing: works of sincerity and truth. It has no use for the machine-made, formula story."[6] *The Anvil,* edited by Jack Conroy in Moberly, Missouri, was successful in discovering and publishing young writers. Babb's short story, "Dry Summer," appeared there in 1934. The publication gave Sanora a needed boost; many years later she still recalled with fondness Conroy's generous encouragement.[7]

The Depression had a galvanizing effect on Babb and other young contributors to the little magazines. "There is a vast piece of the USA," Babb remembered, "between New York and the West Coast that still has not had its due in our literature, especially in that period, which for all the terrible suffering of people then, was a rich source for artists. I remember the high awareness (of others) in the air then; we were shaken out of our private lives."[8] The cultural movement associated with the political left made space in widely-circulated magazines like *New Masses* for literary radicals. New magazines pushed up through midwestern soil in Davenport, Iowa *(The Left)*, Rock Island, Illinois (*The New Quarterly*), Des Moines (*Hinterland*), Mena, Arkansas (*Windsor Quarterly*), and elsewhere. An active participant of the little magazine circuit of the early 1930s, Sanora Babb drew upon contemporary social reality and the responses of those who experienced the Great Depression. Some of her writing appeared in the form of reportages on mine strikes, dams, and labor theater in *The Daily Worker, New Masses,* and *New Theatre,* alongside the work of established writers like Ernest Hemingway, Dorothy Parker and John Dos Passos. It was a "magic time," Babb would later note.[9]

Editors offered criticism, and established publishers like Alfred A. Knopf and Covici-Friede would search for promising new writers in the little magazines. Through a long literary apprenticeship in the most difficult of forms, the short story and poetry, Babb honed her writing skills, gaining a lifelong appreciation of the writing craft. She also refined her political sensibilities, organizing migrant workers in California fruit orchards and enlisting support for the Spanish loyalists.[10] Ignoring conventional wisdom and standing firmly for her beliefs Sanora Babb remains a "born rebel" today [1995] at nearly ninety years of age. Clear-eyed, compassionate observer of both human distinction and folly, she has always held herself to high standards of discipline in writing.

Because Steinbeck's *The Grapes of Wrath* (1938) appeared in the meantime, Random House decided not to publish Babb's novel manuscript, "Whose Names are Unknown," after having accepted it. Both novels are based upon the lives of migrant workers of California's

San Joaquin Valley. The Random House editors argued that "the market" would not sustain two novels on the same subject. It was a bitter blow; organizing migrant workers had given her an "insider's" perspective that Steinbeck, who made several investigative trips to the migrant camps, did not possess. Putting the manuscript aside, she edited *The Clipper* (1940-41), sponsored by the Hollywood chapter of the League of American Writers, and a decade later, *The California Quarterly,* offering, as the little magazines of the 1930s had done, a lively forum for new writers and social criticism. Her involvement in progressive causes and marriage to James Wong Howe, Oscar-winning cinematographer, made increasing demands on her time. An early member of the Los Angeles Writers' Workshop, Babb continued to publish short stories and poems, accompanying her husband, with whom she shared a deep love of craft, to filming locations. On one of these trips—to Mexico City—with "Jimmy" Sanora began in earnest to write *The Lost Traveler.*

In the 1940s and early 1950s, the "Red Scare" left deep fissures in Hollywood's artistic community. FBI agents interrogated actors, writers, and directors who were suspected of "un-American" views. Leaving their Hollywood home and the overheated, oppressive atmosphere of McCarthyite intimidation, the Howes moved to Mexico City in 1951 where they had lived several years earlier during the filming of "The Brave Bulls." Saxe Cummings of Random House, which had accepted, then rejected "Whose Names Are Unknown," encouraged Babb and gave her editorial assistance. "Throw out everything that doesn't have to do with carrying the characters forward in the narrative," he advised. When he saw early drafts of *The Lost Traveler,* he asked her whether she really hated her father as much as the story seemed to imply. She "backed off a bit," not wishing to give a false impression of what she wished to convey in her story, namely, a balanced portrayal of a very complex man.[11]

A rough-cut version of that portrayal appears in her short story, "A Good Straight Game," published in the *Kansas Magazine* in 1951. The father, Dan O'Connor, is a hard-working man who has a passion for gambling which conflicts with family responsibilities. "His first wife had called him irresponsible, it's true, but he was not afraid of hard work," the narrator says. "It was the humdrum and working for somebody else."[12] Foreshadowing the tragic compulsion that underlies Des Tannehill's behavior in *The Lost Traveler,* the story concludes when

Dan slips out at night to gamble, believing in luck as the means to recoup financial loss and dwindling self-respect.

Babb sent *The Lost Traveler* manuscript to Mary Abbot, agent with Macintosh and Otis in New York City who sold it to Reynal Publishers after Random House released its option. (Random House and other mainstream publishers backed away from critical realism in the Cold War period.) Eugene Reynal, who had split off from Harcourt and Brace, died when Babb's novel first appeared. His wife warehoused the entire book inventory, including *The Lost Traveler,* suspending sales. Another publisher picked up Reynal's list and marketed *LT,* but the initial sales momentum had been lost.[13] Babb's English agent, Patience Ross, who had sold a number of her stories to English publications, persuaded Victor Gollancz, Orwell's early publisher, to bring out an edition of *The Lost Traveler.* The English prefer American writing that is distinctively "American," Ross argued; the strength of Babb's novel, she said, is its perspective on what is different and unique about America. The English edition appeared the same year as the American, to favorable reviews both at home and abroad.[14]

The *London Times* "strongly recommended" the Gollancz edition. "A fascinating story of a professional nomadic gambler who starts by being a hero in the eyes of his wife and daughters and ends in lonely disgrace: occasionally embarrassing, frequently funny, and as an account of the development of family relationships good by any standards."[15] The Newcastle-on-Tyne *Evening Chronicle* called it "a splendidly written novel," and the Ottawa *Evening Citizen* reviewer agreed: "It grips you without release from the moment you turn the first page until you have read the last one and ever after, wondering if the author has not left herself plenty of room to follow with a sequel."[16] It's a very American novel, *The Times Literary Supplement* reviewer noted, "in its combination of honesty and sentimentality ... obviously deeply felt, an odd novel whose awkwardness is part of the total effect." The unbridled vigor of Babb's novel was apparently *too* American in the reviewer's eyes who found "a perverse attractiveness about the gaucheness of the telling." "Weakly, the reader may yearn for more Hemingway," the review concludes, "and less domesticity: much of the latter is hard to take."[17]

Perhaps the "unflinchingly honest picture of a wandering gambler and his family" (*New York Times,* March 1958) touched a sensitive nerve of the *TLS* reviewer. More significantly, *The Lost Traveler* was at odds with contemporary portrayals of family life in 1950s' American popular culture. In film and television drama of the "Silent Decade" domestic order and happiness are managed by a self-sacrificing mother and teenage daughters who extend the mother's role, participating in household work, making the home a comfortable place for father, and preparing for marriage.[18] An early, notable exploration of the backlash that women experienced following World War II appears in Betty Friedan's *The Feminine Mystique*. Middle-class white women, Friedan noted, suffered the isolation of suburban domesticity beneath a facade of decorative respectability and contentment. The "good" wife in the 1950s stayed at home, dressing for her husband's return from the office.

Class issues were central to fiction in the 1930s; by the 1950s, however, sexuality and gender roles had become the dominant focus. *The Lost Traveler,* appearing near the end of the Eisenhower era reflects the earlier pre-war view of women who despite unequal opportunities persist and push out into professional and personal domains that had been reserved for men. The spirit of buoyant resilience, so memorably dramatized in *The Grapes of Wrath,* of people who come back despite hardships and deprivation, yielded in the 1950s to a conformist desire for acceptance. In the shadow of "the bomb" one was instructed to crawl under a table. The consumerist society we know today shaped its horizon of expectations in depictions of the happy family familiar to viewers of "I Remember Mama" and "Father Knows Best." [19]

In remembering her early years on the western prairie Sanora Babb brought to bear a subtle yet powerful critique of social forces that bear upon family life. In coming to terms with an anguishing past she settles a long-standing account that envelopes family relationships in a larger social web. Given the prevailing climate of literary reception of the late 1950s, *The Lost Traveler* seems an unlikely candidate for favorable review; but perhaps reviewers (and readers) were ready for an honest, unblinking look at family life. Subsequent events—the reaction against conformity in the 1960s—proved this to be so. It is unlikely that Sanora Babb would have written a novel that conformed to contemporary standards of conventional behavior, given her convictions and long record of struggle for personal freedom and social justice. Nonetheless, she was a very able author of romantic fiction. Her story, "Night of Yearning," published in *The Saturday Evening Post,* the year following the publication of *The Lost Traveler,* reveals her skills at "reading" the market and providing entertainment.[20]

    The Lost Traveler is quite at odds, then, with the dominant ideologies and cultural icons of the postwar era; like the figure of Janus it looks two ways at once: back to the critical realism of the 1930s and forward to our own time when value questions are polarized, and young people are thrown on their own resources, failed by adult prescriptive models of behavior. Writing about the 1950s, Oscar and Mary Handlin noted that

    The poverty of aspiration was the product of upbringing and of a yearning for security. The desire to avoid risk was not a response to anxiety about the future. Young people in the late 1940's and 1950's married and bore their two or three children without forethought or concern .... Meanwhile, they settled easily into the ruts they dug for themselves, expecting to spend the rest of their lives undisturbed.[21]

    How different from today when college graduates flip hamburgers in fast-food restaurants and white collar workers are let go in mid-career. But the situation Babb describes is one in which neither educational nor cultural expectations play a determining role, simply because they did not exist for women at that time. Financial security, complacency, job stability are completely foreign to the Tannehills. And the struggle to survive is shared collectively. Responding to the uncertainties and privations of their collective existence, and to the problems these pose for her individually, Robin Tannehill neither crawls under a table nor succumbs to bleak prognostication. It is not a tale Ernest Hemingway might have written; yet there is abundant evidence of "grace under pressure" and personal courage in Babb's portrayal of "domesticity."

    The main characters are, taken by themselves, attractive, admirable people, despite their human failings. At times they share happiness; other times they suffer cruelly, violating their own standards of admissible conduct. Family therapists call such behavior dysfunctional.

    The Tannehill family's dysfunctionality is centered in the father, Des. The Tannehills are locked together in a complex interplay of shame and love. They are bound together, as Robin says, but not "related." Des is a complex figure, a kind of prairie titan, charismatic and disreputable, heroic and frightening. A family patriarch he dishonors himself, disentitles his authority. His strengths—robust vitality and risk-taking— undo him because they are inextricably linked to his chief weaknesses: a capacity for prideful self-deception and a destructive devotion to "chasing" luck.

By the early days of the Great Depression, when this story takes place, individual gamblers, such as the legendary Poker Alice and Luke Short, who plied their trade alone or in small teams, were a disappearing breed, like harness-makers. Casinos, race-tracks, and organized crime absorbed them or drove them out of business. Gambling is a compulsive activity, psychologists tell us; it is also a skilled trade, requiring intelligence and practice. Gambling is part and parcel of Des's personality, character, humanity. He makes little effort ever to resist, to overcome the compulsion. Des begins as a life-embracing adventurer and ends, like Shakespeare's tragic heroes, metaphorically (and actually, in Des's case) blinded by his obsession. His forthright acceptance of his gambling activities is part of the fascination of his character: strong and willful, he pursues his disreputable profession without apology.[22] Gambling is an escape from the probabilities his birth and class have assigned him. It takes him to the borders of ordinary existence, to dangerous, forbidding areas of risk and gain that investors and land speculators know.[23] Here the narrative connects with gambling's "respectable" counterpart: commercial life in small-towns.

The capitalist businessman knows these borders—their demarcations are grain futures, land deals, speculative enterprises. Indeed, much links Des to his businessmen clients, like Jim Charters, the automobile dealer. But if this borderland of risk and reward offers the adventure that Des craves, then it also sponsors the destruction of personal relationships and financial ruin. The burden of the expense falls upon the family who become agents in the adventure and the destruction.

The Tannehill's desire for respectability is the source of the family's shared secret: in order to ingratiate himself into the community, Des's wife, Belle, and daughters, Robin and Stevie, must lie. In mirror-like fashion, the respectable "town fathers" and the police (taking bribes) mask their own illicit behavior in lies. Babb's tale of gamblers and small-town commercial life functions like satire, by exposing folly and greed, unmasking hypocrisy. It suggests that by defining the conventions of "respectability" a patriarchy of pecuniary-minded "good people" are able to maintain the status quo. This becomes ever clearer as Des, who would rather play fairly, is forced to cheat to recoup losses. The balance of cheating and fair play is tipped finally beyond the limits that respectability allow. The city fathers send Des packing.

Like the "boneless woman" at the carnival, with whom he feels a strange identification, Des is a pattern-maker of illusions, a master of the bluff. His games of chance involve harmless deception; they are powerless against the betrayal of "respectable" people who permit his gambling as long as it suits their needs. His tentative acceptance and subsequent expulsion underscore the deep ambivalence of communities in which risk and acquisitiveness as economic practices are in conflict with establishment standards of prudence-morality. A marginal figure like the carnival freak, Des bears the wrath of those whom he exposes. Rebel against conventionality, "a clean man in a dirty business" (303), he is forced to "travel" when his tricks wear thin.[24]

"Traveler" has, in American lore, several connotations: itinerant salesman, boomer, migrant worker. A boomer is one who follows in the wake of new industries—oil production, mining, railroad shops—setting up business where there is easy money to be made. Restless spirits like Des are travelers, springing for better opportunities. That Des is after more than money is part of his attractiveness as a fictional character. He possesses the stuff that has raised unknowns from mid-west small towns to national renown, like the legendary baseball player, Walter Johnson.[25] Des's charismatic attraction, despite the ugliness of his reckless, obsessional behavior, is modeled after Babb's father who appears memorably in this verse portrait:

> Sunday afternoon inside the drugstore
> After the baseball game,
> Papa, the hero circled by his team:
> Pitcher of bush-league fame.
> Marble-topped tables, vanilla ice cream,
> Cool green-rivers in glass;
> The fountain is swamped, sun beats on the town;
> Players are served first class.
> Papa looks handsome (he had Irish charm),
> Even with sweat-limped hair;
> Worshipful girls in voile and organdy
> Lean on cases and stare.
> Diamond runners from store, farm and office,

By weekday commonplace,
Transformed by Sunday's baseball game, smile back
With a hero's face.[26]

Des comes from "good strong stock" (309), the end term, as it were, in a sequence of generations in decline. Large bread factories have rendered obsolete his small-town bakery. He is willing to do hard work and enjoys the comradeship of harvesting, but he perceives too clearly how "men [are] sloughed off like the waste of the world" (43). Men are fools, he reasons, to work for another man with such meager return for their sweat. "As a boy with no chance, he had made up his mind to manipulate chance for his own ends. He would not be deadened and destroyed inch by inch, day after day, until his life came to a welcome end" (36). By gambling he means to make his living and escape this dismal prospect.[27]

If *The Lost Traveler* submits small-town pecuniary interests and patriarchal power structures to scrutiny, then it also tells a tragic story of family obligations and conflicting needs. The emotionally charged settings of family life have been the occasion of tragedy and comedy since ancient times. The appearance of the family as principal structural element in Molière's *Tartuffe,* is possibly the earliest example in modern western literature of kinship relationships and interior domestic settings as unifying features.[28] In both classical Greek and the seventeenth century French drama of Molière, the eccentricities of a family member dislocate family harmony, which is the situation of *The Lost Traveler.* Similarly, Eugene O'Neill's *Long Day's Journey into Night,* D. H. Lawrence's *Sons and Lovers,* and Tennessee Williams' *The Glass Menagerie* portray individual demands and needs in conflict with affiliative obligations of loyalty. Ideas and situations resonate across the ages, renewing their meanings ever and again. In Babb's novel, kinship ties are the structural feature within which powerful emotions and the quest for truth slowly unwind a tangled ball of family loyalties.

Robin feels impatient with small-town narrow conventions of respectability; yet she is complicit in attempting to preserve a lie that binds the family together, violating her sense of justice and honesty. Critical of her mother's complacency, Robin nonetheless participates in the violation whose source lies in the father's compulsion. Tensions build to a crisis that serves violently to correct an imbalance that is created in the loyalty scales of affiliative needs within the family. The conflict between Des and Robin prepares the way for her disengagement from childhood family loyalties so that she is free to develop peer relationships and commitments outside the family. In the violent, melodramatic fight with Des, Robin comes to terms with the unjust loyalty accounts that have caused her embarrassment and humiliation. Out of this experience she becomes more self-reliant in the quest for autonomy as a young adult; ironically, new family commitments and obligations evolve, ones that she, as an adult, can give of her own free will.

If Robin shares the strengths of her father without his self-destructive failings, then Stevie, the younger daughter is the ultimate casualty of what Freud called "the family romance." By playing the role of her father's "little girl," his favorite, she avoids his criticism and anger, and is martyred in turn through her dependency. Belle, scarcely more than a domestic servant in the family, finally breaks the terrible yoke of exploitation that her marriage has become, acting resolutely to settle the unbalanced loyalty accounts that pliantly over the years she has established.[29] Female friends encourage and aid Belle in reframing her commitments. Sustaining Robin, on the other hand, is a young black friend whom the community has placed in a position of blame and condemnation, as Robin is scapegoated by her father.

The story is almost entirely autobiographical in origin except for the figure of Blackie, Robin's lover, who appears to be a novelistic device, a Doppelgänger figure, the gambler-self that Des seeks symbolically to destroy in directing his terrible rage toward Robin.[30] Family tension at the bursting point, fears about health, and a failed "chase" after the luck that might restitute Des's damaged pride, climax the story in a violent scene, in which the family fragments like an exploding star, forming a new constellation of interconnectedness. The bonding remains; the energies are simply redistributed.

There are moments of joy and pathos in the family's collective existence, for instance, when Des, in a generous gesture of impetuosity, lavishes an expensive gift on Stevie, or, on a trip to the city, puts them up in a luxury hotel. The family is joined, happy; worries are temporarily banished. The affection the Tannehills feel toward one another is expressed in the reprieve granted them from turmoil and corrosive anxiety. The pathos of such scenes is a powerful contrapuntal melody in

The Lost Traveler, preparing the reader for the tragic recognition scene that concludes the story.

Family relationships preoccupied a number of novelists of Babb's generation whose literary work was colored by Depression-era social concerns: Tillie Olsen's *Yonnondio,* Fielding Burke's *Call Home the Heart,* Thomas Bell's *All Brides Are Beautiful,* Josephine Herbst's *Pity Is Not Enough,* Erskine Caldwell's *Tobacco Road,* indeed, William Faulkner's *As I Lay Dying.* Kinship structure and roles were topics of numerous short stories Babb penned in the 1930s, for example, "An Old Man Waiting," which looks forward to her memoir, *An Owl on Every Post* (1970).[31]

In our time, nearly one-half of all marriages fail, and broken families are the rule rather than the exception. One of the strengths of *The Lost Traveler* is its comprehensive depiction of character *and* social circumstance as ingredients in the making and re-making of family ties. It wisely avoids the generalizations about family life that our sectarian age encourages, for example in ascribing fault to a single gender group or class or race of people, or blaming "society." Life, it appears, slips easily out of theory's reach and statistical nets.

A writer must have strong legs, Thoreau wrote. Sanora Babb has run a very long and difficult course since first starting as a printer's devil in a prairie town. She has lived long enough to enjoy the recognition that is finally and deservedly hers. Wise, witty, tough, yet tender *The Lost Traveler* stands firmly on its own feet, showing few signs of ageing.

Douglas Wixson
Austin, Texas, 1995
English Professor Emeritus and
Author of *Worker-Writer in America*

NOTES

1. *The Lost Traveler*, 303. All page references are to the Reynal edition.
2. Carson McCullers' *The Heart is a Lonely Hunter* is an example of this form.
3. See Boszormenyi-Nagy and Spark, *Invisible Loyalties*.
4. *The Portable Blake* (New York: Viking Press, 1946): 268; 278.
5. Boszormenyi-Nagy and Spark, 8.
6. *Clay* 3 (spring 1932). How fitting that Babb's two novels should find their way to Albuquerque in the two new editions!
7. Conroy's letter of acceptance to Babb, 7 August 1933, is with Babb's papers. Also, see Babb to Wixson, 18 September 1983, in my papers.
8. Babb to Wixson, 18 September 1983.
9. Interview with author, 21 October 1983.
10. An excerpt from Babb's unpublished novel, based upon her experiences among migrant workers, entitled "Whose Names are Unknown," appears in the *Michigan Quarterly Review* 19 (summer 1990).
11. Babb, interview with author, 20 September 1994.
12. "A Good Straight Game," *Kansas Magazine* (1951): 6.
13. Babb, interview, 21 September 1994.
14. Following the publication of *The Lost Traveler*, Ross suggested that Babb write a memoir. The result was *An Owl On Every Post*, published in 1970. (See the University of New Mexico Press edition, published in 1994, with Babb's Afterword.)
15. *London Sunday Times* (August 1958).
16. *Evening Citizen* (May 1958).
17. *The Times Literary Supplement* (5 Sept. 1958).
18. See Walters, *Lives Together/Worlds Apart*.
19. The following provide general background here: Walters, *Lives Together / Worlds Apart;* Tufte and Myerhoff, ed., *Changing Images of the Family* (see especially Billie Joyce Wahlstrom's "Images of the Family in the Mass Media: An American Iconography?").
20. Literary radicals like Paul Corey, Walter Snow, and Henry George Weiss, wrote for the "pulps," to them harmless, income-producing fare. See my *Worker-Writer in America*.

21. Handlin, *Facing Life,* 253.

22. During a visit, Sanora's father, at her request, laid out cards in an imaginary game of twenty-one, which accounts for the accurate detail of Chapter Twenty-one.

23. My sources on gambling: John D. Rosecrance, *Gambling Without Guilt;* John M. Findlay, *People of Chance;* Henry R. Lesieur, *The Chase.*

24. Similarly, in Melville's *The Confidence Man* a marginal, disreputable figure serves to expose contemporary mores and conventions.

25. A pitcher, Babb's father did in fact play for a Kansas City semi-professional team and organized the first all Native American baseball team in Red Rock, Oklahoma where the family lived.

26. "Old Snapshots," *Prairie Schooner* 39 (winter 1965-66): 303.

27. Sanora's father read early versions of *The Lonesome Traveler.* Proud of her work, he said, "I don't care what you write about me." Interview, Babb, 21 September 1994.

28. See Perry Gethner on Molière.

29. In her role as self-sacrificing mother, Belle is scarcely different from the figure of the domestic ideal popularized in post-World War II fiction and media representation.

30. The strong autobiographical pull in Babb's novel is evident, in authorial intrusions, such as the following: "Belle was still behaving as if she were afraid of him; she had run off down the alley to her friend Penny, the Christian recruiter, who didn't know God from Santa Claus" (308).

31. *Kansas Magazine* (1938): 98-101.

REFERENCES

Babb, Sanora. *An Owl On Every Post.* Albuquerque: University of NewMexico Press, 1994.

Boszormenyi-Nagy, Ivan and Geraldine M. Spark. *Invisible Loyalties.* Hagerstown, Maryland: Harper and Row, 1973.

Findlay, John M. *People of Chance.* New York: Oxford University Press, 1986.

Gethner, Perry, "The Role of *Décor* in French Classical Comedy." *Theatre Journal* 36 (October 1984): 383-99.

Handlin, Oscar and Mary F. Handlin. *Facing Life.* Boston: Little, Brown and Company, 1971.

Lesieur, Henry R. *The Chase: Career of the Compulsive Gambler.* Garden City, New York: Anchor Book, 1977.

Rosecrance, John. *Gambling Without Guilt.* Pacific Grove, CA: Brooks/Cole Publishing Company, 1988.

Tufte, Virginia and Barbara Myerhoff, ed. *Changing Images of the Family.* New Haven: Yale University Press, 1979.

Walby, Sylvia. *Theorizing Patriarchy.* Oxford, England: Basil Blackwell, 1990.

Walters, Suzanne Danuta. *Lives Together/Worlds Apart.* Berkeley: University of California Press, 1978.

Wixson, Douglas. *Worker-Writer in America: Jack Conroy and the Tradition of Midwestern Literary Radicalism, 1898-1990.* Champaign: University of Illinois Press, 1994.

The Sun of Morn in weary Night's decline,
The Lost Traveller's Dream under the Hill.

—William Blake

PART ONE

ONE

DES PAUSED before the window and looked out over the flat, sandy town with disgust. No trees shaded the unpaved streets and meandering paths, and the small houses sat on their bare yards in ugly nakedness. Sand blowing in the hot winds had cut the paint from their boards, and where no screens covered the windows flimsy curtains waved with a melancholy air from the heat-stilled rooms. The thick dust over everything made a monotone of the town.

Des resumed his thoughtful pacing, his low moody whistling, his stops at the front door, when he gazed at the house across the street or farther, over the ripening wheat fields south of Tumbleweed.

In spite of the heat, the house was filled with purpose. A regular, determined brushing sound came from the kitchen. Quiet turning of pages with intervals of silence and pencil writing went on in the bedroom.

Although his feeling was one of detachment, of self-absorption, a moment of irritation and affection flickered in his thoughts as he looked at his wife, Belle, sitting on a neighbor's low shady porch across the street, her pretty legs awkwardly relaxed as she sewed, talked, laughed.

"The older a woman gets, the less she knows what to do with her legs," he said.

No comment came from either room. He went to the window again and looked at the town, at its one oasis, the church, painted white, surrounded by frail trees, neatly set aside like the Sunday religion of its members, rigid and severe.

"That damn church," he said. "A bunch of damned hypocrites."

In the quiet, he heard the sand ticking against the house.

"Christ!" he said.

He glanced into the small bedroom at his younger daughter, Stevie, curled up on the bed, surrounded by thin white catalogues. She was utterly absorbed in mapping out her life.

Stevie did not look up.

He went to the kitchen and watched Robin. Her heavy dark hair was tied on top of her head like a feather duster and perspiration ran down her face. She was painting the last big numbers in the field of the canvas Do-or-Don't layout, a gambling spread.

3

"Going around naked as a bird's ass!" he said.

"*Where* am I going?"

"You have no shame!"

"You have?" Robin was wearing a piece of bright cloth tied around her hips.

"Well, a man's different."

"How?"

"You're a woman. By God, you're sixteen years old."

"That's no argument."

"You're always looking for an argument," he said, thoroughly delighted.

"Maybe I'm looking for reasons for the things you say to me."

"Well, you'll find out soon enough."

"You threatening me with life, Papa?"

"You need it. Always naked. Bad as a whore."

He watched her cheeks redden and her eyes flash angrily. He enjoyed these bantering conversations and it pleased him to make her angry. He almost smiled.

"You—!" she said impotently, and he watched her hand reach for the scissors, which he knew she would not use. Her good sense would come up and save her. It was the only thing that saved her from all the rest. She had got that from him.

"It's hot!" she said impatiently, and began making sure strokes on the canvas.

Des was pleased with the whole neatly painted design.

"Queenie." His voice announced softly its familiar mockery.

Robin glanced up sharply.

"Queen of the Underworld."

"Oh-h-h-h!" Robin said in a low voice. "I'll kill you! I'll ruin this darned layout!" She lifted the brush.

"Hey, hold on, you spitfire! Can't a man have a little fun?"

She laughed.

"Say, you know," he said looking at her impersonally, "if you don't get some breasts on you, how do you ever expect to get a man?"

"Easy! But I'm not trying to *get* one. It just happens naturally. Remember, Great Aunt Hannah boasted that her husband had never seen her with her clothes off and yet she had thirteen children. Breasts or no breasts. What is your opinion of that, Papa?"

"She was a good woman. Those were her ways."

"Well, all these ways you object to are mine."

"Your ways are a little wild."

"Maybe. You suspect me of a healthy nature as if it were a crime." She looked directly at Des. "I hate a dirty mind."

"Say!" he said, pretending to slap her. "Are you talking about me?"

"Not only you," she said, dodging his hand. "That's part of my private pattern."

"It's not much."

"Oh, I have other ideas!"

"What, for instance?" Des asked suspiciously.

"Well, I feel so alive I could burst!" She leaped up from the chair and whirled to the door, turning her back on him, pretending to look out, saying passionately, "I feel connected with everything, buffalo grass, meadow larks, lizards, rocks, wind—everything! I feel in tune with the universe!"

"And a little off key with the world," Des said, smiling at her youngness.

She turned to face him. "Do you really think so, Papa? I feel completely at home on earth, and the earth is a part of all the rest."

"That's not the world," he said.

"But I feel at home in the world, too, don't I?"

"That depends on what you want."

"I want to be everything I potentially am!" Robin said grandly, making a wide sweep through the air with the paint brush.

"Well, I can tell you right now you'll never make it. Nobody does."

"But I expect to!" Robin said intensely, her face glowing.

"It's not in the cards. Too many things against us. I felt that way and my father before me. It won't be all your fault, understand. But aim high anyway. That other don't make sense."

"Doesn't."

"All right, doesn't."

"It makes sense to me. Why are all these mysterious feelings stirring around in me?"

"I had them too," he said forlornly. "It's just being a kid, I guess."

"Not 'just'. It must mean that when we're young we feel what we are."

"Life soon gives that a few calluses."

She looked at him with sudden tenderness.

"I know that already. Those feelings you had meant something, you see, Papa? And they still hurt you. I think they're like seeds, moving in the ground, bursting with sprouts, ready to grow into beautiful and useful plants. Like wheat or a peach or a rose, or even a weed. Weeds keep the soil from blowing off into the universe. And *we* eat them when we can't buy vegetables."

"Human beings are different," he said.

"They're not less than plants! They're more! Whoever would think of asking a seed to stay in the ground? When it has to, it dies. Or is already dead. I always feel sad when I uncover a poor little dead seed."

"Well, you get a little older and look around in people and you'll see a lot of dead seeds."

"But I'm going to try to raise every seed that's in me!" Robin declared.

She stood up and displayed the layout for six-eight-and-the-field. "For the best gambler in Oklahoma!"

"It's all right," Des said. "Thanks. Just let it dry and tonight we'll all have a game. I want to practice. I'll be the banker and we'll use real money. What I've got, anyway." He picked up a leather cup and shook it and rolled out two dice onto the table. "They do or they don't, they will or they won't," he chanted. "These are pretty little dice."

"I hope you aren't going to cheat those poor harvesters, Papa."

"Hell, no! This game is straight. The odds are in my favor. I can make money and they can have some fun. We've got to get out of this town. I don't want to stay here after what happened last week."

"Well, what about me?" Hurt and angry tears shone in her blue eyes, and she lifted her head and blinked them away.

"You stay right where we are till we all go," he ordered, then handed her a cup of water.

"Germs!" she said and turned the cup around.

"I never had a damn germ in my life!" He dashed some water on his face, and looked admiringly into the kitchen mirror.

Robin came up and splashed water over her eyes.

"You know, Robin," Des said proudly, "you're a pretty good-looking girl. You look just like me."

She raised herself on tiptoe to see his handsome face in the mirror. "I do, don't I? Thanks for your pattern!"

6

He wet a comb and ran it through his dark hair. "The Irish and the Welsh are a hell of a fine people. Don't forget that."

"How can I? Aren't they your profession?"

"No, by God. I'm a gambler, an honest gambler."

"I can never figure that out when you play with marked cards and loaded dice."

"Well, it's my state of mind—I'm no crook. I've got no use for dishonesty. If I ever catch you telling a lie—"

"Don't worry!"

"Listen, I'm going in and devil Stevie for a while. She's in there ordering a tailor-made life for herself. I'll try to talk her into a hand-me-down."

"I think you'd better stay in your temple, O, Tannehill. Stevie imagines you to be a god."

"Imagines? I'm as good as any god."

"A while ago you sang a different tune."

"That was a while ago." He went out whistling like a bird.

At the front door he looked across the street. "I wonder what your mother's talking about over there? You know, she's kinda cute, but you didn't get your brains from her."

"She has other qualities," Robin called.

Des sat down on the bed, shoving the booklets aside. "Let's talk, Stevie."

"Papa, you're ruining everything!" Stevie gathered her catalogues close as if she were covering a secret. "I'm planning four years of college, maybe five or six. I want a B.A., a Master's, and maybe a Ph.D., but that would cost too much."

"Why, you're not even in high school yet. You're only twelve."

"I'm thinking of the future."

"Future, hell. Live today."

"That's what sister says."

"Well, I'll take care of her."

She smiled at him, and he could hardly bear the sweet innocence of her face. She reached for a sheet of paper on which he was leaning, and her blond straight hair, cut short, slid forward like small wings on either side of her large blue eyes, much lighter than Robin's. For a moment she looked like Belle when she was fifteen and they had just married.

"Papa! Careful! That's Vassar! A girl's college, Papa."

7

"You go there. No boys around."

"Oh, now, where's Wisconsin gone to? It's a university. I might go there."

"Take Vassar," Des said.

"Here's Wisconsin! Look, Papa. I've got these two all figured out and three more nearly done." She placed a sheet of paper between them. "See, Papa? I even went down to the station and found out the train fare to all these places."

"You shouldn't bother the agent when you're not going anyplace."

"Oh, he said he enjoyed it. Most people aren't buying tickets outside of Oklahoma, and it was fun."

"I suppose you *were*."

"Well, we pretended."

"He's a good fellow."

"I didn't put down the fare for coming home Christmas like the other students here, but if you make a winning, then I can. Here, board and room. Clothes. Books. Laundry. Music, extra. I've *got* to study the piano, Papa. Do you care?"

Des's face had become serious. "Sure thing, Steve."

"I think I can play the piano. I hear some music in my head." She said, dreaming, "Maybe I can even make up some! Imagine!"

"If I ever make a big winning again, I'll buy you a piano, Stevie."

Her eyes were on his face, believing and worshipful. "Listen, Papa. Do you want to hear the clothes I'm going to buy? Not too many, but good."

"Let's hear them." He looked at her faded cotton dress with the snags carefully mended, at the old white slippers cracked and broken across the toes.

"One plain winter coat, no fur. One green suit. Two shirts. Three wool skirts and three sweaters—two slipovers and one that buttons. A dress, although I don't care a thing about the dress. I might have to have it. Low-heeled slippers, two pairs. Stockings. Scarf. Cap. Three real nice cotton dresses for spring. One summer jacket. Underwear. Clothes brush. That's all."

"No evening dress?"

"Well, not if I don't have a beau, and you said I'm not to have any."

"That's right, Stevie. You can have a beau when it's time to get married."

8

She made a face at him. "I don't want any old beau. I'm going to marry you."

"All right," he said.

"Papa, I'll need money."

"Stevie, by God, there are a few other things in life besides money."

"How do we get them without it?"

"Well, you've got me there."

"We have to plan ahead, Papa. It costs quite a lot. When I get through, I'll teach in college and you can live with me. I'm saving in my bank. I have nine dollars and twenty cents. Maybe you can save some too. In a bank."

"I'll help you, Stevie."

"Papa," she said urgently. "It's nineteen-twenty-eight now, and I'll need this in nineteen-thirty-three. It'll be several thousand dollars, Papa."

"One big winning like I used to make at Blackhawk—remember? and you can go. You had a little fur cap and muff and so did Robin."

"We don't remember that. I remember most about being hungry."

"Well, you want to forget that. The big winnings will come again. I've got to send you to college."

She pinched him on the shoulder and whispered, "Robin wants to go to the university this fall."

"Well, by God, that's too soon."

Stevie leaned closer and whispered again, "Don't tell, but she said she'll run away and get a job and go to school. She means it. You know Robin."

"Since she's been working after school on that one-horse newspaper, I can't do a thing with her."

"You better watch her." Stevie got up, gathered her catalogues and notes into a shoe box, and placed them on the closet shelf, afterward pulling the curtain securely over the closet door.

"Straighten up your shoulders, Steve. Watch those long steps! You walk like a boy."

"Mama said you wanted boys."

"I did, goddamn it. I wanted a couple of ball players."

"I'm a good ball player."

"You sure are, Steve. If you were a boy I'd have you in the big league before long. We'll have a game after supper when Tobey comes home. That dog is a good outfielder."

"Robin walks like a girl."

"She's as independent as a man, though," Des said. "I feel sorry for her husband."

Stevie laughed. "You'll be disappointed, old hoss. She says she won't have one, only lovers."

"Where did you get that word?" Des demanded angrily.

"Where do you think?" she said, teasing him. "In books. Then I looked it up in the big dictionary at school. I don't think it means anything bad, Papa. It said, 'One who loves. A friend. Usually, a male lover. Plural, a pair in love.'"

"Well, by God," he said, awed and shocked.

"She said she won't be bossed around like Mama by any husband."

"She's as wild as a range filly," he said. "I'll have to tame her down."

"Ho-ho," Stevie laughed.

"Don't you worry, I know how to handle her."

Stevie turned her fist softly against his nose. "That's the only thing you don't know how to do, old hoss."

"I'm not too old to learn," he said smartly, giving her a wink, "but I'll have to look out for myself, or you damn kids will get the best of me."

"Papa, it's so hot. Can we afford to buy some lemons and have lemonade for supper?"

"Why, Stevie, we can afford anything till the money's gone."

Belle was sewing rather haphazardly but with real sincerity. "If I don't get these collars turned just so, Des will have a fit. He just loves to look perfect."

"Well, I swear," Mrs. Thayer said, "you're one of the prettiest families ever been in Tumbleweed. We just look for each one of you to come out of that poor little house over there looking like you just came out of a bandbox."

"Oh, fiddle!" Belle laughed.

"It's the gospel truth. I just hope you won't go away after what happened to Robin."

"How would you feel?" Belle asked. "Not letting my daughter make the valedictory speech!"

"Now I'm a member of that church, and maybe I'm a heretic for saying so, but I don't care who got the highest grades in high school. If it's a gambler's daughter, give her the honor! Don't let her folks come there for the first time in the church because a cyclone blew the schoolhouse down, and then insult them. It's outrageous!"

"And she worked so hard on the speech, too," Belle said. "I could have cried. I did too, I cried all night long."

"No wonder."

"I'll never understand it," Belle said stubbornly.

"That's because you're kind. Now, if it hadn't been in the church itself, maybe this wouldn't have happened. In the school auditorium, they would have let Robin be honored."

"The mean thing is that they didn't tell her before graduation night. And shamed us all—poor little Stevie and Des and me."

"It's mean, all right, but maybe they call it the wrath of God."

"But what did Robin *do?*"

"Well, there you are. Sometimes I can't make head or tail of religion."

"She won a scholarship, too, from a fine eastern college, but the druggist's wife told her she shouldn't go there because she has no family background."

"O, tarnation!" Mrs. Thayer burst out.

"She won't go for the simple reason that we haven't a cent for train fare and she hasn't a stitch of clothes. If my mother knew all this, she'd be saying I'm paying dearly for marrying Des. But do you know what my own mother said after she saw Des waiting in church just so he could take me home?"

"What?"

"She said he had the hands of a gentleman, that there was no hard work on his hands."

"I should say not!" Mrs. Thayer leaned back in her rocker and laughed. Then she was suddenly sober. "But there's nothing wrong with hard honest work, child. Whatever was your mother thinking of?"

"Mom was good. But she said she didn't know how she had me, that I had no grace, that I was common."

"Shame!" Mrs. Thayer said. "You're a dear, good little thing. Too easy for your own good."

"Mom was a Virginian," Belle said seriously. "She was English and German, and stiff as a poker. Papa was Irish, and Mom used to say he was common too. But he was a gentleman. He was a court judge."

"Really, child?" Mrs. Thayer said. "Well, you ought to march right down to that church tomorrow and raise Cain!"

"Oh, what's the use, Mrs. Thayer? I'm just myself. And Robin's herself. She's proud like her dad. Pride sticking out all over her."

"What did Robin say that night after the graduation exercises?" Mrs. Thayer leaned forward to listen for a secret.

"She didn't say anything. She went out the back door of the church after she wasn't called on when she was printed on the program and all. On the way home, we found her cap and gown in the weeds by the path, and when we got home she was down by the shed, playing ball with the dog. You know, our neighbor's dog can catch balls like a human. Robin wouldn't talk, and Des said I ought to leave her alone."

Mrs. Thayer sighed. "So often we Christians don't know, let alone live, the meaning of Christianity."

"Not long ago," Belle said, "when there was a wild revival meeting and the students had to go, and a lot of them were going up to be 'saved,' Robin wouldn't go up and the school board didn't like it. She called it voodoo, and that didn't set well."

"I heard that."

"She's a good girl, though, Mrs. Thayer. She's just willful and outspoken."

"Robin's rebellion against the church, dear, is not against true belief. Deep down most of us recognize our spiritual ties. I wouldn't worry if I were you."

"You don't need to say that to comfort me, Mrs. Thayer."

"I'm not. Indeed I'm not. But Jesus is love, God is love. To me, privately, God is the principle of creation, of love. And how much and how little love there is in the world!"

"I don't think Robin's worrying much about the trouble, Mrs. Thayer. She's real high-strung, as you know, but she's level-headed."

"But you can never tell about the young," Mrs. Thayer said. "Anyway, I just hope you won't go away."

"We're always going away, darn it; we've lived in twenty towns since we were married. The kids have never had a decent school year until we came here, and then see what happened. We've been as poor as Job's turkey and as rich as Croesus. Well, not rich, but you should have seen the beautiful clothes I had when we were first married, and the way I dressed the girls when they were babies!"

Mrs. Thayer leaned back and smiled and rocked while Belle described the baby dresses.

"I've always wanted some adventure," Mrs. Thayer said dreamily. "I'll never have it."

"I hate adventure!" Belle said. "I just want to stay in one town for the rest of my life. Here, or someplace. I'd like a place with trees. But I love my friends, trees or no, and I just keep leaving them."

"That handsome husband of yours is looking over this way," Mrs. Thayer said. "It's a sin to be so attractive."

"Pretty is as pretty does," Belle said.

"Now, now, Belle. You're overwrought. Your husband may get in a nice business someday and settle down."

"He charms you even from across the street."

"Well, doesn't he charm you?"

"I guess that's the trouble. Always has been. From the first time I saw him. He had a date with my older sister and I thought I'd die if I couldn't have him."

"Well, that's nice."

"Sometimes I wish she had him."

"You're upset about the graduation."

"I suppose so."

"You just live for your girls and your husband."

"You know, Mrs. Thayer, I was just crazy about my dad, too. He was very strict. We kids couldn't even talk at the table. But he was fun, too. At home we used to sing together almost every evening and he liked for me to start. He'd say, 'Ring, my little Belle.' I just loved that! I guess he gave Mom her troubles though."

"Maybe gentlemen are no better husbands than all the rest," Mrs. Thayer said. "My Will is just a hard-working man and he's as good as gold."

"I know he is," Belle said. "But when Mom said I couldn't even carry myself like a lady, I was bound and determined to get a gentleman just to show her I could. I'll never forget how proud I was of the way Des looked at the wedding." She was quiet for a moment. "But I always wanted him to be more like other people. He just won't work, Mrs. Thayer, he doesn't believe in it."

"He's a *real* gentleman, dear," Mrs. Thayer laughed.

"Well, it all certainly got mixed up." Belle looked at Des standing in the door of the unpainted house across the street. The front porch had no steps and was too high for anybody but children, so that everyone came in and went out through the kitchen in back. "I'd better go home. He may be thinking I'm visiting too long."

"Oh, tut," Mrs. Thayer said. "He doesn't look very fierce to me."

"He is, though," Belle said smiling.

She crossed the dusty road, the hot wind blowing through her summer dress against her small body. Des came out on the porch to wait for her. She wished he wouldn't, because she wanted to think about God's being a principle of creation. It was a startling idea, much too hard to figure out just now.

"Belle!" he called out through the strong wind.

"Oh, why the deuce can't he wait till I get decently in the house?" Belle grumbled patiently.

"Say, Belle. Hurry up! All the women in the big cities have cut their hair off real short!"

She had a vision of thousands of women cutting their hair off at the same time.

"I'm going to cut yours."

"What!" She had resisted the first wave of "bobbing" several years before. Now as if to forestall this one, she called, "What did you say?"

"Cut your hair off. Give you a stylish bob."

"Oh, lord!" Belle said to herself. She touched the thin knot of long pale hair that had been hers for years. "Doesn't even ask me."

"I want you to look like the new, free woman," Des called.

"*Look* like," Robin said over his shoulder. "And *be* the humble wife."

"You stay out of this," Des said.

Belle saw Stevie at the bedroom window. "Mama," she cautioned. "Don't you do it!"

"For heaven's sake, stop shouting at me, all of you. I'm coming."

A neighbor's cow came slowly but determinedly from the vacant lot, dragging a long rope with a stake at the end.

Belle hesitated. "Des!" she cried out. "You know I'm deathly afraid of cows." She was nearly crying.

14

"Come on!" Des commanded. "A cow never hurt anybody."

Belle started again. Stevie came out on the porch.

"She pulls up her stake every time she sees Papa. See, Papa, you're a bad influence."

"She and I are well acquainted," Des said. "Poor old cow, she's lonesome." By this time the cow had reached the porch and was looking at him with a devoted lack of expression. He scratched her ears and then shooed her off home.

Belle went around to the back door, into the kitchen, and straight to the mirror. Des came in.

"Can't we think it over?" she asked.

"What's the use? I'm going to cut it. Don't you want to look like something?"

"Mama, do what you want. Speak up!" Robin urged her.

"But if Des wants me to—" Belle said resignedly.

Stevie began to cry and ran to the bedroom to hide her tears.

"Now, what the hell's the matter with you?" Des yelled.

"A mother with short hair!" Stevie sobbed.

Belle took the pins out of her hair. Then she started for the bedroom and Stevie. Des held her back.

"Sit down, Belle," he said. "You can't listen to these damn kids. They'll make an old woman out of you."

"Oh!" Belle said, exasperated and fearful. "Shave my head. Get me a wig. Anything for peace."

"You'll be a good-looking woman. The first woman in Tumbleweed with her hair cut."

"I'll be embarrassed to death. Why should I want to be first?"

"Because I want you to be. I like to keep up with the times."

Belle sighed loudly.

"You haven't seen Robin yet. She found some pictures in a magazine and *asked* me to cut hers."

"All right, cut it off!" Belle sat down in the chair and Des draped a towel about her and clicked his scissors together with delight. She raised her face to him and he saw the pained and pleasurable submissive love. He slid his free hand into the neck of her dress and pinched her breasts.

Belle sat without a word while her long blond hair fell onto the floor.

15

TWO

A PAN of melted paraffin was cooling on the kitchen table. Des tested its heat and molded it over his fingers and palms, patiently waiting for it to set.

The day was like a cotton cloud pressed against breath and body and mind. Belle passed him with an armful of freshly ironed underwear and bent to kiss him.

"What are you doing that for if you're going to the harvest?" she asked.

"You know as well as I do I've got to take care of my hands. These are the tools of my trade."

"But the wheat will ruin them."

"I'll wear gloves all I can and be careful. Here." He indicated a catalogue from a card company. "Open that up to the dice. I'll be reading while I wait."

She found the page and looked at it without interest. "I hate all that stuff!" she said suddenly, and closed her full lips as if they had betrayed her.

"I know you do, old gal, but I'm the provider. This is the way we eat."

"Don't call me old gal."

"Say, old gal, you look like a kitten with your hair cut."

"Oh, shut up," she said smiling.

"Come here and I'll give you a kiss."

She obeyed with gentle pleasure.

"Now, go pack my suitcase. I want to think a little bit."

He was wearing a pair of overalls and a work shirt, which he had seasoned by hoeing weeds, chopping wood, and cleaning out the shed at the end of the yard. His face was tanned, and the sweat-band of his hat had made a red crease across his forehead.

Through the back-door screen he could see the shimmering heat hanging over the low, dun-colored town. Already a fringe of the huge army of migratory workers was drifting through in its movement northward to Canada. The grain ripened early in the South and later and later as the men worked their way up the middle of the United States, cutting the wheat that grew like a golden mane on the American continent. They left a ridge of stubble on the land like the stiff, cropped hair of that yellow mane.

These men sat on the low curbs of Tumbleweed, waiting. Some of them were ragged and morose, broke, having sent their last earnings home to families. Others wore sturdy work clothes, had money in their pockets, and lent the scene of their presence in each town an air of freedom and good spirits. Mothers kept sharp eyes on their daughters, but in spite of the warnings and extra vigilance lonely girls considered this a time of romance, and young harvesters were occasionally remembered in both fanciful and concrete ways long after the yielding time.

Des studied the new catalogue, selecting a pair of dice he would order from his harvest winnings. These catalogues contained the latest gambling devices for trapping the unwary, the descriptions expressed in legitimate terms and the purpose made clear as amusement. He turned the pages with his paraffin-coated fingers, passing over a roulette wheel and a chuck-a-luck cage, hesitating with pleased superior scorn over a ring "shiner," a tiny palm mirror, and a pair of eyeglasses. He needed none of these tricks; he was a good player with a foxy, lightning mind; he could remember every card, and figure out the game a dozen ways ahead, and when he was surprised his mind raced into calculations that made him glow with an absorbed creative fury of invention.

I'm a good card player, he thought in cool recognition. Few men could beat me in a game of skill. But I'm no sucker. I've got to make a living; a professional gambler has to cheat.

The word nicked him. I'm no crook, he assured himself. Goddamn son-of-a-bitch in hell, a man has to make a living the best way he knows how.

He ripped the paraffin off a forefinger and turned the pages to "Cards." As soon as he had money again he'd buy a supply of fan-backs and bee-backs and mark them in obscure places that the card company never thought of. Now, he searched the illustrations of new designs for which he would create his own series of infinitesimal cuts or inked signs.

He removed the paraffin from both hands and flexed his fingers, spatulate, the tips curved upward from years of dealing. Twenty-eight years. He examined his right, larger than the left. A good male hand. He was forty-one. A gambler had taught him a few tricks when he was thirteen, hanging around a saloon looking out for a free lunch. From then on he began to pick up a little money to live on. Not long after that, Burley Wellington saw him playing ball; he trained him for three years and sent him to St. Joe in the Western Association, where he won eight straight games, the last one seven to nothing. He was a hell of a pitcher with a great spit-ball delivery. Burley used to say he was as cunning as a fox. Another time he pitched a seven-inning game when not a batter got to first base. He and the catcher and the first baseman handled every ball in the seven innings. Des saw one of the fast plays in his mind. Kid Bemis, another pitcher whom Burley had trained and sent to the Kansas City Blues, had taught him a lot of his secrets. Once when they were playing the Chicago Cubs and Charley Arketa, his Otoe Indian friend and a great third baseman—

"Des, honey, shall I pack this canvas that Robin painted?"

"Leave all my gambling stuff alone! I'll pack that myself," Des shouted through the small rooms.

Burley tried to talk him out of gambling. He'd say, "You can't stay up day and night, I don't care how strong you are. Okay, you don't drink, but you've got to have plenty of sleep."

And Burley was right. Next to gambling, there was never anything like baseball. But he threw his arm away and had been playing in small towns ever since, just for the fun of it.

He got up and looked out through the door at the dismal town. Two girls were walking down the path in their summer dresses. They were going to the drugstore where the students hung out. Robin was probably in there, talking to boys. If he had sons he wouldn't have to be worrying about that. Stevie was all right, though; she was on a hike in the sand hills with a bunch of girls.

He sat down at the table again and began his daily practicing. He dealt second and bottom, and played a mock game in which he tested his memory of the cards held by each player, identifying them by the marks on their backs as they left his supple fingers. He turned up the queen of hearts, which he sometimes called "Robin" to tease her.

In the last day or two her rebellion had taken on a different hue. He thought of her defiance of the rules, the town, himself, and he smiled. Like me. But what was she up to now? She was too damn quiet.

He played a game of twenty-one, another and another, and stopped. The afternoon was hot and dull and silent. He shuffled and dealt four hands around. The cards slapped the table in soft, long monotony. An old song came into his thoughts and he pushed it aside to think only of the marks.

Just as this exercise in concentration had reached its pitch and his whole mind was involved in the science of the game, he heard quick steps in the sand and looked up.

Robin was running up the path, carrying a package and a handful of letters. She leaped onto the low porch, came rushing through the door, and dropped the box on the table, careful to avoid his cards. He kept on with the game, frowning when he saw the Virginia postmark.

Robin's blue eyes were flashing pleased excitement and humiliation, as if at this moment she could not feel one without the other. She gave her father a warning shake of the head and began opening the box, lifting out the useless knickknacks, the long lace evening gloves, the crushed silk flowers, the too-large stockings; then a barely worn blouse for Belle and a sweater for Stevie. The sweater had a small stain, which meant that she wouldn't wear it because of the stain and because it wasn't her own.

From the bottom, Robin lifted out two pink silk bed sheets.

"Papa!"

Des looked up reluctantly.

"If these had come before graduation I could have made a dress to wear to dances. I still can!" She draped one of the sheets against her body. "I'll make a tight bodice and a very full skirt, and make a belt out of that purple ribbon Mama found in the remnants."

"By God, all you think of is clothes."

"That's not true!"

"Well, damn near! Where are your brains?"

"My brains don't mean I have to look like the wrong end of town."

"You *live* in the wrong end of town."

"Well, what's wrong with that?"

"The address."

"General Delivery is our home address, Papa."

"I suppose so," Des said, hurt.

"I can be myself at General Delivery," Robin said. She struck him affectionately. "I have my own resources."

Not to give in so easily, he said, "What else is that in the box? Some old aristocrat's false teeth?"

19

Robin unwrapped a pair of black satin evening slippers, and could not resist putting them on. They had heels and toes of another era and were far too long for her small feet.

"Now, by God, you can't go out in those," Des said in angry pleasure. "They're out of style."

Robin toed-out and glided absurdly over the floor. Then she took them off and set them in the package. "Sad, isn't it? I wish I could make shoes."

Des leaped up and grabbed the slippers. He banged one of the round lids off the stove and stuffed the slippers inside. A column of dead ashes rose into his face. He crushed the paper that had held the slippers and struck a match to it. Gray smoke, surreptitious in its slow curling escape, gave an unpleasant odor into the hot air.

"Thanks, Desmond Tannehill!"

Belle came running from the bedroom. "What's burning?"

"Some of your relatives' fine feathers!" Des said.

"What's it all about?" she asked, bewildered, her large, tender eyes already changing with hurt and fright.

"Where's your pride?" Des demanded, and sat down.

"Pride?" Then she saw the box. "Oh, Des!" She put an arm around his shoulders.

He began to deal his cards in the small space left to him on the table.

"What's pride where my loved ones are concerned, Des?"

"Bring in love, Goddamn it."

Belle went back into the bedroom, weeping cautiously.

"Robin," Des said, "get this stuff off the table. I've got to practice."

She put the box and wrappings behind the stove and gathered up the abandoned surplus.

"Silk sheets," she said in a perplexed tone. "I don't think they'd be very comfortable. But isn't it strange how all the good things seem perfectly natural and poverty never does?"

"Sometimes," Des said aloud to himself, "it's awful for a man to have to live with three women."

Belle came to the door looking hopefully at Des's sulky back. "Cousin Della is a good woman, Des. *She* isn't rich. She just sends on the things that Cousin Mollie B. sent to her. I haven't even seen my rich relations since I was a kid, and you very well know it." She went back.

Des looked through the letters. "Here's one for Stevie from the Chicago Conservatory of Music and one from a silverware company back East. By God, she's furnishing a house now." He laughed. "Here's a handful of letters for Belle. If the law ever got after me they could trace me through every town we ever lived in by your mother's mail. Here, take these in to her."

"Yessir, Mister Tannehill, sir!"

"You're damn right, *sir*."

The bag stood open on a chair and Des was placing his card, dice, leather cup, and the carefully rolled do-or-don't canvas layout in the side pockets. His overalls and work shirts lay on top.

"I'll fix supper," Belle said. She patted him affectionately and started away but he pulled her back and held her tightly, kissing her smiling mouth. She was pleased and a little afraid of his passion; it was like an electric storm, wonderful and frightening at once. There was no gentleness in it.

"Send the kids outdoors!" he whispered.

"I can't," she whispered back, reluctantly pulling away. "Leave in the morning."

He pushed her away. "Behave yourself while I'm gone."

"I always do and you know it, Des. Maybe I should say that to you."

He smiled at her, the desire still in his eyes and on his mouth. "You won't catch me with any other woman."

She kissed him. "Aren't you hungry, Des?"

He laughed at her. "If we can't go to bed, I may as well eat."

"You be still," Stevie said from the doorless bedroom. She came into the living room, frowning. "You won't forget, will you, Papa?"

"No, I won't, pard."

"Apache, Kansas. Go there before you come home! A junior college with credits accepted at the university," she said rather loudly, motioning for Des to speak up and nodding toward the kitchen where Robin was helping her mother. "Papa, it is the best town yet! Seven thousand population. Two newspapers. A park."

"You've told me all that a hundred times!"

"A high school for me! Trees, too, for Mama. The folder says it is in the breadbasket of America." She swung on his arm.

21

"You're always after me like a lot of little ducks," he said with mock crossness. "The thing for you to do is to grow up and marry some professor and live in a school."

Stevie climbed onto her father's back, fastening her arms around his neck and under his chin, her long legs around his waist. "Get up, old hoss!" she shouted, slapping him hard on the shoulder, clasping her hands again quickly as he started suddenly to imitate a horse.

Des trotted sedately in the crowded room, shied at furniture, bolted for the bedroom, giving Stevie a rough ride.

"You're shaking the whole house!" Belle said.

Des came back through the living room at a gallop, into the kitchen, shying violently at Belle. He stopped, raised his head, whinnied, and then nuzzled the back of her neck. Belle giggled. Stevie struck Des a jealous blow, pulling his right ear like a rein. He jerked his head away and leaped into the air. Stevie held on and yelled.

Des turned back into the living room and tried to buck Stevie off his back, but she clung expertly. He trotted primly for a long time.

"I'm riding fence," she said. "I'm lonesome out here on the lone prair-ee." She began to sing in a thin plaintive voice. "All day long on the prairie I ride, not even a hound dog to trot by my side ..."

Des trotted faster in time to the song. Abruptly he stopped, bent forward without warning, and pitched, and Stevie went flying over his head. She landed on the old wire davenport. A spring wing screeched and gave way, dropping her to the floor.

Belle came running in. "Now what?"

Des was puffing and laughing. Stevie crawled forward and bit him on the leg.

"Damn you!" he laughed, and sent her sprawling.

"Such an uproar!" Belle said. "Tomorrow she'll start in. When you're gone she does nothing but moon around and wait."

"Come on," Robin called, "to black-eyed peas and a ham bone!"

"By God," Des said, "it's about time we had some good meals again. My luck's going to change, I can feel it."

After supper in the early dusk, the four of them ran foot races in the dirt street. Belle did not care for such violent pleasures, but Des commanded her and she joined them, running without desire to win until his teasing made her stubbornly determined to beat him. Then the two ran together and once he let her win. He matched Stevie against Robin over and over, and they ran close, but Stevie won. Stevie was the best runner of them all. At last Stevie and Des raced each other, the dirt of the road rising like powder under their swift bare feet, their faces set and their bodies straining to get an inch ahead. They crossed the finish line, marked on the road, at a tie.

The moon came up in splendor over the dismal town. Des and Stevie ran again. Neighbors peered from their windows. The dog Tobey came home from a ramble and joined the final race. The Tannehills went tiredly into the house. They were perspiring from head to foot, and took their turns at sponge baths in the kitchen.

Des dressed in work clothes to go to the harvest. He was whistling "Shine On, Harvest Moon."

"Papa!" Stevie scolded. "You're *happy.*"

"Of course I'm happy. Any law against that?"

He picked up his suitcase and kissed her and Robin, then Stevie again. She clung to his arm while he tried to hold Belle and kiss her. Belle put her arms around his neck. They swayed against him.

"When I'm away from home, I tell the boys I've got a harem."

They tried to laugh.

"Now," he said sternly, "I want you kids to behave yourselves and don't give Belle any trouble."

"Pooh!" Stevie said.

The three of them stood in the back yard and watched him go down the narrow path.

He stopped and waved. "I'll be back with a million dollars!"

"When?" Stevie called.

"When you see me!"

In the moonlight they watched him until he turned into a street at the foot of the easy hill. He was going to catch a night ride to another town where he was not known.

THREE

FOR SOME TIME after the other men had fallen asleep Des lay wearily awake. The ground was hard against his body and the cool night air made him pull the cover up to his chin. The single forms of the harvest hands loomed dimly all around him, sprawled on their thin pallets. The rhythm of breath declared itself like a common agreement among them, a comradeship of sorts, while their discordant snoring plagued the air with strife.

Des turned on his side away from the men. The black shape of the barn became friendly with the quiet rustle of cows and horses nuzzling hay or chewing a last stalk of fodder before sleep. Now and then one of the horses gave a great sigh, as if troubled, and Des was carried away with thoughts of this creature related to him by work and hunger and thirst and a need for companions.

The night sounds quieted, save for those of the snoring men, the distant yapping of baby coyotes left alone by their mothers in search of food, and an occasional stealthy marauder nearing the chicken house, frightened away by the scent of men. Des turned on his back, unable to sleep. The hard work in the wheat field had assaulted his great energy, his body wanted rest, but his mind, long set in nocturnal habit, demanded activity. Used to intense concentration for hours at a time, it stood apart from him like another being, rebellious, impertinent, ready to perform, refusing to give up consciousness at this odd hour.

He thought of the day, of the men working, talking, laughing, swearing, all of a color with wheat dust muddied with sweat. In spite of the burning sun, deepening the brown of the men come up from Texas, turning to fiery red the new harvesters, cracking their dry lips and blistering their damp hands, in spite of the first day's tiredness that was like pain, Des had taken pleasure in the hard, shared work. He felt reluctant to admit it. When at evening he had looked back at the wide swath of stubble and compared it to the golden acres of standing wheat he was suddenly filled with pride. Yet his own pride was like a betrayal; he thrust it aside, saying to himself what fools men were to work like this for another man. His way was better, at once an escape from monotony and a pursuit of freedom in which he might find himself, his own meaning. And when he found that, the way was clear sailing, nothing could stop him. The Tannehills would have a turn for the better: up. And, by God, it was time; they had been going down for three generations. They were still good people but their fortunes had declined and with them their chances. As a boy with no chance, he had made up his mind to manipulate chance for his own ends. He would not be deadened and destroyed inch by inch, day after day, until his life came to a welcome end. He would never put his life in another man's pocket a year at a time until it was used up. He wanted to live in his own life the way he lived in his skin: filled out, no sags. It was tough going sometimes, like cutting his own path through a forest that ran alongside a highway. He wanted to be close to the highway, maybe walk on it at times, but he wanted his own path in the forest.

When he was a small boy living alone with his father after his mother died, he had actually had his own path through the woods between the homes of his grandparents. The old Welsh pair, his mother's people, lived in town. Grandpa Davies had cleared timber and made a farm from virgin land but he had left woods on his place, saying that nature would have the last word if he stripped the land of trees. He had become an unofficial legal adviser for so many settlers that he had moved to town in order to be more available. As his services were free, he opened a store to make a living and to provide a convenient place to enjoy his gift. They were fine people; Des remembered many of the ways they had taught him, and passed them on in his own style to Stevie and Robin.

His Irish grandparents, the Tannehills, lived on an ungiving farm several miles from town. They were a wildly quarreling, religious old couple, either too strict or over-indulgent, who preached at him and scolded him until all he could think of was violating their commands. He smiled now to remember the dominating old man and the devoted old woman who would not be dominated.

He was five when his mother died, and his father lost himself in drink and silence and forgot his son. Thereafter until he ran away at thirteen, Des lived in all three places, staying with his father, where he most desired to be, when he was least wanted by the others. His grandparents loved him, or pitied him, he knew, but found him hard to handle. He was a mischievous, strong-headed boy whose energetic pleasure in living often saved him from the bursts of anger he felt toward his father for neglecting him. He could see his father now, a tall, shy man with fierce black eyes, and a consuming memory of guilt (his wife had died in childbirth), with never a moment for him. He was a baker who let the bread go and spent his time decorating fancy cakes. Through drinking he lost his shop and drifted away, walking all over the country like a hounded man. Once, before this, when Des was twelve and his father had come home drunk and fallen unconscious on the floor, he, Des, had beaten him hard with his fists, crying tears of rage and loneliness as he dealt his blows to the groaning, whimpering man. They had met again a few years later and his father had taught him the baker's trade, which Des had practiced in the early years of his marriage.

Soon after that, failing all cures for his drinking, his father had filed on a homestead of government land in another state and lived like a hermit in abstinence and poverty until he was free of his curse. They had tried to be friends but had not succeeded. The final irony, still raw in his memory, was his father's death. Des had gone to his bedside eager to offer his love in final release, and his forgiveness, and to ask for them in return, but his father lay watching him, dumb and paralyzed, his fierce eyes neutral, and Des never knew if he understood his words or his tears, or if his father absolved him of his violence.

Des turned on his side again. The night was darker, the shape of the barn merged with the dark; silence was like a clock ticking in heaven. He felt lonely. He yearned for lighted places and movement. He liked being up at night, dressed, living. Here, lying on the earth, looking into the endless space of the sky, he could not sleep for loneliness. He would have got up and walked on the road but for the aching muscles and the tiredness that drugged his flesh.

It seemed to Des that he had no sooner fallen asleep than a rooster began crowing. A thin mauve darkness still lay over the land, as if the night withdrew reluctantly. Through this phantom air, Des saw the dim flame of the lamp in the kitchen window of the farmhouse and knew that the women were preparing breakfast for themselves and the hands. As night retreated to another continent scarcely ahead of the sun, the hens in the chicken house began hopping and flying off the roosts, jolting clumsily against the walls. The men leaped from their pallets. A commotion of dressing, washing, shaving, and hair-combing began alongside the house, where a bench held several basins. In many places they had a cold shave, but this farmer's wife had set a large bucket of steaming hot water at one end of the bench.

A little girl ran from the house and unlatched the chicken-house door. The crowding hens rushed out in joyous panic, surrounding her like a huge undulating flower on the barren earth. She clung to the door, calling some of the hens by name. At sight of the roosters she fastened the door back and ran fearfully for the house. The men teased her, but she kept her eyelids down and hurried shyly inside.

The farmer came through the back door and joined them, sitting on a keg at one end of the long table that had been set up in the yard. He lowered his head and gave brief thanks to God for the food and the good weather. As his face lifted, solemn for a moment, he waved his hand at the food and called out, "Wade in, you fellas. There's more in the kitchen!"

The men fell to eating their food as if they had just succeeded in capturing it and pinning it to their plates. The women brought huge platters of fried eggs and thickly cut bacon, pans of hot biscuits, and fragrant coffee. When the meal was finished, the men stood about, smoking, before going into the fields.

By seven o'clock the heat had begun; it mounted higher and higher throughout the day, cooling about four o'clock.

Des worked and listened to the steady click of the binder, waiting for night. In the evening, no matter how weary the men were, one would be speaking of women, another telling obscene jokes, another describing a drunk or a fight. Some men spoke of their homes, of their wives or their children or their hard luck, or they told tales of other jobs. But Des had sized up this crew from the first; these men would be raring to gamble before the week was out. Since they either spent their money on Saturday nights or sent it home to their families, they wouldn't have much in their jeans. But by Saturday night he would have a little stake from the spenders. He couldn't do anything without stake money.

The next night he and the other harvest hands were sitting in the deep night shadows of the barn, talking and smoking, their cigarettes winking like stars in the dark.

"How about rolling a little dice before we turn in?" Des asked, without urging.

"Say, how about that, you fellas?" said another excitedly.

"I'm on."

"You'll have to excuse me, gentlemen," said one of the men. "I'm hittin' the hay. Some other night I'll shoot my wad."

"Bring out a lantern."

"Better in the barn."

"He wants to be a stud horse."

"Who says *wants?* Boy, I *am!*"

"Quit braggin'," Des said. "Somebody's liable to think you're scared of women."

"Me?"

"If you boys want to play do-or-don't, I've got a layout I made myself."

"Bring her out. Got a chuck-a-luck cage in your hip pocket, Tannehill?"

"They get one small enough I will have. Say, we'd better all quit smoking, by God, we don't want to burn the barn down. Everything's dry as a bone around here."

"Yeah, douse the lights, boys."

They filed into the barn—the ones who had not gone silently to bed. One of the men took a lantern off a nail by the door and lighted it. The horses looked around curiously, the cows continued chewing. The men found a place on the side of the bam away from the house so that the light would not show through the cracks. Des spread the layout on the floor. A mother cat came running from a dark corner, rubbing against the legs of the men, who petted her and called her gentle names.

Three of the men had dice.

"Use any of the dice you want, boys. They're going to be shaken in this cup. No monkey business."

"What the hell, shake the dice."

The men knelt around the canvas spread with its large numbers showing up clearly in the light of the lantern. Its unquiet flame threw slashes of light and shadow on the faces of the men, enlarging their eyes, and sent long trembling ropes of light into the darkness of the barn.

"Come on, boys," Des said.

The men leaned forward, placing their quarters and halves on the line.

"They will and they won't, they do and they don't," Des said in a low singsong. He shook the dice and rolled them out.

One of the men made his point. He sat back on his heels and smiled. Des pushed the money forward from the bank, a small pile of coins and bills on the edge of the canvas at his knees.

"Let 'er ride," the man said. He passed again and Des paid him.

One of the men cautiously put down a half-dollar and threw a seven out. He sat quietly for a moment and then placed a silver dollar on the line. That too disappeared.

"Seven away, nobody to pay," Des chanted, but he gave the man a sympathetic nod.

A Texan rubbed his coins together between his palms, blew on them, and dropped them with mock elegance onto the canvas. As the dice shook in the cup he said in the secret, intimate tones of a lover, "Come on, little babies, I'm talkin' to ya. Sweet and low." As the dice rolled onto the layout, he purred, "Come six, come eight. Don't give the bad man my sweat money."

He made his point, and kissed the dice. "You have to talk to them little dice, boys. They hear ya, they got little ears and hard hearts just like a woman."

"They ain't nothin' as mean as a woman," one of the men said slowly.

"Ain't nothin' quite so nice when she aims to be, but mostly she ain't aimin'."

"Reckon they talk likewise about us when our backs is turned."

"Shoot dice, boys," Des said. "Women are all over. You pick 'em like daisies. The fields are full."

Early in the morning he separated his bank from the winnings and found them to be over twenty dollars.

The next morning it rained and the hands moved their bunks into the barn. The wet wheat was too tough to cut, and the men gambled all day and part of the night. In the afternoon the sun was so hot that steam rose up from the crop and the ground, and the next day the wheat was dry enough for them to go in again with the header. Des had over sixty dollars to add to his stake for the week-end in town.

Crowds loitered about the main street. Men leaned against the buildings, sat on curbs, stood thick on the walk so that the citizens of the town, especially the women and girls, had to press through their ranks. They filled the small cafés and jammed the Saturday-night public dance. As there was not enough hotel space for the men, cots were set up in vacant buildings and rented. Trains of boxcars carrying hundreds of hands northward disgorged new crowds. Farmers came in town on Saturday nights to round up crews, and on Sunday nights to take them to their farms.

Drunken men were everywhere. Many of the men stayed sober and gambled; some tried to combine liquor and gambling. Others sat lonesomely on the curbs or wrote letters on lined tablets placed on their knees. Merchants sold more than they had sold for months. The little bakery was swamped; men lined up to buy hot rolls and sweet buns, cakes and pies and cookies. They carried the pies and cakes into the street, cut slices with their pocket knives, and ate their fill. Pop-bottle tops littered the gutters. Enterprising little boys collected the empty bottles and sold them. Often the men gave them pennies and nickels or bought them ice-cream cones.

Des rented a hotel room and arranged with the owner to cut him in on the games. His sunburned face and roughened hands inspired confidence among the men who needed confidence. Most of them did not care. They were restless for excitement. Des ran a dice game Saturday and Sunday nights. This was hard work, especially as the heat made sleeping by day difficult. The hot wind blew; the drawn blind flapped monotonously. The dingy hotel curtain fluttered forward and back like a feeble dancer shedding stale dust from the folds of her old skirt. Acrid smoke from the night before was a long time blowing from the room. Beneath the odor of dust and smoke the room exuded its own slyly offensive smell, collected and stored over the years in the wool of its dim carpet, the pores of its cheap furniture, the shabby wallpaper, the boards and plaster. No wind could blow this air of old and transient life from the room. It smelled of trouble and loneliness, of worry and sleepers' dreams, of boredom and degradation. It smelled of life in the under seams. Its scent of joy was gone.

Sometimes he sat on the side of the bed and smoked a cigar. The country scene came back to him with its clean air, and the strangely festive joy he had felt among the men and in himself as they worked together in the wheat. There was a sense of *rite* lost in the chaff of old centuries and remembered again. A sense of celebration.

Sometimes he went into the street. The stragglers were there. He sat with them and talked. A few were professional men, ruined by financial trouble or love or drink; others were men sloughed off like the waste of a world, by ignorance, by war, by superfluity. *"What's it all about?"* *"Who the hell was I dying for? Not myself."* Des listened. He knew they wanted an ear, an ear unattached to a face with eyes to scorn or a tongue to judge.

The steady-working, saving men had stories top. They were separated from their families because they could not make money at home. They went through the harvest from Texas to Canada, saving their wages like squirrels storing nuts for the winter ahead. They stayed North for the threshing and went home with a bankroll to pay the grocery bill, to buy clothes, to hand the landlord three months' rent in advance.

Townsmen drifted into the hotel lobby to talk about the price of wheat and flour and bread, about bank loans and mortgages, the price of land and straw hats. A few of them found their way cautiously into Des's room. They asked for news of other places with which to regale their friends. Des reported and invented, and separated them from their dollars.

He went ahead of the harvest to a town and made arrangements with the sheriff and his deputies. If a sheriff could not be bought, Des moved on. His bankroll grew. He went to the post office, bought a stamped envelope, wrote a hasty note at the public desk, and stuffed several bills into the letter, sealing it carelessly. The bills of like denomination in his pocket and in the letter to Belle were different in his mind. The ones in the letter were larger, more valuable, and capable of buying more than any he kept.

Robin stood in the Tumbleweed post office reading a card stamped at Dodge City. The quick, forward-slanting letters raced:

Dear Wife and Daughters, Pack up, move to Apache. Nice town. Bring furniture. Hell of a house but best I could rent for fifteen dollars. 317 Burkett Street. Dodge City sure nice place. May live here someday. Just been out to Boot Hill, a graveyard for men who died with their boots on. Leaving this a.m. Don't know when I'll be home. Love, Des.

Robin read the card twice and looked into the back of the post office to see if all the mail was sorted. A harvester stood at the public desk, laboriously writing a letter, wetting a stubby pencil with his tongue, gazing into the quiet street for ideas to fill out the page.

31

The old postmaster came to the window and looked fondly at her through his silver-rimmed glasses. "Going away, you folks."

"Yes, Mr. Holliday."

"Going to Apache," the old man announced. "Moving to *Kansas*. Hate to see you go, Robin. Going to miss putting all your letters up. Leaving the Oklahoma Panhandle. Well, I declare."

"I'll write you a card from Apache."

"Now, I'll be right proud to get it, Robin. I already taken your address off your dad's card so's to forward your mail."

"Thank you," she said, "but I'll be in every day till we leave."

"Oh, wait," he said. "I've got a little something or other here for your sister." He handed her a thin package of sample stationery. "New York! You girls sure do put some life in this post office!"

The harvester was waiting to buy a stamp. Robin said good-by and went into the street. The wind was blowing sand. Men in overalls fringed the walls, keeping in the shade of the cement-block porticoes. Main Street had a Sunday look. Two little boys were playing a game of marbles in the recess of the wooden movie house. She passed the hotel and lunch counter which was called Dakota's Place. Dakota was sitting at the counter, gazing into the quiet afternoon. Robin waved to him and hurried along the walks and paths toward the end of the town. The wind was strong and she bent forward, pressing against its strength, hooding her eyes against the sand.

At the foot of the hill two bay horses ambled along, drawing an old wagon filled with watermelons. The dark green melon skins shone coolly in the heat. A young girl sat very straight on the seat, her face hidden in a large starched sunbonnet. Beside her sat a tanned little boy, holding the lines slackly.

They were Irma Branscomb and Johnny. Her father was in prison. Her mother had been dead a long time. When Irma had a baby, Henry Branscomb was arrested and taken to the county seat, where he pleaded guilty and was sentenced to prison. Irma said nothing against her father; she nodded her answers in court, and once she said, "He never meant me no harm." Some people said he was a good enough man but was just plain lonesome, and maybe Irma was the same, away out there on that sandy farm.

Irma never smiled at anybody.

"Did my mother buy a watermelon?" Robin called to her.

"I went by. She didn't come out."

Johnny pulled the horses to a stop.

Robin wished she could see Irma's face. Would it show anything? Irma always wore her sunbonnets.

"Then I'll take one with me," Robin said.

The girl stepped down easily, placing one foot on the wheel hub. "You can't carry too big a one." She thumped several melons. "Want it plugged?"

"No, you can tell."

"I sure can."

"Did you have a good crop this year?" Robin asked, hoping Irma would look at her and smile. She wanted painfully for Irma to know that she wasn't against her.

"Nothing to brag." Irma selected a melon, took a knife from her apron pocket, opened it, and thrust the long blade into the green rind. She cut a small triangular plug, which she speared on the blade and showed to Robin. The bright red fruit dripped its juice onto the dusty road.

"Go-o-o-o-d!" Johnny said.

Irma gave him a commanding word and he turned his face toward the horses.

As Robin paid her she saw that the girl's hands were hard, with cracked nails and axle grease imbedded in the pores.

When Irma handed the melon into her arms, Robin looked directly at her and smiled. Irma's eyes looked back, steady with suspicion.

Robin walked slowly home, thinking of Irma. I'll send her a card from Apache. Then she'll know. She won't have to answer.

FOUR

THE LITTLE black Model T crawled along the dirt road like a decrepit but determined beetle. The dry wind blowing across the plains was colored with sand. The heat was intense.

Old Mr. Duvette clutched the nervous wheel. Belle sat beside him. The loose buttons of the hard leather seat pressed against her flesh through the clean gingham dress. Long silk gloves which reached above her elbows and a plain black straw hat tied bonnet-like protected her fair skin. Now and then she glanced back through the small window at Stevie and Robin sitting on the floor of the built-in box with their legs dangling over the end. Only their farm-straw hats and tired slumped backs were in view. The jolting was severe.

Emerson, the drayman, and a son who owned a truck, had gone ahead the day before with the furniture. She and the girls had spent the night with Mrs. Thayer. Belle had given the key to the drayman and asked him to hide it under a morning-glory vine which Des assured them grew up the east wall of the house.

Old Duvette was the janitor at school. When Robin and Stevie had gone to tell him good-by, it occurred to Robin to ask him if he would like to drive them to Apache. He agreed but he wanted no pay, and as they did not wish to take advantage he settled for gas. He was proud of his Model T and the trip to another and larger town would give him a tale to tell and retell for the rest of the year.

"Do you think we look respectable?" Stevie asked Robin, stretching her dusty legs in front of her. "Let's see your feet."

Robin imitated Stevie and the two of them looked at their bare feet.

"I think they're pretty," Stevie said, "and delicate. Are mine prettier than yours?"

"Yes, big baby."

"Well, do you, Robin?"

"Do I what?"

"Think we look respectable?"

Robin watched their old tennis oxfords bouncing about on the floor of the truck. They would put them on just before they arrived. It was better to enter a new place with worn shoes than with none at all.

"Are we?" Stevie asked.

"Certainly. We're clean. Why?" Robin looked at her crossly.

"Because Papa is always harping on that word. You know he is. Sister—" Stevie hesitated and looked into the distance as she spoke. "Do you think we'll be more respectable in the new town?"

"Of course, if Papa makes enough money!"

"Or if they don't find out about him," Stevie added, "and they always find out."

"What do you think respectable is?" Robin teased her.

Stevie's face was thoughtful. "Having some money, and shutting the windows when you quarrel and things like that. And working at a job you can tell so you don't have to be ashamed."

"*We* don't have to be ashamed. What are we doing?"

"Nothing. But nobody just says Robin and Stevie. They say 'the Tannehill girls.' ..."

"Let them!" Robin said. "We will respect ourselves. That comes first."

"I am not sure about that."

"I am. I'll do as I please!"

"You'll make it worse!" Stevie accused.

"What I please may be something good."

"Well, I hope so!"

"Oh, Stevie, you make me tired! Can't you be a little gay? We've been perfectly respectable. Remember the silk dresses Mama used to wear to the ball games on Sunday? And Papa in his baseball suit? We'll be all right, money or no."

"I remember locking and unlocking the bakery door," Stevie said. "That was *ours.*"

"I remember my pinto pony that Chief Flying Hawk gave me."

"You used to leave me alone all the time, and ride to camp and just live with the Indians."

"Well, you wouldn't come with me."

"I was afraid. You rode too fast."

"When my horse was going home, he wanted to run. That's why they named me Little-Cheyenne-Riding-Like-the-Wind."

"You," Stevie said, "were going to run away and ride your horse all alone back from Colorado! When I was your age I had a better sense of the impossible."

"But you've changed," Robin said, and Stevie pushed her off the car.

35

Robin ran along as fast as the laboring machine and swung on again. They giggled and fought until they were tired, then sat watching the road in silence.

After crossing the Cimarron River, with its wide, white sand dunes on either side, they stopped to drink. Old Duvette waved his bony, big-knuckled hand toward the flat plain dotted here and there with sagebrush and yucca and huge Russian thistles.

"Not so long ago," he said, "this was No Man's Land, with Indians following the buffalo herds. Nothing would do the consarned new settlers but to kill off every last buffalo and sell his hide, and then his bones. Man is a destructive beast. It's a wonder to me he gets on as well as he does."

Stevie and Robin took off their hats to wet them in the stream.

The old man ruffled Stevie's blond hair and fixed his black eyes on her face. "Who is Coronado?" he asked. "Quick!" He snapped his fingers.

"A Spanish explorer," she said.

"Well sir," he said, "Coronado was around this country in fifteen-forty-one and he thought this smooth, level tableland beat anything he ever saw. He wrote in his report that a man could see the sky between the legs of the buffalo, and if a man lay down on his back he lost sight of the ground!"

Duvette drank again, wiped his mouth with the back of his hand, and started for the car. "It's a hard land, you might say, but once you've lived in all this space, it ain't likely you'll ever get over the spell of it."

Belle wanted to say that she did not like it, and that she wanted to live closer to people and trees. She watched Robin and Stevie; their faces were tender with some deep agreement she could not feel. This gray desert had no claim on her.

"Are you hungry?" she asked, calling them back to her.

"Yes!"

"Then let's eat here in the shade of the car." Belle unpacked the lunch she had prepared that morning before sunrise. They ate hungrily their ham sandwiches, whole tomatoes, potatoes in their skins, and fat slices of the devil's food cake that Mrs. Thayer had made for them. Sand blew into the food and gritted between their teeth, but the little party was filled with pleasure over the good lunch and the cool stream sparkling nearby.

"Let's be off," old Duvette said. "We must not forget we are travelers!"

For many miles over the gray land they did not speak. The heat grew and the dry, hot wind was like a tongue of flame licking them as they passed. Robin and Stevie sank into a boneless torpor. In the morning they had watched with delight the small, many-colored wild flowers nodding in a fringe of swaying grass beside the road; or made objects out of the great white clouds piled stilly in the sky far above the wind. Now they sat looking only at the brown road as it ran like a snake from under the car. Grasshoppers with their long droll faces and direct, critical eyes jumped thickly in the grass and onto their arms, appearing to study them humorously before their sawlike legs propelled them away. They spat their "tobacco juice" on the girls' clean dresses now dim with sand.

Belle glanced back anxiously from time to time.

Ahead, the heat waved over the plain like dipping and rising flocks of silver butterflies, and far beyond in the center of the road shimmered a lake with gleaming white castles edging its shore. This mirage retreated as they approached, and mocked them with the shining cool of its water and the fairy-tale richness of its alabaster walls. The road lured straight into infinity; it broke at the far horizon and tumbled off into space, world's end.

Soon after four o'clock the wind quieted; it became gentle, playful, as if proudly apologetic for its bold day-long arrogance. The vast cooling plain released a medley of austere perfumes, locked under the sun, odors of sage and sharp-breathed weeds, of buffalo grass and the earth burned dry. The high, clean air came over them all like a fragrant shower. They sat erect, yawned, stretched, felt renewed. A meadow lark flew out of the grass and rocked on the barbed-wire fence, singing a crystal song. The song lived in the afternoon, deepening the silence.

Robin and Stevie leaped from the car and ran behind to awaken their sun-drugged bodies. The powdered dust under their feet was feathery-soft and warm.

Old Duvette pushed his hat high on his forehead; it slipped off and rested on the back of the seat. He let it stay. He looked like an old blackbird with a white topnotch.

"Cooling down now," he said as if he were nature's spokesman for the climate of the high plains.

"What will you do about sleeping, Dad?" Belle asked. "What if we weren't along?"

"If I was alone, I'd keep a-goin' till I got there, but I don't aim to treat you womenfolk to my ways."

"I'd as soon go on," she said, "if we could stop at dark while I unroll the covers in the back for the kids."

"Kids—babies." He laughed. "They're as big or bigger'n you. We'll stop some place; you'll have to work like sixty when you get there."

"I've covers enough for all of us," Belle said. "Can't we just sleep on the prairie?"

He looked at her sharply. "Broke, eh? Now, lookee here, I'll lend the money for a room. We'll come to a little town directly."

"No. I've some money but I want to be careful with it till I hear from Des. We've often slept out in summer because we wanted to."

"As you will," he said contentedly. "We'll drive till dark and shorten the journey tomorrow."

Far ahead they saw a few buildings and a windmill.

"Warsaw is just a wide place in the road," Duvette said. "I was there some years back to visit a widder but she moved to Ulysses and married a broom-corn grower."

"Oh," said Belle sympathetically.

"It's no mind. I just heard she was in the market for a husband and figgered we was both lonesome. The grower o' course was better fixed in cash, and I don't hold that agin her."

"That's nice," Belle said.

"I'll find me an old woman one of these days got no better sense than to marry me."

They stopped at a lunch counter by the road. Warsaw was a general store, post office, gas station, and café for truckers. They ate hamburgers and pie, rested over their coffee, and read the signs stuck around the edge of a smoky mirror. The largest sign read: You Wouldn't Ask the Bank for a Sandwich. Please Don't Ask Us to Cash Your Check.

When they drove on, the sun was going down like a holocaust. Afterward there was a moment of pearl-like clarity over the whole plain; farmhouses unnoticed before shone in isolated splendor. Then they were lost in the rising dusk which grew on the land like a magically hasty purple grass waving gently in the evening wind.

With the first faint darkness, owls scooped over the road and settled on the posts, their great eyes staring from feathered moons.

"Your man," Duvette was saying, "is a handsome cuss, and dogged if he don't have a friendly way I take to. But, puttin' my foot in it, I don't hold to his other ways. How in tarnation with a fine wife and kids did he ever take to gamblin' for a livin'?"

Belle was too tired for this kind of talk. "We had a bakery once," she said, determined to say no more; then she thought of the old man's loneliness and went on. "He was a very fine baker. We had friends, and money in the bank, and Des managed a baseball team and played every Sunday."

"You don't say!"

"When machinery came in, the big shops began to ship bread all over, and put a lot of small bakeries out of business."

"Machines are fine in their places," Duvette said. "I wouldn't drive this trip now with a team of horses, though many's the time I've drove farther."

"He was stubborn about working for someone else. Finally, he *had* to. An old woman in a small bakery. He hated it so that he began to gamble." She looked at the great fan of sunset coloring the world of the plain. "In earnest," she added.

She thought of that other husband, the baker of bread, dressed in white, with flour dusting his eyebrows and gloving his hands. Impertinence then had been on his face like a part of the flesh.

He began to hold out money from his small wages. Those were the days when they drank hot water seasoned with salt and pepper, and called it "pepper tea." In the summer they gathered weeds and greens for cooking but all this took place in the winter, and the winter was long.

After work, he sat at the small kitchen table, cleared of the quick evening meal, and dealt the cards over and over again. Some nights he worked with the pen and ink and the children would be let out to play, or, if a blizzard kept them in, they must be careful not to bump his elbow or jar the table. The cards were left to dry, and the next night he would sit at the table, preoccupied and silent. He was ruthless and disciplined, training his eyes, his memory, his hands, his mind.

The soft ripple of cards fluttered in the room like a bird's wing, into their waking and into their sleep.

One night he came home and ate, and as soon as the table was cleared he sat down and dealt the cards around to the absent players, gathered them up, and dealt them again. He moved quickly and the pupils of his eyes were dark with interest. He got up, took his coat from the back of the door, put it on thoughtfully as if he were trying it for fit, and dropped two blue-fan decks into his pocket.

"I'm going to town," he said in a voice that was low, preoccupied, and strange. He forgot to kiss them good-by.

He came home about five o'clock the next morning, emptied his pockets, and went to bed, sighing with weariness. They heard him in silence. When light came into the room, Stevie went barefoot to the table. Her eyes were large with wonder. "Thirty-two dollars!" she whispered to Robin, and went to bed and to sleep.

The next day Des quit his job. He began to sleep in the daytime and go out at night. The pattern of their life had changed.

"He was half right and all wrong." Duvette startled her. "He can only come to grief. You should guide him a little."

"I can't."

"Well, he's a strong branch, but the wind's twisted him in the wrong direction. Look out you all three don't get in the way of that wind."

Belle could feel old Duvette waiting. She could tell him more; perhaps if every job Des had had as an orphan had not been a lesson in bitter disadvantage—oh, to heck with this old man's curiosity. In spite of the gambling she felt proud of Des. He might change, now that the girls were growing up.

The old man pulled off the road and the car bumped over the tufts of short grass. "It's nigh dark," he said.

They shook the dust from the bedding while Duvette shone his flashlight over the grass. "Looking for button cactus," he announced. "Worse than a danged snake bite."

Belle made his bed first, and nearby spread another wide enough for the two girls and herself. She placed quilts on each pallet, for although the day was hot, the night was cool, almost cold. They hung their dresses in the car and put on their nightgowns over their slips.

"It'll be real cold about four in the morning," Duvette said. "I'm a mind to sleep in all my clothes."

"You'd better, Dad."

The plain was black now but they could see the shapes of the car and the old man sitting on his bed with his back to them, smoking his pipe. A cloud bank lay far off to the southwest like a dozing wildcat opening its sleepy eyes, sending a flashing blade of fire into the dark.

"I like the storms," Robin said.

"I don't," Stevie said. "The lightning is pretty but I'm afraid."

"Come on now, you kids, get in bed," Belle urged. "We'll have to be up at dawn and on our way."

The three of them lay down, facing the great starry sky, so wide, so tall they could never put the wonder of it easily aside.

"Now," Stevie said, "the sky is a big magic bowl over us, turned upside down on the earth." She sat up. "Let's look at the edges."

"Don't say that," Robin said. "It makes me want to run to the end of the world and pry up the side of the bowl and get out!"

"Where?" Stevie asked wonderingly.

"Where," Robin said, dreaming.

"Kids! Kids! Go to sleep!"

Coyotes barked not far away. Belle looked at old Duvette's dark form in the night and felt secure and protected. The plop of his pipe being struck on his palm was heard like the cork being drawn from the jug of their sleep and dreams.

FIVE

AFTER DRIVING all morning through fields of wheat, the travelers from Oklahoma entered Apache from the east highway, turned left too quickly and rattled through Dirty Spoon, saw the depot and turned back right, crossed the railroad tracks, and drove the length of Main Street to the school square. They looked at the new town in awe and admiration.

In Burkett Street they drove under large trees whose leaves met above them. The houses were old. Greenish-tan lawns were out front like welcome mats.

The houses grew older and smaller, the lawns browner, chickens appeared in the yards, but the street was still a good street. It was better than any they had lived in for years, in view of Dirty Spoon, but separated by the railroad tracks. Stevie saw it first.

"Three-seventeen!" she yelled excitedly. "Mama! Three-seventeen!"

The house was gaunt, and a faded, peeling green; it looked like a stringy, neglected female. But they did not care. Everything about it seemed wonderful—the broken cement walk, the patchy grass, and most of all the two great trees. They were speechless with pride and pleasure at the sight of the black tin mailbox beside their door.

As they started up the walk, the three of them saw it at once at the window next door: a stealthy hand pulled the old lace curtain back a little way, and from behind in the dark they felt two eyes taking them in.

The curtain dropped.

"You see!" Stevie said fearfully, and stopped on the walk. "They already know."

"Sh-h-h!" Belle whispered.

"I'll hide!"

"Sh-h-h!"

"Mama! We can't live in whispers!" Robin scolded.

There was a door with a frosted glass pane. Stevie traced its design. "I like this."

Robin searched for the key. The morning-glory vine was sparse at the roots but its trumpet flowers and heart-shaped leaves spread over the window above.

"Well, I suppose Emerson carried the key back to Oklahoma with him," Belle said.

Robin dug into the earth with her fingers and felt the key close to the roots.

Stevie discovered a small metal bow on the door and turned it. A screeching bell sounded through the empty rooms.

"Sh-h-h!" cried Belle again, and inserted the key.

The door opened into two rooms straight ahead. Their furniture stood in the heavy stale dust. To the left a low door led into another room darkened by a cracked blind at its one window. In the kitchen, Emerson and his son had set up the stove and wired its tin pipe for security. Belle unlocked the back door, which was so near the stove that one would have to take care in passing. The yard was a large oblong of hard, bare ground reaching to the alley, where an unpainted outhouse stood near a coal shed.

All the rooms were small but there were four of them, forming a box. The two girls shouted and laughed and chased each other until their outgrown slippers pinched their toes.

"It's ours!" Belle said reverently to herself. "A good house. Separate rooms. You kids can have this bedroom off the front room," she said, dispensing her bounty.

"It hasn't any door!" Stevie announced with bitterness.

"Well, poor old Mr. Duvette," Robin said, and ran out. The car was there with the suitcase and quilts. She went to the corner, looking for him. Had his feelings been hurt?

A half-block down a side street was a neighborhood grocery. She ran on toward it, unpinning the dollar bill from her slip. Through the window she saw old Duvette tipping a bottle of near beer to his mouth. When she went in he smacked his lips and gave her a smile.

"It's grand, Mr. Duvette! Won't you come to lunch?"

"Indeedy I will." He pointed to his purchase. "Ham, mustard, bread."

She bought four apples and a half-pound of Tillamook cheese.

"Tut, tut," old Duvette said.

They entered the house, feeling important with their surprise.

"Vittels!" he shouted.

Belle made sandwiches on a packing box, and they stood about eating. From another bag, Duvette took two bottles of buttermilk.

They talked and laughed so much that Belle said right in the middle of laughing, "We'll all be crying before night."

"Fie!" Duvette said, putting the remaining food in order and folding the paper sacks as if he were alone. "I'll be staying this afternoon to help you set things right."

"Smoke your pipe and rest," Belle said. "Why don't you stay several days and see Apache?"

"I'll be leaving at sunup. Want to get back and tell everybody about my adventure."

"We'll have to scrub this place from top to bottom," Belle said, searching for pails and rags and soap.

By nine o'clock that night the house was almost clean and the beds were set up. After a warm supper, Duvette went for a brief excursion to Main Street.

"I saw the bright lights!" he said. "The town's too big for me. But I'll tell you, I enjoyed it!"

They went to bed exhausted, the three women in the bedroom and old Duvette on the davenport in what they had begun to call the middle room.

Belle watched the old man drive away in the first sunlight. She went in slowly, noticing that a tree root had broken the walk. Mocking birds were singing in the cottonwoods. Morning sparkled with newness; under the birdcalls the leafy street was silent. She felt joyous and lonely at once, and made a wish like a child to live in this town forever.

She hummed at her work. As she was setting the emptied boxes outside, someone spoke to her. A thin, dun-colored woman, standing in her yard to the east, appeared to be taking the sun. She was closing and opening her eyes, clucking softly like a hen. Her sorrel hair, twisted into a high knot, let a shower of loose ends down upon her neck. Her long face was fine-boned, once handsome, and there was an elegance in the way she wore an old beaded dress.

"Good morning," she repeated. "I'm Mrs. Polk."

"Good morning," Belle said, smiling. "I'm Mrs. Tannehill."

"I hope we'll be neighbors," the woman said coolly, and turned aside.

As they were eating breakfast a light knock sounded. Belle glanced down at her soiled apron before she opened the door. A plump, lively-eyed woman came in and looked at them all in delighted curiosity.

"I'm Mrs. Weeks. Just want to welcome you!" She held out a plate of warm, fragrant rolls, and took from her apron pocket a glass of jam. "I made them both."

Belle offered coffee, inviting her to share the gift.

"Oh, fine!" Mrs. Weeks said, sitting down on an old chair with its back off.

Belle protested.

"I live down the street, Mrs. Tannehill. My husband has the Weeks Hardware store."

"Mrs. Weeks," Robin said, "you must be a very good cook. The rolls and jam are delicious!"

"Thanks, I really am!" she laughed. "What does your husband do, Mrs. Tannehill?"

Stevie blushed.

The amiable expression that had come to Belle's face on meeting Mrs. Weeks changed to one of helplessness.

"We used to have a bakery," Robin said brightly.

"How nice! Then you'll start one here?"

"No. Papa says individual bakeries have lost out to the big companies that ship bread."

"What a shame! If he's looking for work, I'll tell Albert right away and—"

Belle's face recovered to smiling.

"Oh, no!" Robin broke in. "Thank you, but he's decided to travel. Some companies have made him an offer, but he hasn't made up his mind which—"

"It wouldn't be right to trouble you unless—" Belle stammered.

"No trouble," Mrs. Weeks said. "If nothing turns up, let me know. Albert is such a good man." She rose. "I must get back to my housework. Come and see me," she said, going out the door. "In the yellow house." She turned back and asked through the screen, "What's your first name, Mrs. T.? Mine's Penny."

Belle watched her out of sight.

"What a narrow escape! Robin, you're the limit!"

It was after two in the morning. Stevie and Robin, asleep in the new room in their old brass-postered bed, heard a noise and stirred awake, slowly at first, the sound crunching along under their sleep. The silence of the town throbbed like a pulse; they felt its strangeness all around them, mysterious in the dark. Stevie moved nearer Robin, sliding her cool feet over her sister's warm ones. The sound came steadily, made secret by weeds underfoot. It enlarged the silence. Robin sat up in bed and looked into the black dark, which churned in furry violence, shapes loomed in odd places. She lay down, remembering where she was. The alien sound came from far off but traveled closer, toward them.

"If it's a robber, what will you do?" Stevie asked, and dived under the covers.

"Chase him out," Robin whispered with mock boldness.

There was the swish of trouser legs and the rhythm of fast walking.

"It's Papa!" they shouted together.

"It's my old hoss," Stevie said happily. Then, warily: "Something must have happened! He wasn't playing in this town last night or we'd know, so why does he come home in the dark?"

"He always does."

"Not from a trip."

"Sometimes."

"Do you suppose he's running away?"

Their father's hurried steps came to the back door, which he shook impatiently. They heard Belle padding in her bare feet, unlatching the screen; they heard the kiss and the whispers.

Stevie sat up in bed. "Something's happened for sure!"

"He's caught! We'll have to move someplace else where there isn't a college!" Robin struck the pillow and pulled the covers violently over her head.

"Don't worry, sister," Stevie whispered. "In the morning I'll look at my list of junior colleges."

Robin subsided into a fierce silence. Her intensity made Stevie's heart pound but she thought calmly of the situation, feeling important with her sister's need. It was necessary—she rehearsed herself—to control all emotions; she was training her own, like innocent little beasts, to regard cautiously, to perform coolly.

The voices of her mother and father droned beyond the wall. Suddenly the middle door was flung open and her father's quick steps crossed the small living room and stopped. Stevie's heart thumped faster. He was coming to say good-by; he was running away again; he might be put in jail.

"Get up!" His voice was intimate, secret, excited. "Come on, get up! Steve, you awake?"

Stevie, feeling paralyzed with fright, crawled out.

"What's the matter with Cleopatra?"

Robin sprang out of her fury and threw the covers back. The hated nightgown, placed at the foot of the bed by Stevie for emergency of fire or storm, she put on as if the unexpected had come at last.

Des snapped the light on and the exposed bulb swung overhead. They stood blinking at him in the flat hard glare. His hat was pushed back and a small wing of damp hair clung to his forehead. He was smiling. The skin at the corners of his eyes crinkled with the good humor of his news.

"Come on." He snapped on the living-room bulb and glanced around to see if the shades were well drawn. Stevie was at his heels like a puppy.

Belle was standing in the doorway looking on. A shapeless nightgown torn at the armholes hid her small body. Her fine hair was mussed; this and her large eyes, gay with innocent excitement, gave her the appearance of a very young girl.

Des waited like an actor for their full attention, his smile steady and suggestive, teasing. He made a soft sound in his throat. Then he slid his right hand into his pants pocket and drew out a large and crumpled wad of bills, fanning it about triumphantly so that a small created wind nipped one of the bills away. As it fluttered downward, Stevie captured it expertly with one of her long hands. Des swiped at her.

"Give it back, Stevie honey," Belle said.

"No!"

"Let her have it, then," Des said, pleased.

He shoved the money back into his trousers and dipped both hands into his sagging coat pockets, from which came the pleasant sound of silver. He threw the coins high into the air, moving out of their way as they fell, watching, smiling. Stevie and Robin ran under them, catching by luck and skill, laughing, yelling, bumping each other. Des caught a few coins in mid-air like a juggler and flung them up again. The silver sped up to the ceiling and showered down, thudding upon their bodies, clinking on the furniture, rolling over the carpet and singing along the floor into dark corners. His hands plunged again and again and tossed the coins until his pockets were empty.

Stevie squatted down where she was, spread her nightgown around her, and shouted, "King's X!"

The game ceased. She drew her skirt away and picked up the silver, counting. "Twenty-nine eighty!" she announced. "Papa, how much did you win? You can't fool me with this." She jingled the money, enjoying the intimate and hopeful sound.

"I don't know. I'll count it before I go to bed." He looked at her with love. "God, you're tall, and still just a kid."

"Not in all ways." She frowned. "How much, old hoss?"

Des hesitated but brought out the money and motioned them to sit on the floor with him. He placed the bills in separate piles of ones, fives, tens, twenties. Belle stood over them, watching.

"Come on, Belle. We haven't had any money in God knows when."

Belle dropped to her knees, filling the circle.

Des looked at her with desire, but a flash of jealousy hardened his face. She wondered at the disparate looks he gave her; then she kissed his cheek and his gaiety returned.

"Eight hundred and ten dollars!" Stevie said with awe, and snatched a five-dollar bill.

"Eight hundred and five," Robin laughed.

"I haven't counted it yet, by God," Des said, flicking through the bills.

"I have," Stevie said, and pinched him.

"Take a twenty," Des said to Robin.

Stevie then took one.

"Here," he said, handing Belle a hundred dollars, looking at her faded nightgown with distaste. "Buy something for yourself."

"It's too much!"

"Take it while I've got it."

"Imagine!" Belle said. "It's been so long."

"There'll be more," Des said.

He was fingering the money, his eyes gone dull in abstraction. "I'll hold out two hundred for a bankroll, we'll pay the rent for three months and be safe, hold on to a little for groceries, and buy some clothes with the rest. Belle, you get a new dress and hat, and you kids, buy something for school. Don't get any cheap stuff. We've got the money now; get a few and get the best. I need a new suit. My ass is out."

"The mark of your trade." Stevie giggled.

"Is that any way to talk to your father?" he asked seriously.

Robin could see that this was one of the times he felt like a father.

He began to separate the bankroll from the money he would spend, a sober expression sitting on his face like a guest in a hurry to leave. "Buy the stuff tomorrow. You can't tell what will happen."

"We ought to get the house in order first," Belle said.

"The hell with the house. Spend the money. I might lose my wad and have to gamble with this." He tossed the bills to Belle.

"All right, Des honey."

"That's the way I like it." He turned to the girls and said, "She thinks she has a mind of her own. You know, when I was going with your mother, I used to ask her, 'How would you like to go rowing on the lake?' She'd say, 'I don't care.'" He twisted his shoulders and looked down, imitating her shyness. "That was what she said to everything. 'I don't care.' I should have known then."

"Ah, you like her," Robin said.

"Of course, I like her. Why, by God, I love her. But what would she do without a man like me?"

Belle sat very still, her expression changing from delight to hurt and back again.

"We sure caught a chump," Des said.

Robin saw her mother smooth and soften at his change of mood. The gambling details would go in one ear and out the other, but Belle would salvage his trust.

Des leaned back against a box and his hat slid over his forehead. He sailed it expertly onto Belle's head. Stevie reached for it quickly and placed it on her own.

"There's all kinds of chumps in the world just waiting to be taken," he said in the tone of a man imparting profound knowledge, feeling as if he and he alone had been chosen to warn these three unwise women in his charge. He was in no mood tonight, however, to attend to this responsibility. The hell with it; he could tell them about the ways of the world another time. "Well, I don't find one like this very often, but when I do, he's a dead pigeon. I take him, girls, I clean him. This fellow was crazy. He *wanted* to lose. The damn fool, he threw away his money. I hated to take it. I wanted the fun of playing. I told him once, I said, 'Look here, straighten up and gamble! I'm no hijacker. I'm a poker player and a damn good one; I can win your money fair and square, but, by God, let's have a game.'" Des hesitated and lowered his voice. "I was cheating him, see?"

"Naturally," Robin said.

"No, not naturally," Des said. "I play on the level plenty of times. But I was cheating *him.*"

"Why? If he wanted to throw his money away?"

"You can't tell. He might hold some good cards. Sometimes these dumb clucks are lucky. You have to be careful. These are games of chance, girls, even when I can outplay 'em. If you're going to make a living, you have to cheat."

"I know all that," she said.

"Papa." Stevie pointed an admonishing finger at him. "I'll bet you play fair a lot more than you tell us. That's why we're always so poor."

"Hell, we're not always so poor. Look at the traveling we've had. All over the country."

"That's just it. Our life is uncertain."

"Life is just as uncertain in one place. Now, you take this fellow, he's growing here like a cottonwood tree; yesterday he had a pocket full of money, today's he's broke."

They listened attentively as he continued with the story of how he met this gullible man whose money they had already divided. He related who played, what cards they held, what cards he skillfully dealt them, how tired he got in the stuffy hotel room, how thick the smoke was, how one fellow was drunk and he, Des, was disgusted and threw him out. He sighed. "It's a tough life." His eyes were shining. "Well, the poor devil, he lost every cent he had. I gave him back twenty dollars, and he said, 'Tannehill, you're a gentleman, sure enough.'"

"Poor man," Robin said thoughtfully.

"Poor fellow," Belle said. "We've got his money."

"But why did he play?" Stevie asked.

"That's something we'll never know, pard."

Des yawned and got up. "Come on, Belle. I've got to get some sleep. You know, this is a pretty good place to live. If I can make it, we'll stay here awhile."

SIX

THE TOWN of Apache squatted on the plains like an Indian squaw in her green velvet skirt. Trees, planted by early settlers, stood in the vast flat lands whose surface undulated in spring with the green of wheat and in summer with its yellow ripeness. In winter the plain was still and frozen, the short gray buffalo grass curled against the earth, huge fields in its midst green with winter wheat daubed with snow blown into drifts by the strong winds. Far apart, because of the large acreage of wheat farms, were nests of country buildings, scattered like the snowdrifts over the prairie. Good county roads led to other towns, and a national highway passed through Apache leading southwest and northeast.

East of the town, isolated sand dunes attested to centuries of shifting of the channel of a river. A dry creek with a clean sandy bed and treeless eroded banks made a sharp gash in the plain to the northeast, rose to the surface like a cow path, farther south, and a mile outside Apache sank again gently into a narrow sparkling stream edged with willows and cottonwoods and wild plum bushes, which soon gave out, the creek wandering aimlessly and without water over the gray land, hiding itself in a wild erupted place of great boulders, burro-gray and smooth as a hoof. Beyond this spot the creek retreated underground and was lost except to experts, who traced its rise in a safer place.

Indians in battle had dropped their stone arrowheads among the rocks, and, later, outlaws had hidden there; now, the Sunday picnickers sat in their hot shade, and little boys climbed in and out of their crevices, whooping like the painted warriors whose natural fortress the rocks had been less than seventy years before.

The Santa Fe railroad passed along the east side of town, separating, as if by design, the shanty town called Dirty Spoon—a mean term, since the place for the most part was neat and clean. Its old houses, scoured paintless by the sandy winds, had a soiled appearance as often do the worn clothes of the poor. Here the Negroes and poor whites lived with barriers of their own. A few cottonwood trees sparkled their brilliant green leaves in the hot, swift air; other trees, stunted for lack of water, left the sky open to sun and storm. The yards were bare and hard and brown.

51

This was the original town, built forty years before, old for these plains; and as towns in America grew westward, it had been left behind, uncared for, but profitably sold and rented to the poor.

The Negro men worked in the hotels, and at driving trucks and various hard labor; others were mechanics; a few owned small stores, there was one prosperous farmer, and one man more prosperous than all the rest made corn whisky and sold it to whites under the thin curtain of Prohibition. Their wives stayed at home and kept their houses, but the young women worked across the tracks as cooks and hired girls in the white wooden houses of the well-to-do.

The poor whites known as "Spooners" scrabbled around for odd jobs, did hard labor, and some of them worked in the harvests, but they were a sad lot. Having lost their place in the scheme of things through origin, or the misfortune of ignorance or event, they appeared to the outsider to live in bewilderment, dimmed hope, and even shiftlessness. For some reason known only to themselves they assumed a superior attitude to the Negroes but excused themselves for living in their midst by reminding listeners that Kansas had been a Free State. They were known occasionally to mention the safely dead John Brown. These historical references were not, however, expanded into practice, but it gave them pleasure to point out that this was hardly the only mixed neighborhood in Apache, since three or four Negro families lived over west with "the others." Dirty Spoon was a very small part of the whole town.

Immediately to the north of Dirty Spoon was the Apache depot, a red brick structure with a long loading platform of the same red brick. A row of dark red boxcars off their wheels lined the tracks south of the station, housing the Mexicans who worked on the railroad in their bright red coats and wide-brimmed hats. A short distance of weeds and track separated this small community from Dirty Spoon.

The Mexican women kept to their boxcar homes, doing the work of the family and the church. They tenderly nursed the stunted red geraniums growing in old syrup and lard cans which bordered the cars or lined the window ledges. The only other colors in the bare yards were bits of broken glass shining in the sun and their washed bright clothes on the lines ballooning in the wind. Young sons in springtime played their guitars and sang love songs, and daughters married early and settled alongside their parents or were sometimes forced to move "down the line" in search of work. Summer evenings were touched with their music, and if the wind was blowing from the east, songs carried faintly into ears across the tracks. A Catholic Church quite large for the Mexican community stood in a dry little clearing beyond the boxcars. The padre could often be seen coming and going, his long black skirts sweeping the dust of the grassless yards.

A quarter of a mile north of the depot, visible to everyone in Apache, a long line of grain elevators, tall and thin, housed the wealth of the surrounding land. They stood close to the tracks, ready to pour their wheat into the arterial trains running through the body of the nation.

Main Street ran west from the depot. People walking along it could see the fuming engines taking water or waiting for freight to be dropped or loaded. The fastest passenger trains whistled and sped through, but two of the big trains stopped for seven minutes, giving the citizens a sense of their town's importance.

All the children from east of the tracks walked through the main street of Apache to the public school at its western end.

The red brick school buildings stood in a square similar to those of older towns in the eastern part of the state. The town should have gathered around this square, but the western influence had pervaded, and the long, straight main street went its way. Its two-story buildings faced one another boldly. The old Royal Hotel and the new Bella Brock each had four floors. The Bella Brock was the scene of Apache's smartest social events.

Leisure was sternly for Sundays and holidays. Even among the handful of people who lived off large incomes from wheat lands, the men went daily about some routine in their land offices or on the farms. A man who did no honest work was not well tolerated by public opinion. If he chanced to enjoy his lazy life, he need not look forward to more than a poorly attended funeral.

As in many Western towns ungracious in the acceptance of death, Apache's cemetery lay unfenced on the open plain.

"What kind of suit will you get, Papa?" Robin asked, as she and Stevie admired the new clothes they had just modeled for Des.

"I've ordered it already. Tailor made."

She looked at him with surprise. He laughed.

53

"Papa!" Stevie said. "You were right here all the time! Didn't you care if we hadn't any money?"

"I was at the hotel playing," he said. "The Royal."

Belle came in. "Your breakfast's ready. I'll get out your clean clothes while you're eating." She kissed him. "Oh, Des, we had the most fun this afternoon shopping!"

"I've got to wash," Des said, and sprinted forward as if in a foot race, roaring with pleasure in his being.

"Hot water on the stove," she called after him.

Presently there was a shout from the kitchen so urgent that they ran through the rooms. Des, still in his underwear, with a wet washcloth held against his face as if he were paralyzed in motion, was looking out the kitchen window to the west.

"I'll be Goddamned!" he said dully, slowed by shock. "Come here, all of you."

They crowded round him, looking into the next yard, where they could see nothing but its neat bareness, a few heavy work clothes on the line, and a small unpainted house.

"Watch!" Des commanded.

A tall Negro boy came out of the shed with an armful of kindling and a scuttle of coal. He carried them into the house and came back for the clothes on the line. A light went on, pale in the early dusk, swinging slowly from the ceiling. A woman, perhaps in late middle age, moved about the kitchen. The boy came in from the yard and promptly pulled the shade.

"Niggers!" Des said.

Belle caught her breath but she said nothing, moving to the first task in sight. Robin reached up and turned on the light bulb as if she hoped to clear the air of a coming storm.

"I'll knock that damned landlord's head off!" Des said, walking up and down the small room.

"Wash your face," Belle urged gently. "Your breakfast is getting cold."

"To hell with breakfast! You haven't a bit of sense. How can I eat now?"

She did not reply.

"What would your Southern folks say now?" Des asked maliciously, as if he had discovered one facet of good in the situation.

"Well," Robin said, "I certainly intend to be as friendly with them as anyone else, if I like them. What have they done to us?"

"Nothing," Des said. "They're black. But don't mistreat them. I don't believe in that."

"We were all friends with the Indians—you most of all," Robin said. Belle was making signs at her to be silent.

"I've got some nigger friends," Des said, "but I live out in the world. Things are different out there. Besides, I'm a man."

"I suppose when you leave here you go through a big gate and you're out in the world. Men only."

"You're too damned smart. It's tough out there. Sometimes you have to be tough. You can't go around wagging your tail believing in everybody."

"Papa," Stevie said, "they're very clean. Maybe they're nice too."

"Maybe they are, pard, maybe they're good enough people, but it's the idea." The anger had gone out of his face, leaving it crumpled with misery. "I want to raise you kids right." He went into the middle room and closed the door. They heard him dressing in a hurry.

The girls hung about the kitchen, saying nothing. Belle stood at the stove; her tears fell onto the hot iron top, sizzled and spat with faint deprecation, and rolled away in little spheres which vanished in steam.

"We mustn't mix," she pleaded carefully, very low.

"But Mama," Stevie whispered, "there was colored at school a lot of places we've lived."

"That isn't next door."

Robin and Stevie exchanged looks.

Des came into the kitchen fully dressed and wearing his hat. He took a deck of cards from his pocket, glanced at it, and tossed in onto the table. The seal was broken; the cards had been used. Tomorrow, he thought, I'd better order a new supply while I'm in the chips.

"We'll move," he said, but the other three knew that the fifteen-dollar-a-month rent would dissipate this decision. He picked up the cards he had thrown down and placed them farther back on the table away from the food. His eyes were dark with suppressed excitement and his voice was passionate, remote. The three stood away from him as if they were fixed by his mood, and he remained clear of them as if they might invade the intensity of his emotion and force him prosaically away from his caprice, vague and unrealized as it was in his mind. He reached for the deck, then let it be.

Stevie lunged against his chest. "Papa, stay home!"

"I can't," he said distantly, and went out the back door.

They listened to his quick steps going away over the bare yard to the alley and the vacant lot beyond to the sidewalk that led toward Main Street.

"That's it," Robin said with a curious acceptance that made the others turn to her. "Chicken one day, feathers the next. May as well lock the door."

When Des entered Matt's Store for Men, he gave the place a quick expert glance of approval to please the owner, whom he liked. Merchandise was displayed with taste, the best quality alongside the reasonably priced, but nothing shoddy, all of it dependable. A poor man need not feel embarrassed here; his price was not in another department to the rear. The whole store had an air of quality and decency, no bargains but no highway robbery either.

Matt, looking calm and good-natured, was standing behind a tie case, drumming softly on the glass with the eraser end of a pencil. He came from behind the case and held out his hand. "Good evening, Mr. Tannehill," he said with genuine pleasure. "Your suit will be ready in a few days now. The tailor took the day off for his daughter's wedding."

"No hurry, Mr. Gregory. Let me see some white shirts. Size sixteen."

He bought six good shirts, two ties, black socks, a pair of shoes, a hat, all very quickly, not rushing but in a concentrated way that Matt Gregory admired. Des tried the new hat several times and kept it on. Gregory set the old hat, still shapely and good, into the box.

"Give this to some fellow," Des said.

Matt smiled, knowing better than to protest with a customer like Tannehill. "I know just the man, had a stretch of hard luck lately. A good honest chap."

"I'm not well acquainted yet."

"This is a good place to settle," the shopkeeper said. "What business are you in, Mr. Tannehill? I'd like to introduce you around." He looked at Des with real liking and trust.

Des thought, He's a good fellow. I wouldn't cheat him. "No business, Mr. Gregory. I'm a baker by trade, but I never work at it. Doesn't suit me."

"I can see that."

"I'm a gambler by profession," Des said, lowering his voice although the place was empty. "I work at that."

"Sounds like an interesting life to me," Gregory said, trying to conceal his surprise. "This whole kaboodle of existence is a gamble. You must meet a lot of interesting people."

"I do. The best and the worst."

"Well," Gregory said, "I'll introduce you around just the same, maybe in a little different circumstances." He laughed. "You wouldn't want to join the Chamber of Commerce. It's a place to go, and we do look after certain interests of the community."

"No, that wouldn't be right. I'd have to lie, and I don't want to do that."

Matt Gregory glowed with vindication. "A good many of the businessmen gamble, the ones with money. Myself, I don't. I've no objection to the fun of it, but it's too risky. I've a fair-sized family, fine wife, two boys and three girls. I want to take good care of them, and that keeps my nose pretty close to the grindstone. People are a bit strict here, though not too bad. A fellow feels the pinch sometimes, but it's a good town. No rough stuff." He hesitated. "A gentleman like you won't have any trouble."

Des paid for his purchases and said he would leave them until he was ready to go home again. Gregory followed him to the door and watched him go down the street. That man has courage, Gregory thought, unaware of the routine courage of his own everyday life. He went back into the store, lifted Tannehill's old hat from the box, and tried it on before the full-length mirror. He studied himself a long time. The hat was so shaped to the other's head that, thinking also of a certain Irish look they dimly shared, he fancied himself for a moment the adventurous man of the world, at home in any company, and somehow pleasing to them all. But there was something lacking, he admitted. He had the build and the friendly good looks, his own intelligence and ways, but he hadn't the *air* of Tannehill. Keeping the hat on, he selected a new one, reasonably priced, placed it in the box, and set it aside. "I'll give that to old Barnes," he said aloud. "It's his right size. I promised him one even if he doesn't know it."

Gregory went back to an alcove he called his office. There he removed Tannehill's hat and ran his hand around the slight roll of the brim, looking with possessive pleasure at the stained sweat-band. He tried the hat on once more, then shoved it with a falsely casual air onto the shelf of a little closet, closed the door, and stood reading the gold lettering on the wood. For the first time he recognized its profound meaning: *Private.*

Des was absorbed in the sudden sensuous desire to spend money on himself; to go to the night-lighted barber shop, to enter the soft cushion of moist air, articulate with bay rum, witch hazel, and other tonics; to lie back in a chair under a steaming towel and luxuriate in the warm, male world of a public shave. Men would be talking and he, under the heated towel, could listen to them, to everything—the stropping of the razor, the flick of cloth disposing of hairs, the competent sound of the hot-water faucet turned on full, the long, artful strokes of the blade; scissors snipping, the lazy metallic snarl of the door opening, closing, and the voices, idle, easy, friendly.

When he came out of the barber shop onto the street again, none of the indistinct, excessive urge had abated. Instead, it was pressing him, against his will, into the unknown, enticing him away from the clean decision to work. Street lights sparking the dark intensified his sense of excitement.

Two women passed and one of them had a pretty behind, as shapely as the ace of hearts and as quivering soft as an unbaked bun. He watched it for a while. Maybe he ought to go home to Belle and he'd feel all right.

Suddenly he remembered how at times in the bakery when he was rolling and shaping dough he held one of the loaves in both hands to his loins and chased Belle about the large floury room, roaring and laughing. She ran among the bread troughs, the heavy wooden tables, the pan racks where the breads and confections were rising or cooling, to the huge brick oven, and threatened to crawl in; or she grabbed the long wooden peel pole and held him away. Usually she only hid her face and squealed; Belle wasn't one to defend herself in any way. If the little girls were present, they watched in sober perplexity their mother seemingly frightened, their father yelling with laughter. Once they joined the chase. There were other times, of course, when pursuit had excited him so much that he threw the loaf back on the board and forced Belle down on the clean-scrubbed floor.

Well, a woman was not what he wanted now.

He heard a train and walked to the station. Five or six university students were surrounded by a party of friends. An old woman and a small boy alighted from the train and hesitated near Des.

"This child's parents were just killed in an auto accident," she said. "The poor little waif has no one in the whole world but me, and I'm only his great-aunt. Too old for a child too, but he's a dear."

"Hello, young fellow," Des said.

"Oh, here's Catherine for us!" the woman said, and tugged the child away.

Des walked back the length of the main street, forcing his thoughts into order. He had already learned that the law in this town could be paid off, and as soon as he had a game set in the hotel he would talk to the sheriff, find out how much he wanted for letting him run without raids. Or if his deputies had to raid the place before elections to keep up appearances, they would warn him, giving him a chance to stay clear. This sheriff was no crook; he was a good fellow with a big family and he needed money.

Des liked Apache. It was one of the best of the wheat towns; and it looked like something, it was no wide place in the road.

He started walking fast toward the Royal Hotel.

The Royal (which had once been spelled Royale) was Apache's popular hotel. It was admirably situated on Main Street. Although there were vague rumors about its extracurricular means of revenue, they remained rumors. The big, gloomy lobby, crowded with nondescript furniture of questionable comfort, was lighted by dusty chandeliers and lamps wearing dark fringed shades. In the back was a large square cage made of wrought iron with an open front in which Farquarson, the night clerk, presided over the guest register and a glass case of sundries.

Des stared down at the tumult of cigars, cigarettes, gum, playing cards, and a spool of black sewing thread with a needle stuck in its top.

"Farquarson, you ought to dust those old cards so they all look alike. Dust everything and shine up this glass. Put the cards between the cigars and cigarettes."

The clerk nodded with respect.

The two Negro porters who had just come on night duty were working about the lobby. One of them, Bowman, signaled toward three men facing the large window. They were complaining that Apache was "out in the sticks." Wherever they were from, their own source on the map made them feel superior.

Farquarson's prune-wrinkled face showed no curiosity. Bowman and Winston pantomimed to Des a call for revenge. Des was suddenly aware of a thrill of resentment like an electric current which dissipated in a glow of loyalty to Apache. By God, I'll give them a trimming.

"Anything doing around here tonight, fellows?" he asked the porters. "This is my birthday. I want to celebrate."

"No liquor in Kansas," Bowman said. "Looks like you gonna haf to contrap yuhsef some amusement of yuh own."

After a few more exchanges Des said, "I might as well go back to my room and go to bed."

They protested, saying Apache hadn't waked up yet. Des picked up a *Kansas City Star* and sat down to read in sight of the men.

"Hell of a town," one of them said to Des, "sitting around here waiting for nothing."

Des bluntly suggested poker. It was apparent that Apache was the last place they would expect to be taken in.

"You fellows any cards on you?"

No one had.

"Then we can get some at the desk. I just noticed them over there under a lot of dust."

As the four of them went toward the cage, Farquarson leaped up and flicked the dust off the cards. He reached for one of the marked decks that Des had given him. Des spun a silver dollar on the glass above the unmarked decks. Farquarson's hand, feathered with black silky hairs, wavered over the cards like a bird of prey. He lifted an unmarked deck and brought it out in an agony of indecision.

"How much?" Des smiled, trying to ease him, but it was clear that Farquarson was not to be eased. He would have to talk to him; he was too nervous.

"Where's your room?" one of the men asked.

"First floor."

"Let's play there." He laughed. "Gambling's against the law, isn't it?"

"Sure," Des said. "Everything good is against the law or unhealthy. Let's go."

"Every damned thing's a gamble," one of the men said brightly. "But in poker we fool 'em; we set right down and gamble in the old girl's face. Come on, Fate!" He raised his hat in imaginary greeting.

Des led the way across the lobby down a murky hall, lighted dimly by elbow-shaped lamps with amber frosted globes designed as tulips.

"Think we're safe?" someone said.

"Sure," Des answered. "The law's in bed like everyone else." He had purposely taken a room on the first floor back with a window opening onto the alley. In case of a raid, they could all be outside in a few minutes. He had already unhooked and loosened the screen. From experience he knew the players would be businessmen, and an occasional working man on a spree. Respected citizens needed assurance against scandal. Once they were acquainted with him and knew he was running a game for their pleasure as well as his living, they would come around of their own accord.

"I wouldn't live in a farmer town," one of the strangers said confidentially to Des.

The angry red eye of the naked exit bulb glared from the end of the hall. Des stopped and unlocked his door, and the men filed into the windy room. He had left the window open to drive out the stale tobacco smell from nights before.

In a backward glance toward the lobby he saw Bowman's stringy shape outlined against the stronger light. The porter raised his hand and swiped it down in a gesture of negation; he was worried about the cards. Des smiled. Bowman had more brains than that groveling clerk; he'd pay him this winter to keep an eye out for restless travelers and any deputy sheriff who was no good and wouldn't take a bribe.

The men stood together in the room. Des flipped the heavy cover off the table and laid it over the foot of the bed.

"Be better, I guess, if we left it on," he said, and replaced it.

"Sure," someone said expertly, and they all relaxed.

Des studied the men as they sat at the table. He hoped they were good players; he wanted a contest.

Bowman long-stepped down the hall and tapped lightly on the door.

"Portah," he called softly.

"Anything wrong?" A stranger's voice.

"Nawsuh." He directed his voice toward Tannehill. "Want anything, sir, 'fore you get started?"

"No, thanks."

Bowman went back along the hall, shaking his head. "Dawgone."

In the lobby he looked at the agitated clerk. "He don' want nothin'."

"Man, you talk more like a nigger every day," Winston said.

"You black scamp, you growin' up with no manners and no respeck for nobody."

"How you like being *nobody?*"

"Nevah min' that," Bowman said calmly. "I'se somebody same as you. I got a diff'rent approach. Ain't nobody knows what ah'm thinkin'."

"Ah dee-clare," Winston mimicked him good-naturedly, "ain't that somepen!"

"Leave me be, now. I gotta he'p out Tannehill. Down under the skin he's a friend a mine."

"Tannehill's okay," Winston said.

Farquarson drooped over the case and mournfully studied the playing cards. "I was going to get a washing machine for my wife for Christmas with the money I'd get between now and then, and in the spring, maybe, a lawn mower."

"Don' give up so easy," Bowman said. "I'm ruminatin'."

As the men continued to play and he looked for the game to go on till daylight, he decided on one of his plans. He had faith in Tannehill's playing but there was no use taking chances, and, besides, Farquarson was in a mess. The lobby was deserted but the clerk did not take his usual nap. Winston was asleep in a deep leather chair.

Bowman jingled the silver in his pocket and went out. He came back with four cups of coffee and slithered along the hall, carrying the tray with expert abandon. He listened at the door. The small tick and slap of the cards were the only sounds. He knocked and called out his identity.

When he entered the three strangers were pleased, but Bowman caught an annoyed glance from Tannehill, who handed him a dollar bill. The men had their hats pushed back, collars open, and ties pulled loose. The air was heavy with smoke. Cigar butts filled an old bronze ashtray the edge of which was a coiled snake with metal scales and raised head.

A single green eye glittered, the other lost, giving it the expression of an evil wink.

Bowman watched Tannehill's face for a sign, knowing better than to interrupt him while the gambler's eyes were on his hand. He wondered painfully if Tannehill was in trouble. There was a peculiar look about him tonight, like something almost let loose. His face was soft, slack, but his eyes and mouth were intent with controlled fury. He's a mean man, Bowman thought, when he wants to be, but he ain't one a them no-good men, he got lotsa points. Somepen's jus' stirred up his bile, I reckon. It's that weak-kneed Farquarson givin' him a straight deck of cards.

Bowman's eyes were drawn to the single glass eye of the serpent. That thing tryin' to work his black art on me, he thought, and quickly denied believing in any such trash.

Tannehill took a drink of coffee and Bowman gathered all the pretense in him and said casually, "Looks lak to me you fellahs done wore out them cards. They all beat up. 'Speck I bettah bring some fresh ones. What you all think?"

"These cards are all right," Des said shortly.

The green eye stared at Bowman with malign satisfaction. Jus' a piece a ol' glass, he reassured himself. Jus' 'cause I'm black don't mean I'm that ignerant.

Tannehill's face was set again, soft and hard, easy and mean. Bowman leaned against the dresser and his arm slipped on a Gideon Bible. Some people looked in the Bible for a sign—just opened the book blindly and placed a finger on a verse, and the words were a piece of advice from heaven. He didn't dare question this as a superstition; he was afraid of God. In spite of his fear, this action reminded him of consulting the dream book, which was one of the most foolish things he had ever heard of. Blasphemy, git outa this black man's mind. You'll beat me outa heaven, and I ain't got nothin' ahead but heaven. Excuse me, Lawd. He was in no position now to open the Bible, but he reckoned Tannehill wouldn't let himself be helped.

Bowman watched the three men. Two of them were ordinary poker players, but the third man was playing right along with Tannehill, the two quiet and skilled, wily and daring. Bowman saw Tannehill's face change with pride in his own ability, and pleasure in the challenge.

"If you're going to sweat this game," Des said, "get us some cigars first, all around, two or three apiece."

"Yassuh!" Bowman went gloomily back to the lobby. The look in Tannehill's eyes as he played took the form of disturbing knowledge in his thoughts. He hurried over to Farquarson. "Twelve cigars, Tannehill's brand."

"What's that?" the clerk demanded sourly.

"I disremember," Bowman lied.

Farquarson brought out a half-empty box of Santa Fes, glancing accidentally at Bowman's face, mournful in repose.

"What's wrong with *you?*" the clerk asked resentfully, as if he had a corner on sorrow.

"Tannehill's gone clean outa his wits," Bowman said as if betrayed. "He ain't jus' no col'-headed gambler the way I thought, he's a *gamblin' man* besides. His eyes on them cards like they wuz a woman. His whole heart and soul in them little cards. An' he hot after them big-town strangers like a hawk after three little chickens. I ain't gonna worry 'bout him no mo' tonight. He playin' fine. He col' an' hot at the same time. Ain't no bettah combination, I reckon."

"He'll lose," the clerk said. "Those fellows have luck. I could tell the way they acted."

"Nex' time you see me actin' lak luck hangin' round me, say so."

"I can tell," Farquarson said. "I can feel it in my bones."

"Man, you all wet. Gimme them cigars."

Bowman was quick about leaving the cigars but he stole one good look at Tannehill's concentrating face, and as he went back along the hall he clicked his tongue smartly.

In the lobby he stretched out in a chair and went to sleep.

About three-thirty in the morning the men trooped wearily through the lobby and into the all-night café. Bowman woke up.

In less than an hour the men came back. The strangers stopped in front of the elevator and signaled for Bowman. The one who had been playing the best shook hands with Tannehill, but the two who were traveling together stood sullenly by.

Bowman took his place as pilot.

As the three stepped in, the one who had shaken hands said to Tannehill, "I may run into you again sometime. We might get together."

"You never can tell," Tannehill replied.

Bowman closed the door and the cage groaned upward belligerently.

"That guy is a goddamn crook!" one of the two said. "He was cheating us all night."

"I ought to go back down there and punch him in the nose!"

Bowman kept the elevator going upward.

"You're wrong, fellows. He just out-played us. He's a good card-player, but he's no crook. There was no cheating in this game."

"Hell, you can say so. You won some of your money back."

"Damn little."

"I say he cheated."

"You won't hear me squawking. He beat us fair and square. You guys have no business gambling."

Bowman stopped the elevator and the two stepped out. As soon as the door banged to, the stranger said, as if to himself, "Poor sports."

"Yassuh," Bowman said.

"This fellow downstairs, is he running a game in the hotel?"

"Nawsuh."

"Come on, now, George, what's the dope?" He held out a five-dollar bill.

"Ain't no dope. He's a stranger jus' like you all."

The other held the money out as if he hadn't heard.

"Mistah, thas all I know, and it ain't worth no money."

The gambler shoved the bill back in his pocket as the elevator halted. "Just wanted to know before I go to sleep." He laughed.

Bowman tried to zoom the decrepit elevator down to the lobby but it rattled along at its accustomed pace.

Tannehill was standing at the window. Bowman went over to the desk where Farquarson sagged like a wilted house plant in stale water. The gambler came over to them, his walk light and springy, his eyes thick-lidded and bloodshot but shining in his tired face, shadowed by the new day's beard. His smile at Bowman was intimate, triumphant. He handed him a twenty-dollar bill. "Kinda looking out for me, eh, Bowman?"

"Tryin'!"

"I might need it sometime, Bowman, but not tonight."

"I seen that, sho' enuf."

Des was pleased. He went over to the sleeping Winston and stuck a ten-dollar bill in the breast pocket of his jacket.

"Farquarson," he said at last, "your heart's in the right place but your brain's in your ass. If I don't give you a sign, you give me my own cards. See? This is no silent movie. I can't give you a five-minute wink that draws up the whole side of my face. Now listen, if I give you the eye, you know I want to play on the square. That won't happen often. I'm a gambler. I've got to make a living. Tonight was different. I had to trim those boys." He shoved twenty dollars across the desk and the clerk's limp hand captured the money. Farquarson folded the bills lovingly into a square and secreted them in the small watch pocket beneath the belt of his trousers, stood back, and tightened his belt one notch. Des watched him and was about to say something to take the sting out of his last remarks when Farquarson looked up and grinned in a completely satisfied way. Des knew right then he could never trust the clerk, that Farquarson would do anything for money as long as it was small and secret.

"You're cut in, you understand that. If I lose, you don't get anything. The more I win the more you get, but nobody wins all the time. You won't ever catch me lying about my winnings, and I don't want to catch you at anything."

"Don't ever worry," the clerk said, smiling, and his hand caressed the small pocket under his belt.

"Give me another room," Des said, paying him. "Take out for the cigars."

"Aren't you going home?" Farquarson asked in surprise.

"That's my business. I'm tired. I want to go to sleep right now, in a clean place." He picked up the key and walked over to the window again, looking out into the gray deserted street where little flights of dust eddied over the pavement. A newspaper blown upright like a sail slid along the shallow gutter. In another hour the empty, lonesome street would be splashed with sun. I might go on a little trip, he thought. The hollow morning filled him with yearning.

Bowman was in the cage, sewing a button on his coat. He watched Tannehill go along the hall. He on his way to sleep like a fast train. I reckon sleep's just a little ol' station to him, like the Chief whistlin' through Apache.

SEVEN

DES SLEPT all day and all night. The next morning he got up early, breakfasted, and was eager to get home. He stopped at Matt's to get the package he had left and to inquire about a fitting with the tailor.

As he crossed the alley that ran behind the Royal Hotel, he noted that half its length was obstructed by the fenced back lots of a feed-and-grain store, a garage, and a sheet metal shop. He passed the low buildings, made of gray cement blocks, housing these shops that hummed and clanged with their work, and began measuring in his thoughts the distance between the back window of his room in the Royal Hotel and the back door of his house on Burkett Street, three blocks south of Main Street and east toward the railroad tracks. If the law ever gets tough, he said to himself, I've got to know my way around. It was certain that he could not take a short cut through these back ways, but would have to run east down the alley, which was dangerous because too far and hemmed in, or come out boldly onto this side street and walk its one-block length before reaching a small park.

He crossed a wide, busy avenue and entered the park. Apache was dotted with small, nameless, block-square gardens. In this one, narrow gravel paths, no wider than cow trails, began from its four sides and converged in the center, which was handsomely occupied by a polished limestone courthouse. When Des reached the southeast corner, he looked up at the third-floor windows ribbed with iron bars. He tried his best to feel afraid, as if this emotion would act as a provision against danger, a mental rabbit's foot to touch each time he would have to cross Jail Park. He felt himself far too intelligent to be dismayed by a superstition, but the thought persisted, and he quickened his step. A series of muffled whistles and shouts from above made him look up once more, and there in the shadows of the deep stone-ledged windows he could make out the dim figures of men. A chill of fear made the hairs rise on his arms. He kept walking and looking upward, and the voices reached him again. At first he thought they were sounds of derision, but he soon realized that the prisoners were merely amusing themselves by greeting passers-by and that their tone was as friendly as might be expected under the circumstance. He raised his hand in greeting and a chorus of pleased replies followed him down the street.

When he returned to the house Belle was stitching in the sleeve of a gingham school dress. Robin was sitting on the floor, cutting out another dress from green wool. Folded blue wool already cut lay beside her.

Des looked at the array of material suspiciously. "Where did you get that stuff?"

"Bought it," Robin said.

"With what?"

"We traded some buffalo hides."

"You know, I could take some of that Irish out of you," he said, and she looked up and smiled.

"Papa, look here," Stevie said, "I am darning your socks!"

He looked pleased and lay down on the bed.

They concentrated on their work, but now they neither spoke nor laughed. He might want to sleep; he had said nothing of the time he had been away.

Presently he sat up, smiling. "Say, I have a new story!" This was a familiar announcement after a night out or a trip.

Robin and Stevie held their fingers to their ears.

"This one is all right," he said. "Open your ears. It's just a riddle. I'll ask Belle, but she'll never guess it."

"Oh, shut up!" Belle said good-naturedly. "If my mind had been any better, I'd have been wise enough not to marry you."

He laughed. "The old gal's got her spunk up. That's the influence of you goddamn kids. You're just like me. Well, here's the riddle. What does a man do standing up, a woman sitting down, and a dog on three legs?"

"Oh-h-h," Belle said triumphantly.

He would have been disappointed if one of them had come upon the answer.

"Shake hands!" he shouted, and when they all laughed he leaped up from the bed.

"Papa," Stevie said, "I have a riddle for you. What shall we say at school is your occupation or business?"

There was a pause.

"Should we say a college professor?" Stevie asked seriously. "But it can't be that, although you could have been one if you'd had a chance to go to college."

"Hell, I'm no professor. I'd have been a lawyer."

"What does your father do? What does your father do?" Stevie chanted dismally.

"We could say he's dead," Robin said, looking at Des, daring to say it because he was filled with high spirits and good health.

"By God, I can't be a ghost. I like this town. I'll be around here quite a bit if I can make a deal with the sheriff."

Stevie's mind prudently selected and discarded trades and professions generally labeled respectable. For herself she did not care. Her imagination, which traveled so fancifully into the future, never followed him into the hotel rooms, through the games. Although he sat at the table for hours at a time practicing with cards, keeping his fingers supple, his eye quick, and his mind alert, this was as ordinary as if he had been a musician, sitting daily at the piano, acquiring skill, perfecting his art. Love for her father was the principal reason that a respectable profession must be invented so that others would not misunderstand and regard him as contemptible or worthless. She wished him to be, if anything else than himself, an expression of her own interests. Why could he not be a scholar? This thought was accompanied by a feeling of betrayal, which she hastily plucked out of her mind.

"It's best to say that I'm a traveling man," Des said. "I represent some company in Kansas City or Chicago. I sell farm machinery, say."

"Good," Robin said. To call him a salesman, a realtor, a banker was no solace to her except as a wedge between him and injustice. "Is that really all right?"

"God, yes. In the last few years these big wheat farms use so much machinery that I'll be just another traveling man. I work only between the manufacturer and the dealer, see? That way, I won't be expected to visit the farmers around here."

"All right," Stevie said. "Say it once more, Papa."

He repeated it, adding details. Another problem, Stevie thought—one she shared with Robin—was that usually the lie failed, the news leaked out, and they were exposed at school in all the embarrassment of pretense. Would Apache be tolerant? New towns were best, less meddlesome. Apache was not new. In every town, she remembered warmly, there were people who were their friends, but Apache, like each strange place, loomed hostile. Robin, more openly friendly, fared better than she. Stevie glanced at her sister in a confusion of admiration and dislike. Robin was basting the green wool dress and in a moment she would be asking Stevie to stand for a fitting.

Des went into the kitchen. They heard the water running and knew that he was washing his face and combing his hair. He came back, straightening his tie.

"How do I look?" he asked them.

"Very handsome!" Belle said.

"Then I'm going to sit on the porch," he said, and went out.

Presently, they saw Mrs. Polk come from her back yard, carrying a rake and broom. Pretending not to see the new neighbor on his porch, she leaned the rake against the house and daintily began to sweep the walk. The yard was a testimonial to Mrs. Polk's consummate surrender to disorder. As an unnecessary postscript, strands of sorrel hair fell upon her slender neck from the stately high roll which slid a little to one side. Her dress was of another era and function, made of amber silk and lace, faded with time and stained in kitchen duty. In spite of all opposition, Mrs. Polk's elegance was undiminished. Her bearing, her manner, her voice, and the quiet assurance with which she spoke, all declared that she had not quitted her past and that numerous aspects of the present were less than nothing to her. Her curiosity, like her amber dress, she retained. It was visible in her back, which she reluctantly presented all the way down the walk. When she turned toward the house, she accidentally, then modestly, glanced at Des, and nodded in proper neighborly fashion.

Des rose and spoke politely. Indoors, the three watched Mrs. Polk smile.

"Now," Robin said, "Papa is establishing his other self with the neighbors. The news will spread."

In a little while they heard Des offer to rake the leaves in her yard, and she in turn offered the loan of the rake.

"I'll bet she never raked her leaves any other autumn," Belle said.

EIGHT

STEVIE AND ROBIN walked home from school the same way old Duvette's Ford had brought them two months before. They looked, as if not looking, at all the houses they passed; they gazed discreetly at the few persons they met, feeling the privileged alien pride of the stranger unsated with familiarity and experience. They were so accustomed to adjusting themselves to new surroundings that the first day was long ago in their minds. Apache, though still in the arid lands, enchanted them with its trees.

The trees disguised the shabbiness of Burkett Street at its east end, but now that leaves were falling the old houses were daily more exposed; they appeared embarrassed and ashamed, as old beauties might, caught unawares, forced to reveal the damage of many seasons. One house sat neatly within a wrought-iron fence, and as the girls approached Stevie slowed her step to prolong a pleasure. The fence was the key to its special being; its iron had the abiding quality of trees; it was a symbol of permanence that she and Robin had never known, and would reject, and to which she was drawn. On still nights when they sat on the low porch of their own house, Stevie heard this gate click with intimate assurance as someone passed in or out. On other nights she traced the design in her thoughts, invoking the domestic sound to recur.

Within the fence a middle-aged woman, bending and moving with quick strength, was filling a large basket with brown and yellow leaves. When she saw the girls she stopped and came to the gate. "You're the new girls down the street! I've been trying to catch you but you drift by like two angels and I miss you, the way one always misses angels!"

Robin smiled and Stevie looked away shyly.

"Tannehill, I've heard, but what are your first names?"

"Robin and—" Robin waited for her sister to deliver her own name.

"Speak for yourself, dear," the woman said gently, and after Stevie uttered her name she added, "Always this problem with sisters and brothers. I've two daughters of my own and a son, all grown and gone. Let us get acquainted! Do you know my name?"

"No, ma'am," Stevie said.

The woman smiled at Stevie, and her gray, intelligent eyes shone as if moist. Her rather plain face, of squarish prominent bones, a small nose, and full mouth, all undistinguished in design, possessed an excellence of tenderness and sensibility.

"I'm Mrs. Sutton. Mrs. Lafe Sutton. Lillie Jones Sutton. Now you know me!" She laughed. She looked from one to the other again in her thorough but unoffending way. "What beautiful girls! Blond and brunette, and sort of transparent, not quite real!"

They blushed.

"And modest too! Good! They say beauty is a handicap, but I was always plain, hungering after beauty—inside and out!"

They had never heard anyone speak in this way and it made them uneasy although they were pleased. No words came to their tongues.

"You are rather special beauties, my dears, not usual at all, and you may as well get used to people saying so."

"Nobody ever says that about me. Always about sister."

"It's only because she isn't seen," Robin said. "She likes to stay home and tag after Papa."

Mrs. Sutton laughed aloud. "I have a piano," she said. "You'll both have to come over and play. I'm sure you do."

"No. Stevie wants to. That's her dream."

"Shut up!" Stevie whispered, and pinched Robin.

Mrs. Sutton's quick eyes saw her. "Tonight I'm burning leaves. We love the smell of burning leaves in the autumn evenings. My husband is an invalid. Have you heard that?"

"No, ma'am."

"Gossip must be declining in Apache. News spreads like wildfire and so does everyone's private business. Now, I've heard all about you people."

The sisters were aware of each other's alarm but each concealed her feelings.

"Well, I always bring my Lafe out in his wheel chair while I burn the leaves. It is one of our finest pleasures. Would you girls like to come over about seven-thirty?" She looked at Stevie, waiting for an answer. "Do come! And it would please Lafe."

"Thank you," Robin said. "We'll come."

Mrs. Sutton's eyes were grave above her smile, and Robin was sure that she saw an expression of gratitude.

At first the girls walked in silence. Stevie's face was set with her troubled thoughts. Then she said firmly, "I'm not going."

"Why? Don't you want to?"

"I might, but I'm not going."

"I think she's lonesome," Robin urged.

"I'll bet she knows everybody. And she knows about us!"

"Maybe. I think she's lonesome in a—well, a very private way."

"Ha-ha," Stevie replied scornfully. "You think you're big like Mrs. Sutton or John Greenleaf Whittier or Papa. Being lonesome is always a private matter."

"Special, then." Robin stared at Stevie's flushed, angry features. "You sound as if you have a big lonesomeness."

"That is my affair. She only asked me because I was along."

"Oh, silly, she especially wants *you*. I saw that, and I don't care."

"Why should you? You have your dates. I hate boys!"

"Well, I don't."

"Mr. Sutton is an invalid!" Stevie said.

"Well, poor man, what of it?"

"Invalids make me think of bread mold. Remember the time we came back from a trip and opened the bread box and it was all full of mold? Like opening a grave."

"Mr. Sutton has a clean heart disease," Robin said.

"You said you hadn't heard that. Who told you?"

"The postman."

After they had walked a way, not speaking, Stevie asked tentatively, "Do you think Papa will let us go?"

"Why not?"

"Then we'd better not be late."

Inside the house was dark. The sparkling afternoon reached vainly through the narrow, curtained windows. Des was pacing the floor. He wore his hat as he often did indoors, and now he pushed it back and greeted them. "Well, if it isn't my young professors!"

"Papa, we're going to Mrs. Sutton's tonight," Stevie said. "She's going to burn leaves. She's the woman with the iron fence."

"Well, say now, I want Robin to do something for me. You can go some other time," Des said.

"I can go. Can sister take me to the gate?"

"Sure."

Belle came in from the kitchen. "How was school?"

73

"Better than any other place!" Robin said happily.

"Remember I found it," Stevie boasted.

"Living better now makes us all feel happier," Belle said.

Des looked puffed up with virtue.

An open package lay on the table in a plain brown wrapper. New, sealed decks of cards were in it. A money sack hung from the edge of the table, held there by its long cloth tongue weighted down with silver coins. Calling for their attention, Des held the sack in one hand and upended the tongue with the other, causing the money to slide quickly and safely inside.

"Good for a swift getaway if the law raids me some night," Des said. "I could leave some money on the table if I have to and save all the rest with this."

Stevie picked up a blue deck of cards.

"Put that down," Des commanded. "Robin, right after supper, I'll show you how to mark these cards. My eyes hurt. I've been all afternoon working out a new set of marks for this design. I brought home a big light bulb so we can see."

Robin looked down at the decks, concealing her pleasure and aversion.

"I wouldn't mark those old bad cards," Stevie said.

"I don't want you to," Des said soberly. "I want you to be a lady. Do you hear? I don't want you to have anything to do with this gambling life."

"How can I help it, old hoss?" Stevie fastened her arms around his neck and swung out. She kicked off her slippers and stood on his toes.

"I suppose you're going to groom me like a horse for some low life?" Robin asked, hurt.

"No, by God, I'm not. I wouldn't do such a thing. But you can look out for yourself. Stevie can't. I'm going to protect her. And you're so goddamn willful, I figure you can help me now and then, and go on about your business when you make up your mind what it is."

"Maybe I'll be a foreign correspondent," she said.

"Good. Do something with your brains. If you don't, your looks are going to get you in trouble. You've got too much life in you. Some poor devil's going to fall for you and give you a fur coat and a bank account and from then on you won't be worth a damn. That's what happened to Kate Stephens."

"Oh, beautiful Kate Stephens!" Belle cried jealously. "I'd like to wring her neck!"

"With all her expert technique, you got him," Robin said. Kate Stephens' name was long familiar to Stevie and Robin. They had heard two versions of her adventurous story.

"I wish you had her!" Belle said, leaving the room.

Des laughed. "Listen to your ma. Fix dinner, old gal, so we can get busy with these cards." He then said in a low voice to the girls, "I wouldn't have Kate Stephens if she walked in the door this minute, but your mother's not wise enough to know that. By God, though—" He pulled the curtain back and gazed dreamily down the street. "Kate Stephens was a good-looking bitch, red-headed, and she had the prettiest titties you ever saw." He turned back and studied the two young girls impersonally. "Your mother is pretty good in the breastworks," he said, and went through the middle room to the kitchen. He came back at once. "She's got the door locked. I've made her mad." He looked as pleased with himself as a tomcat. "She's getting dinner, though. I can smell it."

The blind at the one window was tightly drawn and a harsh white light fell upon them from a high-watt bulb hanging overhead. They worked in silence, save for the brief and precise directions Tannehill gave to his daughter. New decks lay untouched. Robin was practicing on old ones, at first with the French pen and then with a small, sharp knife. She marked one pattern with ink, another with cuts, in each method using a series of infinitely small signs denoting the value of the cards. She had memorized the mark for each, beginning with the deuce, up through all the cards to the ace, but, still uncertain, she looked at each card before she made its signal.

She was quick in learning to guide the pen and the knife in their brief, sure strokes which must not go wrong and betray their deception, or, by one slip, ruin a whole deck. A mistake could not be mended, and this, acting as a challenge, caused her to work at mastering the stroke.

"Why can't I correct a mistake by the pen with that ink eraser you've got?" she asked.

"That's for me, not you, and I use it only when I have to. I don't depend on it."

She made the marks over and over again. He held her cards at arm's length to read them and examined them critically a foot from his eyes.

"Looks like a bear track."

She worked through two old decks in silence. Her rebellion at the tedium began crawling along her nerves like tiny bugs. She stood up. "Why in heck don't you buy them already marked from the card house?"

"Sometimes I do, but I like to get them from the factory and mark my own."

"Why? It's so hard."

"I want to know my business! And these marks tonight, they're harder to find. I worked them out myself."

She sighed.

"There are ways I can fix the cards right while I'm playing. What would you say to that?"

"That you have sleight of hand. I don't," she said without interest.

"Some cards are sanded, some are crimped right in the game," he explained. "I can do that stuff if I have to."

"I feel as if I'm going to explode!" she said.

"You've got to learn to be patient. Rest a little bit."

She began to walk around and then she opened the back door and started out.

"Come back here!"

"I want to walk a minute."

"Some neighbor might want to come in."

She closed the door, restraining a desire for the largeness of the outdoors as an antidote to the little tools and the marks which could not be seen without concentration.

"Wash your hands," he ordered, going to the kitchen sink. "Here, like this." He scrubbed like a doctor preparing for surgery, then supervised Robin.

When they were seated at the table again, he opened two fresh decks, tearing away the thin paper that groomed the boxes. Transparent wrappers, ordered from the card company, awaited the finished work.

"Now, watch me." Des handled the cards deftly, as if not touching them. He took the knife and began skillfully marking a new deck.

"Watch the way I hold the knife, the way I make the stroke, and where I'm putting the mark."

"All at once?"

"Sure. You've got to learn to concentrate. You can't let your mind be wandering around. If you do, you'll make a mistake sure as hell."

At his suggestion of concentration, her thoughts crowded with distracting images; the most troubling was one of her mother's face revealing her tender concern and suppressed opposition to this new venture. Des had noted it too, and, taking advantage of Belle's gentle nature, her reluctance to quarrel, had urged her to take her friend Penny Weeks to a show. When Robin kissed her mother good-by, she whispered, "It won't rub off on me, Muz. Don't worry!"

"Here, Queenie! Get your mind on your business!" Des scolded.

"It's not my business. I don't like it!"

He stopped and looked at her. "Now, what the hell's wrong with it? I suppose you think society bridge games aren't gambling?"

"I don't like society and I don't like bridge!"

"I'm damned if I know what you like, but I can tell you right now that a lot of people with the cleanest fronts have dirty backs. That's the way to get along in this world—be a hypocrite. If people lived more natural lives, they wouldn't be sneaking into the Royal Hotel and gambling, and I wouldn't have to cheat them."

"Or sneaking upstairs to the girls," she said.

"That's a little different."

"Natural, isn't it?"

"Taking a chance is human nature, too."

"I'm going to live a natural life," she said. "Purely natural."

"Pure?" he asked.

"Not dirty."

"That's for the Greeks."

"I don't feel natural marking these cards," she said.

"I'm not asking you to gamble, am I? This is a skill. You can help me a little."

She liked the thought of helping him.

"I don't have to worry about you gambling," he said. "You know damn well by now that it's a sucker's game. I wouldn't be on that end of it. I've got better sense."

He went to work again, and she concentrated all her attention upon his hand and the cards.

When they were finished, he assembled and returned them to their box. He resealed the opening with the excise stamp, and placed the box in a new wrapper. The stubborn ends were folded into place and pressed together. The deck presented its original appearance with no sign of tampering.

"Now, listen here," he said. "You take this new deck and mark it. I'll watch. Use the pen."

"A *new* one?"

"Do what I tell you."

Robin had not her father's steadiness of hand and had constantly to be aware of the strictest control. He gave her no praise but his silence; he spoke only when she made a mistake. She could not remember the marks, and halfway through her hand began to cramp. She rested and went on. How did he remember? How did he find new combinations in these familiar designs? What power in him had disciplined his concentration? She made a mistake, and tried to correct it.

When the cards were dry, he looked at them. She could tell nothing from his face. "Look here!" he said suddenly. "You've got the ace of spades and the ten just alike!"

"Oh, I've spoiled the deck!"

"I was just wasting a new one to see what you could do if you thought I was going to use it in a game. Not bad, but not good." He shuffled the deck, dealt her a hand, and told her the cards she held. Then he dealt fast, with only a small supple movement of his fingers and wrist, sailing the cards accurately to a stop across the table, reading them as they flashed from his hand. She saw the easy mask of his face, the concentrating, unrevealing eyes. All this she had accepted before tonight without any thought of his skill or the quality of his mind.

"Papa!" She interrupted him. "You're wasting your good mind."

"Do something with your own and leave me alone. Maybe you'll amount to something."

"I didn't mean that."

"My right eye is tired," he said and put the deck in front of her. "I wish I could make a real winning again soon. I'd get me a pair of glasses. And we'd move out of this nigger neighborhood."

Robin cut the cards and slapped them together. "Chris Garrison is in one of my classes, and he's just as good as anybody there."

"No nigger is as good as a white man," Des stated flatly.

"All people named Smith have six hairs in their eyebrows."

"You're too foxy. I'll take you down a peg or two."

"Think so?"

"Well, you're always trying to argue with me. I never saw anything like it. Your own father."

She laughed delightedly and began to read the marks off to him, making mistakes.

By the thoroughness of his directions she knew that this was not to be the help of a few evenings, but was the beginning of a collaboration, which filled her with contradictory thoughts. A suggestion of risk and adventure pleased her; the mild lawlessness enticed her; his acceptance and trust gave her a secret joy. Against these were a sense of vague disgust, and a desire to escape. She guessed that for her the adventure beyond this room was shabby and hollow, that her need was for something quite different in which she could involve her mind, emotions, body, spirit, a cohesion of feeling and intellect and that high nameless dimension—an experience of whole self. This need had no name. She asked herself if she would ever have the wisdom to give it a name, or must she find it by seeking with parts of herself, at variance and separate, contending toward a whole? It would be enough to understand the need; working out its satisfactions was the inexhaustible process of living; and this process was private, public, and universal, involving the life of her deepest self, of people, the world, and the unknown, or the intuitively known.

She would like to tell him what she was thinking, *speak* to *him,* to reach through to someone who *might* be there. She would like for him to *speak* to her. But now that she felt herself to be growing up, with even more of a secret life than before, almost any serious or intimate conversation with her parents was an embarrassment. They were all strangers to one another, as perhaps they had always been, but the knowledge was now more acute; and with it there was a sense of guilt for the unspoken breach, the need for a separate life.

"Papa"— she ventured, hesitated, then went on with a reckless tenderness—"do you ever wish you were something different—not a gambler?"

79

A small derisive sound exploded in his throat, a sound part mockery, part affection. "Think you're pretty wise don't you? But you don't know it all."

"I don't know much of anything."

"You'll get wiser," he said. "I can tell. But you've got a streak of wildness in you—you're like me. We're not like other people."

"Everybody is different," she said.

"There's a lot of moss-backs."

"Do you think we are special, Papa?"

"Maybe not special, just a little off-trail."

"I don't mind that."

"But," he said, "this kind of mixture is tough to handle, and nobody can handle us. We have to handle ourselves. Remember that."

She nodded, believing him.

"I've got a lot of different men in me to contend with," he said. "The best one's lost." The controlled melancholy of his voice reached out to her. "Lost in the shuffle," he ended flippantly.

"Maybe not," she said very low.

"I don't know how in the hell it happened," he said.

Two tears ran down her cheeks.

"Oh, I'm not so bad off," he said lightly. "I'm doing what I want to do."

"I don't think you are," she dared.

"Don't ever worry about me, Queenie. Now, even some poor bastard you may think hasn't got a brain in his head or a feeling above his belt—he has these times too. I've listened to 'em. They could all be something better than they are, according to their dreams. Well, maybe they could and maybe they couldn't."

She smiled at him. "Could you?"

"Who knows? I missed some chances."

"But you didn't have much chance to begin with, did you?"

"That's the gods' truth, I sure as hell didn't. But I want to tell you something, Queenie. That's only a part of the whole works. And if anybody starts handing you that kind of sympathy—and it'd be easy with some of the hard times we been through—don't listen! That'll take the iron out of your blood. Do the best you can with what you've got. Maybe I didn't do that, but it's right."

"That's what I want to do, Papa."

"And don't ever take advantage of anybody, you hear me?"

"I won't! I don't even want to."

"More like somebody taking advantage of you. And you've got to learn how to handle that wild streak, Queenie. Look out for yourself." He hesitated and finished lamely, "And be a good girl."

She glanced up and saw a reluctant tenderness on her father's face. The terrible barrier of intimates was down, and, before he could conceal himself again, she said, "You seem to expect a lot."

"Well, how would you like it if I didn't?" His rebuff, friendly though it was, had the snap of a lock. "You've got to practice every night a little while and maybe in a week or two you can start marking new decks for me. But you've got to *practice.*"

"Oh, lordy," she said, "maybe I can never do it right."

"Yes, you can. One of these days I'll teach you to use a brush for shade work. But now you try with the French pen. I like it best for blot-out."

"Can't you really afford the glasses?"

He ignored the question and spread a deck of cards along the length of his arm, the cards holding, evenly spaced.

She watched his swift hand running the cards together again. Was he too vain to wear glasses, or was he afraid?

Robin picked up the delicate pen and cleaned it. She would do what she had to do, and in the pride and arrogance of her youth, she pronounced herself inviolate.

Stevie stood at the Sutton gate in the protective dusk and pressed the iron catch that admitted her. After she had closed the gate, she stood with her hands on the black metal scroll, and looked into the street from the security of the enclosure. An indescribable sensation of longing and pleasure filled her. She had come to the Sutton's alone after all in order to possess this experience without sharing. Still holding to the gate, she leaned back and let herself down gently until she could see into the night street through the iron design. She whispered, "I shall never forget this moment. I shall hold it in my mind forever."

The fragrance of burning leaves surrounded her, and when she turned she saw the smoke rising above the house. She took the path to the back garden and there the tentative flames of a beginning fire were exploring a pile of leaves.

On the side away from the wind, Mr. Sutton was sitting bundled in his wheel chair. Mrs. Sutton was standing by the fire, controlling its flares by the pressure and movement of a rake.

Stevie walked near the fire and stood looking into it.

"Why, my goodness, hello!" Mrs. Sutton said.

"Hello." It was very difficult to say such a casual word to a stranger.

"Here, Lafe," Mrs. Sutton called out. "This is Stevie Tannehill."

Stevie enjoyed hearing herself announced in this important way, but she went slowly around the pile of leaves to meet Mr. Sutton. She was afraid to look at him because he was an invalid.

"Good evening, my dear," Mr. Sutton said in the quietest, gentlest voice Stevie had ever heard.

She looked up and he smiled, ignoring her shyness. His face was thin and pale. Hooded fierce eyes, a great beak of a nose, and a thick spring of black hair made him look like a subdued eagle.

She could not speak.

"Lillie," he said, "you were right. This is quite a beautiful young lady. But she has a secret she isn't giving away."

"May be." Mrs. Sutton laughed, turning the remark into something easy and flirtatious. "But we are not prying into any secrets. We're burning leaves."

"Never pry," Sutton said. Then he turned to Stevie again. "You won't mind us after a bit, my dear. My wife and I enjoy talking to each other, and according to all the propieties this shouldn't be."

Stevie gazed into the fire, unable to think of anything to reply to this strange, lively man with the patient voice.

"Would you like to tend the fire awhile, Stevie?" Mrs. Sutton asked.

"Yes, please." She took the rake from Mrs. Sutton, who sat down on a garden bench beside her husband's chair. Stevie began to feel at ease with the pleasure and responsibility of the fire. Now and then a burning leaf rose on the wind, darted about on its fiery wings, and lighted on the grass. She chased it with the rake and pulled it back into the bonfire. The Suttons sat together, watching, calling after her gaily when she ran after an escaping flame.

When the fire sank down, reaching with less and less interest at the remaining leaves, Mrs. Sutton dragged the garden hose near and sprinkled it all into blackness.

"We'll go in and have some hot chocolate," she said.

Stevie's delight turned into dread at the thought of eating away from home. Papa would urge her to have a good time. How was it done? With what seemed no effort at all, Mrs. Sutton rolled the wheel chair up to the back door, lifted it over the one step, and sent it on its way into the lighted yellow kitchen. Mr. Sutton took charge of his own course and turned the chair around, pulling up to the table. Stevie was aghast. Both seemed to make a joke of Mr. Sutton's helplessness. He began taking cups and saucers from a dish cabinet and setting them on the table while Mrs. Sutton washed her hands and prepared the chocolate. When there was no danger of being in the way, Stevie went to the sink and washed her hands. Mr. Sutton rolled about the kitchen, filling a plate with cookies and dates.

Once Mrs. Sutton said, "Out of my way, Lafe!"

He looked at Stevie and asked, "Shall I run her down?"

Stevie smiled for the first time, and Mrs. Sutton suddenly put her arm around her shoulders and gave her a peck on the cheek. Stevie felt as if she were whirling and flying away like a burning leaf, but she was also curious about the dates, which she had never tasted. At the table when she finally bit into one, it tasted of the whole exciting evening.

As soon as they had drunk the chocolate and washed the cups, Mr. Sutton wheeled himself into the living room, turned on the lights behind a baby grand piano, and beckoned Stevie to a chair near his.

"Time for our little evening concert," he said.

Mrs. Sutton came in, rubbing her short hands along her thighs to dry them well, and sat down on the bench. Stevie was miserable, wondering what she would be expected to say. But nothing was expected of her, it seemed, except to listen and enjoy herself. Mrs. Sutton simply began to play with great strength and startling delicacy. The room filled with beautiful sounds. There was a vague familiarity in the music, and Stevie remembered that once Papa had bought a phonograph and a lot of records, and when she asked him what kind of music they were, he said, "I don't know. I just like it."

Stevie looked cautiously at Mr. Sutton. He was leaning back in the chair; his eyes were closed and his pale face looked like a mask with a candle light behind it flowing through the skin.

Stevie did not know what she was feeling, and she could not, this first time, sit back like Mr. Sutton, who let the music stream over and into his very being. Her emotions were singing and sorrowing, rebuffing and accepting; her mind tried to explore and discover and recognize—and gave up. The music was unknown to her, a whirling pattern of ideas and emotions that she despaired of understanding, and yet an elation and a desire filled her with a familiar sense of obligation. In a space of expressive delicate single notes, she found the connection: her catalogues of plans for the future, the piano of her own, the music she would play!

At the end, Mr. Sutton remained silent for a while. When he opened his eyes, he turned to Stevie and said, "That was the C Sharp Minor Impromptu of Chopin."

Mrs. Sutton came over to Stevie and rumpled her hair. "Lafe, look at this child's sensitive face!"

"Do you like to play the piano?" he asked.

Stevie made a tremendous effort to speak from her tight throat. "I can't, but—it is what I would like to do."

"Would you let me give you lessons, Stevie? I'd like to pass on whatever I know. And I can see you like music."

"I'm in favor of that," Mr. Sutton said to Stevie, "Are you? Or, would you like to think it over?"

"Oh, no!" Stevie said, forgetting herself, feeling the offer might escape her, but beginning to worry about the money. "But I'll have to ask Papa first."

"All right, dear," Mrs. Sutton said. Then, guessing Stevie's reason, she added, "If you learn to play well, it will be your gift to me. If I can teach you it will be my gift to you."

Stevie thought it all sounded something like a fairy tale and she looked at Mrs. Sutton as if she might be a genie who would disappear at any moment.

Mrs. Sutton laughed. "That's the way it will have to be. You see, I'm not a real teacher, so we'll have to work together."

Stevie stood up and her knees were trembling. "I have to go tell Papa!" she said in a rush.

Mrs. Sutton opened the door for her. She forgot to say "Good night" or "Thank you" until she had opened and closed the iron gate. She called back but she could not be sure that they heard her. When the door closed, Stevie began to run fast toward home, aware of the smoky fragrance of burning leaves all about her.

NINE

IN THE EARLY WINTER Des and Robin spent many evenings marking cards. Stevie was often at the Suttons', practicing her piano lessons. Belle usually sat in the kitchen, writing letters to friends in other towns. On Thursday and Sunday nights she went out.

This Thursday evening when the light knock sounded, Des called from the middle room where he was working, "Shut this door!" And Belle jumped up to obey before she answered the knock.

Penny Weeks leaned in and whispered, "Oh, he hasn't gone yet!"

"Sh-h-h-h!" Belle shook her head at Penny.

"Now, Belle," Penny whispered, "don't tell me you can't go to choir practice again."

"I can," Belle said. "Wait till I get my coat on."

Belle went out and came back, opening the door just enough to slide through, speaking to Des as she did so. "Penny and I are going to a movie, Des honey."

Mrs. Weeks was alert, trying to see into the middle room. When they were outside, she said, "I'm absolutely fascinated!"

"Oh, for heaven's sake, what for?" Belle asked. "I wish we had a decent business."

Once, in a rush of affection and trust, she had confided to her friend that Des was a professional gambler. Belle, expecting a look of shock followed by quick sympathy, was disappointed. A disclosure of such piquant savor caused Penny to roll her brown eyes in sinful pleasure before she caught herself and expressed the proper reaction. True, she was stunned, she said gaily, and would never have guessed it, but it made not a particle of difference. This opened the way for mutual confidences dredged from all the years past. Penny tried hard to equal the adventurous misstep of her friend. There was no end to their outpouring of emotions; their brief satisfactions stirred new appetites; their relationship flourished.

Penny's amiable gossiping scattered the secret. A betrayal Belle found hard to forgive was not viewed as such by Penny, and the rupture was mended. Apache soon knew that Desmond Tannehill gambled for a living. Few accepted it with Penny's relish, and neighbors and students were now in the process of withdrawing or asserting their friendliness.

A church bell rang out across the town. As the two women went along the autumn streets toward its ringing, Penny said, "You won't let me down, will you, Belle?"

"No."

"When will you join, then?"

Belle was silent.

"It's just that they may think it's kinda funny, you singing in the choir and all, and—"

Belle stopped in the street, and without looking at her friend said in a grieved and angry voice, "Then I won't sing in the darned choir!"

"Oh, dear, what have I done?" Penny said. "We need your good voice. We were talking about you as maybe a soloist—when you're a member. That was the only reason I—"

"At least you don't have to work on me and convert me," Belle said, pleased with the compliment to her voice, but not so easily placated as Penny thought.

"Well, I should hope not," Penny said. She had never thought of converting anyone. She was no religious fanatic; on this she based a certain pride. The hereafter was amorphous, and seldom came to mind, but, in any case, it was pleasant; there was no hell. Church was an attachment to the community, which spread her life beyond the confines of busy housewifery; it was more local than cosmic, and this suited the bounds of her interest. While her mother had thought of God as a grand old man above the sky, to Penny he was more the shape of wind than of man; he invented birth, created lightning and thunder, incredibly concocted the organs of man and beast, magically originated the patterns of the vegetables and flowers in her garden, and kept the whole general order of things in hand.

As they passed beneath a corner street light, Penny looked at Belle's stubborn face. She felt commanded by God to patience. Time was on the side of good; sin was always in a hurry. Mrs. Coleman over on Arapahoe Street, who seized all the best strangers for the Methodists, was certainly not going to get Belle. She wanted someone in the same block of Burkett Street to walk to church with.

"Are you mad at me, Penny?" Belle was disturbed by the other's unusual silence. She could not bear to think of losing this new friend. To be one of two women walking alone together in the soft summer evenings or the cold winter nights was a very fine thing. It was something you could never explain to a man, and that you didn't have to explain to a woman. And she loved to sing. She wanted to hear someone say, "Why, Mrs. Tannehill is one of our best singers." The *our*, the belonging, would be the same satisfaction as the public singing.

"Good lord, no!" Penny said relieved, and gave Belle a quick hug.

Belle laughed happily, wanting only to prolong the warm glow of her imagination as it created one small scene after another of her singing in the choir, singing with Penny, singing a solo. But best of all she liked blending her voice with the choir.

The stained-glass windows of the white wooden church gleamed softly, and smoke from the chimney was climbing the autumn air, blowing away on the wind.

TEN

AT NINE O'CLOCK Robin left the *Monitor* office and walked west along Main Street. The gutters were patched with frozen snow. Few people were on the street. The big windows of the Royal Hotel were misted. Over her collar, turned up about her face, she glanced discreetly in and saw Des sitting with two men. He was talking, slapping his knee for emphasis and causing the men to lean back in their chairs and laugh.

At first he had been very angry about the job; he had said people would think he couldn't support his own family. Then she heard him boasting about her independence to Mrs. Polk next door, and after that he teased her about when she would be a good enough reporter to get his name in the paper. How? she had asked. Well, he had said, in case I tangle with the law.

On press nights she stayed late at the office, not so much because she was needed but because she liked being there in the lighted dark, with everyone busy and purposeful.

The rhythmic click and roar of the press filled all the space with its living sound and left beneath it a field of solitude. The others were felt and seen but, in the dense atmosphere, unheard. Now and then someone shouted, but this intensified the throbbing silence after.

Mr. O'Brien, the owner, was always there working with the printers, the pressmen, his daughter, and his sons.

When she applied for the job, a part-time job after school, the very day Hilda Bensen eloped, Mr. O'Brien had ended his questions by asking in a friendly way the work of her father.

"He is a professional gambler." She had said it without challenge, without shame.

This was the first time she had said it, and Des would not be pleased if he knew, but she could not reply to Mr. O'Brien in any other way. Besides, since Mrs. Weeks had spread the news, it was all over town. Nothing dramatic had happened; it seldom did. There was an invisible difference, a silent change. Friendliness at school ended off the campus. A few friends remained among the girls; all but a very few of the boys behaved as before. But, with two exceptions, there were no more invitations. The mothers objected. From that time on, Robin and Stevie did not see the inside of any Apache homes except those of the Suttons and the two friends each had.

It hardly made a difference to Robin. She had dates to the school dances and ice skating on the river. She was not invited to bridge games or evening parties or weddings. Stevie went ice skating or hiking or stayed home and read; she withdrew before the blow could be struck.

Robin left the lighted streets to cross Jail Park. The night was clear and windy and cold, but since she had a warm coat the winter could be enjoyed. The bare trees in the little park exposed the square black shape of the courthouse-jail, unlighted and bleak. The sky was black and glittering with cold, fiery stars. She felt reluctant to go home, and walked slowly along the path, in the pleasure of her coat, saying something to herself.

Steps crunched on the frozen path and curved past her slow, preoccupied walking. It was Chris Garrison in his old overcoat, and the wind like a blade.

"Hello, Chris. Did you hear me talking to myself?"

The tall dark boy waited on the path for a moment, spoke, went on, and, arrested by the question, hesitated once more.

"No," he said, "I didn't."

They had moved only a short way together when he stopped abruptly and turned on her. "Why don't you just let me walk on?" he said. His voice, which was rich and gentle in class or when speaking to his mother, was now angry and impatient.

Robin's temper flew up. "Go on, then!"

He went on, lost in the dark along the courthouse wall; then she heard his steps end, waiting. When she came up to him, he laughed quietly. "I'm sorry, but I thought you were being nice to me."

"I didn't get that impression of *you!*"

"Don't you know what I mean?"

"Yes. Do you suspect *me?*"

"Why not?" But his tone now implied that he did not. "Over there"—he gestured toward the dim street light on the corner—"it won't be so dark. Honestly, this is just a little thing, maybe, but if we meet someone it will be a big thing. People will be talking."

"Let them talk," Robin said stubbornly. "Can't we be friendly? If they get used to it, there won't be anything to talk about."

"I'm a few years older than you," Chris said. "My mother has been a long time trying to teach me not to spit in the wind."

"Has she succeeded?"

"Well, I don't give up, but I'm not looking for trouble."

"What would it be?" she asked, not wanting to cause him trouble.

"I don't know. This is a pretty decent town. Maybe nothing but a warning."

"Warning?" A warning, with all its implication of foul thoughts, ugly hints, cruelty, was a sickening idea. The warnings Des had received from the law, the warnings she had received from Des, the warnings of other parents to their children not to be "too friendly" with the Tannehill girls—galling as they might be—were small beside the awesome warning Chris had mentioned. One night in Oklahoma she had seen a Ku Klux Klan cross burning on a hill; she was a child and had not understood when Des said, "Those hooded sons-of-bitches are giving somebody a warning."

"A warning is disgusting, insulting—and—and worse!" she said aloud.

"All of that," Chris said dryly, then, "What were you saying back there?"

"Poor Akaky Akakyevitch," she repeated mechanically, curious about the warmth of Chris's thin coat. Akaky in his greatcoat walked across her thoughts; she could imagine him going along this winter path, in Kansas.

"Akaky Akakyevitch! So you know him?"

"We've just met."

They began to talk together of Gogol's poor official, and walked on.

They stopped before their homes. The fronts of both houses were dark and the kitchens alight. Bright window shapes fell on the ground, almost meeting in the black strip of yard between. The wind mourned through the heavy branches of the old trees and hooted plaintively into an empty bottle. They listened to the long, low whistle of an eastbound train going through Apache.

"It's the ten-twenty-two," Chris said longingly. "Some night I'm going to flag that train."

"So am I," Robin said, "and I don't care whether it's going east or west."

There was not much doing around the Royal Hotel that night, and since Des had a good bankroll in his pocket he decided to go home early and surprise Belle. She'd be writing letters; he had never known such a woman for writing letters. And drinking coffee. She'd jump up and pour him a cup of coffee and stand beside him waiting for a command. By God, didn't she have an ounce of pride? You wouldn't catch Robin doing that. But then they were different. Belle just couldn't do enough for him; she wanted him to tell her what more she could do. When you came to think about it, it was pretty good for a man to have a wife like that. She'd be happy as a lark to have him home early. They'd go to bed and make love and Belle would talk in a low voice, as if it were a continuation of love, about every little thing that had happened during the day, and he'd fall asleep, half-listening.

When he crossed the alley and came into the yard, he heard two "Good nights" and saw Robin walking slowly around the house to the back door.

"Hey," he called, and she waited.

In the faint light reflected from the windows and the street lamp on the corner, he could see the animation in her face. Her cheeks were red with cold and excitement, and her eyes were luminous.

"Who was that?"

The Garrison front door closed in answer.

"I suppose you're going to tell me you were talking to the old woman—his mother?"

"No. Chris."

"What were you doing?"

"Talking."

"What about?"

"Books."

"Books?"

"Books."

He hesitated, trying to down his regard for the reading of books.

"Oh, Papa!" Robin said in a confiding rush. "It was—"

"Now don't give me any of your blarney."

"It was," she repeated, ignoring him, "wonderful! He's read so many books and he even owns some of his favorites and he'll lend them to us."

"If he's so smart what's he doing crawling around in the grease, fixing cars down at George Charter's garage?"

"That's the way he earns his living. What does your friend George Charter do in *his* spare time? Sneaks in the back door of the Royal Hotel and gambles, and I don't know what else."

"Now, that's none of your business."

"Well, anyway," she said, "this is spoiling my mood. Chris knows a lot more than I do, but he seemed to respect my mind. I was feeling so good when you—"

"Since when are you prowling around in alleys like a stray cat, looking for respect?" He had an urge to slap her but she was standing up to him, getting ready for some sassy answer, and he wanted to hear what she'd have to say for herself now.

She began to smile at him and then she struck him softly with her small fist and said, "Papa, shame on you. That was the best conversation I ever had in my life, and I want to go in and think awhile."

"Conversation!" he said, and he spat on the ground, aiming expertly an inch from her slipper.

He watched her look down at the ground and up at him, more horrified, he thought, than if he had struck her. She turned and went into the house. He heard her greeting Belle, as gay as if nothing had happened. He followed her in, smiling to himself. She went sailing to the bedroom.

Belle's face was almost as lighted up as Robin's had been and he looked at her with unusual interest.

"I'm home early," he said, and when he kissed her hello he pinched her breast.

Belle seemed flustered. "I wasn't expecting you," she said and turned to the table, which was littered with sheets of paper, each one with a few lines of writing on it. "I'll clear these away."

"What the hell you doing?"

"I was going to keep it a secret. I'm trying to write a letter for a contest, and I have to tell in twenty-five words why I like this laundry soap. I can just fly through letters, but this—well, the darn soap practically takes the skin off your hands and I just hate it but I thought I'd surprise you and give you the money for some glasses."

"I don't need glasses," Des said, and he didn't know why but this kindness hurt his feelings. "And how do you know you'll win? You're like a kid."

"I'm determined to win. I have a feeling, and I have all the wrappers."

Des snorted.

"Glasses won't hurt your good looks," she said. "I've noticed that every time you play, your right eye is tired longer than the left one. It's a little red right now."

"I haven't been playing."

"That proves you need glasses, honey."

He started to say that if he did he had the money to buy them, but he decided to keep that to himself. A man had to have a little privacy.

"I'm going to bed," he said from the middle room.

"I'll be right there, Des. Maybe I'll just write one more letter. Do you care?"

"They're just trying to sell soap," he said, taking off his suit and laying it carefully over a chair.

The latest *Monitor* was lying on the table where Robin had left it for him. He got into bed, propped himself up on his and Belle's pillows, and began to read. It was all local news except the wheat market, which reflected the locality's connection with the rest of America and the world. The thought of this exhilarated him, but out of curiosity he read through the first page, then, unable to control his restlessness any longer, he called out, "Come in here, Belle!"

She came with a stubborn expression on her face, interrupted in the best letter of all.

He was surprised, but in a generous mood he saw, beneath her desired and irritating docility, an unaware selflessness. It wasn't just the soap letters and the glasses; it was all their life together. He tried to turn away from the foolish, prideful pleasure it would give him to let her know that he had the money for the glasses any time he wanted them. Also he couldn't explain to her, or to himself, that they would be a humiliation, not a gift. Their generosities were oddly different; he thought of hers almost for the first time, so commonplace as to be taken for granted, rooted in her secret strength and endurance. He knew she hated their life but she loved him. He loved her, but he wished that he had not in this moment sensed a firmness unknown to him before. It all but spoiled what he wanted to say to her out of a spirited impulse. She waited with a kind of furtive impatience.

He shook his burdensome observations off with the same swiftness with which they had crossed his mind. Animation came back into his face.

"By God, let's all go to Kansas City for a week and have some fun!" He gave the *Monitor* a grateful and enthusiastic tap. "It says here school's out for Christmas vacation."

Utterly astonished, and less flexible than he, Belle could not adjust at once to this news, any more than she had to the years full of other impromptu decisions. She looked stupid, then undecided; then she began to smile. She'd have something new to talk about to Penny Weeks and Mrs. Saunders!

Des was taking her in; he seemed to strut sitting down.

"Tomorrow," he said, "we'll catch the afternoon train."

"Tomorrow? But—"

"Sure. If we're going, let's the hell go."

Belle hesitated, then dared. "But—can we afford it, Des honey?"

He smiled, male, confident in his rights, pleased with his subterfuge. "Don't you worry about that. I've got enough for the trip, and I can make more when I get back. I'm flush!" He saw the new amazement on her face, and added, "I've been winning pretty steady lately. We'll get some new clothes, and stop off in Wichita on the way back and you can visit your old friend Edith McAllister."

Belle came fully awake and began to laugh the way she had laughed as a girl. "Oh!" she breathed. Her eyes grew moist. "Oh! Can I?" She forgave him for the secret money. Maybe he'd been planning this trip, but it wasn't like him to plan. She said, "I'll go tell the kids!"

"No. Surprise them in the morning. You'll have to pack for Stevie, anyway; she's too slow. When the Queen of Hearts finds out she's going to the big city, she won't even pack. She'll be buying all new clothes there."

"Edith McAllister," Belle said dreamily. "I never expected to see any of my old friends again. Do you remember how she made me some extra-thick hip pads to wear after Robin was born so I'd look like a woman?" Belle came over to Des and kissed him.

He was delighted with the sensation he had created and could hardly wait for morning. "I'll look up Barney Lockwood there and we can talk over some of our old baseball games." He flexed his muscles. "What an arm I had! I think I'll play ball again next summer!"

"Robin will have to get time off," Belle suggested in a careful voice.

"That's the trouble with a job," he said, without his usual hostility. "But O'Brien will let her go to K.C."

Belle set up the ironing board, humming a popular song from her unmarried youth, and began to press their best clothes for the journey.

ELEVEN

A TRAIN TRIP was always an adventure. The familiar life was arrested from the moment they entered the small, inelegant station with its medley of travel smells, its quietness accented by the handling of thin-paper reports behind the grilled windows, and made solemn and romantic by the somehow lonely clicking of the telegraph.

On the train, the busy everydays from which one could never be spared were abruptly left behind without upheaval or catastrophe; the false necessities were deferred, the habitual postponed. One was suspended in movement and change, lulled into reveries, aware of minute joys and roused to ineffable longings. Observing the unknown people of an unknown town, or contemplating a strange landscape, one seemed at times to be on the very edge of recognition. For that instant the journey became timeless; fossiled memories were compressed into one mercurial sensation.

Appetite for food and talk and sleep brought one crashing back into the world of the train that had been forgotten. No longer was it a pause, but a continuance; then once again its rhythmical progress, its muted screeches of steel on steel, its swayings and strainings all became music for the traveler away from his fixed place.

The Tannehills sat together, the girls across the aisle from the parents. At first they had been scattered, but as passengers left the train at Hutchinson the family had shifted about until they were joined again. Stevie debated the temptation of a window seat or one on the aisle nearer Des.

"Behave yourself," he commanded in a low voice, and she sat by the window.

Des maintained a formal bearing in the rare public appearances with his family, and, watching them critically, he gave a series of commands regarding correct posture, staring, pointing, table manners, low voices, and courtesy toward himself and Belle and all others. Actually he had little to complain of, so that he reminded Stevie for all the meals ahead not to put too much food in her mouth at one time, and cautioned Robin against her habit of "looking at people."

In spite of all this, he turned their way now and then with his whole mobile face smiling, as if to say, "Well, we're off on a lark!" His sensuous emanation of expectancy and mystery enfolded them.

Belle alone sat enclosed in her dream, which the others might misjudge to be small; but, as with all dreams, only the manifestations were less; her yearning was immense. The landscape flying by, more and more softened by snowy hills and old trees, the towns' houses more staid and secure, shook old memories to fresh hopes and fresh hopes to new resignations.

Robin sat lost in a reverie, eyes shining, filled with the little drama of the trip. She looked past Stevie at the cold earth, snow-blown and harsh, at the cattle and horses with their backs to the wind, in attitudes of cold, still and accepting. Her sympathy reached out, and her sense of relatedness to every alive being centered on them. A man sighed in a doze and her attention turned to him and all the people she could see from her seat. Forgetting, absorbed, she stared at their clothes, their faces and hands, curious about their lives and the reasons for this journey, until she was brought back to "courtesy" by a "Pst!" from Des.

Stevie, bemused by the cadenced motion of the train, watched from her window the gray winter plain, living only in her impressions indelibly received. Some of them, she knew, would lie fresh in her memory forever—not just the sight, but the sensation evoked.

Suddenly the landscape was cut off as the lamps came on. Reflections of the coach glowed in the dark window. Stevie looked up at the ceiling, painted a pale glossy green, and then along the aisle at the red plush seats, and the place seemed cozy and warm and safe. She sat back again and gazed at the white globes and the silky sheen of the ceiling, conscious of the gentle rocking motion of the train, and she wished they could go on and on, never reaching their destination. In all their trips from town to town, she had never liked reaching a destination.

The train stopped and they left the car. A bell was ringing, quick and clear in the evening air. At supper in the railway café, they were only partially emerged from their separate musings, and spoke little and remotely, but they all felt themselves drawn together in special intimacy by right of their difference. They finished before the others as if by silent agreement and walked up and down the station platform, their breath entering like blades and coming out in little warm clouds. Stevie and Robin lowered their faces from the freezing wind and in the same moment they looked at the platform and then at each other in recognition of a lasting impression: they thought the red bricks were beautiful.

In the train, after the lamps were dimmed, Des's preoccupation with his family role slid out of his mind like the light out of the sky into the quick winter dark. He wanted with an aching intensity to be free, free perhaps to enter the world of night where he went alone. His dreams were amorphous and huge and they ran before him like an unknown beast that he must catch and tame before he grew old. But how do I grow old, feeling so young, feeling so free? And he didn't really know what he meant by free, what he would ask for if suddenly by magic the beast were caught and offered him his dream.

When the windows were black with night, he rented four pillows, and all but he fell asleep in the simple pleasure of being unusually well fed, and rocked to sleep by the swaying of the train, seeming now to have a secret life of its own, as it sped through the dark with little tremors and sighs.

In the city they changed again, into the full regalia of their worldly selves. At first the largeness of the station, the clamor and uproar, the purposeful commotion, engrossed crowds, all astonished them. Each person so intent on his progress lunged in from the streets or away from the trains like a fugitive. The Tannehills kept close together, warmed by their personal union against the avalanche of neutrality. Des, again inspired by the spirit of husband and father, went along the remembered ways of the station; the three women followed their leader and protector into the wilderness of yet more people rushing through high, cavernous rooms, and finally into the gabbling conflict for taxicabs. He gave the porter a generous tip; the porter smiled them into the taxi; and Des gave the driver the name of a good hotel in the very heart of town. As they, fleeing like all the others, rode through the dismal city streets, Belle and Stevie, in rare agreement, saw through the windows the grave possibility of getting lost, and determined to go forth only with Des, no matter how much Robin wanted to explore.

The quietness and courtesy of the hotel lobby eased them. The too warm, steam-heated room with an alcoved bed for the girls released their delight in the journey. As it was early in the day, they rested and took turns at baths, luxuriating in the long white porcelain tub of deep, steaming water, such as they did not have at home.

As soon as they were dressed, Des was eager for them to go out and walk in the streets. Confinement in the train had made them restless, so in spite of the indifferent sun and the slashing cold wind they spent the afternoon walking. But first, Des took them to a familiar restaurant where the owner remembered him, and his sense of importance and worldliness before his family grew. In this city he was known, and that was not the end. As the week went on, and they walked in the streets, shopped, ate in other restaurants, and attended shows, Des was often hailed by old acquaintances and now and then carried off by them to a male world of bars and reminiscences and roars of laughter.

When this happened, Belle timidly took over to look after and protect. They spent their time in stores, looking more than buying; or sinking into the cushioned dark of movie palaces, quiescent under the resonant organ music, enchanted by the fairy-tale splendor.

They all wore new clothes, and Robin had observed and adopted a new hair fashion which made her appear older. The dress she selected was more sophisticated than any she had. It seemed to her, and to Belle looking on, that within these few days she had gained several years. People mistook the two of them for sisters, since Belle retained an innocent girlish appearance and showed no parental authority.

One day she remained in the hotel with a headache. "I don't see how people stand to stay dressed up and eat out all the time and go places one after the other!" she said to the girls. "I'll be glad to get home." But they knew she had enjoyed herself, and was simply surfeited with this rootless life in a very short time.

With some trepidation Stevie accompanied Robin, but as soon as it was decided they would visit the public library and a bookshop she was willing. They wished to see some "real paintings" but they did not know where to search and were too shy to admit their ignorance by asking. They had already spotted the library and a bookshop.

In the silence and the lighted winter gloom of a large reading room, the library seemed to them a real heaven. They did not read but sat side by side without speaking, amazed, overwhelmed and utterly happy in the presence of so many people reading!

After that, they walked half frozen until they found the bookshop in a side street; there they longed to browse, but were again shy and unsure of their privileges. The proprietor ignored them and they were grateful, but a woman clerk made them ill at ease by watching them with a little smile, which they were afraid revealed her amusement and prescient knowledge that this was the first bookshop they had ever seen. At this moment the band of understanding between Robin and Stevie drew so taut that their thoughts and feelings were in complete harmony. Stevie looked to Robin's self-possession to protect her from any unforeseen insolence; and Robin, her fierce protective feelings aroused, was ready in an instant to show her strength. They were used to the friendliness and good manners of the towns and did not understand the more impersonal manners of the city, which at times they mistook for rudeness. They looked through the books as much as they dared, and then purchased three, the third one to be a present for Chris.

"Such pretty girls, and you like good books!" the woman said appreciatively, and they felt ashamed of their country suspicions.

Outside, Robin kept to herself the sting of humiliation she had felt in the shop at her own inadequacy. All those books she had not read, and those only an infinitesimal fraction of the books in the world! She could almost hear Stevie thinking the same thoughts. Near the back of the shop, Robin had heard a young woman say to a man, "Shakespeare is as dead as a doornail! How much longer are they going to stuff him down our throats?" This heresy was unimportant. What struck Robin was the fearless authority, dubious as it might be, to make such a statement. When she heard it, she believed the speaker must have great knowledge of books to be so daring; then it occurred to her that it was possible even to conceal a superficial knowledge by making a large, shocking statement. It disturbed her to think that such tactics might be used in the worlds of literature and art, which gleamed pristine and radiant, almost blinding, to her eyes. But this is only a small part, she consoled herself, and clung to her veneration.

The clanging, the unpleasant city smells, the growing press of people as the day ended alerted her senses, and she began to feel involved in the life around her. How hungry she was for living! And yet, wasn't she *living* in their own life at home? Why did the city give this illusion? She found the city distasteful; she felt disjoined from nature; and yet she wanted to experience its choices and advantages, its freedom from home. Not this city, but many cities; she wanted to move in ever-widening circles, within herself and without.

"We will always live together," Stevie startled her by saying in an uncertain voice, as if they were already separated. "Won't we, sister?" Robin hedged. "All four of us?"

"That would be nice, but it won't happen. I mean you and me."

"We should have our own lives," Robin said firmly. "When you're older, you'll want yours."

"Papa says, 'This is the life,' but it scares me. I would like to live in the library."

"Why not, if you like it?"

"I feel so ignorant."

"I do too, but we'll learn."

"When we go back," Stevie said, "everyone will ask you about the city and you'll tell them. But I'll go to school, and no one will even know I've been away, probably, and I can't start talking about something, so it will be as if I've never been here. Just some more stuff stored away in me."

"There's Papa now!" Robin said with relief. "He's waiting for us in front of the hotel." She smiled at Stevie. "Feel better?"

That evening Des invited another couple, old friends of their early married years, and they all went to a Chinese restaurant, the first for Stevie and Robin.

The Tannehills were resplendent in their expensive new clothes. Next to her gold wedding band Belle wore a glass-diamond engagement ring she had bought in the five-and-ten for fifty cents. It gave her more pleasure than her elegant hat.

The restaurant was a lantern-lighted place up a flight of steep stairs; the furnishings were red with black and gold carvings, and on the walls were long silk panels with embroidered or painted birds and flowers. Somewhere beyond the quiet dining room a clatter of voices spoke a strange language in unfamiliar rhythms, and now and then two enchanting little children, laughing in a game, ran from the kitchen, as if from a painting, and were promptly called back by one mysterious word. The air of the place seemed made of the exciting fragrance of food and sandalwood incense. With a thrill it occurred to Robin that here was an exotic experience and she was in the midst of it. Their young waiter, in soft slippers and a feminine jacket, came and stood between her and Des to take their order. While he was busy, she looked at him unashamedly, admiring his black-black hair, his alabaster skin, his sloe eyes, and his startling lack of whiskers—at least, there were very few and those were in an artistic design! These people are more evolved than we, she decided, and stared at his smooth cheek, which she thought would be nice to touch. She blushed. Just then he moved his hand in a gesture, and the scent of ginger root came into her nostrils. Afraid that Des or Stevie would notice her excruciating pleasure, she began a pretended search of her new purse, looking down, savoring her experience, and feeling a sophistication the others could not guess. She glanced sidewise at Stevie, such a little girl still, tagging after Papa; and she knew that this trip, with only a series of daily events that others might find ordinary but to her were adventurous, had helped her change into a young woman. The future, full, varied, colorful, invited her; and she, eager, daring, atremble with self-knowledge, accepted. She sat under the alien adult laughter at the table as under a parasol that shaded her new restless knowledge.

She heard Des say, "I've never laughed so much in all my life!" and knew she had heard him say it before and mean it each time.

The couple, a lawyer who had played catcher to Des' pitching in the baseball of their energetic youth, and his wife, who had sat many a Sunday beside Belle at the games, and whose assurance Belle envied, were genuinely glad to see them.

"Remember ... ?" the flying sentences began, followed by a clue that sent the four friends into shared memories and fountains of laughter.

Once Des caught the flash of the glass ring on Belle's finger; their eyes met and her easy smile wavered. She felt poised against gravity, fixed in imbalance. He hated anything cheap on their persons, and it did not occur to him that Belle's longing for an engagement ring was in part an expression of her romantic attachment to him. Instead, the surprising appearance of the "diamond" under the low lights of the place roused his pride in himself as a family provider before his friends. The traditional ring on his own wife's hand belonged to the world of the lawyer. For a moment the abiding conflict between his feeling for his family and his umbrage at the responsibility was in complete abeyance. He enjoyed an instant of utter freedom and of rare, pure rapport with Belle. His eyes released her. She was so startled that she had a dizzy sensation of falling *up*.

Robin and Stevie, with senses highly trained for these swift weather changes between them, observed the subtle impasse. Then Stevie returned to her self-absorption, exploring the familiar sensation that one of the two persons she was stood outside her, watching her every move. She saw herself looking rather scared and mousy, and she disdained the others for not knowing how busy she was with her intense and turbulent impressions. She was stung awake by Des' remark—"Stevie's bashful, but she can hit a ball a mile!" She blushed and scowled in embarrassment and remained silent, accusing her father of having a good time without any concern for her.

This baseball remark reminded the lawyer of their favorite memory—the time when Des' pitching had won against a hard rival team and his fans had showered the ball diamond with silver dollars. Des sat back in his chair, glowing with past acclaim and present delight. His pleasure involved the others so powerfully that each felt the acclaim as his own. Under Stevie's shy mask, she reveled in the joy of living borrowed from Des.

On the last day, without a word to Belle, Des went to see an eye specialist recommended to him by a friend. With a week of good times behind him, he was able to admit that whatever was wrong with his eye might need professional diagnosis. He had even brought himself to the idea of wearing glasses. "I'd better get them while I've still got the money," he told himself. "You never know what's ahead."

The handsome interior of the doctor's office, with no outward signs of the clinic, reassured him. He was getting the best attention and advice for his most valuable asset.

He did not have to wait long, and the doctor had reserved full time since Des had telephoned him that he was from out of the city and wanted to leave the following day. The examination turned out to be rather lengthy, and at one point Des was asked to wait while the doctor called in another for consultation. This made him uneasy, but the nurse had gone out and brought him a sandwich and coffee. Fortified, he felt better when at last the doctor invited him into his office to hear the results.

The doctor was a quiet-voiced man, and he sat for a long moment looking at Des. "Is there any history of blindness in your family?"

Des felt the hairs rise on his arms, and his throat was suddenly so dry he wanted to cough. "Never!" he answered with cold pride.

"This is an old condition, and I'm afraid it won't get better," the doctor said with genuine sympathy.

"You mean I'll have to wear glasses the rest of my life," Des said. "Well, that's all right if I have to."

The doctor shook his head.

Des felt oddly chilled.

"I just thought it was eyestrain." He lied hurriedly, recognizing the hidden fear that had plagued him.

"It's that and more now. What is your profession, Mr. Tannehill? Does your work require the intensive use of your eyes?"

"I'm a printer. I need my eyes, all right."

"Yes, indeed. I don't want to alarm you; no good will come of that. I just might say though, you'll doubtless someday find it more comfortable and advantageous to be in some other work, possibly a related business. Since you are a young man, that shouldn't be too much of a hardship; you can plan for it in advance."

Des felt himself bristle at this concealing talk, no matter how sympathetic it was, and yet he wanted this controlled professional concern with a desperation born of his resolve never to reveal his trouble to anyone else. Here, today, in this room, from this man he didn't even know and who knew him even less, was all the sympathy he would get, and he needed it to remember and use on the rough days.

Some other business, Des repeated in his forlorn thoughts. The old high-flying big-money days are over when I could make enough to start a gambling house of my own.

"At this point," the doctor was saying, "I don't see any need of glasses."

Des didn't even care now. But he had to say something. "Why is that?"

"Well, the left eye seems fine now. Rather remarkable, in fact, perfect vision. Take care of it. The truth is, all sight in the other eye will soon be gone. I'm sorry to tell you this."

Des fiercely tested his right eye on a framed medical degree on the wall, listening as from a far place to the technical explanations of his difficulty. He had never been sick in his life, and even now this news seemed to have little to do with any physical infirmity. He was seized by a terrible suspicion that he had begun to disintegrate piecemeal, the whole of him, even his power and confidence. Fury flashed and went out like a match in the wind. Where was his huge anger?

A dull panic shook him. A revelation gleamed in his quivering thoughts like a red light over an exit door.

I've got to get hold of myself, he said in his mind, seeing this urgent statement spelled out. And all the time he sat looking at the doctor with respect and apparent calm. I've got to get hold of myself, he repeated with ruthless scorn for the blow.

When he stood up to go, his strong legs trembled with dreadful terror. Well, by God, it isn't that bad, he told himself with familiar bravado. He spoke a few pleasantries to the doctor and was amazed to hear his voice steady. He wanted to get away, out in the cold winter air, where his mind would clear and his legs give him firm support.

"I want to pay you now, doctor."

The doctor smiled. "That will be fine."

While Des was waiting in the reception room for the nurse to bring his bill, he had a powerful desire to pick up a heavy chair and crash it against the wall just to assert his healthy animal prowess, and to drive out the kind of thought that was badgering him. The flaw in his superb health, a flaw that refused to heal itself, was an omen of hidden deterioration.

He went back to the hotel late that night, and announced to Belle that they would leave the next morning, but that he intended to go straight home. She and the girls were to stop over in Wichita and visit her old friend. As he appeared haggard and would explain nothing, she said she wanted to go with him, knowing she could not enjoy herself for worry, but he objected, and she obeyed him.

In the train he spoke only the barest civilities. He chose to sit with Stevie, and when she asked playfully, "What is the matter, old hoss?" he emerged from his bleak mood for a moment, and replied, "I'm studying about something, pard."

"A new game?" she asked innocently.

"You might say." He gave her a bitter smile that she could not understand.

At Wichita, Belle got off the train in tears, wondering what wrong she had committed, or if Des had suddenly fallen in love with someone else. She and the girls stood on the platform, watching him framed in the window as the train moved away from the station. Des waved, but his eyes were on Stevie and she yearned to be with him.

"What do you suppose has got into Papa?" Robin asked with a wondering urge to know.

"The Lord only knows. I don't!" Belle said with a small flare of anger, now that she was safely out of hearing.

PART TWO

TWELVE

SNOW HAD FALLEN ALL DAY. It was the snow of their second winter in Apache. Des sat hunched down in a big lobby chair in the Royal Hotel, gazing moodily into the swirling white world of the street. He had lived a year with the knowledge of his dying eye, this ominous knowledge that was like a marauder rooting in his vitals for another weakness. After forty, he thought, the years were swift, the last one swifter than the others, rushing him toward a fearful depth.

He had told no one of his eye but he thought about it all the time. If, in the end, he couldn't gamble as a professional, what then? What would become of Belle, of Stevie? At times his obligations seemed right and they gave him a kind of sweet pain; but most of the time they weighed heavily. And when Belle inquired about his eye, he didn't know why, but her concern made him angry. He expected more of her, a second sight to see his dilemma.

"What's wrong, Des?" she asked him in the nights when he was home. "Ever since last winter you've been changing. Did I do something wrong in Kansas City?"

He heard her bewilderment without his old amusement. Sometimes, when she wept, he said to her with fierce impatience, "Goddamn it, haven't you a bit of pride?"

"No! What good would it do me?"

"Keep you from crying."

"All you think of is pride!" she dared because she was weeping.

"Shut up and go to sleep." Then he had to lie awake in the swollen silence, but he'd be damned if he'd tell her. He had to keep it to himself; he had a hunch about it.

All year he had made no spectacular winnings, but he had been able to depend on small steady money, and he was as much a part of the secret life of the Royal Hotel as the girls on the second floor. It was the steadiness that irritated him like a rash. When he couldn't endure it, he rambled around the country for weeks, and came back to the Royal. Bowman looked out for "live ones." Farquarson, that cowardly and greedy clerk, did only what was required of him, folding his pay-off money into a wad and stuffing it into the pocket under his belt in a way that made Des despise him. "I hate that damn clerk's guts!" he kept telling Bowman, and the porter nodded in agreement and warning. Farquarson whined once when the winnings were small, and again when they were none, but Des cursed him relentlessly, and the clerk was filled with respect and fearful pleasure.

When gambling was slow, Des and Matt Gregory, who had become his friend, played cards together, without money, for the fun of it and the companionship. By now, as in all the other towns, Des knew a good deal about the vices of certain respectable businessmen who frequented the hotel, more often through the back door than the front. He looked upon all this with private disdain and a kind of tribal loyalty and tolerance.

He ran his hand in his pants pocket and felt the thin fold of bills. Although he knew the exact amount, he was tempted to count it. The thought of family expenses stirred a resentment in him. It was a pleasure to give money impulsively, but the routine and certain demands peculiar to domesticity were a mounting irritant. Stevie wanted a piano and he dreamed of buying one; he had promised her repeatedly, but there was seldom a lump sum of money on hand because of the daily, commonplace drain. Belle managed on whatever he gave her, and he was glad of that, but there were always the rent, the food, the lights, the water, the coal. The coal bill was large; the winter was cold.

He had other problems. They were working in him like yeast in dough, and he remembered the quiet bread in the clean wooden trough expanding until it rose to the top, pushing up the lid and hanging over the sides, revealing its strength by not falling, by clinging to the mass. He always reached it in time, but a little while more and it would have broken away. His whole being was filled with expanding resentment as the trough was filled with dough. He longed to battle the strange emotions as he had battled the dough, punching it with his strong fists, folding it, lifting it, and throwing it back into the trough, tamed for a moment until it rose again and demanded this violent attention.

The peaceful days of having two little girls were over. This thought rang in his head with the doleful monotony of a cowbell. Stevie at thirteen was childishly knowing and innocent, but he could see, in her tallness and the subtle curving growth of her body, the hints of the woman to come, and he was stung with fear. Stevie, his Stevie, must always be pure, untouched, unharmed by the world. The impossible logic of this struck him a daily blow.

Robin, at seventeen, was a woman, and nothing he could do or say would change that. With her, his worry was immediate. He might have another year or two of grace with Stevie, in which time he would warn her, make her understand. Stevie was made of frailer stuff than Robin, and she loved him devotedly. She would listen.

With the full-time job at the *Monitor*, which Robin had taken when there was no money to go on to the university, she was more independent than ever. Des liked to remember the day O'Brien offered her the job; he had acted the same as every day, then he asked her to go back in the plant with him. She followed him clear to the wash bowl. Above and to one side was a long board nailed to the wall, with hooks on it, from which hung the ink-stained towels of the regular workers on the paper. Above each hook was a name. O'Brien never said a word; he just pointed to a clean towel on a new hook, and above it her name. She wanted to thank him but was too worked-up; she grabbed the bar of Lava soap at the sink and ran out the back door. When she got home she was crying. She burst through the door and stood there bawling, and when her mother, frightened, asked her what was wrong, she handed her the Lava soap. She said, "Smell it! I'll never forget this good smell! I've got a real job! I'm a reporter!" They all laughed and Belle said, "Why, honey, aren't you glad?" "Yes," Robin said, "but I'm scared," and she went in the bedroom and cried some more. Yes sir, that was one time her proud feathers were drooping, and every time she had to write a news story she was scared she wouldn't do it well enough to please O'Brien, but he was always encouraging her. He must be a pretty good old man, Des thought; Robin listens to him, and she works hard. He felt a moment of jealousy and pushed it aside. O'Brien didn't have to raise her, he didn't have to watch her like a hawk, and worry about the boys.

How many times he had warned her, "You'll come home with a kid in your belly, and I'll kick your hot ass out on the street!" All she'd say was, "You make me feel dirty." She was a big-hearted, tender bitch, but hot-headed and independent with the boys, and the damned fools liked her.

How did he know whether she was still a virgin, as she insisted the last time he accused her? He knew she didn't care much about any boy yet, but that was because she had her own way. Maybe he ought to trust her a little more; she had plenty of common sense, and some high ideas about what she was going to do with her life. Des snorted aloud, laughing, and he looked around the deserted lobby, but the day clerk was asleep at the desk. He would have to get her worked up again pretty soon and try to find out something. The last time, she shouted, "I haven't! I haven't! But I will when I'm ready!" That was going pretty far. He should have boxed her ears. It would have been safer and easier to bring up boys, as he had wanted in the first place. They could have their fun and be no worry to him.

The wind went down and the snow fell gently in a pure white curtain parted only by someone passing the hotel. The early winter dark was already tinting the light and obscuring the snow. He wished he had a drink of good whisky to warm the cockles of his heart.

He seldom drank, except for a roaring New Year's Eve. He kept a bottle of good Kentucky bourbon in the house, and this, at Prohibition prices, was a luxury he enjoyed. When one of his gambler friends dropped in on his way through town, he liked to offer his hospitality with a drink. This New Year's Eve, he bought a gallon of bonded whisky for a hundred dollars and gave part of it away to the boys at the hotel.

He got drunk and had a gay time for a few hours. Over a trifle, he fought a man in the street, and afterward they shook hands. The only trouble was that he sometimes hurt his hands, but what the hell, it was worth it. Fighting made him feel good, drunk or sober, but he really enjoyed fighting without a drink. He should have stayed downtown, but when the exhilaration was partly worn off and the whisky gone he went home, and, feeling quarrelsome, unsatisfied, and still not tired enough for sleep (he could have stood another fight) he scolded Belle over Robin's being out to a New Year's dance. Didn't Belle have sense enough to know that New Year's Eve was a treacherous time? Hadn't she told Robin to be home at a certain hour? Why didn't she lay down the law? Belle wouldn't open her mouth, just looked at him glum and hurt; he felt powerfully invited to slap her across the face, and he did. He struck her harder than he knew, and she cried out in surprise and fright. Stevie came to the door of the middle room in her nightgown and gave him a look that sobered him. She wouldn't listen to a word he said and when he cried, because he was drunk, she made fun of him. He could hardly believe it. In this moment of weakness he nearly told them about his eye, but just in time he remembered the promise he had made to himself last winter in Kansas City.

When Robin came home at one o'clock, he met her at the door in his underwear, and threatened to drive her out of the house. She said her feet hurt and stubbornly went to bed. Stevie said solemnly in the midst of the racket, "I'll never have a quarrel in my life when I get away from here." That, the thought of her wanting to leave him, and Belle's sobbing, and his great energy wearing down made him want to say he was sorry. The dawn of the New Year lighted a quiet house. He smiled now when he thought of the pleasure of fighting.

The lights came on in the lobby, and it was suddenly dark outside. People were walking by the hotel, going home from work. He heard Bowman in the back urging Winston to be on time, and Winston singing, not answering the older man. Farquarson came in for the night shift.

"Keep the cards dusted," Des reminded him.

"With a prayer," the clerk said.

Bowman came up front and looked at Des. "How yu eye feelin'? Nothin' don't show, looks same as the other one."

"Feels bad, but I can still see those marks."

"Reckon yu oughta get some glasses."

"Hell, I don't need any glasses," Des said. "Bowman, listen here, I don't want you saying anything to anybody about my eye. Just tired; it'll be all right."

"Not a word." Bowman looked out into the thinning snow and the growing cold. "'S cold, nearly all the gals gonna get some sleep up there tonight," he said, indicating the second floor.

"Too cold for sin tonight," Des said.

"They's a new red-headed whore sho' make a lotta noise," Bowman said. "The others say she puttin' it all on to make mo' money. Cost ten dollahs! Mos' all the big-shot respectable men in town been up there day *and* night. She gonna be rich."

"Now, old man," Winston said, "there's plenty men in Apache not been up there."

"Plenty has," Bowman insisted. "Some the best men in town." He leaned over to Des and spoke low. "She jus' tol' me she wants yu to come up an' see her. I'll tell yu what she wants. Wants yu t' sleep with her when she ain't busy. She ain't got no man."

113

"By God, I'm a gambler. I'm no stud!" Des said, so loudly that Farquarson jumped and leaned over the cigar case, listening, running the tip of his tongue over his upper lip. "Times may get tough, but I don't want anything to do with a damn whore."

"I tol' her yu ain't gettin' messed up with no whore," Bowman said with satisfaction.

"What'd she say?"

"She said right then, watch yer tongue, nigger. You know," he said, smiling at Des, "that don't bother me none. I'm a portah. I ain't no pimp er no whore."

"That's right, Bowman."

"Then she said, 'If Tannehill wants to call me that, that's a different story. Yu tell him. Tell him he can have eight dollahs, I'll keep two.' Then she give me this for tellin' yu." Bowman drew out a five-dollar bill and showed it to Des. "I reckon she's lonesome."

"Well, I can't help that." Des was angry. "Eight dollars! The damn fool."

"I tell yu she's sick lonesome for a plain ordinary friend. But everything with her is buy an' sell, that's the tight place she's in now. Ain't room for a gnat's soul."

"Some of them are pretty good old gals. They've loaned me money a time or two, but I always paid them back. But, listen here, Bowman, I don't want anything to do with her."

"Sure not," Bowman said hastily. "I done assured her yu ain't gettin' into that kinda indecency!"

The door opened and snow blew in ahead of the man who entered. Winston hurried over to take his bag. Farquarson put on his manners. Someone had come in on the evening train. He walked easily, a slender young man of medium height, well dressed and with the undemanding assurance that let Winston say "Yes sir" without his usual irony. The young man registered without speaking, and then pushed his hat back and turned toward the stove. Des glanced up curiously, seeing the smooth olive skin as beautiful as a woman's, the cheeks red with cold, and the black eyes not yet turned his way. He jumped up, glad, smiling.

"I'll be goddamned! It's the Prince! Why, Blackie, you young devil, where'd you come from?"

"Tannehill, you big stiff! I'm looking for *you!*" He rushed to meet Des and they shook hands. "If you weren't here in the Royal, I was going to start looking for you tonight."

"How'd you know I was in Apache?"

"I picked up a message on the grapevine in Amarillo that you were all set here."

"Like a trap," Des said. "Live ones are scarce. I was hoping you'd be a victim when I saw you come in in these good clothes."

They all laughed, and the young man looked at the clerk and the two porters.

"The fellows are all okay," Des said, smiling at Bowman. "By God, we run this hotel, don't we? There hasn't been a soul come in here for the last two hours."

"Too cold," Bowman said, and winked at Winston. "Too cold for ev'rything."

"Come on into the café," Des said to Blackie. "Get some coffee and warm you up. Say, I haven't had my supper yet. I'll take you to supper, by God."

The two sat at one end of the long, deserted counter. While they were eating, Des observed Blackie. The boy must have something lined up or he wouldn't be looking for him. He hadn't seen Blackie for four or five years; he was a kid then, wanting to be a gambler, always after him, hunting up chumps, proving himself to Des. He was pretty smart, and he knew how to keep his mouth shut.

"What are you up to?"

"I've got an idea."

"Have you learned anything?"

"I'm a good card player," Blackie said in a low voice, proudly.

"The hell you are."

"I don't lose much money unless I'm running a streak of bad luck. I've been out-playing some damn good card players from Tulsa to Tucumcari and up through Colorado Springs. The only time I've taken any real trimmings was when I was cheated."

"Not too bad," Des said.

Five schoolboys came into the café, sat down at the counter, and noisily ordered hamburgers and milk. Des and Blackie returned to the lobby and sat in the leather chairs facing the street.

"I'm ready to turn professional," Blackie said earnestly.

"That's a hell of a note. That means you're going to have to start cheating. Why, I never wanted to cheat anybody. But there's so goddamn much cheating going on I had to do it to survive."

"Have you ever been to Las Vegas or Reno?" Blackie asked.

"Sure."

"Well, you see how the gulls fly up there to be taken? The house doesn't even have to cheat 'em. They've got the fever for anything from the wheel down to beano. Once you see them parting with their money, cheating doesn't mean a damn thing any more."

"Well, that's right, but there's a lot to learn about cheating."

Blackie hesitated. He had been perfecting his card playing for years. Tannehill was an honest man and he had a mind like lightning. To be associated with him would be an honor among gamblers. "I practice all the time, Tanny, and I'll practice what you teach me the same way, every day."

"Can't you think of anything better to be than a gambler? By God, you've got a college education, and the highest ambition you've got is to be a crook. Most gamblers nowadays are the lowest class of people on earth. They double-cross their best friends, borrow money, never pay it back. The old-time gambler was honest, his word was good. Now his word doesn't mean a damn thing. They think it's smart to double-cross. You ought to know that. You'd be better off shoveling manure."

Blackie smiled. "Same old Tannehill. You can't change my mind. I don't want to be a sucker. I don't want to be a crook. I want to be like you."

Des snorted. "Hell, I suppose I'm a crook, but people want to gamble."

"That's what I'm saying, we don't tempt them."

"Business is crooked, too," Des said, "but that's within the law. We give the boys a chance to take a little time off from good behavior, blow off some steam. The law is crooked; you can buy 'em up like second-hand suits. So, what the hell, I'd rather be an open honest crook any day. But you ought to think of something else."

"Listen, Tanny, I'm bound to be a gambler. I can't explain it but there's no use your trying to talk me out of it."

"What about your folks? They're fine people."

"Too fine. They haven't stopped telling me I'm a big disappointment since I was fourteen. I got tired hearing it. They didn't even like my little old French harp." He drew the instrument from the inside breast pocket of his coat, pressed it to his lips, and blew once softly. He looked at Des and smiled. "Listen, Tanny." The music came low, private, defiant, sorrowing and swaying, "Gambler's Blues." At the fourth line, he held the harp away from his lips and sang hardly above a whisper, "To let the Lord know I'm standin' pat," then beginning the last verse, "O sixteen coal-black horses, to carry me when I'm gone ..." Winston's richer voice from the back of the lobby joined in and carried the song through once more. "I went down to Saint James Infirmary, to see my ma-a-a-ma there..."

Des liked the music, although he could whistle but one tune himself, a Viennese waltz, and then only when he was unhappy. He did not like it that Blackie interrupted a serious talk in this way, and he took it as a sign of weakness. Blackie was probably a drifter.

"You could get a tin cup and play on street corners," he said.

Blackie placed the harp in his pocket. "Aw, Tanny, I want to join up with you." As soon as he had heard by the grapevine that Tannehill was having trouble with his right eye, he knew his chance had come. He never had been so crazy about anybody in his whole life as he was about Tannehill. But he would have to keep still about his eye. Tanny was proud.

"Well," Des said, "it's your business if you want to be a gambler."

"You like it yourself, Tanny. Admit it."

"Sure. But I'm over forty and you're twenty."

"Twenty-four."

"A few years one way or another on either side." Des studied him, thinking how he would be as a partner. He wasn't as good-looking as when he was a kid, and this was better.

"I'll put my cards on the table," Blackie said. "I may not be much damn good to you, but I'll be some, and I'll work. I'm a straight-shooter. You know that."

"I don't *know*. You and I have been on different trains."

"Man, you can trust me."

Des didn't really want a partner, but if Blackie was all right, he wouldn't have to hunt every day like a coyote, or sit in this damned hotel all the time, afraid he'd miss something. Blackie could do some of that and maybe a little more. He'd teach him to play marked cards, to deal second and bottom, and to run up hands. You had to be smart to give the other fellow a good hand and then take a better one yourself.

"Can you run up a hand?" Des asked him.

"No." Blackie flushed.

"You ought to know that."

Blackie was silent.

"That's not all, either," Des went on. "You have to be a good card player along with your cheating. You've got to be smart to win money and keep the players from thinking you're cheating them. Too many fellows get caught because they don't use any judgment. A smart gambler can go a long time, then maybe he's caught." He looked hard at Blackie. "Most fellows get caught doing business with some other gambler. He'll say, So-and-so can sure cheat. Before you know it, the players get wise and watch to catch him cheating."

"I know how to keep my mouth shut, Tannehill."

"See that you do." Des watched his face and said, lying, "I heard around the country you're a short-changer."

"A short-changer? What the hell, I never did anything like that! I'm a gambler."

Des smiled. "What've you been doing then?"

"I've been rambling around by myself, playing for a couple of years, and right after college I worked with Mark Collins, and then with Dutch Wagner—you know him—but he was always cheating me and I quit and started out on my own. I could learn a lot from a gambler like you." He paused. "Tanny, you could have been a big guy if you'd wanted to."

"I never made it," Des said. "And it's too late now. Gambling isn't a sport any more. It's big business—a racket, mixed up with bootlegging and murder. I don't want any of that for mine. I'm an independent operator, Blackie, and the independents haven't got a chance. We may make some big money now and then but we won't get rich any more."

"I know that."

"If you want to hook up with me for a while and see how it goes, okay. If you want to be a millionaire, you'd better join a gang."

"Not me."

"That's up to you."

"Tanny, it isn't as bad as you think, maybe. We're the gentlemen gamblers. We could travel around, hit the resorts, and really make something."

Des looked up, interested but dubious. Before tonight he hadn't spoken his thoughts about the state of gambling. It depressed him. Maybe it wasn't so bad, as Blackie said. In a country as big as the U.S.A., there ought to be room for every kind of gambler.

But it wasn't a question of room. His kind of gambling was over and done with, as old-fashioned as harness-making. Sometimes he'd be thinking about his eye and feeling low, then, before he knew it, the feeling was all mixed up with the one about modern gambling. It haunted him in the same way. There was no place for the real gambler any more, no need for his skill and individual cleverness, and there was no adventure for him in a *crowd* of suckers in a room. When he got old, he wouldn't mind having a small gambling house, if he could find a state that still had open gambling.

"Tanny! You look as low as a snake's belly. I'm telling you, it isn't that bad! We've got it all over mass gambling. *We're* exclusive, hand-made, imported from Oklahoma."

Des smiled at last. "By God, they'll never factory-make an Oklahoman!"

"That's what I'm telling you! No roulette wheel or chuck-a-luck cage or slot machine will ever take the place of live gamblers like you and me!"

"Why, Blackie, they already have," Des said, but his tone had changed to one of humorous indulgence. He felt ashamed that he had given way to his fear. "What the hell, we'll keep the strain from running out."

"*That* sounds like Tannehill!" Blackie said, pretending to look around the lobby for the speaker.

"You'd better move into the Bella Brock Hotel tomorrow," Des said, "and think of a good excuse for living there. That's class. We'll branch out. And no monkey business around that hotel, understand? No gambling. I don't want to get caught. I'm protected here. I pay off the law every month."

"What about the idea of the resorts?"

"Keep that on ice. I'm staying in Apache for a while. My daughter Stevie wants to finish high school here."

"When do we start?"

"I'm going home and go to bed," Des said. "Nothing going on tonight around here. A lot of men in town play regularly with me, but money's tighter since that goddamned stock market crashed this fall. No business. People are afraid. Maybe you can catch some travelers."

"Tannehill," Blackie said soberly, "I'm proud to be with you."

"Listen," Des said, ignoring him, "if you get lonesome, there's some pretty good whores on the second floor. Ask Bowman or Winston."

"I don't go for that. When I'm lonesome, I'm lonesome. You can't buy anything for that. I'll find a nice girl here in town."

"Nice?"

"Sure. Nice girls are human."

"When I was your age," Des said, "all of us boys went to Kansas City to the whore houses on Saturday nights and had a hell of a time. They used to make better men than they do now."

"There's nothing wrong with me, Tannehill. I know what I want. I never hear of you chasing around."

"You won't, either." Des got his overcoat and put it on. "Better go upstairs and learn something. I'll see you tomorrow." He called good night to Bowman and Winston and gave the startled Farquarson a friendly wave.

120

THIRTEEN

ROBIN SAT in an old straight chair, tilted dangerously far back, with her feet resting warmly on the open oven door. She was reading from a book of Keats' and Shelley's poems. Stevie had spent from her savings to give her the book for Christmas, savings obtained from her old and regular source of income: shining Des's shoes, shaving him, and, for ten cents additional, massaging the crown of his head, where the provident Stevie suspected a future thinning of hair. She boldly asked for a quarter from each winning, and with this and the payments for chores, she accumulated in her bank a small but steady sum of money which represented to her a growing wall against perilous time. Together, Stevie and Robin were also accumulating books, ordered from publishers' catalogues. Of all Stevie's catalogues that came in the mail, these were the only ones from which orders were placed. The others were studied and filed with notes for the future. Stevie's life was now planned up to the age of thirty.

Robin's plans were wild and vague. She was going to earn money to help her parents and Stevie; she was going to live her life, she was going to travel all over the world. She wanted to infect everyone she met with her own joy of living. She had no savings; she spent her salary on clothes and books and useful gifts for Belle and Des and Stevie. She bought an electric iron, new curtain material, a German etching, and a second-hand typewriter. She had money in her purse.

Her father's snoring came from the middle room as if he were scolding her for hazardous ways. "The future will just happen," she'd say. "How can I stop it?"

"What the hell kind of future is that?" he'd demand.

"I'll make it happen!"

"That sounds better. But, by God, how?"

"Who knows?"

He would be infuriated.

The snoring stopped and he slept quietly. He had been asleep all day after playing all night and winning only a small sum of money. Belle had gone to church with Penny Weeks and Stevie was at the Suttons'. It was pleasant to have the warm kitchen to herself. Last night, Stevie and she

121

and Chris and his girl Marie had walked to the frozen creek and skated until ten o'clock. They had built a campfire in a hole in the sand and skated in the darting, eerie light and shadow made by the red thrusts of its flame.

Robin opened the Keats and Shelley again. She was far away in the poetry when footsteps made a crisp sound on the frozen back yard. She glanced at the silver dollar-watch hanging on a string beside the kitchen mirror. After eight. A sharp knock struck the door. *Who?* A flash of memories of other towns and other times when she had had to talk to a deputy sheriff through a bolted screen, while her father escaped through another door, made her heart beat hard with fear. Had her father been unable to make the pay-offs? There was no way to see the person at the door because the one window in the room faced the Garrison house. Des suddenly snored again. When a second knock tattooed on the door, the snoring ceased, but Des still slept, breathing evenly. The knock came again, gentle, secretive. No sheriff would knock like that. She opened the door, and through the old summer screen she saw a stranger who had stared at her on the street. Why did he come to the back door? She waited a moment, leaving the hook on.

"I'm Blackie," he said. "Blackie Collier."

She let him in, surprised that he was her father's partner. She did not know what she thought he was when she saw him on the street, but it was not a gambler.

She edged back past the stove to the center of the small kitchen. He closed the door quietly and removed his hat. She picked up the book from the chair and held it against her breast in the curve of her left arm, her right hand pushing back her hair, curling wildly from the morning's shampoo. She felt disheveled, and she was wearing boy's overalls. What did it matter how she looked before a *gambler*?

"Is your dad awake?" he whispered.

"No. I'll wake him." She turned.

"Let him sleep. He's tired. I'll wait a little while."

"Then you'd better take your overcoat off and sit down."

"Do you mind?"

"No." She could think of nothing more to say, and was annoyed and embarrassed that he was young. But hadn't Marty Gates been a young man too? And he had hidden in their house for a week. Des had felt only pity for him, and so had she, because he was a drug addict.

122

Blackie sat down in the chair with the back off after she had seated herself by the oven. He opened his coat but did not take it off, although he seemed at ease in their silence. Robin looked at him and thought that if he were not a gambler she might admit the attraction that had passed between them before she knew who he was. He was flexing one of his hands, testing the suppleness of his fingers in the same way Des did. His hands were lean, with the tendons moving just under the fine, pale olive skin; they were all oblongs, the palm, the fingers, the well-kept nails. She watched them, fascinated with their contrast of strength and weakness. Or was it gentleness? Or patience? Or cunning? His face was impassive. With the lids down and the flesh molded without excess over the bones, he appeared as remote and secret as a carved head which gave her an aesthetic pleasure quite apart from the charged response she felt when he suddenly looked up. It was the way he had looked at her on the street, as if he were unsealing an inevitability. This disturbing exchange had a fated quality which invited her, but now that she knew who he was she reluctantly determined to set her mind against him.

"I see you every day on the street," he said.

"That's because I work on a newspaper."

"Tanny says you're very intelligent. He says—"

She remembered the inscription beside her picture in the high-school annual. "Nature has smiled upon her, giving her brains as well as beauty." What bosh! Here I am, not even in college, and stuck in a little town! And attracted to a gambler! "I'm very ignorant," she said. "I wish he wouldn't brag!"

"He wasn't. He's proud."

She felt the rebuke.

"You never speak," he said. "When we meet, I mean."

"I don't know you."

"I know you, at least in a way, and I think you know me in the same way."

She realized that he was referring to the silent recognition when they met, and she felt embarrassed and hypocritical trying to deny it now.

"And didn't Tanny tell you who I was?"

"No. And Papa wouldn't like it if we spoke to each other."

"'Papa wouldn't like—'" He smiled at her. But then his mood changed and he bent forward, resting his arms on his knees, seeming to study his hands. "Are you serious?" His clear black eyes, soft a moment ago, demanded a truthful answer.

"Yes. He won't even let me speak to him downtown."

"Oh. Well, I understand."

"But he wouldn't like it anyway," she warned.

He made an effort to conceal his offense. "I should have known Tanny is strict by the way he lectures me. And I don't ever want to do anything against him."

The necessity to keep their voices low was creating a feeling of shared secrecy, and after this declaration a sense of conspiracy grew. They sat uncomfortable in a new silence.

"You are all girl," he said after looking at her a long time, "but you have on boy's clothes. Do you want to be a boy?"

"No. I want to be a woman. It's an old idea. A lot of wonderful women have tried it."

"Are you being sarcastic?"

"No, I'm serious. Women don't have to imitate men. I like men, but women should be themselves, equal and different."

"Well, that's right," he said.

"Do you really believe that, Blackie?" After speaking so eagerly and using his name, she blushed.

"Oh, Robin—hello!" he whispered, as if he had caught her.

"Curses," she said, "the conversation is over." She stood up. "I'll wake Papa."

He rose and held her arm. "Not yet."

"Why not?" she said crossly.

He let her arm go but stayed so near that she could smell the winter air on his coat.

"You've got to practice your honesty a little more," he said. "'Why not?' Isn't that dishonest?"

"Yes." She frowned. "Oh, well, it serves me right."

"Then say you'll meet me someplace tomorrow—maybe at the matinee?"

"No! I'll be working."

"You could take an hour off."

"No. You said you wouldn't do anything against Papa."

"Robin!" he whispered. "Robin, speak for yourself."

124

She felt as if she were swaying imperceptibly and that any moment they might touch, and she would be committed to him and he to her. She turned her face away and closed her eyes, feeling smothered, stricken, beyond all power to move. Opening her eyes, looking down, she saw the worn linoleum on the floor. The feathery snoring came once more into her ears. She broke away as if she were held, and opened the door.

"Papa!" The cold air struck her quivering breath. The room was dark. She shook her father, and when he spoke she said, "Blackie's here. He wants you to go to town."

Des rose up from his deep sleep. "Make some coffee," he said, and sat on the side of the davenport in his wool underwear, rubbing his face, groaning drowsily. "Tell him to wait."

Robin returned to the kitchen, closing the door. She could not look at Blackie until she had placed some wood in the fire under the fresh coffee.

He came near and put his hand on her heavy hair.

"Leave me alone!" she whispered, and her eyes were fiery. She sat abruptly in the chair. Blackie leaned against the door and watched her, his intent and sensitive face filling her mind. She wondered if anything in him matched the glow and eloquence of desire in his fine black eyes. The coffee began to perk, thumping like her pulse; drops of water bubbled from the coffee pot and spat on the hot iron stove.

"I have to fix Papa's coffee." She got up. "Do you want a cup?"

"No, thanks." He lighted a cigarette and his hands were trembling.

Des came in, dressed and ready to leave. Robin handed him his coffee and he drank it standing.

"Don't you want breakfast, Papa? I'll make it."

"I'll get some later. Better see what Blackie's been hustling up." He looked at himself in the mirror and said, "I ought to shave, Blackie. Have you got a live one?"

Blackie seemed reluctant to speak of gambling before Robin. "I think so."

"You know," Des said proudly, "Robin here marks most of my cards now. My eyes get tired playing in all that smoke."

She blushed, and Blackie stared at her in amazement.

"You ought to see her—she uses the pen and the knife and the *brush*, by God. You ought to see her do that shade work. A regular gambler!"

"Well, hardly," she said.

"That's so. She can't learn to play anything. Something wrong there; she's got a good head. She can read the cards a mile away but she can't play a thing. Now, Blackie, I don't want you to mention this about Robin. She's got to be halfway respectable."

"I never heard it, Tanny."

Des turned again to the mirror. "You can trust Blackie. By God, if he was younger, he could be my son. I always wanted a boy."

Blackie's eyes spoke to her in a guileless candor of feeling. Robin thought that no other man had looked at her in such a contradictory way.

"Disappointed?" she asked him.

He did not reply.

"Blackie, I think I'll give myself a quick shave. I hate to go out looking like this." He opened his coat collar, stuffed a towel about his throat, and pushed his hat back. "Give me some hot water, Cleopatra."

Robin poured water from the tea kettle into the wash basin in the sink, and Des wet his face with a steaming cloth. She looked at Blackie again, her face still burning. He smiled, but not unkindly. She smiled back. He was standing at the table, turning the pages of the book, reading here and there. At last he folded the corner of one page and closed the book, waiting for Des, his face smooth and impersonal.

As soon as they left, Robin searched through the book for the marked page, and there, under the poems written late in 1819, was Keats' Sonnet to Fanny.

She read it, hearing Blackie's deep voice, and burst into tears. "Blackie," she whispered. "You are in my mind and feelings and all my nerves. I was all right this morning! And now—" She felt invaded. "Oh, get out, get out!" She closed the book and swung round, burying her face among the coats that hung on the back of the door. She cried hard in angry despair. "It's no use," she said after a while. "Everything's changed. In just one minute everything's changed! But why does it have to be Blackie Collier? Even that silly gambler name!"

The front door clicked open. Robin ran to the sink and splashed cold water on her face, dried it, and sat down, bending over the book, pretending to read. She tried to console herself with the thought that one hundred and ten years ago Keats was speaking to her through Blackie.

"What a come-down for Keats!" she said to herself. "And for me, too. A gambler!"

FOURTEEN

THE MIDDLE ROOM was only slightly warmed by the kitchen fire. Des sat on the davenport, whistling the Viennese waltz, the one bit of music he was able to produce. He loved all kinds indiscriminately, favoring the piano and the violin and, in periods of money, paying indigent musicians to play for him; sitting alone listening raptly, or sharing his pleasure with anyone nearby at the moment. The old waltz, whistled low and pensively, was a sign to all in the house to leave him alone.

He could hear Belle in the kitchen at one of her endless household tasks. She was careful not to interfere with his mood. Robin's quick steps and Stevie's slower ones sounded on the linoleum-covered floor of the bedroom.

A stack of books waited on the table for Stevie or Robin to return them to the library. By God, they'd have the shelves read clean at this rate. Why was Robin late for work? It was her habit to be on time. Was something brewing? Because of her job and her friendliness—like his own, he thought with pride—she knew nearly everyone in Apache. Like him, she appeared deceptively open and accessible. Was she hiding something from him now? For as long as he could remember she had been going her own way. She had taken care of herself and come to no harm. What was he concerned about? Girls! Having girl children was probably the worst thing that could befall a man.

He thought about these things while whistling, abandoning them, returning to himself. Selecting a small design in the faded wallpaper, he held a hand over first his left eye and then his right, a test he repeated often. The right sight was blurred and he felt the added strain on his left eye. He reached into an open traveling bag at the foot of the davenport and took out a deck of cards. He dealt these for a while, reading accurately but with effort, all the work falling to the left eye. Because the shading could not be seen in close playing, he must catch the flash of the mark as the card was thrown to a player. This brushwork was the most exacting of marks, and yet to give it up would be to admit a defeat he could not afford. In time he would drop the use of shading, he decided, but he would still have, if he was lucky with his left eye, the inked and cut marks, and, of course, loaded dice. After that, a job in a gambling house, himself dressed up like a penguin, was all that remained. If he didn't have the price of good clothes, if his partial blindness gave him too much trouble, he might even end up as a shill in cheap card rooms that opened their public doors in shabby streets, catering to men and women with anything from a nickel up to place on Chance. His whole being rebelled at the thought of a job. He got up and paced around the small room and sat down and lowered his whistling.

Belle came in from the kitchen and patted his shoulder. He kept on whistling. She patted him again.

"Goddamn it, leave me alone!"

She drew her hand away but stood near him, listening to the sad song. Finally she said, with effort, "Have you fallen in love with somebody else, Des? Have you got a girl someplace?"

"God, no!" He looked up at her in astonishment. "What's the matter with you?"

"What's the matter with *you?*" Belle cried, the tears starting.

"That's my business," he said gently.

"Ever since New Year's Eve—"

"What about New Year's Eve, what's wrong?"

"You slapped me. Don't you even remember?"

"Oh, I was drunk."

"You slapped me once before, too, and you weren't drunk. When we were first married, and you said you'd never do it again."

"That's when you made me jealous. You said you'd never mention it, too, remember? Now, you're dragging it up."

Belle wiped her face with her apron. She thought it might be better to keep still but she couldn't stop talking. "After you hit me New Year's I began thinking."

"Well, by God, it's about time. Love won't solve a damn thing."

"That's mean, Des."

"I know it. I feel mean."

"You know very well I think and worry a lot. And I don't care what you say about love, it's nearly all I've got, and—"

"That's the truth. It won't be long now till it will be *all* you've got."

"I know that means you don't love me any more."

"It don't mean any such thing, God damn it."

"After you hit me, Des, I thought a lot. I thought I used to be the happiest-go-lucky girl before we got married, and I don't know how in the world I lost all that. I never even missed the way I was for a long time. And then I thought maybe it was just growing up. I was only fifteen, remember?"

"You were just a kid," he said.

"When we went to Wild Horse right after we got married, and there was all that shooting when we got off the train, I was just scared to death, and I was scared of the Indians, too, till we got acquainted and they liked me."

"They wouldn't hurt you."

"How did I know? I never told you before, but when you used to go out at night and leave me alone in our rooms behind the bakery, I got so lonesome, I used to sit on my little round-topped trunk and cry to go home to Mom. Sometimes I used to rock my old doll I brought from home and sing so I could imagine I wasn't so lonesome. Then you taught me how to play solitaire, remember?"

Des did not answer.

"And there was something else I never thought I'd tell you. Sometimes those nights I used to go out and play run-sheepy-run with the kids. They never told on me. We used to have the most fun! There was another running-and-hiding game we played in the pecan woods, too—"

"I was just out having some fun with the boys—playing cards. I didn't know you were so lonesome, Belle, you were such a kid."

"Kids get lonesome," she said. "You know, Des, I've always just been crazy about you, but I don't remember being very happy. I guess you didn't mean to, but gradually I just got blotted out."

"You should've stood up for yourself more."

"I didn't know how."

"Here," Des said. "Sit down here by me a while. No use thinking of all that stuff in the past. It's over."

She sat down and leaned against him and held his arm and touched his hair.

"I thought I was going to amount to something," he said.

"All I ever wanted was just to have you and the kids and a nice quiet life, Des."

"What's wrong with our life?" he said, teasing her.

"I guess I just wanted it more respectable for the kids."

"They'll take care of themselves," he said. "Look at all the books they read."

"Books don't make a bit of difference about what I mean, Des."

"Well, you never can tell."

"They're growing up now—" Belle was bringing up all her courage to ask him if he would think of getting a job or starting a small business.

Stevie came in, taking short steps, almost mincing, teetering uncertainly in her new gait.

"Look out there, Steve! Be careful! You'll fall flat on your ass trying to walk like a damn girl."

"I am a girl, and quit using those awful words."

They watched her pass through the room; then Des said, "Where is my old baseball player and my foot-racer?"

"I don't know," Stevie enunciated clearly.

"Well, then, how's my piano player?"

"You'll never find out since we'll never have a piano."

"Well, I'll read about you in the papers."

"Please don't make fun of me."

"Or," Des went on, "I'll buy one of your records. People will say, 'By gosh, that girl can play like a house afire. You'd never know she was the daughter of a small-time gambler.'"

"Boo-hoo!" Stevie said.

"Hey, Papa!" Robin yelled from the bedroom. "You just sound awful saying 'by gosh.'"

"Well, I've got to reform now. Stevie's going to be a lady. I always wanted her to be but I didn't think it would happen so soon."

Stevie came back through, eating a piece of bread with her lips closed and a large lump in one cheek.

"Now, by God," Des said, "you've got to stop putting so much in your mouth at once. I've told you that before. It looks like hell."

Stevie changed her pace, taking her natural long steps toward the door. Des jumped up and grabbed her, laughing, and in the tussle he accidentally touched her small breasts, hardly visible through the wool dress. She jerked away, her face reddened, and she struck his arms with her fists. "Keep your hands off me, you—you—fool!"

Des stood back stunned. Belle stared at Stevie in dismay.

"Listen here, Steve," Des said soberly. "That's going too far. One more time like that and I'll box your ears."

Stevie leaned against the wall, her face sullen. She began to nibble at the bread.

"What's going on around here, anyway?" Des said. "Everything's changing."

Robin came part way through the door. "Safe?" she asked.

Des looked at her with interest. Belle smiled.

"So you've decided to dress for winter!" he said. He gazed at the red wool stockings that came to her knees. "If you haven't lost your job, what are you doing late for work? If you've got a job, do it, don't start taking advantage."

"I don't, and I'm not late." She smiled at him because she had heard the waltz, signifying trouble. "I'm going to the country to look at winter wheat and talk to farmers."

He snorted.

"Those are my orders," she said. "Mr. O'Brien wants to see if I can write a feature story. He said anyone can write one on sensational news. I'm to try one on everyday living."

"Winter wheat," Des announced. "It's all up and the stock are grazing on it. There's plenty of snow for a good stand. That's all there is to it."

"Not just wheat. People too."

"What the hell do you know about people?"

"I'm learning. People, like charity, begin at home."

"By God, you'll never get anyplace working."

"Well, how will I live?"

"Get married."

"Not until I know how to support myself. And a long time after that."

"Working is no good," Des grumbled.

"I like working!" She hesitated. "Has it ever occurred to you, Desmond Tannehill, that *gambling* is a tyrannical profession? As much as any job?"

"Take your smart words and go to work before I box your jaws."

Belle looked intimidated; then she said, "What makes Mr. O'Brien think everyday living is the opposite of something sensational?"

"He isn't familiar with us," Robin said.

Des gave her a critical look. "Who's driving?" he asked suspiciously.

"Kate O'Brien, Papa, ha-ha." Robin gave him an easy poke with her fist.

"Well, I don't know what you're up to, but you'd better behave." He looked out the window into the snowy yard. "Poor old Demeter's still grieving for Persephone. I'll be glad when the old girl gets her daughter up from Hades. Like to see some green grass and flowers around once more."

Robin and Stevie shouted with delight and threw themselves upon him with such force they almost downed him, hitting him, kissing him, and pushing him about.

"Say some more, Papa!" Stevie demanded.

He could hardly speak for laughing, but he said, "Your mother and I read some of those books, you see. I read all about those old Greek and Roman gods. Why, say, I'd like to have lived then. That was the life for me."

"So would I!" Robin said.

"I liked the poems," Belle said.

The girls tugged her into the tight circle with them.

"All about love," Des said. "Belle hunts those love poems down like a bird dog."

"Oh-h-h!" Belle protested.

"Say some more about the Greek myths, Papa!" Stevie begged. "We won't take the books back to the library today. You and Mama can read them all."

"No," Des said, "I don't want to get too smart. And I don't want your mother, there, getting ahead of me."

The winter sun sought delicately through the cold air. On the black earth glazed patches of snow flashed diamond fire. Robin felt masterful, walking in the clean morning to an assignment all her own, and freed of the clashing, turbulent emotions of the three weeks since her meeting with Blackie. So lightly touched by sorrow as to see it clear, she felt as one emerged from an affliction which was to have lasted forever. The barren earth of Demeter's grief, like the landscape of all grief, had its own somber beauty, its hint of fertility locked for a season. There is no permanent grief, she thought, not caring that there is no permanent joy; they are inseparable and usually out of balance.

She went along asking herself questions that she knew had been asked by youth thousands of years before her but they had the newness of love's repetitions. Feeling reasonable and superior to love's single obsessiveness, she was unprepared for the tremulous, exquisite sensation at seeing Blackie standing on the far side of Jail Park, the smoke from his cigarette rising slenderly in the cold, still air.

After their first meeting, he had come to the house only when there was urgent business about gambling; he had made no pretenses to Des in order to see her. They had passed each other with secret looks on the street, and twice he had waited in the early winter night on the path she took for home. Once they sat briefly on the steps of an empty darkened house and kissed, but even in the desiring kiss it was apparent that his emotion contended with his loyalty to Des. When the image of Blackie's face persisted in her mind, she was like a tenderly remote spectator enjoying the little drama in which a strange young man suffered for love of her.

She had never known anyone who could stand so long in one place with so much ease and interior occupation. This was a part of his deep reserve. When she was on the path that led toward him, he moved out of his stillness and came decisively to meet her, took her hand, and walked beside her without speaking. His touch destroyed all her sense of spectator, but his rightful air was a new source of resentment against him; yet she realized at once that she would feel contempt if he behaved meekly. She withdrew her hand.

"You are blushing!"

"It's because you embarrass me. I don't like your possessiveness."

"I'll be more careful," he said, "but sometimes you're tender and sometimes you're proud, and I'm never sure which at first, and then sometimes you're both at once."

"I'm usually more predictable when—"

"When you're not in love?" he asked.

"When I know how I feel at all," she said firmly. "I am not sure that I even like you."

"I believe you—this morning, Robin." At the street crossing, he took her hand again and guided her round to face the courthouse in the center of the park. "People get married there," he said gravely.

"Let them," she said very low, feeling sorry at once for this meanness.

He continued to gaze at the courthouse as if it were a temple and he had come a long way to enter. Its gray had a stately gleam in the winter sun. Her mind filled with the Greek myths, her imagination gave him the identity of a youth in ancient times, and momentarily she admired in him this quality of forthright surrender to love. His acceptance had the dignity of respect for sudden feeling. Her own spontaneous joy in being alive, not dead two thousand years, gave her an absurd sensation of being rooted in the earth like a tree and moving in the sky like a wind. She bent forward and barely touched her lips to his cheek. When he looked at her in a confusion of pride and humility, she knew, with all vanity deposed, that his feeling was not one of abasement before her, but of almost impersonal humility before his own sure emotion. There was a splendor about him that she did not dare disturb.

She saw him interpreting her stillness to please himself. The young man of Athens was gone. The little park might yet be an ancient wood in which she sought the temple of Athene as well as that of Aphrodite. The one alone would not do.

"I have to go to work," she said, feeling endangered by the unsafe present. "I'll be late."

They crossed the street and walked on together in silence. She turned abruptly into a side street, saying good-by. At the door of the *Monitor* office she looked back. He raised his hand and she felt it like a caress. Then he walked on with purpose, but, she thought, with the unmistakable air of a man who does not work for his living.

FIFTEEN

ROBIN SAT on the ground in a border of wild spring grass that ran along the back of the coal shed. The night was black; the stars in the big sky were soft and remote, giving no such light as their steely flashes gave in late autumn. A cool wind was blowing off the waking plain.

Her eyes were beginning to distinguish the outlines of houses when the kitchen screen door gave out a cushioned thud and Des's footsteps came over the bare yard toward the alley. Robin stood up as he came around the corner of the shed.

He came close to her and spoke in a low voice. "You all right? See anybody sneaking around?"

"It's too early."

"You can't ever tell. That damn law, they may stake out a deputy to watch, and just about the time we all get in the game, three or four of these half-asses will break in for a raid."

"I wish you could make a good winning, Papa, and pay them off again for two or three months ahead." She kept her voice as low as his.

"You never do that! A month at a time. They'd raise the ante."

"Well, it's just awful to play in the house, Papa."

"What can I do," he asked impatiently, "if I can't pay for protection at the hotel? These are hard times."

"I know, but—"

"Now, listen here, you stay out of this. I've got enough on my mind."

"I'm sorry." She wondered if he meant something more than was known to her. "You know, it will be hard for me to warn you if anything happens."

"Why do you bring this up every night I play? Nobody can hear you running in your bare feet, and you throw a couple of little rocks on the side window as you go around the house. I keep one ear cocked. That'll give us time to clear away if the law does come in."

"They'll *know.*"

"Sure they'll know, but there won't be any evidence."

"I hope not!"

"I'm going in now," Des said. "Just do the way you've been doing and everything will be all right." He turned and came back. "Now,

135

Queenie, don't go to sleep! It's kinda tough on you working all day after these nights, but it'd be tougher if I got caught."

"I'm all right," she said.

"And don't walk around! Every little sound carries when it's still. You'll scare the hell out of these town fathers, and me too."

"I'll get watcher's cramp!" she said.

"Tomorrow's new moon. You can sleep nights till it's dark of the moon again." He leaned nearer and whispered. "The fellows will come first, then Blackie. After Blackie, if anybody shows up, do your stuff." He left her alone.

Blackie. She was filled with distaste and torment at the thought of him. Since that winter morning he had spoken of marriage, she had avoided seeing him. He had gone with Des on gambling trips, and the whole town seemed empty, and all that interested her in the streets was dull. But when he came back, she kept out of his way.

A man left the lighted sidewalk a block away and cut across the vacant lot between two houses and came toward her. The dark was so intense that he passed by without knowing she was there. Des and she had agreed to keep her chore a secret. The other men came soon after the first, and one of them startled her by entering the alley at the west end and walking past her. She had been unable to catch even a glimpse of him outside the dark, but she heard his safe entrance into the kitchen and felt relieved.

After that her ears were alert to every sound. She could see well enough to identify the men as they arrived. When she heard Blackie's familiar steps, as easy as a cat's, she pressed back into the deepest dark and held her breath, but he stopped anyway, calling her name very low. She did not answer. He came directly to where she stood and reached out and touched her.

"Aren't you afraid out here?" he asked with a tenderness that hurt her. "This is a pitch-black night."

"I can see a lot now. Anyway, what's there to be afraid of? Just some harmless little animals scouting around for food and—" She stopped, withholding the word. The air was bittersweet with spring.

He laughed, very low. "Speaking of love, or not speaking of it, are you in love with that reporter I saw you with?"

She didn't answer.

"I shouldn't ask," he said. "I can see that he's in love with you."

"He isn't! And I'm not! There are a few other emotions."

"A few." He waited.

She did not reply.

"I can't bear to have you out here, Robin. Good God!"

"I sort of enjoy it," she said. "I'd rather be here than in the house."

"Yes. That's no good."

"You'd better go in so they can start."

"You feel so close here in the dark." He pulled her to him and kissed her hard, and was gone into the house, all so quickly that she sat down on the grass and leaned against the shed, forgetting for a moment to watch and listen. The kiss was in every nerve; the memory of it was like an endless kiss that would go on and on, disturbing her the rest of her life.

She made herself think of Drake Bishop, a new young man in town, working on the *Globe*. No matter how one felt in winter, not being in love in the spring was unbearable. They had begun having dates soon after he came to Apache, and everything about the friendship was just right. It had a known temporary quality. Robin was involved with her feeling for Blackie, which she was determined to destroy, and Drake was engaged to a girl in his home town. Nevertheless, they had fallen a little in love, and Robin had come upon a bit of new knowledge. She could love more than one without feeling guilty or divided. Her response to Drake was simply another of her selves; and his response to her was not the self known to the girl at home. What she and Drake were to each other, they were not and could not be to anyone else. From one basic self there were endless variations. This understanding between them created a free and good-natured relationship with its own contained excitement—the periphery of love. They shared certain interests and argued in stimulating disagreements. He was attracted to the unconventional in her, but afraid of it too, cynically sure that his choice of the safe and accepted life would end by making him a big man in a little town.

Sometimes, in the middle of an argument about idealistic values, he would say, "Don't talk like that, damn it!" but his plain, freckled face revealed more humor than pain at his predicament. Drake had not the depth and range of Chris, or the intense and labyrinthine attraction of Blackie, but he was more fun than either; and, with life at home strained and complicated because of her father's frequent sulky moods, she welcomed the fun and the nonsense that she and Drake shared between arguments.

There was gossip about her going out with an engaged young man, but she paid no more attention to it than to all the other gossip that trailed their nomadic life.

She drew up her knees and leaned forward embracing them, and was reliving being kissed by Blackie and by Drake, when she heard a stealthy footstep swish through the grass near her, and, before she could remember to move as stealthily, she leaped up, nearly crying out in fright.

"You out here again tonight?" Chris asked in a secretive voice. "I can't see you."

"Oh!" she said aloud, then caught herself and spoke low in anger. "Why didn't you warn me!"

"I did. What are you doing? Napping at the post?"

"No, thinking, but not very nobly." She had to say something flippant to recover from the sudden senseless terror that had lifted the hairs on her arms and legs, and even on her scalp.

She raised one hand and ran her fingers under her hair. Her skin felt cool. "You scared me, Chris!" she said. "But I should have been listening."

Chris laughed. "If this keeps up, you'll have to take up Braille. You could get a lot of reading done."

"I seriously will if this keeps up."

"I'm sorry I scared you, but now that you're here, I'll bring some of Mom's camomile tea. It'll calm you down, and we'll talk awhile before I go to bed. If I didn't have to get up so early, I'd keep you company."

"I might forget to look and listen," she said. "Sometimes I feel silly sitting out here all night, but it's a serious matter."

"I know it is."

Chris went away and came back in a few minutes with the herb tea and they sat down on the grass together.

"My upright employer is in there. I heard his handsome voice as he spoke to Des."

"I'll never see my boss here," Robin said, "but I do see quite a cross-section of respectability."

"I hope you won't turn into a cynic," Chris said with sober concern. "It'll stop you where you're going."

"I won't. I'm like a dog—I'm attuned to the best in every man. But where am I going at this rate?"

"That's up to you. And I mean it. This is thin ice for a girl as complicated as you are."

"Are we going to read Eugene O'Neill aloud, or not?"

"Sure, as soon as you're off duty."

They sat drinking their tea in affectionate silence, enjoying the night and the dwindling small noises of the town going to sleep.

After Chris went in, Robin tried not to think, but to hold her mind still and open, just to see if she could; and to grasp what would float up to the surface or enter from the night. This game helped the long hours to pass. At night her senses were more alert, her whole being more aware. Unknown faces, drawings, dances, and poems fabricated themselves, but she could not remember them in the day.

Cats prowled the alley and quarreled and courted, but when they discovered her they carried on their vociferous nocturnes in other back yards. Now and then a dog trotted by in the darkness, sniffing along the way as if reading the night news of this alley world. One of them growled, low, surreptitious, half-threatening, half-afraid, suspicious of her odd habit of sitting in such a place at such a time. The toenails of rats ticked on the coal in the shed, and the tiny feet of mice ran sweetly back and forth across the alley. Beneath the silence she could hear the smaller sounds and movements of insects in the grass, and came to be aware of the enormous activity of the night. When a male cricket signaled somewhere nearby, Robin felt befriended.

About three o'clock the night was as silent as it was black, and, as at this hour every night, one mocking bird sang alone, trilling and whistling through his complicated song many times, varying the beginning with a swift imitation of another bird. He stopped as abruptly as he had begun, creating a sepulchral hush.

The hush was like a soft black fog in the air, enveloping and smothering the smallest noise. Robin longed for a bird to call, or even a rat to topple a piece of coal.

The night was changing; she could feel the silence and the blackness intensifying. Her eyes could no longer see, isolating her, blinding her. In this blackness and silence that had its own eerie presence, deep and secret and primeval, she felt urged to hide or to run, to shake off the primal fear, the fear of the mysterious and awesome presence of this darkest hour. She tried to see, feeling as if she were lost in the first night of the world.

Then she heard the sound, a soft silky, ominous sound of heavy movement that continued with secret purpose for a moment, then stopped, and began again, coming closer and closer. Although she could see shapes of houses, she could see no one in the direction of the furtive movements. Her heart began to pound. She got to her feet and stood dead still, listening. The steps—for now she knew they were steps, the stealthy steps of two men—came nearer, and she realized they were moving in the denser night shade of one of the houses that edged the vacant lot before her. Did this mean they had waited in the dark until their eyes could see her? Two men meant two deputy sheriffs. She pressed her body against the shed and edged along its length toward the outdoor toilet. A space separated it from the shed; she darted through this small corridor and into the outhouse. She feared that she was too late to warn her father because the men, more stealthy than she had anticipated, were now within a few feet of the alley, but an idea flashed into her mind. She seized the flashlight that was kept in the toilet and turned it on, knowing that when the men crossed the alley they would see the long cracks filled with light, and hesitate.

She looked toward the house and its back was dark, the bedroom window and the solid back door revealing no hint of the wakefulness and the illegal gambling within. The side window of the kitchen was certain to show strings of light around the edges of the drawn blind, although now and then, when Des felt a hunch about the law, he tacked a blanket over the frame. The lot was long and narrow, but the low mumble of voices seemed to reach through the night. This was the imagination of her fright, she knew, but she knew also that if the deputies managed to get near the house they would hear the monotonous burr of talk, kept low, but not low enough for concealment.

The two men stepped across the hard ground and came in sight of the lighted toilet. They stopped and she could almost hear their surprise. They whispered a moment, waited, and then, as if decided, went forward. They must have thought a light was accidentally left on. Cautiously, they were going toward the house!

Robin pushed the door open and it flew back without sound enough for Des to hear. She walked out, pointing the flashlight toward the ground, going toward the house as if unaware of the men. They stopped; she could hear them breathing, very near. Suddenly she gasped and turned the flashlight full upon them, and stood still as if too frightened to move. She gave a small whimper of fear and said almost in a whisper, "Please don't hurt me!"

The faces of the two men showed their stupid and utter astonishment at this unexpected judgment of them; they turned in disgust and walked back the way they had come. Robin held the flashlight on them until they had gone beyond its beam. When they reached the sidewalk, their footsteps sounded for a long time, but she knew they might wait awhile and return. She put the flashlight back in its place, and returned to her post behind the shed. A peculiar elation came over her like a flush, but her legs were trembling so violently that she sank down in the grass, and might have fallen asleep from weariness if the incident had not alerted every nerve and changed the whole pattern of her quiet pleasure in the night.

She began to think of her mother and Stevie shut up in the suspect house, in the ugliness of these suspect nights.

Indoors, all night the staccato betting, the mumbled conversations, the swearing, penetrated the thin wall between the kitchen and bedroom and kept Belle and Stevie awake. They dozed and dreamed and were aroused from their half-sleep. Tobacco smoke crawled under the middle door and hung in the two rooms like fog. The clock ticked determinedly as if to emphasize the long hours of night. Belle began to worry that the men would not leave before daybreak as they usually did, although Des had told her many times before that he would not risk having the house raided.

Such a catastrophe would bring disgrace down upon them all at a time when Apache had become home, in a long line of homes, and when a subtle acceptance by friends they had earned made their precarious life seem more stable. The lives they led of poor respectability and uneasy subterfuge were not simply two—public and private—but four, the dissonant pair operating together in both places. Belle felt the strain and Stevie felt it more. Robin lived cheerfully in the whole complicated mess, so much like Des, both of them carried away with the mere act and idea of being alive. They got up every morning celebrating their breath, almost as if they didn't care what was happening one way or another. But maybe this wasn't true. Robin kept her problems to herself except for an occasional violent quarrel with Des. Actually, they all concealed their problems, revealing them only in furious or sly or sulky or abject or silent ways. Belle wasn't sure what the other three were thinking of these vile nights, but she knew she was afraid; afraid of Des and afraid for him, and afraid for Stevie and Robin.

They were growing up. What would it do to them, hearing these men night after night? Fearing the sheriff's raid? Fearing that Des would be put in jail? Fearing such news in the papers and on the town's tongue? And she and Stevie fearing a new town? What about Robin sitting watch in the dark alley? What about *everything?* All, it seemed to her, because Des would work at nothing except gambling.

This was the first year he had brought his gambling home. Maybe he hadn't meant to, ever, but she knew it would be dangerous to play at the Royal Hotel without giving protection money to the sheriff.

And Des was changing. He didn't seem to mind; he made less effort to find another place. Even before the stock-market crash, before people lost their money and jobs, he had begun to change a little—ever since Kansas City. She could feel that money was not his only problem. Good heavens, that was nothing new in their ups and downs. No, there was more than one reason or two or three, and she was so shocked that she nearly sat up in bed, shocked to realize that she didn't *want to know*. It was as if the part of him that had been so bent on respectability was going bad. This suggested a maze of reasons, and she liked things simple and clear. She felt plunged into and locked in a cellar of Des's self that was strange to her, that she never before had entered. It was a place of corridors and shelves; on the shelves were the unknown factors like foreign fruit in smoky jars with faded labels. She was to name them. She didn't want to know. The skin all over her body felt stung by a thousand infinitesimal bites of mean little nerves that detested farrago. Well, this was the limit, feeling her nerves!

She lay puzzling about herself in this odd state, and about him who was someone else, when a spittle of obscenities oozed through the wall.

"No smut, you fellows," she heard Des say. "My family's in there."

Gratitude pure and simple flowed over her; and then a wave of shame like dirty water. She was used to Des's talk; it was a part of his energy and high spirits, unless he was brooding, and then his swearing was dark and evil.

Beside her Stevie sighed with disgust. "I hate men. They're dirty!"

"Sh-h-h!" Belle said. "Try to sleep. We'll be half dead tomorrow."

142

They finally slept from exhaustion.

A chair scraped on the floor, the back door was quietly opened and closed, and the footsteps of one player sounded loud in the still night. Another left, then another. Belle, half awake, sighed with relief.

Robin came in from the middle room, and Belle rose to give over her place in bed.

"Are you all right, honey?"

"Yes, but I'm going to stay up about fifteen minutes longer and fix this new deck for Papa." Robin had just told Des about the deputies coming into the yard, but he was too tired to be alarmed. He asked her to keep still about the law; and to wash her hands well and put the new cards away before she went to sleep. He had won only a little money.

Robin had marked the cards after work and left them on the table to dry. She began to put them in order. All that remained was to seal the box with the excise stamp and fit the deck into its thin outer case.

"You'll be sick!" Belle said.

"No, I won't. I had a good sleep for the last three nights, remember? And I'll sleep tonight; there'll be a moon. Tomorrow night I'm going to a dance with Drake."

"Don't mention to him these awful nights!"

"Of course not, Mama!"

They heard Des get heavily into bed. If he had made a good winning he would have come in. Belle went to join him for a few hours of undisturbed sleep.

Robin undressed and put on a robe the three women shared and went into the living room and opened the door. The cool spring air came into the smoke-bitter room. She closed the door part way to conceal herself and sat down at the table. Des had just told her that Blackie had found a man with money but it wasn't known yet whether he would play.

Darkness was still in the doorway, but before the stealthy gray light or the blue light or the rose light or the white, long before the sun, the night continued to change. She knew the night by heart.

Somewhere a bird woke and murmured. Another murmured as if half asleep. One awoke and sang a brief song; another cheeped as if in answer, then another sang and another. These songs in the dark went on until dawn, when a chorus of utmost joy greeted the day, as if, Robin thought, the birds had not taken for granted the morning, and it had come, a wonder and a miracle of light and sun.

Robin listened to the birds for a moment and thought of Blackie. She was pleased with her display of will against him, but there was no satisfaction in it.

Stevie groaned. "I wish those birds would be quiet, or else get some new songs."

A mocking bird joyously repeated his song.

Stevie followed him. "Shuffle up, shuffle up, shuffle up! Cut 'em, cut 'em, cut 'em! Deal! What you got? What you got? Two pair. Two pair. No-o-o g-o-o-d! No-o-o g-o-o-d! Shuffle up, shuffle up, shuffle up! Cheat 'em, cheat 'em, cheat 'em! *Y-o-u w-i-n!*"

"Go to sleep, Stevie."

"I want to hear the notes but instead I hear that darned thing. Papa has spoiled the mocking bird's song for me."

"Quiet, Stevie."

"Are you and Drake Bishop about to build a nest?" Stevie asked deridingly. "You've been flying around together quite a bit lately."

"What do I want with a nest? I want some wings!"

"Tell the truth."

"I am."

"Don't think I didn't see that Blackie looking at you, and you looking at him, too!"

"Is that any affair of yours?"

"He's the romantic-looking type. I'll bet you like him."

"I don't go out with him."

"He might be nice if he weren't a gambler," Stevie said.

"But he's a gambler."

"Are you going to marry Drake?"

"No, silly. We don't want to marry each other."

"Then, are you going to have a lot of love affairs?"

"Certainly."

"I think you're bad."

"I don't. It all depends on the attitude."

"It seems a lot of women in history did like that but now people think it's bad, and I *don't* think it's very nice."

"I have something to do. You'd better go to sleep, baby. I'm coming to bed in a minute and no talking."

They slept until eight. Stevie went off to school without breakfast after a brief visit to the kitchen, which her mother was quietly cleaning. As Stevie passed through the middle room and Des stirred, opening one eye, she gave him a chilly look which he absorbed into his sleep like an ominous potion. Stevie imagined everyone in the neighborhood to have seen the thin, clandestine light along the edges of the drawn window blinds, and the men leaving furtively just before dawn. This evening, she thought, I'll go over and ask Chris if he heard them; he'll tell me the truth.

Robin came sleepily into the kitchen, bathed at the sink, tiptoed back to the bedroom, and returned, dressed for work. Even the clean spring air and the aroma of coffee could not dislodge the stench of dead cigar butts and stale smoke. She and her mother sat at the shaky cooktable and ate their breakfast. Des had moved the old round table back to the middle room.

"At this rate," Belle said in a low voice, "it won't be long till we're back to pepper tea."

"Papa will make a winning. This can't last forever. Or maybe I'll get a raise."

"Hot water with pepper in it," Belle said, as if she had not heard Robin. "That's kinda like our life."

Robin smiled at her.

"Robin honey, you won't get a raise in these times."

"Tell Papa," Robin said, getting up, "I left the cards on the table, all marked and sealed."

Belle looked guilty.

"It doesn't bother me, Mama. I just do it and forget it. I have my mind made up against it."

"Well, I won't worry about you because I know you don't like it. I'm worried about Stevie and all those notebooks she's writing down the future in."

"That's her private burrow."

"It's too private."

"Now, Mama, she's playing the piano, too, and Mrs. Sutton says she's remarkable."

Belle's sad face lighted up. "I nearly forgot since I never get to hear her play."

They kissed good-by, and when the door closed Robin heard her father run barefooted into the kitchen, calling her. She went back. He had the cards in his hand. His eyes were bloodshot.

"Here, take these to Blackie. He'll be around on the street later, and if you don't see him, take them up to his room at the Bella Brock, three-fourteen. He thinks he's got a live one but we can't bring him here." He handed her the deck of cards and she wrapped it in a handkerchief and place it in her purse. "Now, listen! Tell him to go get my old room at the Royal, the same one, so we can get away if the law comes. Tell him to plant these cards."

"All right."

"Tell Blackie to fix it with Bowman and Farquarson, to fix that damned clerk good, he's liable to turn us in. I've got to get in shape for tonight."

"That all?"

"That's all." He shook salt into a cup and filled it with cold water. "No, by God. If you go to Blackie's room, you stand in the hall."

"You needn't worry! Why can't I write a note and leave it with the cards in an envelope at the hotel?"

"No, you bonehead! I can't take any chances. We may make some money tonight and I want everything fixed in advance. If I make a real winning we'll lay in a supply of groceries and pay the rent for three months." He turned to the sink and began splashing salt water into his eyes. "I'll see Blackie at the Royal tonight. Tell him to stay away from here today."

SIXTEEN

AS ROBIN crossed the alley and the vacant lot, she traced the way the deputies must have come last night and might come any night hereafter. What would it be like at the *Monitor* if it carried a story of Des' arrest? The other paper would run a banner head, but Mr. O'Brien, an admirer of the policy of the *Kansas City Star and Times,* would not. Which, if any, of her friends would remain openly faithful in such an event?

She now had three friends among the town girls—Florence, an intimate, whose home she must not enter, but who came to the Tannehills'; Molly, whose warmth led her to bumble and choose by her feelings; Iona Lester, the daughter of Apache's oldest and most important family, who was more interesting than the other two, and, because of her position, was bolder and invited Robin and Drake to her occasional parties. Would Iona's social security or her affection—which?—permit her to ignore an open scandal? Iona could not give the direct and laughing companionship of Molly, whose invitations conferred no favor but asked for shared fun. Iona was stern and demanding of Robin to prove her friendship, constantly searching for the purest honesty to match her personal code, which was that of her father and grandfather, good, high-minded pioneer men. But along with this demand and her faithful, dignified affection, she caused Robin to wonder how much of it was based on curiosity, as every meeting was taken up with answering or ignoring the stream of frank questions Iona asked about her personal life. Their strong liking for each other came to be restrained by their mutual distrust, and their friendship limped along, half realized.

When Robin had occasion as a newspaper reporter to call on Iona's father in his land office, he inquired seriously about her work and ambitions, offered his recommendation for any future jobs, and often sat for an hour or two telling her pioneer stories of these high plains he loved. Once he had asked, in the same quizzical manner as Iona, "How are you and Iona getting along?" His question was not casual, and Robin had replied, "Better if she would not ask me so many personal questions." And, added to herself, sometimes offensive. "Perhaps she is lonely," he said. Robin was surprised. "But she has so many friends, and every year she travels, and—" The list could be long, and the old man knew what she was thinking. He smiled and said, "But you are not lonely.

Perhaps she'd like to know why." Robin wanted to absorb his generous understanding, make it her own. "And you don't know why, do you?" he asked. "No," she said, "because sometimes I am lonely—in a way—for something—I don't know what." He nodded. "That's another matter. That's our grand insufficiency." "Then what about Iona?" Robin asked. "Iona," he said, "wants people to live up to her ideals of perfection. And I must say she tries to live up to them herself. As a result, she suffers from mortal distrust—of herself and others. The trick is to develop one's understanding while maintaining essential ideals. I'll keep my eye on you two young ladies."

After that, she was more patient with Iona, and answered all her questions in some fashion; but their friendship did not flourish as it might have, because, Robin finally decided, Iona could not help thinking of her as an outsider, while Mr. Leslie considered her simply as another person. If Iona knew about Blackie, her curiosity would be really offensive. She had to take care to prevent that in defense of Iona, in defense of herself—and of Blackie.

But why "in defense"? she asked herself. Were Iona's questions, which echoed the town's, making her doubt her own genuine qualities, which gave her strength, and those of Blackie, which made her wish to forget his sordid ambition?

At the *Monitor* she worked all morning in the conscious pleasure of her job, surrounded by the multiple activities that concealed the daily routine. She left the office a little after one o'clock and walked along Main Street, looking in shop windows and glancing along the street for Blackie. She wished to avoid going to his room, and she wished to go, perhaps standing in the hall, delivering the message in a low, impersonal voice, watching the unshielded expression in Blackie's eyes and knowing that he would be far too provident of Des's friendship to speak as he once had. She felt strong and was almost aching to show her strength.

The distaste she felt for last night flared up against him and sent her into a café where she usually met Drake when she stayed downtown for lunch. Molly Bassett and three other girls hailed her from a booth to join them and they all sat talking and laughing together in a way that made her feel unexpectedly related to them. She didn't want to belong; she wanted to feel related; it gave her a quivering sense of freedom; freedom to like them and yet to be independent of their confined world, leaving her to dream of her own beyond this time and place, beyond this self she was now. They dreamed of living in Apache all their lives. And why not? Belle might ask; but Robin could not understand it. She sat with her secrets, her eyes shining.

One of the girls began to speak of a luncheon they were giving at the fashionable Bella Brock. In the small, articulate pause, Robin saw them, all blankly embarrassed. The girl hurried on, with desire in her voice, "That good-looking, mysterious Scott Collier lives there!"

Robin was amazed to know Blackie's first name, and yet *they* knew it! A fire went through her because he was hers, not theirs, if she wanted him.

"About the luncheon—" Her friend Molly Bassett's good-humored mouth was fixed in a half-smile of painful sympathy. "I won't be able to come," she said, as if the event had none of the importance the other girls lent it.

Robin distinctly heard the light thud of Molly's slipper kicked against the foot of the girl next to her. She could feel herself waiting for the humiliation she must seize and conceal before her face could reveal it. Instead she was pervaded by a new and surprising amusement at the puffed-up importance of this moment.

"Why?" she asked with reckless delight, rejecting Molly's confused effort.

Molly, rebuffed and adrift, snapped back at them all, "I'm washing my hair."

Robin was soothed by Molly's anger, but now she too was angry at the others, and her head buzzed with retorts that seemed clever and sarcastic, but she pressed them back.

"I've got to go to work," she said, and rose. Then her humor returned, shattering her stale anger, and she thought how much fun it would be to give them an uneasy few days. "See you at the luncheon!" she said, smiling, and went out, again made aware that through her job she had a friendly acquaintance with nearly everyone in town, and yet had been asked into only three homes. She had pretended to ignore the humiliation for so long that she almost believed her pretention, but, now admitting it, she walked along the street, thinking of the ostracism without malice, even without her usual contempt. Her pride, she realized, may have been false, but it had held up her courage until today, when she knew she truly respected herself.

149

When she came to the Bella Brock she went in, took the elevator up to the third floor, and walked along the carpeted hall. She passed number 314 and went back, paused before it, wishing to go swiftly downstairs before Blackie should appear. She held her hand out to see if it revealed the trembling that was shaking the whole inside of her, but her hand was firm. She doubted if she could speak, and wished she could try her voice. Perhaps he was asleep after playing all night. She knocked lightly. In the silence she heard a drawer pushed to, then his light easy steps on the carpet. He opened the door, and his indifferent face changed with astonishment. He did not even speak. She handed him the deck of cards, beginning to recite the directions Des had given her.

In the midst of her communication Blackie said, "You can't stand out there in the hall."

"I can too," she said, feeling secure in the words she had yet to deliver; then, in spite of the adult replies invented on the way, she added, "Besides, Papa told me to."

Blackie hesitated.

"He wants you to go to the Royal and"—she faltered against the powerful tide between them—"and get his old room back and—"

Blackie reached out and pulled her into the room and closed the door. He let her go and she stood clear, but the sight of him in his white shirt was of such special intimacy that she guessed it could never be repeated, and she stood a long, stunned moment absorbing the experience. Then with a cry that surrendered all the effort she had made against him, she pressed into his arms. He held her and said in a grieved tone, "My God, how I've waited!"

They were wild with release of waiting. They could not look at each other or touch each other or kiss each other enough. All time was theirs and the world diminished.

"Oh, my beautiful!"

She was silent.

"You are my love!"

She murmured sounds without words, wary of full commitment. Their voices were low with passion and enchantment.

"Robin, how I've waited!"

"I've waited too!"

Their repetitions created a spell, and all that had been intricate and obscure between them now appeared simple and clear, with out question or cruelty, with tender and pure and joyous admission.

They had waited a long time; there was no need for evasive ritual. He unfastened the buttons at the throat of her dress, and she slid her hand beneath his hand so that he would not yet touch her sensitive breasts. She had permitted no one to touch her breasts; she did not know why or question the reason. Perhaps they were waiting as she was to be overwhelmed by love, holding back from the meaningless gestures of small passions. Now the points rose, aching with desire, and pressed against her blouse, acquiescent at last, sensuous and sure. It was as if their language spoke to her, pledging her own right at a momentous and hazardous time.

Would he mind, she wondered, that she was slender and undeveloped?

She drew off her clothes shyly. In *love,* she thought, how strange it is that I am timid! In the *other,* the slight, inconsequential kissing loves, I felt free, and gay—but that is over. A little gust of regret swept through her, followed by a trembling urge toward this new knowledge. A cool curiosity in the urgency filled her with dismay. Is my wish for experience betraying me? Is my mind simply wanting to know? As she bent forward to step out of her slip, she risked a cautious glance at Blackie, and all thought was devastated by the electricity that streaked through her body. She felt grateful. *All* of me has to *know;* I don't come in parts! She said a simple good-by to that other self so soon to be amended. I shall always be in love! The other was fun; this is not; this is beautiful and awesome. We are more than ourselves, or were we this all the time? She stood free of her clothes, and in that first moment she was aware of an intense and defiant solitude, a secrecy filled with longing against itself. But in the place of the shyness of a few moments before, she felt exactly herself. It was a fine, unadorned feeling.

As if they were going for a long walk he took her hand for the brief journey to his bed. She wanted to smile at this but she felt solemn with a fearful acceptance. When they lay down he put his arms around her and laid his face against her breasts, and all the fear went out of her. She shuddered in release, and mistaking this for fright he held her all the more gently. He felt as if he had captured a wild bird whose only show of alarm was the pounding heart beneath his ear pressed against her small, perfect breasts. A clumsy gesture, a careless word, and this lovely pulsing girl, so like a wild creature in her complex simplicity and incorrupt spirit, would escape. Like a wild creature, too, she was at home in the world, intuitively self-reliant; she had no need of him. But this was wrong, he thought, holding her, giving her time to trust his love. *She is here.* The meaning of this simple fact almost caused him to abandon his caution.

"Are you afraid, my darling?" he whispered, hoping to learn if this was her first time to make love, wanting desperately to find that it was.

"No," she said very low; and he tried to think that it didn't matter; it was only that he wanted her all to himself, to secure her with her first experience. She'd call me "backward" if she knew, he thought, and decided not to expose himself to her ridicule.

Robin lay blushing with shame of her virginity, sure that he valued its unimportance in a way that she would never understand. In itself it meant nothing; it was simply a time *before,* occurring naturally; and the next state was a time *after,* occurring naturally. Her possession of virginity implied no value; she was not ready before, and she was ready now. She asked herself his question: was she afraid?

"A little," she said, "a little afraid."

"Oh, my beautiful darling!" he said in a rush of love and relief. He lifted his face from her breasts and kissed her hard on the mouth and she responded with such passion that the first pain of this love was lost in the whirlpool of sensation that spun her down and down, helpless in the dark swift current of innocent joy. Oh, such a pure delight of body and spirit! Let it never end! And when it did end, she was still submerged, floating slowly up, up, from the deep primeval waters. When she looked at him, she was shining with sensuous and reverent feelings. She could not speak but could only lie close and feel, feel her quivering flesh, her bewitched emotions, her soaring mind. She lay singing in herself an earthly-unearthly song of praise for the mysterious source of love. She sang this way in silence for a long time, and then she didn't know how or why it happened but such an acute and piercing sense of loneliness came over her that she turned away from his touch, sobbing.

He was alarmed and took her back into his arms. "What is it, my darling, what's wrong?"

"I don't know," was all she could say, and the appalling emotion soon went away.

"I'm in love with you, Robin—more than ever." His dark eyes searched hers for an answer.

I'm in love with you, she said in her thoughts, but the words would not be uttered. She could only return his grave kiss.

Before today she had been self-enclosed, complete; now a fulfillment ironically had created a new need. In making her more, it made her less; in answering a passion, it had roused a longing—a longing for all the meanings of love.

"You've got to love me, Robin!" he demanded, then ended tenderly, "I want you to love me!"

She tried to escape her thoughts and his words.

"You know, I'm like Tanny—I'm a one-woman man when I find the woman."

"But I'm not a woman yet," she said in a dreamy evasion, knowing in the midst of her love for him that she wanted more than one love, that she wanted to be free for years and years. She had something to do that she could only sense, but the sense was strong and urgent.

"You are now."

"I am what?"

"A woman."

She laughed. "Oh, I am not!" She wanted to ask him hundreds of questions about himself and his life, and while they were speaking she raised herself on one elbow and looked at his lean and satiny body, darker than her own, its passion still and hidden and remote. She lay back, seeing her body beside him, and she thought that one of the loveliest things in the world must be a boy and a girl lying together in quiet pleasure, talking with intimate ease and fullness after love.

"After this," he said, "we must go back to work."

"Yes," she said, and for only a brief moment she thought of his work.

They came suddenly awake as if the dusk outside were an alarm.

"Oh, good God!" Blackie said, and sprang up, rushing into his clothes.

Robin hurried into her own, saying "Oh, my job! Where have I been? And, Papa! *Papa!*"

"That's *it!*"

It seemed that they might be angry with each other.

"It's because we had so little sleep last night," she said.

"No," Blackie said, putting on his tie. "It's because I've never been so happy in my life!" He slipped on his coat, dropped the marked deck into his pocket, and interrupted her dressing to kiss her. "I've got to find that fellow, Robin, and then go to the Royal. I've got to leave first. Forgive me."

When he was gone, she felt as if she were waiting for him to return "home," and this wonderful suggestion burned along her nerves. She went into the clothes closet and pressed her face against his suits, breathing in the faint scent that came from his skin, that was particularly his, different from her own. After she finished dressing she went downstairs and moved through the door with a group of strangers.

At the *Monitor* office she worked an hour late, placed her copy on the hook, and gathered up her notes to take home.

The lights were on when she came into the street again, and when she reached the little park she saw Blackie walking nervously back and forth on the darkest path that ran alongside the courthouse, dark also except for the barred windows on the top floor. He came to meet her and led her back to the path. He was desperately upset.

"He got away! He was just checking out when I got down to the lobby."

"Oh!" Robin whispered, fearful for Blackie.

"He asked me where I'd been all afternoon, said he was looking for company. I tried to get him to stay, I told him we'd scare up a game someplace, but he had his bags in his car and wanted to be on his way."

Robin clasped his hand, feeling bleak and guilty.

"That wasn't so bad," he went on, "but I didn't keep my word with Tanny. That's the worst."

"You're not keeping it about me, either," she said, not caring that he had not, but wondering at his logic.

"I didn't give my word about you, and I love you. That makes a difference."

"I doubt if it would make a difference to Papa."

"Don't say that!"

"He won't know it."

"He'll have to sometime."

"No!"

154

"Robin! I'm serious, I'm dead serious." His fingers gripped her upper arms, hurting, and he shook her, hardly knowing that he did it.

She struck one of his arms furiously. "Stop shaking me and hurting me!"

"Robin," he said gently, "You know I wouldn't hurt you. But *you* nearly broke my arm."

She smiled.

"And you're pleased."

"No. But don't—ever! Don't touch me like that!"

People were walking along the paths, going home.

"Listen, Robin, you must help me. Tell Tanny that the man left early. I hate to lie to Tanny," he said miserably.

"You aren't, really, and it can't be helped now. I can stand to tell a small lie if it keeps him from feeling bad."

"You don't mind?"

"No. I think being honest about everything is just getting something off your conscience at any cost to the other person. Just think how Papa would feel if we really told him the truth!"

Blackie looked at her for a long time, deciding whether or not he could agree, but he said nothing. He had his own secrets in a maze of intricate ways and in the odd purity of his expectations.

"I'm going back downtown," he said, "and see if I can get up a game. Tanny needs the money, and he ought to get back into the Royal. Last night I could hardly play for thinking of you and your mother and sister. That's not right—playing there. I could rent the room at the Royal, or I could live there instead of the Bella Brock, but Tanny won't listen to me. I want to make the payments to the sheriff, but he—"

"Leave him alone," she said. "He doesn't want to be obligated, and I understand that."

"Well, tell him if I manage anything tonight, I'll fix it at the Royal and come after him. Or I'll meet him there."

"I'll say you said all this at noon. Remember."

He put his arms around her and they kissed. "This is the last time we're going to lie."

"Oh!" she said in alarm. "Whatever you mean, please don't say *anything* to Papa!"

"He likes me, Robin, and I like him."

"I know all that, but I have a feeling that he wouldn't like *us*. Daughters are a great strain on a young man like Papa. It isn't anything against *you*."

Before he could answer, she kissed him, then ran along the dimly lighted path toward Burkett Street and all the way home.

SEVENTEEN

WHEN ANOTHER WEEK had gone by without a game of any kind, not even on Saturday night, Des and Blackie went on a trip around the country. Blackie was to stake the games but Des' hatred of borrowing would not let him accept a loan and his pride would not let him go as a guest. He ended by borrowing all Robin had, a small amount from Stevie's bank, and as much as he dared from the "grocery jar" in the dish cabinet. Belle urged him to empty the jar, as she had managed after each winning to put a few coins under the shelf paper and leave them untouched even on days when there was nothing to eat.

He had been around the house so much, awake and moody all day, that she was glad for him to leave, as much for herself as for him. Besides, she had a plan—a plan she could not possibly carry out while Des was home. At church, which she still attended as a nonmember, she had become acquainted with a number of townspeople, and friendly with a few. Next to Penny Weeks, who remained her best friend, was Mrs. Saunders, the wife of a bank manager. Mrs. Saunders was an older woman, educated, traveled, bored with Apache's social life, and secure enough to like whom she pleased. She liked Belle. Belle sometimes visited her in the afternoons when Des was asleep. When the Negro woman who did her fine laundry, her personal things, moved to California, Belle asked for the work "until things were better at home." She caught the surprise in Mrs. Saunders' face, but, much to Belle's relief, it was quickly followed by understanding and acceptance. Mrs. Saunders had said, "You won't let it make a difference in our visits, will you?" And Belle took the laundry home. She returned it two days later, washed, ironed, and mended, a neat package of silk underthings with labels from New York and Paris and Rome.

Instead of a trip that lasted for months, Des and Blackie were back in two weeks; gambling was as dead in other towns as it was in Apache. On the afternoon of the second laundry, when Belle was ironing a beautiful silk slip, Des opened the back door and walked in. At first he paid no attention to this commonplace chore and began to tell her about the bad luck of the trip. When she cautiously tried to cover the luxurious garment with a pressing cloth and pretended to continue her work, he looked at it and asked, "What the hell's Robin doing now, buying expensive underwear when we're living on pinto beans?"

"No," Belle said, for Robin had paid the rent with her salary check.

"I don't want my kids supporting me, but, by God, that's going too far. She's got to learn some sense, and when she comes home—"

"Calm down, now," Belle said. "I'm just doing this for a friend. Nobody else knows it, and it will help out a little."

As this news penetrated, his face sagged; then he shouted in outrage, "Calm down! Help out! Haven't you got a bit of pride? By God, taking in laundry." His voice was so scornful that Belle began to tremble. "I go out and try to make some money, and before I can turn my back you're on your knees."

"Des honey, I know how you feel, you're proud, but I don't feel that way. I can't help it."

"You feel the way I tell you to feel, if you don't know any better than that! We'll starve before we live on that kind of money."

"Any work that is honest work is all right, Des, and I'm not ashamed. We haven't had a decent meal—"

He slapped her hard across the face. She staggered back against the kitchen table, open-mouthed, shocked. He ripped the silk slip off the ironing board and threw it across the room. It fell on the stove. A strange mixed odor of scorching and perfume filled the air. Smoke rose, and Belle ran to the stove and grabbed the slip; she ran to the sink and turned on the water, then, seeing the ruined silk in her hands as if for the first time, she turned the water off. Des passed by her without looking. He sat down on the davenport and bent his face into his hands.

"This must have cost more than a month's rent," Belle said in a dazed way to herself.

"You can buy her another one," Des said very quietly. "I'll get the money some way."

"We can't. It says 'France.'"

He said nothing more.

Belle folded the ironing board away and placed the remaining laundry out of sight. A chill desperation shook her, mingling thoughts of money and the cruelly unjust blow. She looked cautiously at Des; he still sat with bent head. She felt his penitent silence and was sorry for him. He would never be able to say that *he* was sorry, so it was up to her to give him a chance to be nice at supper. She went out the back door, as if she were going to the outhouse, but at the alley she turned and hurried to Penny's house to borrow a can of salmon and a little butter. She'd make a salmon loaf and hot cornbread and tea; Des liked them all. She'd make a dish of greens from the young thistles growing along the splintered fence of the Polks' lot. It would be hard to earn enough money to pay for Mrs. Saunder's slip, but she thought of washing in the days and ironing in the evenings when Des was out; and with this image came a sweet and satisfying sense of devotion. Self-sacrifice was one of the secret pleasures of the long and isolated years; it had filled out the sagging contours of her self.

Feeling happier, she realized that she could use what was left of the ruined silk and lace to make Robin a pair of panties. On the underneath side, along the seam, she would sew in the label that said 'France.'

I should have stayed away longer, Des was thinking, I should have stayed away for good, maybe, and that would teach Belle who was head of the house. He pictured himself never coming home again and the muscles of his face ached with the effort not to cry. What the hell was happening to him? He'd been broke before. They'd been poor for years but something always happened, those sudden "chicken days" when they'd take a trip, buy clothes, spend money, and have a good time. Now he couldn't even make a dime. When a man couldn't make a living, he got to thinking about everything too much. Why, there never was a time in his life before when he was afraid he couldn't make *something*. Blackie should have listened to him; they should have gone over into the oil towns in Oklahoma and picked up a few dollars the way he used to. Money might still be loose there. The oil workers made plenty and spent plenty. He could have used the dice layout. Or they could have set up a game somewhere and he would have made money just taking off the pots, not burning his eyes out on marked cards. He could do that here, too, and it would be a lot easier, but there wasn't enough steady playing. Blackie kept saying they might as well be back in Apache, it was no worse.

Stevie came in the front door and he could see that she was glad to see him and that made him feel better.

"What are you sulking about, old hoss?" she said. "I thought you would never come back."

"Did you miss me, sprout?"

She nodded. "I like Mama and sister but I like you better."

"Now don't say anything about it," he said, joking, "but you're my favorite."

"Well, were you sulking?"

"Hell, no. I didn't make any money, just a few dollars over expenses."

"What else?"

"That's none of your business. I've got my troubles."

"I hate to grow up—there's nothing but troubles."

"Now, you mustn't say that; there's a lot of fun in life."

"Where?"

"Now, listen here, Stevie, we might move."

"I knew that was it," Stevie moaned. "I was just coming along the street looking at the locust buds and thinking that maybe Apache is *home* at last."

"I've got to be where I can make a living," Des said, appealing to her. "We ought to do a little more rambling."

"I don't like to ramble! *You* can. I want to finish high school right here!"

"Wouldn't you like to meet some new people, maybe make some new friends?"

"No!"

"Well, how're you going to stay here if I can't make money here?" Des was impatient but he tried to conceal it because Stevie was such a baby he hated to upset her.

"And what about my music lessons?"

"You can take music lessons anywhere, Steve."

"Not *free!* And not from Mrs. Sutton! She just teaches me because she wants to, and I learn a lot faster this way. Next year she says I can be in a recital with some students of a friend of hers. *Now* I can't be!"

"We haven't gone yet," Des said. "By God, you'd think we were packing up."

"I know you when you start brooding." Stevie said the last word sarcastically.

"I like to wander," he said, and he was separate and remote, thinking of himself now, feeling misunderstood.

Stevie felt the change and she was afraid he might go away alone and not send for them. "Did you find a nice new town, Papa?"

He didn't answer. He took a pair of dice from his pants pocket and rolled them on the bed cover.

"Did you?"

"I'm thinking about going back to the oil towns." He kept rolling the dice, not looking at her.

"I didn't like the way they smell."

"I can stand that. You just go on and play your music."

"You don't like me any more," she said, and she wanted to cry, but, No one will ever catch me crying, she thought; I despise showing emotions, I despise people, I despise myself, I am going to be a hermit! "I am going to be a hermit," she said aloud, "and live wherever I want to."

Des looked up and smiled. "If you're going to be a hermit it won't make any difference where you live."

Belle came in the back and put something down on the table and came into the middle room. Her face was lighted up with the visit she had been having with Penny. "Hello, Stevie honey, aren't you glad to see your dad home?"

"Uh-huh."

Belle looked at them. If anything's wrong, she thought, it can wait. I'm darned if we won't have a good, peaceful meal. She bent over Des and kissed him, and when she rose she shook her head at Stevie.

"You just rest, honey," she said to Des. "We're going to have a scrumptious supper. A celebration." She felt as if she were walking on eggs. "I used the money I'd been hiding from your last winning," she lied, following the advice Penny had given her. "Now that you're home, it's safe to spend it."

Des felt just a trickle of his high spirits returning. He doubted her for a moment, but for years he had been amazed at her artless and tactless remarks, and he knew she had no deception or cleverness in her.

They were sitting at the round table in the middle room when Robin came in. Belle had put a white cloth on the table and Stevie had polished the old silver until it gleamed in the flat light from the overhanging bulb.

"Well, here comes the Queen of Sheba," Des said, "and you're over an hour and a half late."

"I know it," she said. "I'm sorry." She kissed him and twisted his ear. "Bossy!"

"I'm the cock of the walk around here," Des said, spreading butter thickly on the cornbread.

When she saw the good supper she could not imagine what had happened; Blackie had said the trip was a failure. He had telephoned her at the *Monitor,* and after work they had had a brief and lyrical reunion, making plans at parting for meetings which Robin insisted be kept secret. Blackie objected to the secrecy but acquiesced. She had dropped her casual dating with other boys; and even Drake and she had agreed to part friends. After all, he was engaged and soon would be married. Robin lived in the private intense world of her love for Blackie, forgetting or pushing aside the painful awareness of his profession, lost in her silky immediate dream.

She sat down across from Des, and in the harsh light he noticed how pale she was, but her eyes were a luminous dark blue. She looked the way he had seen himself in a mirror sometimes after a good straight game.

"Do you remember that time," he asked them all, "when we were living in that oil shack and the town was so new there wasn't even a bank and everybody had his money on him, and the whores had on their diamonds night and day because they were afraid to hide them? People were getting robbed right and left, but the stick-up men were afraid of the oil workers. They're tough. Money was flowing like honey. One night—you remember, Belle?—that fellow came in our shack with a gun. I had two or three thousand dollars under my pillow. I had a gun under it too; everybody did. But hell, I forgot all about the gun, and I got up and took after that fellow in my bare feet and ran him out." Des began to laugh. "I ran him clear around the shack and he ran right back in the door again, and Belle began to scream. And you kids were taking it all in as if you didn't know what was going on. When Belle began to scream, both of you began to cry like murder. The poor fellow—I was right on his tail—got so scared he ran out and I never saw or heard tell of him again. I can hear him yet, running off in that oily dirt, yelling for help. By God, I never laughed so much in my whole life!"

"Weren't you scared, Papa?" Stevie asked in admiration. She looked at her mother and Robin to see if they weren't suspicious.

"Hell, no. I wasn't afraid of anything."

"I remember all that," Belle said, and shivered.

"Well," Des said sadly, "all that's gone now. The towns have grown up and they're tame. All that old spirit is gone. A town is kinda like a man."

"It's a good thing you grew up in Oklahoma where the Wild West was still happening at a late date," Robin said.

"Say, you know," Des said, "I'd like to start me a town someplace. You kids are lucky; you've been in on a lot of new towns, right from the first nailed board."

"I wish we'd been born in a big city," Stevie said, "with lots of colleges and opportunities."

"There's nothing like a new town," Des said, dreaming. "I'd like to start me a new town out here on the plains somewhere. We could name it Desmond, or Tannehill. I could keep my name going that way. And I could have a hell of a time doing it."

EIGHTEEN

THE FRAGRANCE of spring vied with the stench of dead cigars and stale cigarette smoke left over from the cheap night games. The men of the town who gambled, the ones who had once been willing to lose small sums for their pleasure, had been persuaded by Des that they could still enjoy themselves if they played in his kitchen for smaller stakes. Some of them could no longer afford even this; the rest were pleased. Regular games began. From these smoky, blinding nights, Des won a few dollars each week, and took off from the pot, still not enough for expenses. He saved his few marked decks for that hoped-for chump with a wad of cash, and played straight. He was more skillful than the others, but some of the regulars had developed into good players, and if he had a bad run of cards, he lost or did well to break even.

Blackie stayed downtown to keep a lookout for strays and travelers, and steer them to the game. Blackie staked him time and again, and although he still had a good bank roll, Des would not borrow money even when Blackie tried to press it upon him. The most he sometimes would agree to was keeping his partner's cut.

Belle cleaned the filthy kitchen without complaint, but unfamiliar questions grew in her mind; tentative resolutions began. Whatever Robin thought she kept to herself, but Stevie revealed her suffering in sulky behavior and virtuous censure that included them all. At home she occupied herself with her future, working over her notebooks and her plans for college as if her life depended on them. She refused to go to Main Street to the post office or shops, saying, "I feel as if every man I meet has been in our kitchen. I'm ashamed."

Chris had told Robin that one night when he came home late, a night when she was not on watch, he had seen two men loitering in the alley. When she told Des, he called off his games for three weeks but he was so broke that he started them again, saying they'd all have to take a chance along with him. A part of Robin's small salary and the few secret dollars that Belle had left over from her insistent payments on the burned slip were not enough. Des did not notice this; he despaired when the jar was empty.

Then one night, when Robin came home at about eleven from a secret date with Blackie, and started around the house to the back, a man who had been crouching behind a bush jumped up ahead of her and ran. She nearly screamed but she remembered the game, and when she went in she was trembling. The house was quiet and Des was in bed asleep. He went out and looked around, but the man who had been waiting and watching was gone. "On the nights we play," he told Robin, "you'll have to stay home and keep watch in the alley till I can afford to get back into the Royal."

Late the next morning, when Belle was standing in the clean kitchen with the strong wind blowing through the door, she made up her mind. The burned marks all over the linoleum gave her courage.

Des was reading a popular novel that Bowman had found in the lobby.

"If the sheriff raids our house I don't know what we'll do. As bad as business is, they could give you a free room at the hotel for all the steady rent you've paid there."

"Bowman would if he owned it, but the manager wants cash. And that damn clerk will have me arrested if I don't cut him in and I can't do it now—the winnings are too small. Don't you know I've thought of all that?"

"Well, you're going to get arrested anyway and disgrace us all."

Des got up and slammed the book to. He began pacing back and forth through the kitchen and the middle room in the same wild way as when he had a toothache. At times he even raised one hand to his jaw, and once he doubled his fist and struck the back of the door where the coats were hanging on large nails. Belle trembled. Her face was white with fear as she remembered the blows that had come her way. She watched his feet; how stubborn, even violent, they appeared. She thought she had ventured to raise only one timid objection.

"If I can't make the pay-offs to the law, where else can I gamble? How will we live?"

"It's just that the kids are bigger now," she said, scarcely above a whisper.

"If they're that big, let them get out."

"If you say that to Robin, she will," Belle said. "And Stevie's too young."

"I don't mean Stevie."

Belle turned her back, the tears had begun, and she was whispering to herself, "My babies ..." which only increased the tears. She dried her face, and, agitated with fright, feeling cold even though she stood in the slab of sunlight from the window, she made a supreme effort at daring, took a momentous risk, still with her back to Des.

"Why don't you try to get a job?" Her voice all but failed and she was not sure that he had heard until he roared from the other room.

"What the hell kind of job could I get now?"

"Any kind, Des, just any kind for a while," she pleaded. "To get the games out of the house before something happens. We'd manage."

"Job! Job! I want money in my pocket, you fool! How much would I have with a job? I can always make more gambling. Money is tight, that's all. The next elections may cure this." He jerked his coat off the nail, slammed into it, and automatically ran his sleeve around the crown of his hat, dusting the brim. He hesitated, then in a fury of revenge said to her, "Well, there's only one thing left I can do."

Just then Stevie came in the front door from her music lesson at Mrs. Sutton's and, hearing the familiar quarrel, went on to the bedroom.

Des paid no attention and continued with cold savagery, "I can take Queenie on a trip with me and let her steer me some chumps."

Belle turned around and stared at him in appalled disbelief.

"With her looks," Des went on, "I'll teach her to give some old boy the glad eye and shake him down for all he's got." He had no intention of doing this; his own words outraged him, but where the hell had they come from anyway? He felt more coming; it was a sensation of convulsive necessity like vomiting. Here they came! "No use wasting Cleopatra's beauty and brains out here in that dark alley, by God. I'll put her to work! She'll make more money than she ever will on that one-horse newspaper."

"Desmond Tannehill!" Belle said in a slow hoarse whisper. "Desmond Tannehill." She repeated the name now in a soft, oddly tender cry, as if reaching far back.

He smiled. It was his attractive smile, not malicious or evil or anything—just attractive. She hadn't seen him smile like that for a long time. "What do you say to that?"

Before she could answer, Stevie came into the room with her face set in pitiful uncertainty. For some time she had been burdened with a guilty dislike of her father, and suddenly, when she heard him saying these reckless and terrible words, a rush of devotion overcame her. She wanted to rescue him.

166

"He doesn't mean it, Mama." Then she turned her innocent eyes upon Des. "You don't mean all those bad things, do you, Papa?"

"Sure, I mean them!" He thought, Here is the place to stop. But he could not. "Every damn one of them! And you stay out of this!"

"You wouldn't make me do that," she said, secure in the knowledge that she was his favorite, free to shame him into the truth.

"*You!*" He turned on her. "You—why you're no use to anybody! All you can do is live in those damn notebooks. You don't know you're alive! You don't even speak to me half the time. You don't even go uptown. People don't know I've got two daughters!"

Stevie stood shocked and still under the incredible attack. At first her face and neck turned scarlet, then pale, and her eyes filled with loathing.

"I don't want to be *your* daughter!" she said with cold intensity. "I don't want anyone to think I am." A helpless expression came into her childish face, and it seemed for an instant that she would give way; then she went quietly into the living room and closed the door on their shared awe.

Des stood fixed, dismayed at himself, at the words that had gushed out of him; and in this vulnerable moment Stevie's retort struck him a crashing blow. He put on his hat, pretending a violence he no longer felt, and as he passed Belle on the way out he gave her a contemptuous look and repeated, "Job!" He slammed the door so hard that the flimsy room shook and filled with tiny sounds of pans and dishes quaking. In the silence that followed there was a soft plop as the old sweater Belle wore for work out-of-doors fell mildly to the floor. Its nail, pointing stiffly upward, was resting in the folds of wool. Belle gazed at it in surprise; then she stooped, jerked the nail free, and threw it hard into the middle room. It clicked against the wall, fell on the edge of the bed, and rolled onto the floor. It came to rest near Des's valise.

She wanted desperately to console Stevie, but she knew better than to approach her now for fear of ridicule. She wanted to talk to Penny, to tell her every detail. When she had confided in her before, Penny had simply announced that she "wouldn't stand for it," that she would have Des arrested, that she would leave. "Get a divorce!" she had said once. "You won't be a widow long. Not in our church." None of these could Belle do, and she could not make Penny understand her obscure and painful reasons. Penny, who had never known real poverty or cruelty or what it meant to be an outsider, was full of ready answers as strange to Belle as her own situation was to her friend, but she wanted to hear them. Out of her silent disagreement might come a way of her own.

She suspected that the girls accused her. She knew they were aware of the monotonous, mumbling quarrels, and sometimes a muffled blow, that went on in the nights when Des did not have a game or go to the hotel. It seemed to her their clear eyes judged her, but perhaps she imagined this. They swore they would never marry; they often stayed away from home in the evenings, or worried her by sitting in the Garrison kitchen next door, in plain view, talking and laughing with Chris and his mother and sometimes Chris's girl, Marie. Robin and Stevie were not unkind to her, but perhaps they no longer needed her as they once had, and this was a growing sorrow.

When she was Robin's age, she had been married three years and Robin was walking and talking. She could hardly remember when she had not been with Des; she had no life away from him. She could look back and see that her adoration had been completely trustful and unwary; he hadn't meant to, but he had taken her spirit away. For the rest of her life people would look at her and know this; the hurt, dumb look she had just seen on her face in the mirror would be there like an invitation to take advantage, to command, to tread upon. Maybe she was a coward. But she could remember quite clearly any number of times when she hadn't been, and she began to ransack her copious memory, like an old trunk, for all the moments of courage.

She was seldom idle, so that now, as her mind searched itself, she went to pick up the nail, and with a heavy piece of kindling wood hammered it back into the door and hung up the old sweater. As she struck the precise blows, she felt vaguely that some decision was called for, but she was too confused with a mingling of hatred and pity and remnants of love.

Stevie listened at the closed door until she heard Belle moving about in her own small, intensely personal world, and then she moved into hers. She was tense with scorn for her mother, whose easy tears seemed more to hide than to reveal a suppressed morass of emotions she could not understand. Stevie belittled them and dismissed them. As for her father, she could not even think in what way she would revenge herself upon him. It must be momentous, for the rest of his life, as he had betrayed her, and wounded her for the rest of her own.

In a dazed, automatic way, she went to the closet and took from the shelf the Sunday shoes and set them in an orderly row on the floor. She placed her father's best hat on the bed. She gazed for a long time at all her catalogues and notebooks and plans. The years of her youth were in them, concealed. The journey to the stove was not a long one in space or time, but the anguish of change and the uncertainty of destination made it a sad and fearful expedition to an unknown place. She carried her treasures slowly into the living room.

She opened the heater door and dropped a booklet in and lighted a match. She sat down to watch, and as the sheets became ash she added more. The fire roared in spite of her care, and once in the space under the door she saw her mother's feet approach stealthily and turn back. When a booklet fell open she watched its pages curl in the fire, its pictures of silver and glass, fences and rooms, its list of colleges and railway fares, its bars of music disappear.

Belle opened the door part way. "What in the world are you doing, honey? You'll set the house afire. What are you burning?"

"Nothing."

"I declare," Belle said, trying to laugh. "You look like a girl burning love letters. I know you haven't any yet." She waited for Stevie to reply. "I'll never forget when I burned my own."

"Why did you?" Stevie asked coldly.

"He wanted me to. Once, when he went away, he wrote me every day."

Stevie ignored her. She could not accept the image of her mother and father in young love. It was unpleasant, almost sickening. Belle may have been giggly and moon-struck, but her father had never been so foolish, and she longed to say so, except that now she was not interested. "I want to be left alone," she said.

Belle, hurt, closed the door.

Stevie placed on the hot coals a brochure titled "Investments for the Wise Woman."

She felt as if she might cry, but she sat very still, tightening the muscles of her throat and face, pressing the tears back inside— where they belonged. How lonely she was!

These years in Apache she had made few friends. At school she was happy; her grades were high and the teachers liked her. There were times of real fun. But she felt herself growing more and more stern, and somehow different, and terribly afraid of what others thought of her life at home. Once an arrogant, coarse girl named Frances, privileged because of her money, had asked flippantly before others where her father "hid his loot." She recalled the tentative gestures of friendly students to pierce the cool, self-possessed exterior of her fears; and the persistence this year of a boy named Max, who wanted to have a date with her. But she had given them no chance to hurt her, or to say a word against Papa. He had made up for them all, until now. She would never let anyone know, not even Robin, or Chris, who understood so many things, and who spoke to her and Robin like a brother.

She hesitated a long time before burning the pages on which she had set up a perfection of qualities she wished to encourage and create in herself; and a long list of demands she in turn would make of life. She was sorry she could not burn the observations she had stored in her mind; they had made an insurmountable wall between her and everyone else. Papa and Robin penetrated that wall with their high spirits and affection, but even they came less often into this private garden, where she tended the brilliant, stunted plants of her dreams, and walked alone along the paths of her mind.

When she had placed the last of the books in the stove, she leaned close and waited. They were heavy and it took a long time. The little mouths of fire burned and closed; a sigh of ash expired like a breath. Stevie's cheeks were hot, and her eyelashes and the fine hairs on her right arm were singed, but she felt cold, cold enough to shiver as with a chill.

She looked in at the black and fragile remains, holding their shape as pages still. She blew on them and they collapsed with an infinitely delicate crash of sound, as if a little van of precious supplies had been wrecked on some far avenue of her mind.

She closed the heater. Belle opened the middle door as if she had been standing behind it all the time. "Did you call me, honey?"

Stevie got up and went into the bedroom. She tried to pull the curtains together across the double door, forgetting that they would not meet. Belle came stubbornly after her and caught her, holding her in her arms.

Stevie pulled herself free, looking at her mother with a tense, set face. "Leave me alone! All of you, leave me alone!" She flung herself on the bed, face down.

Belle stood rejected and stunned, no longer hurt, but alarmed. She patted Stevie's legs. "Did that old mean papa scare my baby?"

"No!"

"You're sick, then, and no wonder—you haven't had a decent meal in months!"

"Go away," Stevie begged.

"I can't, honey. You need me."

"I don't need anybody!" Stevie cried. "And nobody needs me. Go away. I want to die!"

Belle was quite still for a while with her own dismay; then she began to take off Stevie's slippers and stockings, her dress and underclothes. The girl lay like a stone, giving her no help and covering her face with her arms. Belle struggled to pull the nightgown over her head, to push Stevie's arms into the sleeves and slip the long garment down over her childish body. She felt proud of Stevie's fine white skin, her small waist and delicate breasts, swollen like buds. She recalled the fountain of her own breasts, the abundance of milk that the little Stevie could not nurse without illness. A neighbor had said the milk was bitter because Des had quarreled with her all through the pregnancy—young, jealous quarrels over her visits to the doctor, who could not keep his feeling out of his eyes.

Remembering how Stevie had clung, nuzzling and biting, angry to be weaned, Belle again felt the thrill in her breasts as keenly as then. She hugged Stevie to her and patted her and smoothed her soft, pale hair. Robin had been a noisy, crying, laughing baby, but Stevie had been quiet and stern, appearing then to be thinking of weighty problems far distant from her baby needs.

Belle began to feel panicky. Had she failed Stevie sometime, somewhere? Had she not been a good mother? She drew the covers back and lifted the heavy, silent girl into her place. She needs new gowns, Belle thought; this one's a pity.

She went to the kitchen and returned with a wet cloth and placed it on Stevie's forehead.

"Put one on my heart," Stevie said, bitterly enjoying the mystified look on her mother's face.

"Oh, honey! Are you all right?"

"Go away, Mama."

"I will. I'm going to the store. I'll fix you some nice potato soup with milk and you can eat it in bed."

"You might use all the money and there won't be any for tomorrow!" Stevie's voice was suddenly anxious.

"I don't give a hill of beans! I'm going to buy a can of loganberries." Belle watched for Stevie's glad surprise.

"You're going to drop a nice bug in my mouth, aren't you, Mama?" She sounded faint and tired.

Belle's face lighted up. "Yes, honey, I'm going to fly out and get a bug for my pretty little bird." She turned, almost satisfied, and yet bewildered, and went into the kitchen.

Stevie heard her lift the money jar from the dish cupboard and empty the coins into her hand.

"Poor Mama," Stevie said.

NINETEEN

DES CAME HOME the next morning a little after nine o'clock, taking the short-cut, entering by the alley. Polk's shed made a sharp design of shadows on the bare, sun-pale yard; the spring wind was blowing the fragrance of sage into the town from the surrounding plain. He was in no mood for spring, his pride still sore with Belle's daring to suggest a job. What job could he do anyway, and, compared to most gamblers, wasn't he as fine as any and better than most? His bad luck had nothing to do with his cleverness; he hadn't a lot of money because he spent it as it came, never put it away. If he had ever made a misstep it was to marry and raise a family. Free, he might have had even more adventure, he might have ended up in the big resorts. He should have gone off with Blackie a few years ago. He thought of the big ships; he might have had a good life on them, but he was forced to admit that he had no desire to go on the water or to travel outside the United States. He felt mistrustful of foreigners, except the ones he knew. But more than one gambler friend had made money on the liners and urged him to try it because he made a good impression upon all kinds of people.

Des hardly cared this morning that he was coming home in broad daylight, in sight of all the neighbors, violating his covert habits. People in little towns considered it indecent not to work. A man coming home in midmorning had neither a day nor a night job. "No visible means of support," the law called it, and the next thing he knew, the law would be down on him for no visible pay-offs. He had played at the Royal last night, afraid of a raid, but Bowman had kept a sharp lookout. Bowman's loyalty was not for hire as Farquarson's was. A jail sentence, and Stevie might not forgive him the public scandal; he had never been in jail.

Before he entered the kitchen he heard Belle singing at the top of her voice the old popular song, "Meet Me Tonight in Dreamland," and for a moment his mood lightened. When he opened the door he saw that she was pushing a wet mop across the floor in time with the song and paying very little attention to the floor. She turned at once, leaned the mop against the wall, slid her hands down the side of her clean apron, and came to kiss him, holding her gentle face up and putting her arms around him. She had hardly slept all night for thinking she had hurt him, and now, with no words and only a mute, appealing look, she hoped he would forgive her. This half-fearful adoration that had once pleased and amused him appeared now to be the most disgusting groveling, and only yesterday an emotion like hate had flared up when he heard her speak boldly to him. He pushed her away and went into the middle room. The bed was opened for him, the blankets smoothed, the blinds drawn. As he took his coat off, he gave her a savage glance that held her at the door; then, sure of her attention, he drew from his belt a Police Colt revolver and tossed it onto the bed. Its bluish metal gleamed in the dusky light.

Belle's mouth felt dry, her heart wavered and raced, and yet she could not move.

Des coolly watched her face, savoring all the pleasure of the fear he saw there, and then picked up the gun and flung it lightly toward her. She caught it and dropped it and let it lay, and began to tremble uncontrollably.

"That's all I could get last night," he said. "A fellow soaked it to me in the game. Maybe you can take that to the store and trade it for some groceries."

She withdrew into the kitchen and sat down on the backless chair, feeling too weak to utter any word even if one had come to mind. The fear trickled away. Over and through her poured the stifling knowledge that Des considered her a burden, an extra expense; in his mind she was indissolubly mingled with the groceries, rent, electricity, and coal. Every other meaning had vanished. It occurred to her suddenly, as if all her small resentments had gone unnoticed, that she had never asked him for money. She had always waited until he gave it because she had learned early that request made him angry. His generosity, famed among friends and strangers, had not often been practiced at home. She thought acridly of all the times when he had large sums of money and there was little or none for them unless he "took a generous streak," which, of course, he occasionally did. For the times they had been truly poor she had only tenderness, for then he was poor, too, and she was a help with her saving and managing.

Why was she now a burden? This thought so enraged her that she stood up and said to herself that she would get a job and bring her wages home and they would be in plain sight, no secret in her pocket. She would go out tomorrow and find a job. In order to show him her work at home she ought to refuse to cook the meals, clean the house, wash and iron the clothes and mend them, press his suits, or do any of the tasks of daily living. This she had not the courage or defiance to do, but she would get the job and do the work besides. What kind of job? As clear and newly shocking as her thoughts of Des was the realization that she had no experience in any work, except that of a bakery—an old-fashioned bakery without modern machinery. Her brief and angry enthusiasm collapsed. All she knew how to do was the work of a house, and she had to admit that she was not expert at that. She had not even won any money in the soap contest. The company had acknowledged her letter with thrilling courtesy, assured her they were sorry she had not won, and sent her a coupon for a free bar of soap.

"I must be a dope," she said, and sat down. She felt exhausted, a state unknown to her in midday; she wanted to lean forward on the kitchen table and sleep. All the vehement resolutions floated away on her powerful weariness like debris on a flooded stream.

It occurred to her to pray. She could hardly rouse herself to the effort of formulating all the pleas that crowded her mind; pleas for Stevie and Robin and Des—yes, Des—and, at the last, pleas for herself.

"Tell me what to do, God!" she whispered against the oilcloth table cover, eased by hope and a sense of mysterious power flowing through her for the first time. "Give me the courage to do it! I'm an easy mark, God, and I'm scared, too. I'm not stupid, but I know I'm not as smart as Des and the girls. That's all right, it's too late to care. But it means you'll have to help me to do the right thing." Then, in the wonder of her daring, she went on. "Maybe I shouldn't ask this, God, but please give Des a winning so he won't be so mean." She lifted her head and took a long free breath. "Oh!" she whispered, and dropped her head again. "Excuse me, God! Thank you, I feel better, thanks a lot!"

When Des saw Belle rest her face against her folded arms, he picked up the gun from the floor, wiped it off, and took it with him into the bedroom.

On Saturdays Stevie slept late. He walked quietly, seeing her mussed blond hair and pale, sweet face innocent in sleep. His bitterness dropped away. He wanted to make up to her for what he had said in his temper against Belle. Stevie would know anyway that he hadn't meant what he'd said to her, except about the notebooks. He'd got after her before about them. He looked at her now with love and wished she could feel it so that he wouldn't have to say anything at all.

Of the four drawers in the large dresser, the top one belonged to him. He opened it quietly and laid the revolver among his socks. Stevie's school books were in a neat pile on the dresser. He raised the cover of a notebook and read through the outline for a theme, then lifted other pages and found nothing of interest but a small folded piece of paper. It had been crumpled and smoothed. He unfolded it cautiously and read:

Dear Miss Stephanie Tannehill—how's that for the formal approach, eh? How's about a date? A double-date Saturday nite with Beanie and Thelma to the mooin' pitcher show and join the gang afterward at Borg's drug store? Pick you up at 7:30. Answer pronto. YES ONLY. Max.

On one edge of the note was a drawing of a girl with her head in a large book, and across the page one of a boy cupping his hands to his mouth, calling, "Yoo Hoo!"

Des was irritated. Then a sharp pain nearly cut the breath from his throat. He felt shaken and weak. He had a vivid desire to get hold of this smart-aleck Max and give him a whack or two on his young boy's bottom and see if that would stop him from bothering Stevie. He had to protect *her* from the damn boys now!

He looked toward the bed; Stevie was lying very still, with her large blue eyes wide open and as fixed as an owl's eyes on him. He closed the book, wadded the note into a ball, and tossed it onto the window sill.

"Let me catch you going out with a boy, by God, and I'll run him off," he said in a low voice. His throat was so tight he could hardly speak. He glanced down at the open drawer and picked up the gun. "See this? The first boy that comes here will pee his pants. I'll give him a look at this."

"Pooh," Stevie said mildly. Since yesterday, after burning her notebooks, she had felt quiet, terribly quiet, remote, floating. Her unforgiveness of Des lay enclosed and living like a microscopic egg at the bottom of a pond. "Pooh," she repeated.

"Pooh nothing. I mean it."

Stevie yawned and stretched. "Did you get it to kill something to eat?"

"Who is this Max? Max who? What's his father do?"

"What's his father do?" Stevie chanted without expression.

"Well, I'll run him off. He won't come back."

"He isn't coming, ha-ha. I don't want to go out with any old boys."

"Well, that's right. He'd better not, or anyone else. Remember what I tell you: boys only want one thing." His voice was fatherly, advising. "They'll tell you anything to get it. A smart girl will hold out, and that's why men fall for getting married. They're a bunch of suckers."

"I'll bet they want to get married just as much as women. Robin's had a lot of proposals and she doesn't even want them. *She* doesn't try to get anybody and those silly boys just swarmed around her at school."

"That's it. They had to chase her. It's all a trap. Nature fixed it up that way."

"The women get in a trap too," Stevie said.

"Damn it, the women *want* in the traps."

"I don't."

"Well, you've got some sense." He walked out, saying, "I'd rather have a couple of good bird dogs than two she-girls." He went into the middle room and closed the door.

Stevie's mind was busy with pictures of a romping contest between boys and girls, and the ground on which they pretended to enjoy themselves was planted with hidden traps that God had laid in the night of the world. Couples fell unsuspecting into them and dropped onto the grassless floor of an underworld, where they began to work and worry about food and clothes and rent and coal and getting sick. Nobody was reading books. Where were the books being written? She traveled back up into the sun and shade of the first layer of living. Since she alone could see the traps hidden in the grass, she picked her way carefully. Once Max was standing in front of her, looking foolish and running his hand through his brown hair just the way he did at school. He looked awfully nice, and kind of innocent, really. But she was afraid of him because Papa had told her the *truth*. She blushed and passed around him, and thought how safe and sensible she was compared with the other girls.

She got out of bed and looked at the gun. There wasn't anything at all frightening about a gun. She lifted it slightly and twirled the cylinder, running one finger over the pretty flat ends of the shells. She smiled, remembering Papa. Papa would never shoot anybody. Besides, boys were more frightening than the gun.

She looked through the window at the sun on the dead morning-glory vine clinging to the screen. Tonight she might go to the show with Mama. But now, suddenly, she might write a poem and hide it with the scrap of music she had composed one night coming home from Mrs. Sutton's. Together they would make a song.

She lay on the bed and tried to catch the words in her mind, writing one down and crossing it out. She had written two other songs and burned them. "My love shall be," she wrote. Without warning she heard her mother crying and Papa's voice low and angry, and she knew they were quarreling over money again. She clapped her hands over her ears and burrowed her face into the covers. Their voices changed subtly and droned on. Stevie uncovered her ears and listened. "Get undressed!" she heard her father say as if they were conspiring. In a little while she knew that her mother had complied. She despised them both.

She got up and dressed, wanting to wash in the kitchen, wanting a drink of water, wanting to be away from this house. She went out through the front door, taking the notebook and pencil, walked around to the back, and sat on the cellar door. She was trembling and her palms were wet. She opened them and drops of water fell, making ragged stars on the gray wood.

Mrs. Garrison, freshly dressed, came from her back door and crossed the yard on her way to town. As she passed she looked searchingly at Stevie and said, "Young girl like you ought be out havin' fun today, at school all week. Oughta be picnickin' with some young folks this spring day."

Stevie nodded but her mouth felt too tight to smile. After a long time she returned to the poem. She wrote one whole line, then gazed without interest toward the alley and streets beyond, where an unhurried motion of people and cars gave all Apache a quietness in her vision. Two dogs who were friends trotted through the yard as if in eager and smiling agreement on their destination. They were always together. She finished the poem swiftly, almost losing the words, and then changed it and changed it until the page was filled with writing. At last she copied it onto a fresh sheet of paper, and gave it a title which flew into her head.

Aspiration

My love shall be a chaste thing and
As cool
As any silvered moonlight in
A pool,
As deep as the unfathomed lengths
That lie
Between the pond's reflection and
The sky.

Stevie reread the poem a number of times before she folded it into a small square and slid it into her shoe.

The door opened and her father's voice said gaily, "Stevie, you'd better come on in here and eat your breakfast."

She got up from the slanting cellar door, and without looking at him she crossed over to the Garrisons' and sat down on the back porch.

"Come back here," he called. "What's the matter with you?"

"Go to the devil," she said under her breath.

Robin and Blackie walked slowly arm in arm along the empty dirt road. The night was like a deserted place opalescent with moonlight; evening sounds of the town drifted away on the wind. Tall, geometric grain elevators cast black shadows on the road, which lay in such wonderful clarity that last year's lost wheat seeds were distinct. Here Robin and Blackie could meet and walk together unseen. Their voices were low; they were awed by love and the luster of the night world.

"We could live in hotels," he said. "We could travel. You'd like that."

"I don't want to *live* in hotels, I want my feet on the ground. But I'd like to travel."

"All right. You wouldn't have to do a thing, I promise you."

"What a stupefying life!" she said, teasing him.

He stopped and shook her gently, and she laughed at his exasperation, kissing him and speaking. "But it's true! If I did nothing my whole self would wrinkle up like a prune. Couldn't you just have a little stuffed likeness of me to carry around with you, unpack me, and set me on a table in your room? Then I would be doing *nothing*." She was still laughing.

"Stop that, Robin! You're making fun!"

"You have such a funny idea of me. You're making me up. You'd be disappointed with *me*"

"No, I wouldn't," he said rather fiercely, and her face sobered. "You can do whatever you want to, but we're in love. You keep forgetting that."

"I don't," she said with sudden emotion. "I don't!" She held his hand tightly and looked away from him into the magic night, and it seemed to her that she could feel this perilous love growing, that she could even hear it growing like the rising hum of insects all around them. It would overwhelm her in this sly season and she would forget that only in their silent walks or in their times of passion was she completely in love and free of doubt. She wanted to live in *this* love that was enough, and then she could be glad, and kind; he would see how different she could be.

"What are you thinking?" he asked.

"That spring makes me ache to be happy. Why must we always speak of marriage?"

"Because I want to marry you," he said, certainty and a shadow of hurt in his tone.

"I know all about marriage," she said with sarcasm. She hated the thought of it. It was a charade, enormous, prolonged. And yet, in the end, there was no substitute. If any man wants to marry me, she thought, relenting, it is his supreme compliment, I suppose, and I ought to respect that. "There are some other things I have to do first," she said in a voice clear and assured by her inmost dream, her eyes tender and ashamed before his expectant look.

"What? What do you want, Robin?"

They walked through a black shadow without kissing and on into the bright night.

"I want to leave home *alone*," she said intensely. "I want to leave Apache—and all Apaches everywhere. I want to be known for myself, and not as a gambler's daughter, not whispered about, suspected, half accepted and half snubbed." She walked near him and their arms touched. "Blackie, I'm sick of pretending I don't know it, of being 'proud.' Apache is more polite than other places, but it's all here just the same. Why should I stay in it?" She let go his hand. "I want to get Stevie out of it too. I'd like to meet some girls who don't describe men by their college fraternity and the price of the car they drive. 'What's he like?'

'Oh, he's a Phi Delt with a Cadillac!' Or 'What's she like?' 'Don't you know? Her father's the head of the Building and Loan.'"

"Don't mind it, Rob. Your dad's all right."

"I don't mean that. It's just that individuals don't count."

"If that's what you want, we could go away tomorrow."

"No, alone, I said. Don't be angry with me, Blackie. I feel different. Maybe everyone does. But I don't want the same things. I want more than they do and less."

"You'll need money and you like clothes."

"I don't want a lot of money. I do like clothes but I don't want to take off my dress and find myself poor all through. I want to read more books and listen to music I've never heard and look at paintings. I want to wander around. I want to know people—what they're really like. I want to live and change and be whoever I am! I want some work that will use *me*. I want my own door, my own key. Oh, I'd be thrilled with a key in my purse!"

"I want you and you don't want me, that's the whole thing."

"I don't want marriage."

"You will—some day. I hope it's with me."

"I won't want it for a long time."

"You seem to know what you want, but little girl Robin, you don't know *all* about marriage."

"I wish I knew less."

"Well, there are as many kinds of marriages as there are kinds of people."

She said nothing, but she liked his words.

"But you do love me, Robin."

"Not in the way you want. I can't help the way I love you," she said simply. "You want more than I can give now. I want to live my life. It is *mine,* and I can't promise it away!"

"Then I may as well quit trying," Blackie said, changing his tactic, giving her hair an affectionate, un-lover-like yank. "You don't know what it's like to be lonely, that's all."

"I guess I don't," she said, and paused. Then, because it was night, she felt free and extravagant and went on as if she were talking to Chris, whom she'd neglected because she was in love. "I feel full of secrets I have to uncover—secret meanings that hook me up to all of that"—she

181

swung her arm in a semicircle toward the night sky—"and every bit of life there is, everywhere!"

"What a wild little, little girl you are! I don't know why I want to marry you! You'd rise up and fly away somewhere."

"The way I feel doesn't prevent me from being interested in the world!" she said, flaring up. "And you know it! I'm responsible on earth because I live here, but the earth is not such a separate place. It's *all* together, the sky and the stars and the planets, the sun—"

"You're drunk," he said, teasing her.

"Oh, I am!" she said, and whirled around and around ahead of him. "I'm drunk with being alive and being in love!" She ran back to him in a rush of passion and of tenderness for the unknown and the lonely in him. I don't know him, she thought sadly. I can't appreciate the parts of him I don't know. I've been thinking of myself. She wanted to kiss him but instead she placed her hand in his and they walked together again.

He stopped and brushed her hair back with his hand. "You are so young and serious. I don't know what to do with you."

"Can we just be in love?" she asked eagerly.

"Would you rather we tried to be friends?" he said, teasing. He smiled and walked beside her. "You can be in love, then. I'll be in love and want to get married."

"Shall we have a contest?"

"Maybe that's it." His face closed.

"Drake said—"

"Do you still go around with that reporter?"

"You know I don't."

"How should I know on the nights I'm with Tanny?"

"You may do as you please about believing me. I said that I don't."

When they turned to walk back along the road, he pulled her to him and said, "I believe you!"

She felt encircled and smothered by the sense of their closeness, and standing only a little way apart from him she felt isolated and incomplete. Oh, you are *my love,* she thought, but she twisted away and said, "Drake said you are the eternal fascinator, and that half the girls in town are in love with you because they want to reform you."

"How can you listen to that?"

"I believe it. I suspect you're going to haunt me all my life."

"I intend to."

His face changed subtly with its rare humor, and her spirits rose as if a weight had been lifted from them. "Then I intend to fly, my love," she said, kicking off her slippers. She ran so swiftly that a moment passed before she heard him running as swiftly behind her. She ran faster. The powdered dirt of the road was cool beneath her feet. She ran against the wind, parting it, feeling its strong flow past, her mind and body singing with the sensuous wonder of flight. When Blackie caught her they fell down together, laughing and out of breath, on the tough new grass by the night deserted road. They lay facing each other, and between their faces a wild red poppy with its petals closed for the night nodded in the delicate wind.

"It's asleep," Robin said, loving the little flower asserting its courage on the harsh high plains. "Let's move so we won't hurt it." She rolled away and Blackie lifted himself over the flower and rolled to her. She was waiting for his kiss.

"We'll be all dusty," he said, not caring.

"The earth is clean." Their kiss tasted of dust and the coarse fragrance of buffalo grass.

"I couldn't make love if we had hurt the flower," she whispered.

"Neither could I," he said to please her.

TWENTY

DES WAS STANDING just outside the back door when he saw Blackie coming across the vacant lot in the moonlight. He was pleased with the leisurely way Blackie walked, but he could sense that something was up, that the casual visitor had a reason for coming. But to anyone else, Des thought, he's got a poker face and a poker body; you can't tell a damn thing about him.

"Hello, kid," Des said with affection. "Sure a pretty night. Full moon last night. Did you see it?"

"Sure," Blackie said.

Des went in the house and Blackie followed him.

"What's up? You haven't steered me any live ones lately. Thought maybe the spring had got you along with the birds."

"Live ones are scarce in these times," Blackie said, trying to avoid lying to Des. He could hardly bear the thought of his deception, and yet he had not invented it; and it hurt him to think that Des would object to his love for Robin, and, worse, that Robin somehow shared this objection. He was so sure the time would come to reveal the secret, and they would all be better off, that his patience seemed to be wisdom.

"Speak up, Lord Byron!"

Blackie tried to conceal his fright.

"I've been reading like hell with my left eye, but no poetry, that's a little tough for me. Just saw a picture of Lord Byron in one of the books. He was a pretty good-looking fellow."

"He had a club foot," Blackie said.

"Well, I'll be damned."

"Tanny, you don't mean you can't *see* out of your right eye, do you?"

"Can't see much, everything's a blur. I've got to make some money."

"What do I have to do to get you to borrow the money from me?"

"No, I don't want to do that. First time I make a winning—say, by God, where did you get all that money? I thought you'd be broke by now."

Blackie smiled at his suspicion, relieved at last that this was the only real one Des had of him. "I've got a little income from my grandfather's place. Good thing *he* liked me. And I've been saving my winnings."

"Well, now, I never saw such a gambler," Des said, and his tone was a confusion of admiration and disappointment.

"Tanny, I've told you a hundred times you can have every cent I've got, but nobody else, and I get sore that you won't take any when you need it."

"I don't like to borrow. You stake me now and then, that's enough."

"Well, if I can get this fellow at my hotel in a game, I'm going to stake you very soon."

"Why didn't you say so?"

"I haven't got him yet and I may not. I don't want to get your hopes up high. He's an oil promoter, I think, and he's got cash on him, I saw that. I don't know how much, but he sure as hell doesn't want to play with me."

"Well, give him a steer."

"I don't know whether he's ready. I can't figure him out. He seems like a fellow just ready for picking, but he's wary. He's got some business in town another day or two, but he's restless as hell every night. He might be a gambler. It's a long shot but we need a game. You check in the Royal tonight. I've got it fixed. I don't think I can get him in there, so you meet us on the street around the Bella Brock in about an hour."

"I'll be there," Des said, and his face became lively and his good mood even better. "But we won't play tonight unless *he* wants to. I'll just tell him some oil stories. I've got those oil towns on my mind again, anyway."

"Good. I'll let you handle him."

"If we get up a game, and you think he's afraid of you, stay out, make an excuse."

"But Tanny, you need me, with that damned eye."

"Listen, I'm desperate. I'll *take* him with both eyes out."

"Okay, I'm gone."

"If it wasn't for that bastard moon I'd go with you."

Blackie started out.

"Hey!" Des called him back. "Spring's got me. You'd better go by the Royal and plant these cards." He searched his valise and selected a deck of blue Bicycle backs. "Here's a cooler; I'd better protect myself. Robin just marked it the other day, and before I put the cards in the case I had a hunch I ought to make up some cold hands for blackjack. I'm ready for anything now. If he wants to play poker, I'm ready for that too." He looked up at Blackie and smiled. "Put these in your pocket. I'll take a straight deck along, just in case."

As soon as Des was alone he reached into his pants pocket and drew out the contents—a pair of dice, matches, small change. After counting the money and replacing it, he sat down on the davenport and rolled the dice. Blackie reopened the door, knocking as he did so, and came in; he handed Des a fold of bills and left.

"Thanks." Des kept on rolling the dice. "Spring's got him too." He rolled the dice for a long time, thinking. Then he stood up, dropped them into his pocket, and buttoned his shirt collar, then unbuttoned it. I'd better dress up, he thought, and took his suit from under its cloth cover on the back of the door. Hell, this is my old suit; I took my best one to the cleaners. He hung it on the nail. The old gal's cleaned and pressed it and got it looking pretty good. He took a clean shirt from the drawer and tossed it on the bed. He had to go into the bedroom for his tie.

For a moment he listened to the quiet turning of pages; Stevie was in bed early, reading or studying. He went in. With her eyelids down, she looked sick, but he guessed she was all right. Her face was pale and set. She hadn't spoken to him for two days, since she had gone over and sat on the Garrisons' back porch just for meanness. His throat tightened and tears came into his eyes but he blinked them away as he lifted a tie from the mirror frame, hardly glancing at the selection.

"I'm going to town, pard. I might hustle a dice game."

Stevie said nothing.

"I'll be leaving for good one of these days," he said softly. "I won't bother you any more then."

Stevie's face drew taut in nervousness. He thought with painful pleasure that she must be trying to keep from crying. She made an effort to relax the quivering muscles into an unrevealing mask.

"I'll be going before long."

Stevie let the book fall, open, onto her breast. Her large eyes looked at him stilly; the reddened lids made them startlingly blue.

"Oh, no, you won't!" she said, at once fierce and helpless. "You won't go until you've destroyed us, all three! You destroyed Mama long ago." She began to cry.

"You're crazy," he said, not liking her weakness. "I never did any such thing."

"Oh, so innocent, you don't even know it!"

"You wouldn't catch Robin saying anything like that about me."

"Robin!" she said, and her face and voice were sour with scorn.

"Say, by God, don't you like anybody?"

"No!"

"If you say one more word, I'll knock your head off." He turned savagely and went into the kitchen, where he stood tense and white, looking around, craving an outlet for his fury. He raised one of the round stove lids and threw his tie onto the dead ashes.

"Goddamn!" he said, balked, and struck a match, lighting the tie. "Burn, you sonofabitch!" He slammed the lid over the fire. The unpleasant odor mounted into the clean spring air. He ran his hands over his face, feeling his whiskers. This was the first day in years that he hadn't shaved. He went to the sink and looked into the watery mirror. His reflection was strange. He raised his fist to smash it, and stopped. To break a mirror was seven years' bad luck. Only a superstition, he thought in disgust, but with both fists in his pockets he went out and sat on the cellar door. The moonlight lay on the ground in remote and untouchable clarity. The beauty of the night was agonizing, his loneliness bitter. The ivories were warm in his pocket. His fingers relaxed and gathered the dice tenderly into their embrace. He went in to dress.

TWENTY-ONE

DES RAN HIS HAND over the heavy table cover, smoothing it for the cards. Across from him the stranger's tall two hundred pounds caused the old hotel chair to creak. A pint of bonded bourbon and two glasses stood on the dresser. The bottle was full.

Randall's controlled face and cold gray eyes suggested no excess of passion, but Blackie, and afterward Des, detecting his restlessness, expertly noted it as having nothing to do with women or drink, both easily purchased through the hotel porters. The oil man wanted to gamble, but he was afraid. After Des and he had talked awhile he did not have to be persuaded. He wanted to play twenty-one, away from his own hotel; he'd play anything, he said, but he felt like a game of twenty-one.

Des was afraid of him; he might be another gambler mistaking him for a man of means. In the past Des had passed himself off as an oil man; it was the easiest thing in the world, and there was something about the two of them, their self-possession and quiet good clothes, that might belong to a gentleman gambler or a businessman of success. The clothes Des wore were older but the quality was there, and no flash.

If times were better, and he had his own money in his pocket, and Stevie hadn't talked to him the way she had, he'd trust himself to take on anybody; he felt like a good straight game, he felt like beating the hell out of a smart player. But he'd better play safe and pick up some grub money for the next few months.

Randall had him worried. Twenty-one was a sucker's game and maybe Randall thought he was a sucker. It was a fast, treacherous game, no leisurely pleasure, and you could strip a man down to his small change in short order. It was Des's room, Des's game; he had paid for the cards in front of Randall. Gambling ethics gave Des the deal. If, by any chance, Randall pretended not to know this and took over as dealer, Des would be pretty sure that Farquarson, who was missing his cut, had made arrangements with another gambler. He'd have to play through against himself, losing a little, acting like a close player.

Des set the deck before Randall, and when the stranger accepted his rightful role Des decided that his troubles had begun to make a fool of him.

Randall cut the cards and made his bet of twenty-five dollars. Des placed the top card face up on the bottom of the deck, and dealt.

Randall looked at his cards. "I stand."

A pair of nines, Des knew. The cold deck was stacked in hands. Des had an eight face up and a buried four. He glanced at the four and said, "I need another one." He drew a seven, and showed his hand. "Nineteen." He reached over and turned up Randall's cards. "Eighteen." Randall shoved the money across to him.

"How about fifty?" Randall said. "Can I bet fifty?"

"Sure, go ahead." Des dealt.

Randall placed the money on his cards, indicating that he would stand. He lost the fifty and seemed unperturbed. He put down a ten-dollar bill with an air of wisely testing his way. They did not speak except in the language of the game. After a few more hands Des knew by the way the other drew his cards that he was a smart player. A smart player, he thought, but he can't protect himself, poor devil.

Randall slid a finger across his upper lip, where perspiration clung. A summer wind came in around the edges of the drawn blind and puffed the dingy curtain. It waved lank and dusty and settled back in place. A streak of moonlight lay unnoticed on the rug.

When the cooler was dealt through, Des was over two hundred dollars in the clear after letting Randall win a few hands. He had a three-hundred dollar bankroll in his breast pocket for the night. Now, with the deck unprepared in winning hands, he was depending on his luck and on seeing the marks with one clear eye to win. He shuffled; Randall cut and bet twenty dollars. Des gave him two cards; reading fast, Des saw a six and a seven. Before Randall's call, Des's eye went swiftly to the top of the deck. There rested an eight, which would give Randall twenty-one.

"Hit me," he said.

Des dealt the second card and gave him a king. "That's ten," he said, facing the card up.

"I bust," Randall said. He was perspiring and uneasy at last.

By the end of the deal, he had won a few hands but he was still the loser. Des gathered up the cards and shuffled them idly. "Let's play some five-card stud," he said. "It might change your luck. By God, I hate to be the winner every time. It's no sport."

"Well, that's the way it goes some nights."

"I had a run of bad cards one night on twenty-one and lost damn near everything I had," Des said. "I hardly ever play it." He placed the deck neatly in its case, leaving the flap open, and watched Randall's face. Then he glanced at the whisky he had bought from Winston. "Let's have a drink."

Three hundred and eighty dollars had passed into Des's possession, and he had seen more in an inside coat pocket when the other reached in for new bets.

Randall was glad to quit the blackjack, but he was not through gambling and fell in with the suggestion of stud poker. He rose, took off his coat, stretched, and poured himself a short drink, offering Des one. Then he filled his empty glass with ice water and drank it down. Des took one drink and a swallow of water, hung his coat on the back of a chair, and gave Randall one of his cigars. The tension between them slackened.

Footsteps sounded along the alley. Des snapped the light off and went to the window. He listened until the men passed, their voices recognizable and harmless, then turned the light on. He couldn't figure Randall out. He was a wildcatter, no promoter, or so he said. If it turned out that he had anything to do with oil, Des could believe this. He was a singular man, something like himself, traveling alone. They sat down, lighted fresh cigars, and turned them slowly over their matches.

"How do you play the joker?" Des asked.

"Ace, straights, and flushes."

They settled into the game. With nearly four hundred of his own and a good player with him, Des was tempted to gamble on the square and make up for all the anxious nights he had sat in the Royal lobby or lain in bed tasting his life. When he thought of Blackie's three hundred in his pocket to fall back on, he decided. It was a hell of a way to live, anyhow, cheating a man out of his money, but he thought, Randall's money is probably no cleaner than mine.

"The law in this state is tough on any kind of gambling, I understand. No liquor, and a man can't even buy cigarettes!" Randall said. "Think we're safe?"

"Sure. We businessmen play all the time. The only trouble is, the law sees things just before elections they're blind to all year."

"True everywhere."

"The sheriff wouldn't bother us for having a little fun. A deputy might try to shake us down for a few dollars, but what the hell, we're safe."

They loosened their ties and opened their shirt collars, making themselves comfortable for the long hours ahead.

"Gambling ought to be legal all over," Des said, ruminating that if it were he would run a nice little place of his own, decent, no rough stuff, and one eye would be enough. He wouldn't have to cheat; the house percentage would put him on easy street. He would stay dressed up all the time and just walk around the tables and see that everything was on the level. He'd play when he wanted to, for the sport of it. "The government could put out an old-age pension with the tax. Some people are going to gamble no matter what they do to stop it."

"Good idea." Randall laughed. "But too many bluenoses around. Tax the vices as well as the virtues."

"It would keep the crooks out," Des said.

The wind that stirred the curtain was fresh and clean, blowing against the small island of smoke gathered above their heads. Hours passed. They lost to each other and won, playing almost equally; then Des felt his luck giving out in a long run of poor cards, and his eyes smarted painfully. He had a reckless urge to defy his luck, when, in the midst of his calculations, the memory of Stevie's eyes looking cold and straight into his own filled his mind. He remembered the money in Randall's pocket. I'll hit him, by God, I'll give him a good hand but I'll deal myself a better one. What the hell, I'm no rich stiff with new bills in the safe. I'm a gambler. He felt proud of his knowledge and the cleverness of his brain and hand. I hope to Christ I can see the marks for another hour or two.

Randall stood up. Disappointment leaped at Des' thoughts like a bandit from behind a wall. He rose, stretched, and sat down again. Randall took a drink and reached into his inside pocket for more money. They played long past the first light of morning. Randall emptied his billfold onto the table.

When his deal came, Des shuffled the cards, his weary, still-quick eye selecting the marks, his trained memory recording them, his supple fingers obeying. He gave Randall two eights and himself two jacks. Des bet.

"I call," Randall said easily.

191

The second round he dealt Randall a queen and himself an eight. Randall was high. He bet. Des called him. The third round Randall got a nine and Des a seven. Randall, still high, bet. The next deal, he gave Randall a nine and himself an eight. Randall had a pair of nines, a queen, and an eight in sight, and one eight in the hole. High, and coldly eager to win, he pushed his money forward.

That's the end of his money, Des thought, there's no use to raise him. "I tap you," he said, and turned up his buried jack.

Randall leaned back in his chair and squinted at Des. "Well, I'm out of cash so the game's over."

"I'll stake you if you'd like to play some more."

"No. I'm tired." Randall picked up a handful of cards and looked casually at their backs, laid them down, and stood up. Des walked over to the dresser, leaving his winnings on the table, took a drink, and handed the bottle and a glass to Randall. As Randall downed the drink, Des slid one card under the others, scooping them into a pile. He evened and fitted them into their case and dropped it into his coat pocket. Then he set the table back in place, talking with Randall about the last hands.

Day sounds were beginning in the old hotel. An ice truck clattered to a stop at the kitchen door and the alley came alive with deliveries and voices in the cheerful exchange of old jokes. Sun gently warmed the room.

The two men put on their coats. Des reached into his pocket and handed Randall an unmarked deck of cards.

"Yours," he said. "You might want to play a little solitaire."

"Thanks."

"For a while there," Des said, "I thought you had me."

"I was close." Randall yawned. "Let's kill the bottle."

"All right with me." Des had over nine hundred dollars of Randall's money, and he could tell by the look on his face that the other had stopped only because he had run out of cash. Often a man like Randall would cash a check the next day and come back for more.

They went down the long, dark hall. Night lights still burned in their tulip-shaped globes. Morning sparkled over the lobby. The shabby leather chairs gleamed like old dogs snoozing in the sun. Dust motes drifted in bright shafts that pierced the corner gloom. Bowman was shuffling about, his black face weary. He greeted them and continued his tasks.

The two men went into the coffee shop together and sat at the counter, where all was in order for the day. Coffee steamed, misting the window and filling the air with its fragrance. Their waitress, in a starched uniform, precise make-up, and netted hair, appeared irreverent in the natural morning light. When she greeted them they noticed their own disrepair of beards and reddened, smoke-burned eyes. They ate a heavy breakfast of ham and eggs, hot cakes, and coffee. After Des paid the check and the waitress was gone, he asked Randall if he needed any cash.

"Thanks," Randall said appreciatively. "I'll go back to my hotel and cash a check. I'll sleep awhile and be on my way."

They shook hands and parted. Des returned to the lobby and handed Bowman fifty dollars. The porter's eyes opened wide, and, as no one was there, he gave a long, low whistle through his old teeth.

"Keep that under your hat," Des said. "This is the first winning I've had in God knows when."

"I'm goin' right home," Bowman said. "This money goin' in the sock."

"What did Farquarson say last night?"

"He took the twenty all right, but, Tannehill, he sure gonna turn yu in the first time another gambler wants to set up here. He spoiled by that easy money yu give him, and he been missin' it. He thinks yu ain' gonna make no mo'."

"To hell with him," Des said. "I'd better stay away from here. If I have to play here, I'll pay him beforehand, like tonight, the bastard."

"Yessuh. He said yu down an' out, an' ah pert-near knocked him on his white ass, 'ceptin' ah too old for that stuff."

"That's right, Bowman. Now listen, if any chumps come around here looking for a game, stall 'em off and send for me. I'll play at the house and cut you in. We'll see who's down and out."

"Ah'm lookin' out fo' yu, Tannehill, we's stickin' together. This panic still swoopin' down on us wors'n nineteen-oh-seven. We bettah git all we can, and no foolin'. I listen to the talk and it ain' good."

"Don't worry, Bowman, money comes and money goes and gambling goes on forever."

"Yu flush now." Bowman laughed. "So'm I!" He spat through his teeth into a cuspidor ten feet away. "Hoo-eeee!"

"I'll be back in a little bit and go to bed. I'll see you tonight. That fellow may take a notion to play some more."

"Man, yu is got yo' spirits up!"

"Can't keep a good man down, Bowman!" Des went to the barber shop, where he dozed under a hot towel after the barber had put some soothing drops in his eyes.

The thickest bankroll he had carried in many months was in his pocket, where he could touch it every now and then and feel like a man again.

TWENTY-TWO

BACK AT THE HOTEL he slept until early afternoon, but his sleep was restless; he felt too happy to sleep, and after a few hours got up and sent the day porter out to Matt's to buy him a new set of underclothes, a shirt, and socks. He stretched out in a bath and thought over last night's plays. When the porter came back Des wanted his best suit from the cleaner's and the boy hurried away for it.

When he was dressed Des stood before the big hotel dresser, looking critically at his reflection in the blackish mirror. The clean suit, tailored smoothly over his wide shoulders, gave him a pleasant sensation of being the man he was in his own mind. He held the knot of his tie between thumb and finger and straightened it a fraction between the immaculate points of his white shirt collar. The old mirror cheated him. He brushed his hat and put it on before he began filing away in his pockets the scattered possessions — dice, a small knife, a gold watch without a chain, coins, the deck of marked cards, a letter from a gambler in Tucumcari. He admired himself again, removed his hat, and examined his haircut.

His old suit lay on the bed. He held it up to the light and saw how worn it was. When he was in it the suit looked young, but now it had a feeble form of its own, not his but that of an old man wanting to sit down. He stuffed it into the wastebasket along with his soiled shirt and underwear, topping them with his hat. I'll buy a new hat right now, he said to his image in the mirror; I want to see Matt anyway, tell him about my luck. Now, there's a good man, by God. He separated the bills for three months' rent and placed them in his breast pocket, and went out to Matt's.

Later he returned, wearing his new hat, to the lobby of the Royal and telephoned Blackie at the Bella Brock. "Meet me in front of Vinet's right away!"

By the time Des reached Vinet's at the far end of Main Street, Blackie, with a perplexed expression, was standing in front of the large store window. Des smiled, enjoying the mystery.

"I made nine hundred and six dollars!" he said at once in a low voice, though no one was passing by.

"Man alive!"

"I'll give you your three stake and the cut just as soon as we get away somewhere. That's the kind of hustling I like you to do!" Des was pleased with himself; he felt as if his whole body were smiling.

"I don't want half, this trip," Blackie said. "Just give me my three. This will put you on your feet. I've got a pretty good bankroll."

"No, I wouldn't do that, Blackie."

"After this, Tanny, fifty-fifty, but this time, do me a favor."

Des was reluctant, and unwilling to feel obligated. "A hundred. Take a hundred then. I'll be all right now. My luck has changed."

"Okay."

Des faced the window. "There they are!"

Blackie looked in at the pianos and phonographs, radios, furniture, and electric kitchen appliances. "If I ever settle down," he said, "I'll buy a piano. That's one thing I like to play."

"Next to cards," Des reminded him. "You've got your harmonica. That's good enough for a gambler."

"It's all right for carrying around."

"Let's go in," Des said, ignoring the wistful note in Blackie's voice.

Mr. Vinet, fat, blond, and easy-going, delighted with the sale of an electric iron or an overstuffed chair, walked to the front, where the two men waited.

"How do you do, sir," Des said with a businesslike air.

Mr. Vinet puffed and spoke and waited. He was also the undertaker and did not want to make a mistake with a customer.

"I want to buy a piano," Des said.

Mr. Vinet looked as if someone had just informed him that he was inheriting a fortune. "A piano," he said with dignity, straightening his shoulders, becoming taller. "Have you any make in mind?"

"Blackie, go play that one over there," Des said, pointing to a heavy red mahogany upright.

Blackie was as startled as the shopkeeper, but he obeyed. He played a soft, romantic tune, his mind filling with delicious memories of Robin, whom he had seen again last evening after Des had begun to gamble alone with the stranger.

"Play something lively," Des said.

"Would you like to try the others?" Mr. Vinet asked politely.

"I like that one."

"Each one has a different tone, but they are all good instruments."

Blackie played the other three pianos briefly, but Des was talking to Mr. Vinet about the price of the first one.

"Send it to my house this afternoon," Des said.

Mr. Vinet hesitated. Des insisted courteously but firmly that the piano be delivered at once. He counted out the whole sum in cash, and Mr. Vinet's eyes lingered on the money he was about to receive, and then on the thin fold of bills remaining.

"You love music?" he exclaimed.

"This is for my daughter," Des said. "A present."

"Well, well." Mr. Vinet smiled. "Most people make quite a process out of buying a piano and make payments for years. A present! This is a pleasure!" He pulled his ear as if to make sure he was awake. "The piano's tuned, but we'll send a man around tomorrow to tune it perfectly! Now, the name and address. What business are you in, sir?"

Des felt like saying something light-hearted and foolish; he sobered his face. "I work for Chance and Company."

Mr. Vinet nodded seriously.

"My name's Tannehill, Desmond Tannehill." His face changed to smiling. "Burkett Street, three-seventeen."

"Ah-h," Mr. Vinet said, "Tannehill, Tannehill. Ah!" He began to smile. "Ah-h!" He chuckled.

"Come on!" Des said to Blackie, and led him from the store and down a side street and over to Jail Park. They sat on a bench and watched for the Vinet truck. When at last it drove by, the two walked to the house and entered the back door. Belle and Stevie were in the living room, insisting to the men that they had brought the piano to the wrong address.

Des went in, his face alight with suppressed laughter. He put his arm around Stevie's shoulders. She jerked away. She wouldn't do that any more after she realized what he had done for her. He stood back, speaking to Belle. "It's a little surprise. It's for Stevie." He looked at Stevie. She was his little girl again. He thought she was about to dive at him in crazy delight the way she used to do. He waited.

"Well, I never! Oh, Des!" Belle was smiling and brushing her tears away. "It's just like you!" And we haven't got a penny in the house, she added to herself. She was seized by an awed realization that propelled her with haste into the kitchen, where she stood still and spoke toward the ceiling. "Thanks, God, for answering my prayer! I never dreamed

197

You'd do it this way! Thanks again! I've got to go back now." With the others again, she tried to conceal the radiance of her magic power in order not to deprive Des of his own glory. She gave him a quick kiss of appreciation. Then she saw that he was dressed freshly and not even in the suit he wore away last night. As she opened her mouth to ask a question she remembered the men waiting.

"Bring it in!" Des preened himself in their amazement. "This is the place!"

Blackie, who was forgotten in the commotion, wandered into the bedroom. He looked about with a stinging tenderness, wishing for something of Robin's to cast his love upon, a dress, perhaps, or a comb which, would touch her with his feelings.

The men pushed the piano into a space that had been cleared, and handed Des a receipt.

He gave them a five-dollar bill and said, "Here, have a drink on me."

Stevie's heart filled with contradictions. She was tensely happy at the sight of the piano, at the thought of Papa changed, but she could not speak; the gratitude she felt was painful. She could not claim the piano as her own. She looked at Des and he was looking at her with his merry eyes, and just for a moment she saw *him,* the Papa she had planned to live with all her life, the Papa she as a child had proudly announced that she would marry. Unexpected recognition cleared her mind. She too had changed, and, no matter what Papa did for her, even to keeping this old, old promise, she could never feel the same. *Papa* was lost and she was alone. The piano had come too late. She felt like an empty house and Papa was knocking at the door. She looked at him again. He was waiting.

"Well, Stevie, what do you think of it?" he asked with eagerness. "Too surprised to say a word? It's yours!"

"Thank you, Papa," she faltered, almost in tears. "I always wanted a piano."

"How about a kiss?"

She kissed him delicately on the cheek.

"No kick in that," he said, joking.

"Oh-h!" she said impatiently and hit him. He was pleased.

She left the room and came back at once with a dust cloth and drew it softly over the beautiful dark red wood. She lifted the cover and gazed with concealed rapture at the ivory keys.

"Now we'll have a tune," Des said. "Stevie, play for us!"

She glanced at Blackie, whose serenity eased her, and at her mother, gratified, then at Des, expectant, jubilant, commanding; and she could not remember the pieces learned on the Suttons' piano. She was terrified of playing before her father, and yet she knew that she must. They were standing and she wished they would sit, but there were only two chairs in the room. As if he had sensed her wish, Blackie brought a chair from the middle room and they all sat down.

"Something gay!" Des urged.

She sat down on the bench and tried to remember what she knew.

"Stevie's bashful before people," Des explained to Blackie.

Blackie said, "I can always play better when I'm alone."

Stevie played through a little minuet to accustom herself to the new piano and to establish a measure of calm; and because she knew her father was disappointed she rushed into the "Scarf Dance" by Chaminade.

"How pretty!" Belle exclaimed, ignoring her self-conscious fumbling.

"You'll have to do better than that, pard, or we'll ask for our money back. What's next? I like to hear the names."

"'Für Elise' by Beethoven," she whispered, her voice deserting her after the first word. She went through this more easily and grasped at the confidence dissipating in her father's eloquent silence.

She rested, pushing down a black key, which made a bleak sound.

"Well," Des said, "that last one was pretty fair. School will soon be out and you can practice." He waited. "Play some more, Steve. I haven't had enough yet."

Stevie's hands trembled. "This is 'Salut d'Amour' by Elgar."

"All foreign stuff," Des said.

Because the piano was her own, she wished hard to show herself worthy of the gift and its possession. Surely Papa would be impressed by this more difficult composition. Halfway through she groped uncertainly over the keys and almost failed.

"You're just doing wonders, honey, for the little time you've studied!" Belle said.

"No, I'm not."

"The piano's new and stiff," Belle murmured.

"Well, loosen it up, Paderewski! By God, I don't want to be ashamed of you."

Wounded, Stevie dared the hardest test yet. Staring at her arms, red-splotched with nervousness, she mumbled grimly, "'Barchetta' by Nevin." She began well, but, hearing Belle's relieved sigh, she was overcome with chagrin. Stumbling, she repeated the opening. The trying right-hand fingering caused her to break again, but she persisted, hearing the music as she played it when alone, or with Mrs. Sutton listening with genuine concern for her progress, and Mr. Sutton, in his wheel chair, intent, nodding his head in time and pleasure. They expected no more of her than she could give, and at times they spoke earnestly of her talent and her feeling for the music, especially of her touch.

When she finished and sat without turning, Blackie brought her a glass of water and said, "Play something you like best. That was a tough one, and you were darn good." She wanted to thank him but her throat was closed.

Though Des sat alerted for more, she was sure that after today he would not believe in her. Suddenly she felt that, with all grace lost, one venture more could hardly matter; she boldly played a strange and lovely piece that was her own. It was very brief, and at its end the back screen door slammed lightly, and Robin called through the house, "What's that? It's beautiful!" She came whirling and dancing through the middle room. "That makes me feel like a ballerina!" She kissed Des loudly on the cheek. "I heard all about the piano downtown!"

Then she saw Blackie. "Hello!" she said gaily, daring with her eyes to flirt with him and smiling at his discomfort. She kissed her mother, and sat down on the bench beside Stevie. "What was that piece? I like it!"

Stevie whispered in her ear, "It's mine. I heard it in my head. Sh-h-h!"

"She made it up!" Robin announced. "She's a composer! I knew it!"

"In about a hundred years," Stevie said. "And you didn't need to tell."

No one knew what to say. Stevie listened to the mingled polite and embarrassed words; then Des said, "It's all right! But it has no tune. You'll have to give it a tune."

"It has a rhythm of its own," Blackie said to Des, and received a swift, full glance from Robin that shook him.

Stevie wiped the perspiration from her palms onto her cotton dress, and Des, observing, said, "Rest awhile. Let Blackie play."

Blackie refused, though he did not wish to displease Des. Stevie urged him shyly and left the piano. Des sat down in the rocker and leaned back. "I like any kind of music."

"That's what you'll get," Blackie said.

"Doesn't know one note from another," Des said to Stevie, "but he can play anything he hears. Us gamblers used to listen to him when he was just a kid."

After a while, when Blackie stopped playing his blue jazz, Des, as if he could not hear music enough, pressed Stevie to play again. Belle patted her with an urging affection.

As Stevie began to play a simple piece to match her exhaustion, a quick tattoo sounded on the back door and Penny's voice called through the rooms for Belle.

Robin followed her mother into the kitchen to ask news of the sudden riches. Penny was looking through the screen door, excited and impatient. Belle invited her in.

"No," she said. "Come out here. I've got something to tell you!"

The two women stood close together and spoke in low voices.

"I heard all about the piano," Penny said. "Mrs. Kirk called me from Vinet's." As Belle started to reply, Penny waved her to silence and hurried on. "Mrs. Coleman down at the Emporium died last night!"

"Oh, poor woman," Belle said.

"Poor woman nothing! She's dead and out of her misery. Of course, it's too bad. But you're broke and having trouble."

"Well, just the same, I'm alive —"

"Oh, bosh! Belle Tannehill, you go down there the first thing in the morning and apply for that job. Now's your chance!"

"I've never clerked in a dry-goods store."

"Say you have. What the heck!"

"Lie? But Penny —"

"If you're thinking about your husband winning some money, how long will that last? Today, for instance! Besides, that isn't everything." Penny gave her friend a knowing prod with her elbow.

"Wouldn't it be kind of mean to ask for the job the very next day after the poor woman died?"

"Someone else will." Penny started across the yard. "I've got a pie in the oven." When she reached the alley she came rushing back. "If you get the job, will you join church?"

"All right!" Belle whispered. They hugged each other and Penny trotted away, singing, "La, la, la, la, la!" Belle lingered in the early evening, proudly seeing herself as a clerk in the Emporium, as a soloist in the choir, as a member of the community, known and respected. It was time to start supper and Stevie was still playing. She must be tired. Belle opened the screen door, and in the faint dusk of the kitchen she saw Blackie move away from Robin and slowly let go her hand. She was startled, and her anxious fears, which were never far away, leaped up to quicken her pulse. That young man was looking at her with his serious black eyes as if at any moment he would say something confiding. She hoped that he would not dare, because it was clear to her that he was in love, and she did not have the heart to hurt him. She glanced uncomfortably at Robin.

"I should have told you, Mama."

Belle felt helplessly that she should demonstrate her parental authority but decided in favor of speaking to Robin alone. Robin would somehow make her feel victorious, and go on about her life.

"Please don't worry about Robin, Mrs. Tannehill," Blackie said kindly.

The exhausted sounds from the piano ceased. Des came into the kitchen. "Come on, Blackie, let's go to town. We might find another chump."

Behind Des as he went out the door, Blackie looked back, and for just an instant, clearly, through the haze of emotion, Robin saw him again as a gambler.

Belle noted the shadow of pain on her face and said none of the planned words; instead she went to the cupboard and reached into the jar.

"A piano," she said dully. "But what about the rent and the groceries?"

While they prepared supper, Stevie slept. When the scant meal was finished, the girls washed the dishes, and Belle sat under the hanging electric bulb, reading the late *Monitor,* which Robin had brought home.

"Oh, good heavens!" she said in a stunned voice. "Did you lose your job, honey?"

Robin's tears fell into the warm suds.

"You did!"

"No, I didn't. But Mr. O'Brien is gone, and all the O'Briens are gone; the rest of us stay. I don't like Mr. Hauser!"

"It says here Mr. O'Brien sold the paper to him."

"He lost it. The bank sold it. He kept making trips and conferring at the bank and doing everything to save the paper, but we didn't know it was that serious. This morning he introduced Hauser to all of us. He wanted to do it as quietly as possible, but it was terrible anyway. One of the old printers cried, and we all wanted to."

"Well, maybe Mr. Hauser is all right, honey."

"Mr. O'Brien was never a boss, and Hauser was a boss the minute he came in the door. He looks like a bull."

"Maybe that's the reason poor Mr. O'Brien lost his paper. Hard people get along best in a hard world. But don't talk back to Mr. Hauser, honey. You need the job."

"I'll do my work, but it will just be a job from now on."

"If that's all the trouble you have in life, I'll be glad," Belle said.

"I should say so!" Stevie warned.

"Well, another country heard from!" Belle said, pleased. Then she told them about Mrs. Coleman dying and the possibility of her own job. After a silence she said tentatively, "And, I guess when I earn my own money, I'll join church."

"Have you religion?" Stevie asked, and she looked at her mother with curiosity to see if she had changed.

"Well, I like to have someplace to go with nice people, and I want to keep on singing in the choir. I'll even sing solos!"

They looked at their mother's face, all smiling except for the pale, sad eyes.

"Your voice is very pretty," Robin said.

"Do you kids mind if I join?"

"If you have religion," Stevie said severely.

"If you want to, Mama, do it. Promise you won't ask us to join, will you?" Robin asked with tenderness.

"Of course, honey."

TWENTY-THREE

DES HAD only one game in the weeks following the nine-hundred-dollar winning, and that in the kitchen. His eyes troubled him so much that he did not use marked cards but took off a small amount from each pot. There was nothing tangible left from the big winning but the piano and an order of cards. Robin marked the cards, which he sealed and placed in his valise. He was forced to keep the rent money back for his playing stake.

Since Belle had begun working at the Emporium he had not spoken to her, but tipped his hat satirically when he left in the evenings. It seemed to him that if she was going to earn money she might do so in a more private way than a job in a store where everybody in Apache would see her.

The summer days were long and he slept them away, lying even when awake on the couch in the middle room, thinking hard, bitter thoughts. Often at night he did not bother to meet Blackie because there was nothing to do, and Blackie disappeared, going about his life. Sleep was the only escape, and at times Des was surfeited with sleep.

The wind flapped the blind monotonously, letting in piercing blades of sun that stabbed his eyes. The heat stayed in the darkened room, making him perspire even though he lay naked and uncovered. He went to the kitchen and bathed his eyes with salted water, and looked into the mirror with perverse pleasure at his unshaven face. He drew on his underwear and went into the front room, where Stevie sat at the table, which was littered with papers and books.

"What the hell are you doing?"

"None of your business."

"Say, now, I'll tan your hide," he said, joking.

"You can't stay off the bed long enough."

"By God, there's nothing else to do."

She was silent, working.

"What's that you're doing?"

"If you must know, I'm studying! Someday I'm going to take exams for a civil-service job and get out of this sickening house."

"What are you going to work at? You won't even talk to people. Why, you can't even play the piano."

"I can too!" Stevie leaned forward, hiding her face, crying. "I'm just learning. How can I play everything you want to hear?"

"We'll sell it."

"Sell it, then!" she flared, but she wanted it desperately.

"You can have it," he said with sudden self-pity. "I bought it for you."

When she heard the springs of the davenport creak, she returned to her work. A girl she knew at school was coming in the evening to study with her; she hoped her father would go downtown. Presently he began to snore, and even that was better than the knowledge that he was lying awake in the other room, occasionally swearing in a low voice at his luck, and mumbling obscenities at the absent Belle. She got up and dusted the piano slowly and affectionately.

Late in the afternoon Chris stopped by on his way home from work. He smiled at her through the rusty screen. "I came by to see your piano, Stevie."

She asked him in, and they stood together in the center of the room, gazing with rapt appreciation at the piano. Chris's sincere delight in her possession returned her own to her. "It's a beauty! I'd like to hear you play."

She nodded toward the sleeping Des. "I'm not so accomplished."

"You will be."

"Robin said you're going to the university. Is that true?" she asked in secret, jealous wonder.

"True if I get a job stoking a furnace. But not this fall. I can't make it. Maybe next."

His courage impressed her and for a moment drew her out of her self-absorption. "I'm going too, sometime, but I don't think I'm well enough to work and study at the same time. I want to study, Chris, just study. Learning appeals to me. I don't want to work."

"Aren't you well?" Chris asked. "What's wrong, Stevie?"

"I don't know. I feel weak. I just go through the motions; everything seems unreal to me, even the piano. I have such ambitions, but making a living terrifies me!"

"I wouldn't let it do that, Stevie, we all have to earn our living."

"I think sometimes that I don't belong in this world, but here I am, and —" She hesitated and withdrew in a deprecating laugh. "I guess you came by just in time!"

"Don't say that, girl. Maybe —" He too hesitated. "Maybe you're not getting enough to eat, and it makes you —"

"Maybe, but that's not it, Chris."

"What is it, sis? Tell me."

"I don't know. I just dreamed of going to school for years and years and then maybe teaching music in a college. College seems so safe and snug. Papa was going to help me." She ran one hand along the gleaming red mahogany. "I might get a county job when I get out of high school. I'm studying ahead."

"Good! You don't have to keep that job forever."

The exclamation penetrated Des's slumber; he awoke and sat up. Chris spoke and Des replied sleepily. Chris commented on the beauty of the piano. Des nodded and lay down, pretending sleep.

"Come over any time, Stevie," Chris said as he went out.

The back screen slammed and Belle came through the rooms. She kissed Stevie before she changed into her house dress and moccasins. "My feet ache already something fierce, but I'll get used to it, they say." She went slupping back to the kitchen and quickly prepared the scanty meal. The four of them ate without speaking. Robin tried a casual remark, but the three were wound tight in their separate grievances.

As they were clearing the table the strident bell jangled into their silence. Des went to the door. They heard him speaking sociably to a man. He came back into the kitchen. "It's A1 Mabie."

"Who?" Belle asked dully, hoping against a guest, wanting only to go to bed and rest.

"A1 Mabie. You remember him at Dodge City, a gambler."

"I guess so."

Des lowered his voice. "He's got his whore with him out in the car. She works for him. He's afraid to bring her in."

Stevie and Robin looked at their father with large eyes.

"Well, what next?" Belle asked, but her desperate question addressed the powers of the universe.

"Get three glasses and come on in. Bring some water. I'll get the whisky."

"I just want to go to bed. Besides, there's only a little bit in the bottle."

"Enough for hospitality. Let the kids bring the things. Go out and ask her in."

Belle halted stubbornly in the middle of the kitchen, uncertainty and fear on her face. Stevie and Robin looked at him angrily.

"Might as well have a whore, the house is full of niggers." He raised his voice. "Al, go bring her in. I'm getting some drinks."

"Sh-h-h," Belle said. "The neighbors will hear you."

"Go on in there. You're the lady of the house, aren't you?" Des asked with mock respect.

A moment of terror seized Belle for the blow that might come later if she did not obey. She looked appealingly at the girls, wanting them to understand. They stared back at her without a sign. She placed three jelly glasses and a pitcher of water on a tray and went slowly into the living room.

The gambler, a tall, finely dressed man, might well be in some respectable business, Belle thought with slight relief. She set the tray on the table. Mabie came forward and shook her hand, saying with deft apology, "Mrs. Tannehill, this is Wanda. When I saw we would be driving through Apache I told Wanda I'd just have to stop for a visit with Des."

Wanda nodded. Belle had lately seen no one so richly turned out. She longed to examine Wanda's clothes, the porcelain quality of her make-up, and the mascara that multiplied her eyelashes. I wouldn't *know*, Belle thought, enjoying the delicate perfume that filled the air. Wanda pulled the silver-fox fur from her shoulders and tossed it on top of the piano. "This rig is killing me in all this heat," she said. Belle thought, I don't know what in the world to say to a prostitute, the poor girl, but she looks a lot better off than I am.

The doorbell rang, and Stevie ran from the kitchen to the porch. "Can we study at your house, Floss? Unexpected company."

"Sure." The girl looked curiously through the screen and followed Stevie inside when she came back for her papers. Everyone said hello. When the two girls were on the walk, Floss said, "Gee, are they rich?"

"I don't know." They stopped to look at the long black automobile at the curb. "They're taking a trip."

"Golly, did you smell the elegant perfume?"

"French, I presume," Stevie said. They giggled.

"Hey! I didn't even look at the piano! Your dad must be *some* father!"

"He is." They began to speak of other things, taking their time about reaching Floss's home.

Mabie insisted that Belle take the rocker, for which she was grateful, and she sat listening drowsily. Mabie was telling Des of the towns they had been in, and the two men spoke at length of "the trouble with gambling." The young woman spoke to Belle in a desultory way about the fashions, the weather, and men. Once she said, "Men don't know nothing about women," and Belle looked at her with a feeling of relatedness.

Des called for Robin. She came from the kitchen. "Come in here, Robin, and give us a song and a dance. Entertain us a little." He turned to the visitors. "She can do anything. My other daughter plays the piano; she can play to beat the band. I just got her that piano, shot my wad." He motioned to Robin. "Sing the 'Alcoholic Blues.'"

"I can't remember it."

"Why, you sang that when you were ten years old."

"I'm eighteen now."

"Well, sing some real blues. Do a little dancing. By God, let's have some life!"

"Anybody play the piano?" Wanda asked, shedding her boredom.

No one played.

Des looked so changed, so merry that Robin could not disappoint him; besides she liked to sing and dance. "I'll sing one or two songs, but I ought to have some music to dance."

"By God, we ought to have Blackie here to play."

She decided to sing one song for her mother and one for her father. She sang the first one in a slow, low voice, and they were all silent, listening.

> When a woman blue, when a woman blue,
> She hang her little head and cry.
> When a woman blue, when a woman blue,
> She hang her little head and cry.
> But when a man get blue
> He grab a railroad train and ride.

"Ain't it the truth!" Wanda exploded. "The bastards."

"Wanda!" Mabie cautioned.

Robin finished the song.

Mabie said, "Sing another one with me."

I'm gonna lay my head down on that railroad line
So that the Santa Fe will pacify my mind.

They clapped their hands.

"Mama taught me this one," Robin said, smiling at Belle.

The turbaned Turk, who scorns the world,
May strut about with his whiskers curled,
Keep a hundred wives under lock and key,
For nobody else but himself to see;
Yet long may he pray with his A1 Koran
Before he can love like an Irishman!

The gay monsieur, a slave no more,
The solemn don, the soft signor,
The Dutch mynheer, so full of pride,
The Russian, Prussian, Swede beside—
They all may do whatever they can,
But they'll never love like an Irishman!

Des laughed and Mabie slapped him on the back. Robin sang the last verse and as they applauded she left the room.

"Hey, come back here!" Des shouted.

"Entertain yourselves," she called back, laughing. "I'm going to wash the dishes."

The conversation became livelier and Wanda now took part. As Robin finished the dishes she heard Des say, "Look at Belle, she's asleep!"

"Let her alone," Mabie said. "She's tired."

Robin sat down to read but the talk and loud laughter came through the closed middle door. She went outside and threw pebbles at the Garrisons' kitchen wall until Chris came into the yard.

"I was about to come over," Chris said.

"You have to have a written invitation. We're entertaining."

"Who? I saw the car!"

She told him.

He laughed. "Isn't that sort of unusual?"

"Everything's unusual at home lately. I'm ready to leave. Frankly, I'm overdue."

"Don't you hate to leave your family?"

"I'm sorry to leave what we used to be—together. Now, we're all separate; we're all unrelated and unknown to each other. I suppose that's nothing new."

"Are you serious about leaving, Rob?"

"Yes, I am. Mama's working and likes it. Papa'll win money again; we've been more broke than this. Then he can send Stevie to college and she can get to work. I'll be *free*. Isn't that wonderful? All I need is train fare."

"More than that."

"A few dollars. I'll be all right, I'll get a job. I walked all over town today, working in that hot wind, and then I performed, and now I'm tired. I wish we had a fence to lean on."

"A sort of color line?"

They laughed and Robin struck Chris on the arm. "How did you guess?"

"You know what I wanted?" Chris asked. "I saw you through the window reading. Have you finished with *The Brothers Karamazov?*"

"Just."

"I'll trade you a surprise."

"Oh, what? Some more O'Neill?"

"Not yet. Joyce's *Dubliners!*"

"Really? Hooray!"

"Oh, there you are." Wanda's voice came from the kitchen doorway. "Come here, kid."

"I'll get the Joyce," Chris said. "Be right out. Bring me *Karamazov.*"

When Robin went in, Wanda was looking about the kitchen with distaste.

"Say, kid, where's the bathroom?"

Robin blushed. "You'll have to go outside, straight back."

"Any spiders?"

"Take some matches."

"Finish up your business before I go out there," Wanda said.

Robin ran out and gave the book to Chris and said, "Miss Thompson is very modest. We'll have to go in."

"Okay."

Wanda gave her a very searching look and said, "Who's your friend? I couldn't see him very well out there in the dark."

"Who's yours? I couldn't see him in the light."

"Oh, fresh! You could do worse, tootsy."

She watched the young woman walk indolently along in the dusk on her high heels; then Robin sat down at the table and opened *Dubliners*. When she heard Wanda's returning footsteps, she folded her arms over the book.

The prostitute walked past Robin's chair and turned to look at her. "What you moonin' about? In love?"

"No."

The small black hat over her blond hair, the black satin dress, the sheer silk stockings were all expensive and new. She doesn't look "bad," Robin thought, but somehow I'd know.

"Take it from me and don't ever fall for no guy," Wanda said seriously. "They're all right till they get you dependin' on 'em."

"I'm not going to depend." Robin looked at her hard, smooth face, closed against everyone and curiously empty; the flawless make-up gave it a doll-like, inanimate appearance. The blue eyes were glassy-brilliant, and they seemed to defy a penetrating glance from another.

"You're a pretty kid," Wanda went on confidentially, "and with your old man a gambler, it ain't gonna be easy." She stepped closer and Robin smelled the perfume, faint, expensive. Wanda brushed an imaginary speck from her dress and waited. Her hands were soft and beautiful, with long claw nails polished red. "Know what I mean?"

"I know what you mean," Robin said, touched by the implied advice.

"Your dad thinks you're a kid but you ain't no kid."

Robin smiled at Wanda.

Wanda did not return the smile but she went on earnestly. "I want to tell you something, honey, and don't never forget it. *Don't give it away.* Get something for yourself. Know what I mean?"

Robin stared at her.

Wanda smiled. "You're kinda sore, but that's because you're fulla crap. Romance and all that. Just remember what I told you. It's easier than cookin' and scrubbin' and gettin' old and ugly fast, and they don't treat you no better for it, men don't."

"One sounds as bad as the other. I just want to be independent," Robin said smugly.

Wanda laughed out loud and waved her lazy hand. "Honey, there's no such thing as independence. They got you comin' and goin' from the time you're born till you die."

"Who's they?"

"The powers that be. How the hell do I know who they are? But you can bet your sweet life they're male."

A sly stab of panic waylaid Robin's judgment. Was Wanda right? She wished intensely to know what had happened to Wanda, but she was not bold enough to ask; and when her eyes warmly sought Wanda's she felt her gaze sliding over the surface of the prostitute's face as if Wanda had anticipated her concerned curiosity.

"I like men," Robin said. "I don't hate them."

"I don't hate 'em." Wanda was quickly defensive, and then flippant. "I love 'em, the brutes." She paused. "I like strange men, men I never seen before and I'll never see again." She gave Robin a sober wink as if to lighten the confidence. "Well, don't sell yourself out cheap, kid." She turned to go.

"I'm not for sale at all!"

Wanda stopped. "I can't get mad at a kid like you. Maybe you *can* take care of yourself." There was an edge of sarcasm on her generous tone.

"I intend to try first!"

"Calm down. Your old man'll be out here and sock us both."

"Not me."

"Now, a good beatin' never hurt no woman, makes things kinda exciting. You even get a kick outa lookin' at the bruises, and when they're all faded off, it's time for another one."

"You make me sick!" Robin said. Her voice was low and her steady eyes looked hotly into the woman's face, which now wore a conceited, pleasureable sneer.

"Somebody will break you to ride, someday, honey, and—"

"Nobody will break me for anything!"

"And you'll eat outa his hand," Wanda said with satisfaction.

"Leave me alone!" Robin said in cold anger, and she stood up.

Wanda backed off and turned at the door, hurrying to join the men. Her perfume lingered in the dingy room.

Robin went outside. A lone tea towel flapped on the clothesline. She sat down on the cellar door in the pale dark of the summer evening, trying to listen to the quiet, friendly sounds of the town. She tried to think of Apache as all the people she knew, but she could not. That field of light in the night sky over Main Street was *downtown* and *Blackie*. She whispered his name with such love that she believed he would hear her in his mind and come to take her away. The three voices in the house dropped intimately. There was a roar of laughter. She held her hands over her ears and closed her eyes; hot tears ran down her cheeks. She despised the thought of Blackie but she could not despise him. She got up and looked through the bedroom window and saw her mother in the rocking chair with her face turned away from the others, sleeping soundly.

Robin walked to the alley, down its dim-lighted loneliness to Jail Park and on to Main Street. She went to Borg's Drugstore, where in the evenings friends from school and work were sure to be gathered, sitting in the booths, dancing to the phonograph in the pharmacy corner. Drake would probably be there, drinking coffee; maybe they could have a spirited, agreeing, disagreeing talk, and she'd feel better.

TWENTY-FOUR

THE HOUSE was hot and silent. Belle and Robin were at work. Des was asleep. Stevie got out of bed, tiptoed to the closet, and took from the shelf a small bank which she kept hidden in a far corner. She held the bank very steady, so that the coins would not move and make a sound, then returned to bed, opened the bank under the quilt, and counted her secret savings. No one knew how much she had; she would not tell and she would not spend any more. No matter what happened, no one but she would know of this money; it was for the future. She missed the money from Papa, but Robin and Mama gave her money to spend, and in the fall she would sell her school books. If the thought of a job presented itself, she fearfully pushed it away. She might take the county examination with Floss, but that too was in the future. She replaced the bank and carried her clothes through the dark middle room, into the kitchen. There she washed and dressed and sat at the kitchen table, eating a bowl of cornflakes and milk.

She felt lost without school; since vacation had begun, she rose late, did part of the housework, read, and seldom went out. After Al Mabie's visit she had not gone out at all, imagining Apache's knowledge and opinion of the Tannehills' entertaining a prostitute. Robin had tried to reassure her, but she felt severe in her judgment of Robin's view, and severe in her judgment of almost everyone she knew except the Suttons. She feared their judgment of her because she had not gone for a lesson; with her own piano for practice, the Suttons would not understand why she intended to give up her music. She could neither tell them nor explain it; there was no tangible reason. Robin had promised to send her to college; she would tell the Suttons that next fall she was going away. But what of the year of high school that remained? This rose insurmountable before her; she slowly ate the cornflakes and looked out the window into the Garrisons' back yard and tried hard not to think of herself. When she did, her throat closed and she could not swallow.

She washed the bowl, slid the milk bottle down beside the dwindling cake of ice, and looked into the box for something more to eat. There was a jar of piccalilli brought over by Penny; Stevie spread this on a piece of bread and walked about the kitchen, eating. Once she started to hum a bar of music, seeing the notes in her mind. She stopped abruptly. Then she fastened the ice card in the screen door so that the driver could see it as he passed through the alley. Belle had left the fifteen cents on the icebox and written a note that ended, "I hope my baby is well today." The handwriting was round and clear and unpretentious. Mama was very proud of her job at the Emporium. Was she ever troubled with big and painful dreams?

The springs of the davenport squeaked and strained and Stevie knew that her father had sat up quickly. It was strange for him to be getting up in the morning after he had been out late. She heard him drawing on his trousers. He came in, combing his hair back with his fingers. He looked at her and past, without speaking. She stood in the doorway, her features tense. His eyes were bloodshot and his cheeks dark with beard. He did not go at once to the sink, as was his habit, to splash water on his face and blow in pleasure. Instead he walked restlessly across the small floor and back again. She watched him cautiously. There was something desperate in his movements. Briefly, intolerantly, she recognized the misery in his face, and turned away, thinking of her own.

He mixed a cupful of water and salt and dashed it brutally into his eyes. Then he looked at himself in the mirror, rubbed his whiskers, and said, "I don't think I'll ever shave again. What the hell's the use?"

Stevie thought bitterly that she hated the way he looked—handsome even with whiskers.

Unexpectedly Des sat down at the table with his back to her. "This is rent day," he said fiercely. "I've only got five dollars. Go to the store and tell that bitch I want the other ten."

"I'll go," Stevie said in a cold voice. "I'll tell her just what you said."

She went out the front door and was on the walk before she noticed the nervous weakness of her legs. No one was in sight until she came to the park. Two old women were sunning themselves on a bench and a few people were on the courthouse paths. Her scalp was tight like a cap. For a moment the scene shimmered before her. She took a deep breath and turned, avoiding the park. Controlling herself with difficulty but wearing the aloof, shy face that others sometimes mistook for haughtiness, she went along Main Street safely to the Emporium. There she looked for her mother and saw that she was busy with two customers. The store was quiet with low voices and the whir of electric fans. Women lingered at the tables, touching the silk yardage, leafing through pattern books. The sight of Belle somewhat restored her, but

Stevie could not resist the ironic thought that she too was a stranger. Grasping her false calm as if it might fail her at any moment, she went toward Belle with a bland air, savoring her plan. If anyone should startle her with a greeting, the brittle façade would break like glass and her frantic vulnerability would be exposed like a naked dummy in a window of the Emporium.

She hesitated at a safe distance, observing her mother's friendliness with the two women. Belle would be sure to say proudly, "This is my girl!"

Belle saw her with surprise. Stevie frowned and her mother's expression at once became apprehensive. She smilingly listened to the customers and glanced at Stevie whenever they turned away. Then she pulled several heavy bolts of silk from the shelves, laid them before the two women, excused herself, and came along the counter to where Stevie stood, pale and immovable.

"Is anything wrong?" Belle whispered.

Stevie could not speak. Belle was alarmed.

"Papa said to tell that bitch"—she swallowed and rushed on— "that he wants ten more dollars for the rent." She spoke in a low voice, watching her mother's face for a sign of revolt.

A momentary look of hurt faded into resignation. "I just got my pay and that leaves only two-fifty. You'll have to wait, honey, till I can get my purse." She returned to the women. They could not decide. Belle came back.

"You've got to leave Papa and get a divorce!"

"The rent still has to be paid, honey." Belle was uneasy about her customers and hardly realized what Stevie had commanded her to do. Her pleasant face suddenly changed with horror. "Oh, honey, I—"

"Mama! You have to!"

"There was never a divorce in our family—"

"I don't care!" Stevie said.

"Maybe I ought to—oh, I don't know!" She watched the women debating about the silk.

"Well! Will you?"

"I haven't got time with this job."

"You could go to court on your lunch hour. The judge would let you."

"Oh, Mrs. Tannehill—" one of the women called, laughing, "we've finally decided."

Belle measured the cloth, matched the thread, wrapped the package, and talked with the two, smiling prettily.

"She's the *sweetest* thing," said one of the women as they left. Belle took her purse from under the counter, brought out two five-dollar bills, and handed them to Stevie.

"If you don't, I'll leave and never tell you or Papa where I am."

Stevie felt the perspiration running down from her armpits.

"How could you leave, honey? There isn't a place to go without money. If you'll just wait a little—"

"I'll kill myself!"

Belle looked about the store. Dread gave way to panic and she said in a low, cautious voice, "Oh, I couldn't stand that! You kids are all I've got!"

"You've got Papa."

Belle looked at her forlornly. Tears shone in her troubled eyes.

"Will you?" Stevie persisted coldly.

"I'm afraid!" A tear ran down her cheek and she brushed it away and composed her face.

"Maybe when I'm dead, you'll—"

"All right, then," Belle said slowly, as if she were half asleep, all her senses stunned with the shock of decision. She noticed vaguely that Stevie's eyelids quivered and that red splotches had appeared on her face and neck.

Stevie turned and went feebly out of the Emporium.

Des was sitting on the davenport, his head lowered, his hands loose between his knees. He was whistling the old waltz. When Belle came in the front door, he looked at her without interest, bent his head again, and went on with the song.

He heard her sigh heavily as she was changing her clothes before going into the kitchen. She built the fire with too much paper and kindling, as usual, so that the flame roared up the stovepipe. He wanted to tell her to turn the damper, but as he was about to call out impatiently she adjusted the draft. He listened to her washing potatoes, dropping them into a pan of water. The odor of onion roused his appetite.

She came back into the middle room. He glanced up briefly. She appeared to be holding every muscle tight as if it would fly loose-ended from her face.

He looked down. In front of him her feet were stern on the floor as he had never seen them. Her pretty legs still excited him. The whistling kept her from touching him; that was what he wanted. If her feet moved one inch, he would stand up and hit her. They stood still. He would not look up. The song ended and he started it again.

"After supper tonight," Belle said evenly, "you go your own way. I'm going mine."

The finality in her voice slowly penetrated his thoughts. The song trailed on a little while in pride; he forgot it as astonishment seeped into his senses. A small chill, as small as a gnat, bit at every pore. Then a hot rush of blood burned his face and neck and seemed to plunge against the walls of his body as if it had escaped his veins. He heard the words again in his mind and waited for her to repeat them. They tapped across his memory like a shocking news headline, the humiliating words that would never be erased.

Her feet did not move but he watched the muscles of her legs relax. She did not speak again. He listened for the words in his mind. They were there like separate stones washed by the hot blood crashing against his temples.

He did not reply. There was nothing to say to this woman whom he had loved and hated and despised. A part of him wanted her still. What for?

Those stubborn feet were waiting.

"All right," he said.

"I'll get supper and then I'll get your clothes ready."

He thought her voice sounded cruel. He felt hurt and defensive. "I'd like to stay for the rodeo. It starts tomorrow. I'm broke. I've got to make some money to leave on."

He saw Stevie's slow-moving feet go toward the kitchen.

Belle waited. "All right." The hatred mounted in her voice.

Des was astounded. He felt quite alone now. Stevie had heard it all and she too wanted to be rid of him. "I'll have to gamble in the house."

Belle's feet moved tiredly. The right heel of her worn, everyday shoes was turned in, twisting her small foot. She sighed. "Just till you get money to leave. No more."

"No more," he said, merely to assert his being. He found the song again and whistled it, low and bleak, to shut out the small familiar sounds in the kitchen.

He ought to be angry, to declare himself, to tell them how many times he had wanted to leave. He could have had a free and easy life if he hadn't got caught in marriage and a family. It would do them good to hear his side. But he didn't feel free; he felt lonesome.

Something was breaking up in him, exposing all the unidentified longings, the unadmitted hope, the questions never answered. It seemed to him suddenly that he had traveled down a false alley. No, this was a lie, a lie that sorrow was trying to force upon him. He had been right. Maybe he *could* have been more, but, what the hell, he had had a lot of experiences, he had been generous with strangers and friends, he had made people laugh and have a good time when he was around.

He got up, took his hat from the door, and went through the kitchen.

"Supper's almost ready," Belle said.

"I don't want anything to eat. I'm going to town." When he opened the door the melancholy music of a calliope floated in on the wind. They looked at each other for a moment, and then away.

He walked fast across the back yard and turned into the alley. The alley was narrow, with sheds on either side. A dim street lamp glowed at the far end. In the black shadow cast by a tall shed, he stopped. He held his hands over the convulsive muscles of his face and wept.

The carnival was a quarter of a mile outside town. Its cluster of lights made an island in the dark sky; the plaintive mechanical music worked at being gay. Des walked along the dirt road in the black night, drawn to this ephemera of change. Cars passed, he stepped aside, the dust showered back upon him, he walked on. A car filled with shouting boys stopped and they offered him a ride but he waved them ahead and the dark enclosed him again. When he reached the midway he stopped on the edge of the night and watched the crowds, but this isolated observing intensified his mood; he plunged into the light, walking fast, seeing nothing, and then he slowed and loitered with the others. Barkers and come-on girls wheedled from every booth, their cynical faces revealing their contempt for the natives of country and towns. They think these people are suckers, Des thought, resenting their shoddy superiority, and wishing at the same time that he could be singled out and known for what he was, a worldly man who was onto their tricks.

The dirt under his feet was ankle deep, powdered fine and soft from trampling. He glanced down when he stood in the clear and saw that the cuffs of his pants were dusty. He was wearing his best suit.

When he came to the merry-go-round he thought of Belle; she leaped into his thoughts the way a child jumps suddenly from a hiding place where she has been waiting. Belle liked to ride the colored horses with their glass-jeweled harness; she had used the children as an excuse for years, and when they were old enough to sit on the horses alone she sat in a spangled seat and dreamed, round and round in this world of worn magic and old glitter.

Carnivals were the special occasions on which he brought his family out. This was the first time he had tramped around the midway alone like this, and the calliope music, which in other years had made him feel gay, now made him feel lonely and cast aside. He turned away from the merry-go-round and pressed his way through the crowd to the other side of the midway, where he lingered before a ball-throwing stand. He bought three balls, and then another three, and threw them with all his strength at the target. He won a Kewpie doll and a tiny beer mug. He waited, and when a woman went by with four children, all poorly dressed, he gave them the gifts, and, hearing their delighted thank-yous, he gave the children each a dime. They glanced at their mother for permission before holding forth their hands, and when she nodded they closed their fists on the money and ran off like killdeers, the mother following tiredly. Des tipped his hat and walked on.

As he watched the high seats of the Ferris wheel and listened to the screams and giggles of the girls, he wondered what was the matter with Stevie. She wouldn't even ride on a Ferris wheel. When she came back from seeing Belle at the store, she had said she was going to bed for a year, she had made up her mind. She had changed the sheets and placed a chair by the bed; she stacked books on the chair and washed a milk bottle for water and found a glass to fit over its top. She did not intend to get up tomorrow, which was incredible. By God, he had never been sick a day in his life, he was as healthy as a bear. He ought to make her get out of bed before he went away. A group of laughing girls pushed him. Maybe this old world was too much for Stevie; he used to warn her that she'd never make it, that it was too tough.

He felt in his pocket, counting the small change, all that he had, and went into a tent to look at The Woman Without Any Bones. Only a few people stood around the hard, high bed where she lay. She was telling about herself, boasting that she had no bones at all, was born like that, and had never stood on her feet. She had a special bed, she told them in a weak, pleased tone; otherwise she would lose her shape. When she said this, she smiled with innocent cunning at Des and he gave her back his most charming smile and replied in a manner of decent flirtation, "You wouldn't want to do *that!*" The others laughed in a preoccupied way and continued to stare at her. We ought to make the poor woman feel good, he said to himself, but she appeared to have accepted her state and to be happy that she was different, and, as she repeated, "of use to science" by exhibiting herself.

"Not even one bone in my body," she said with pride. "Just think of it, folks!"

He wanted to say, "That's pretty tough," but caught himself and said, "I don't suppose there's another woman like you anyplace in the world."

She was modest for a moment, accepting this supreme flattery; then she said to the others, "No, I'm unique."

Des wanted to ask her how many years she had been in bed, but she might not wish to reveal her age.

"Now," she said with patient finality, "would you all like to feel me? You'll see that I am telling the truth."

The onlookers poked her gingerly. Des stood aside. "I believe you," he said.

"Oh!" she cried in disappointment. "When you tell your friends, they won't believe *you!* More than ten thousand persons have touched me. I like to keep count. It gives me something to think about."

"In that case—" he said, and transferred his hat from his right to left hand. He saw by the touching pleasure in her face that she had noticed this courtesy of removing his hat for her. He touched her pulpy arm. "You're a very interesting woman," he said politely.

"Thank you, sir, thank you, Mr.—?"

"Tannehill."

"I never know anyone's name," she said wistfully. "But that's show business."

There was a brief silence of respect for the transience and enchantment of the entertainment world.

The barker outside the tent was enticing another group of curious customers inside.

"Good-by, Mister Tannehill," she said in triumph.

"Good-by, Miss." He kept his hat off until he was outside.

Des had a powerful, prescient feeling that his luck was going to change.

He tried to look ahead, to plan his days; he would go to the rodeo every afternoon—he could borrow the money from Blackie— and to the carnival every night, in the hope that someone would want to carry the spirit over into a late game of cards or dice. He hated to go home.

This thought sent him into the midway again. He passed a roulette wheel where the prize was a live bird, and stopped to watch an elderly monkey forced through his tricks. Des bent to give him a penny, and when the old fellow reached out his hand he gave Des a searching look that was like an exchange of sorrow. By God, Des said to himself, walking away fast toward a booth where people were laughing, I've got to pull out of this. At that moment he saw Robin with her friend Iona. He admired the tall, handsome girl, much like her father, who observed the social mores of Apache and yet went her honest ways. One of them was to like Robin. And Robin liked her. Iona wasn't afraid to be seen with the daughter of a gambler, by God. Des watched the two girls talking together and hardly noticing the carnival booths. It appeared to him to be an enjoyable conversation and he felt relieved. After he had turned to walk in the opposite direction, he could not resist glancing back, and his eyes met Robin's. In that startled instant her expressive face sent him a single penetrating message of compassion, before she turned back smiling to her friend. He saw her speak quickly to Iona and run toward him. He raised his hand to wave her back. She hesitated and came on. When she was near he said, "Leave me alone, I don't feel like talking."

She stopped and then she rushed close and said, "I won't bother you, Papa! But if you'd like to talk to me sometime, you can. I—" She didn't try to finish, but just looked at him, her eyes luminous with tears.

"All right," he said, moving away. "Go back to your friend. And don't be telling our troubles."

When she was gone he stood, nettled with questions, in front of a fortune teller's gaudy cage.

"Let me tell your future, mister."

He didn't hear. The music and barking and laughter made a canopy for his thoughts.

"Fifty cents! Cards or your hand. One dollar for the whole future!"

The music was circular like the merry-go-round; it slowed, dragged, and started spinning again. A fragrance of his youth elated and saddened him for a moment.

"Your fame and your fortune, gentleman. Be a sport!"

The music labored gaily with an old song. He remembered his baseball days and the laughing girls.

"Go to hell!" the woman said.

He looked up amazed into the painted hag-face of the fortune teller, and turned away.

Matt Gregory came along, surrounded by his family. They all stopped to talk, and Des wished he had the money to treat them. The children were excited and restless, so the Gregorys set off again in a cheerful colony. A good steady man, Des said in his thoughts, as he lighted a cigar.

Near the end of the dusty midway he stopped at a shooting gallery to fire on some moving ducks. He selected a rifle, and, as he was the only customer, he said in a joking, confidential way to the man in charge, "Have to allow for the crooked sights, won't I?"

"They're okay," the man said dully.

Des raised the gun and sighted along the barrel. He closed his good eye for a moment and watched the ducks. There was only a dim whitish blur. The desperation that had enveloped him for weeks tightened and squeezed all the brief pleasure from his mind. He took careful aim and fired a round, missing the ducks; then, finding that the sight was high, he allowed for it and the last two shots hit their targets. Keeping his hand on the gun, he said, "Load it," and paid. The man picked up the rifle and began inserting the shells; but he pretended to have trouble and offered Des another. Des wanted to strike him, the down-and-out little crook.

"Come on, load that gun, you tinhorn. I've found the sight, by God, and now I'm going to shoot with that one."

The carnival worker finished loading the rifle and handed it to him. Des watched the moving ducks with his good eye and fired rapidly, knocking down all but two. He felt better. As he laid the gun on the counter, he noticed the man watching him.

"You don't know where a fellow can get a drink in this tank town, do you?" the man asked.

"I couldn't tell you where," Des said, sizing him up. The man's face reminded him of a worn hat that had been stepped on. "It's against the law."

"So is misery."

"I'm going into town now," Des said. "I might see one of the boys someplace. If I do I'll send him out with a pint."

"Make it two. My buddy'll take one." He shoved the reloaded rifle toward Des. "Have a round."

"Thanks!" Des smiled. He knocked all the ducks down with a clatter. "I'm on my way. If any of you fellows want to play a little poker or shoot some dice, I'll be in the Royal lobby till one or two o'clock."

"Too tired myself. I'll pass the word along to the boys. Be sure and remember that fire-water. Man, I need me a drink."

"Sure thing," Des said. He walked with resolution toward town. Winston would be glad to pick up a few dollars. Maybe some of the carnival workers might want to gamble. He'd take them home. They wouldn't have any real money, but, what the hell, any kind of money would look good now. And if he won a little nest egg he'd try to talk to Belle.

TWENTY-FIVE

THE MOONLIGHT glided over the floor and along the wall like a shining presence. The silence of the town came in through the open hotel window and circled them like the waters of a lake. Beyond the silence, the carnival music went round and round in a solitary ring on the plain. They could hear it like an echo of old sorrows that were not their own. Robin and Blackie lay on the bed tense and apart except that one of his hands and one of hers clasped each other in tight embrace. They had thought to make love but could not and remained fully clothed, speaking in low, constrained voices with long, mute intervals between.

"But why?" He asked at last the question she dreaded.

"I've made up my mind," she said, hating the will in her. She turned her head and saw the gleam of his white shirt in the strange light, and she did not know why seeing him so was such an ecstasy.

"That isn't the answer."

"It is, though, Blackie." Her calm was not calm at all but a cold numbness. "I've made up my mind. It's over."

"I agreed to quit asking you to marry me. But this—"

"I know."

"And why all of a sudden?"

"It isn't all of a sudden," she said tenderly. "I knew it from the very first night, the night you came to the house and we looked at each other. I cried when you left."

"We felt alike then and we still do."

He was speaking the truth and there was nothing to say that would not hurt them more.

"Why do you gamble?" she asked cruelly.

"Because I want the money. I make it easier that way."

"But what a life it is! I'm so sick of it!"

"We could have our own life."

"That's a delusion."

"If I had you I could make more money. I'd have a reason. We might even get rich."

"I don't want to be that kind of reason!"

"Be sensible, Robin. With money we can do anything we like, be anything we want."

"It's sickeningly true if our values are *all* purchasable. It won't—"

"It helps."

"I know money is important. We've been poor and we're poor again; that's the best way to find out. But it couldn't make you a poet."

"I don't want to be a poet."

"That's merely a symbol of what I mean! And you know it!" Her anger dropped away. "But you are a poetic man. A poet might not be."

He was annoyed.

"You like me to sense this," she said, "but you don't like me to say it."

"Why are we quarreling?" he said in despair. "And why are we breaking up? It doesn't make sense. Good God, do you want to suffer like this?"

"No. I don't want to betray myself now and suffer more later, and I want to go on my own. I've said this over and over."

"There must be some people who don't want to do anything important and I'm one of them," he said stubbornly.

"I'm not asking you to do anything important, just something better with what you've got."

"That's for you, my darling."

"Blackie, I want to get a better job, and maybe go to school some more. You should understand that. You've been to college. Your parents helped you. Were they nice to you?"

"Yes, and I never heard the last of it after I was kicked out of school. I couldn't study; I was supposed to be like my father, my mother, my uncles, my brothers, and God knows who else, all successful. Anything but myself."

"What is your self?"

"Damned if I know. Lost in the shuffle maybe. I heard my aunt saying one day that I was going to be a black sheep, just like great uncle Andrew. I felt better after that."

"Is that why you're called Blackie?"

"Yes. I told my best friend about it and the fellows got to calling me Blackie."

"I'm glad. It's such a common name for gamblers and crooks that I didn't want you to have it."

He laughed in a sad way.

She thought of lessening this hurt by placing part of the responsibility upon him. "Would you give up gambling?"

"Would you marry me?"

She was startled and said quickly, "And do some honest work?"

"What work?" he asked evasively.

"Any work you like. Something you can take pride in."

"I take pride in what I'm doing," he said quietly.

While she was admiring this firmness, he asked, "If I were gambling on the stock market or the board of trade, would it make a difference?"

"Not to me. You'd be generally respected but I don't care about that. You're misunderstanding me."

He hesitated for a long time. "If I understand you, it hurts like hell."

"You understand me." She could not look at him or the resolution might fail, and it would have to be gone through again.

They lay in miserable stillness.

Finally he said, "Maybe I don't. Say it right out; it might be better than I'm thinking."

"I can't say it all. I don't know all of it. I'm ashamed I couldn't say it at first, but I wanted you—" She stopped, gathering control.

"Go on," he urged her.

"It was important." She waited for these cool words to restore her; she wanted to give him these thoughts to take away with him, and somehow perversely to secure a part of him forever. Wasn't it her loss too? It was such a deep-down drawing together that it had to happen; it would have been wrong to resist.

He held her hand so tightly that her arm throbbed with pain. He was waiting.

She knew that a part of her and a part of him that had met would meet no one else, would belong to them alone. This too was love. But she could not speak such thoughts. She wanted as much to sooth herself as him. "It has changed us and—"

"Bound us," he said passionately. "You know that."

"Yes! But I won't be bound to *all the rest*. I won't be! I can't help it, Blackie. I won't—" she began to sob, and pulled her hand free, covering her face and turning away sobbing. "I won't—I won't!"

He did not move. "Are you still in love with me?" He spoke as if he were making a decision.

"Don't ask!" she cried.

"Are you?" he said, and his voice was hard.

"Yes!" she answered, hoarse and vehement in denial. She got up wildly. "But it's over! Over! Don't you understand me?"

He swung toward her and pulled her back, into his arms, holding her forcibly. She put her arms around him and they lay together desolate, already remote, crying.

They rose from their chaste embrace when Blackie heard the utter silence of the town. The music of the merry-go-round had ceased.

"It's midnight!" he said.

They looked at each other forlornly.

"I can't go home like this," she said, drawing her hand across her face. "They might still be up."

"We'll go for a walk," he said, putting on his coat. "A last walk. Is it a last walk, Robin?"

"Don't," she whispered.

"I've seen this coming for a long time," he said, "but I didn't want to believe it. You're Tanny's daughter, aren't you? The way he really wants you to be, the way he couldn't be himself."

"I think you and Papa are too good for what you're doing, but you're doing it and you like it."

"You like part of this life too. I know. And you won't give in. Tanny and I—we gave in."

"Then Papa and you belong together, not Papa and me, or you and me."

He smiled. "Got it all figured out."

"Maybe it seems better to you and Papa than it does to me. I guess I don't understand."

"Well, just remember that what we're doing and what it looks like to others are two different things, maybe five or six. The same with you, with all of us."

"I've found that out," she said, contrite. "What people think of you and me together and what we are—anyway, I wish I knew why you—"

"I don't know myself. It's what I want to do."

"Will you not be partners with Papa any more?" she asked, feeling a terrible guilt.

"That's up to Tanny. You know how I feel about him."

"I'm glad," she said softly.

He looked at her for a long time. "I'm not giving up, Robin." He watched her face tight against the tears, and put his fist under her chin, lifting it, trying to make her look at him, but she kept her eyelids down. "I'll leave in the morning on that early train. I can't stay around town and see you on the street and not have you for myself." He hoped that if he left, proving his respect for her decision, she would change her mind. Her love would change her mind. If he didn't believe that, he couldn't leave. "I'll pack tonight and when you wake up, I'll be on my way. Is that how you want it, little love?"

"Where will you go?" She could not control her voice above a whisper.

"Las Vegas or Reno or maybe Colorado Springs. I'll write you."

She said nothing more.

"I'll write Tanny later when I get settled. I'll tell him some gambler out there sent for me. Something quick, or he'll be sore. I hate to run out on him like this, and I can't do it if I see him again. You understand that, Robin?"

She nodded.

"Funny how I feel about Tanny. I figured we'd be together from now on." Blackie opened her purse and placed a fold of bills inside.

"No!" She handed the money back. He would not take it and she put it in his pocket.

They went out, along the hall to its end and down the iron fire-escape stairs into a side street. No one was about. The town was going to sleep. They walked without speaking, through Jail Park, passing the dark shape of the courthouse, on through the old paved streets overhung with trees, to the little dirt roads beyond. The houses were dark. The pinnate leaves of the small honey locust spun like wind chimes in the light of the moon going down. They caught in Robin's hair. Blackie held her hand, which lay quiet within the lean curve of his fingers. The road ended and the town gave way to the land. They came to a barbed-wire fence. The full ripe heads of wheat nodded docilely in the wind, the field undulating like golden water, giving into the cool night breath the fragrance of sun-filled grain.

They rested and walked on beside the fence until they came to the open plain. The plain lay primeval under the moonlight. The stillness was immense. The weave of insect songs was in the silence as the wind was in the night. They walked far out, and a coyote as dim as a shadow, suspicious, curious, moved with them distantly.

Here alone in this hard, silent land, their love seemed continuous, exalted and disclaimed.

Only once as they turned back they stood for a long moment with their arms gentle about each other, their eyes in a deep exchange. There was nothing more to say. Here on the plain, away from the town, they felt a part of all being, ennobled by the sense of earth, of timelessness, infinitesimal in nature, splendid in their separate moment, attached by their very breath to the universe and the whole of life.

"I love you," he said.

She heard his proud words in the great hush of the plain. Love, she thought, and she could not speak. Love, a foreign word, a stone.

TWENTY-SIX

ROBIN STEPPED quietly onto the porch, wanting to take the calm of exhaustion into her sleep. The house was dark. A strange, low, monotonous sound came from within—the familiar night quarreling. She opened the front door. The sinister mumble ceased. She listened for a long time to the stillness, and entered, tiptoeing into the bedroom. The silence was ominous. Her heart beat furiously, her throat closed on her breath. Chill flashed over her skin. She stood still. A raw fear powerfully urged her to run. Before she could move, his bare feet smacked on the floor and he was in the room, felt and heard in the darkness. She kicked off her slippers and leaped into bed beside Stevie, who was awake, trembling. The bed was like a warm, dark cave which would protect her.

Des switched on the overhead light and it swung away from his furious touch in a wide arc, making his giant shadow climb and fall swiftly from the bedroom walls.

"You goddamn dirty slut!" he said. "I ought to kill you!"

She held her breath.

"Where have you been? It's three o'clock!"

Stevie clung to her arm for silence.

"You put the whores out of business," he roared.

She wanted to reply but Stevie pressed her arm.

"Sleeping with Tom, Dick, and Harry."

She sat up. "I do not! The only vulgar thing about my behavior is what *you* think!" She wanted to prove to him, even though he'd never know it, that making love had nothing to do with vulgarity. It was all to do with how one felt and thought.

"Don't start side-stepping and don't lie!"

"I'm not. We went for a long walk. Only a walk. I'm telling the truth."

"Who?"

"I felt bad about everything—you and Mama and everything. I didn't want to come home."

Belle's soft footsteps padded on the living room floor. "Come to bed, Des," she said fearfully.

231

He paid no attention. Robin glanced at his face, ugly, distorted, the handsomeness gone. She lay down warily. There had been similar tirades; he would talk out his anger and go to bed.

"By God, you'll tell me who you were out with, or I'll—"

"Stop yelling," Stevie said calmly. Her trembling shook the bed.

The covers were thrown back violently. One arm felt wrenched from its socket as Robin was jerked from the bed. Protectively she stood on her feet and with fearful strength she twisted free and ran toward the door. Des stepped in her path before she was out of the bedroom, and slapped her hard across the face. She lost her balance and fell against the wall, but righted herself and looked angrily into his eyes.

"I'll teach you to lay around in the grass with a nigger!" he shouted. "That whore saw you out there talking to him in the dark; it was even too much for her."

"I despise you," Robin said with cruel distaste.

He slapped her again, hard, but she stood.

Belle whimpered and moved nearer Des. "Don't hurt her," she pleaded, and then she burst out, "It's that Blackie! It isn't Chris. It's your friend!"

Des stood back, shocked and still, with Blackie's betrayal and Robin's deception clarifying themselves in his mind. In slow, final, utter contempt, he said, "Well, by God, a *gambler*."

He struck her with his fist and she jarred against the wall and sank to her knees. Dazed, and then alert with terror, she rose and backed into the closet, which was open and shallow and too small for shelter. For a moment clearly she saw in his wild eyes a rage that was beyond reason or pity. He came forward again, cursing in a low and terrible voice, and struck at her face. She slid away from the blow, lunging forward against him to try for the door. He shook her free and knocked her back into the closet. She clung to the clothes, fainting, determined not to fall. She heard in his breathing the alarming frenzy of his animal strength; and then Stevie's voice, "—Don't!" as if he could not hear her, "—Don't!" Her mother was sobbing and begging.

Robin opened her eyes, and before the lids weighed heavily down she saw Belle and Stevie struggling to hold him. He flung Belle away with one fierce movement of his arm and lifted Stevie onto the bed, where she stood rigid, stricken. There was a hush as before a great wind, and in that hush, separated, suspended in time, a soft, even sound repeated itself in the room. Stevie.

Robin pulled the clothes down with her. They cushioned the floor where she lay, crumpled, half-sitting, with awareness receding. Blood ran warmly from her nose over her mouth and fell upon the dresses. A monstrous blow came out of the dusk against her ribs, and the breath went out of her lungs like a blade. There was another blow and another. Des was kicking her with his bare feet, but she could no longer resist. His tall, strong body in white summer underwear shone clear for a moment and faded. A hoarse, unnatural voice was signaling through the dark monotonously. She tried to pull herself up from a paralyzing dream. Other voices embroidered the distance, a woman's sobbing punctuated with effort, a girl's screaming—dry, repetitious, shrill. A flash of spare, pure knowledge lighted her mind: he meant to kill her. Incredible strength sprang from her fear; she rose on powerful, instinctive wings of flight into the small, closed room, surprising, striking, eluding him, fierce in her desperation, reaching the dresser, pulling out the drawer. She swung round, facing him as he reached for her; she held the revolver with both hands.

He saw her finger in the trigger curve and backed away.

Stevie, remote, alone, enclosed in hysteria, stood on the bed.

Blood ran over Robin's mouth and dripped onto her breast. Her eyes glowed deeply in her pale, bruised face. Small, curling leaves of honey locust were caught in her tangled hair. She felt cold, steady; her senses soared with awareness.

Belle released her grip on Des's arm and rushed past him toward her.

Robin's voice, guttural, unknown to her, crashed like a rock— "Stay back!"—and Belle obeyed, her lips apart, her eyes afraid.

"Put that gun down!" Des commanded. "It's loaded!"

Robin said in her ominous voice, "You won't hit me ever again. You won't call me any more filthy names. *Nobody—ever—will hit me.*" She saw him fixed with terror. His face was young and frightened, all the cruelty gone.

She fired.

In the instant between the decision and the aim, a clarity like crystal filled her mind. In it she saw the words she was thinking: 'I don't want to do it. I'll ruin our lives.' The impulse for her finger to press the trigger was already in motion. She aimed away. The bullet opened the flesh on the side of his palm, and lodged in the floor. His voice released an animal's desolate cry. "My hand! You've ruined my hand!"

The acrid smell of burned powder floated upward and clung to the air of the room. A Navajo pin on her dress, dangling unfastened, fell; it clicked on the floor, small and neat in the silence.

Stevie's forlorn, abandoned screaming stopped; she collapsed upon the bed without a sound.

Belle stood as if petrified, staring at Des.

The revolver, heavy and warm, was suddenly beyond Robin's strength to hold. She turned blindly and placed it in the drawer with her father's shirts.

The room was quiet.

The doorbell jangled and Mrs. Polk's voice fumed urgently. "I heard a shot! Open the door! I'll call the sheriff!"

Des called out in a controlled voice, "Go back to bed. Everything's all right."

Seeing the blood on Robin's dress, he said, "Change your clothes and get out of here!" His voice was low and cold.

"No, Des!" Belle entreated. "No, please!" She ran to the bed and threw herself face down by Stevie, holding the still girl in her arms.

"Shut up!" Des said. "I don't want Robin around here any longer." He waited threateningly.

Robin did not move to obey; she was trembling violently. Then she crossed the room and took from a closet nail her denim overalls and drew them on, pulling her dress off over her head. She slipped her feet into old canvas oxfords, thinking clearly of flight.

"Hurry up!"

She stooped guardedly and picked up her clothes.

"Leave them alone, goddamn it! Get out of here before I kill you this time, and don't come back! I never want to see you again! I hope you go to hell! I hope you starve to death!" He doubled his wounded fist, and winced with pain.

The town was as dark as the night. The shapes of Burkett Street slowly emerged deeper than the dark. Robin crossed the small park and stopped uncertainly. She thought of going to friends. Exhaustion and pain tempted her. She considered Iona and Drake and Chris and Blackie, but she could admit to no one that she had been beaten. She went down Anadel, avoiding Main Street where lights burned dimly in hotels. Precise catalpa trees loomed blackly in the charcoal night until she came abruptly to the railroad, climbed the roadbed, and walked on the sleepers in the direction of the block signal, that lonesome glare in the night. A narrow dirt road hemmed the outskirts of Dirty Spoon, dark and silent except for a square of light in a single shack. This way led to a small town nine miles distant; between were the fields and pastures, the sand hills and the river.

The darkness became intense; only the starlight giving a sheen to the night revealed the small road on the plain. Dulled with shock, she walked unaware of the soft, wild movements of animals. A gray, desolate light as if from nowhere skulked into the black world and roused her. Shadows lingered on the ground like a field of ripe darkness. The hidden sun bloomed on the fields of night. The wonder of it filled her mind.

Coyotes would soon be going to sleep and snakes waking and coming up from their holes into the sun. Birds that had sung wildly all spring were quiet with nesting. When she was beyond the familiar picnic grounds, she took off her canvas slippers and went down the damp bank, wading into the narrow, drying stream. Minnows swam away from the sudden disturbance of her steps. The place was green and still; it smelled of water-cool shade. She crossed to the other bank and walked under its trees until she came to a willow with branches that fell over the sand. She lay down in the green enclosure of leaves, seeing the red sun rise, the yellow hills curve away from the river, and a cottonwood sparkling in the radiant air. The warm smell of the sweater folded under her head made her think of home and Stevie, and her tears fell on the sand. One small globe, like a world in the universe, rolled away, gathering dust. Feelings of anger and humiliation and despair seeped into weariness that pulled her down into sleep.

At the farewelling whistle of an early-morning train she awoke dimly and thought of Blackie going away forever, but her grief would not rise through the pain and exhaustion, which whirled her again into sleep.

All day and all night, unaware of place, she drifted in sleep that was like the mindless nothing of being dead.

The next morning very early she was awake, bewildered at seeing the green willow leaves instead of the cracked plaster ceiling of the house in Burkett Street. Her body throbbed. She sat up and lay back, moaning. All morning she lolled in feverish, arid space, confused, troubled. When

235

the sun was high at noon she went to the stream for a drink; then, feeling the utter solitude of the place, she bathed in the shallow water. Soothed, dressed, she waded downstream and climbed the dunes, her bare feet sinking into the sand, her bruised body aware of the strain. She picked a handful of wild sand plums and went back down the cushioned hill.

As she sat under the willow, eating the tart fruit, her thoughts groped tentatively, like a finger over a wound, toward the night of violence, and withdrew. She tried to plan and could not. She was strangely at rest; sensation was remote, as if it were not her own. She did not feel like anyone; her special identity was hidden, renewing itself perhaps, but she did not care.

After burying the plum seeds, making a wish for a plant to grow, she had nothing to do. She waded into the river again and sat on a large rock, watching the minnows flash in the clear water running over the pale, sandy bed. Long-legged insects walked on the water, and a lizard sunned itself on a reef. She thought with satisfaction that she could stay here through the quietly humming summer. Edible greens grew along the river and ripe wheat seeds were yellow in the sun not far away.

A cool resolution flicked against the stillness in her mind and lodged like a small, indissoluble stone.

Then the memory of Blackie's tenderness and dignity at the last imposed itself upon her returning strength, and undid it. She flung herself on the sand and wept aloud, since there was no one to hear. His image, his words, and their exchange of awareness burned in her mind. His presence had never been so real, so powerful and urgent. She had denied him with her reasoned will. How much time would be required to wear him out of her very texture? And what would love be like after that? But the thought of any other love was repulsive, and brought on another uncontrollable seizure of tears, after which she lay exhausted and quiet, staring without feeling into the white hot sky of the afternoon.

The heat itself roused her to go down to the stream. She lay in the water under the delicate rhythm of its tide, aware of nothing but nature's infinite quiet commotion around her.

At night she sat on the sand, listening to the whir of insects, the sleepy twitter of birds, sticks breaking as animals moved, the flow of the stream. They with the tranquil days of sun were the poultice that renewed her strength and led her thoughts beyond herself. When she had made her plans and was preparing to go to sleep, her ears caught the even sound of someone walking toward the river. She lifted herself into the slender branches of the willow. The steps came through the brush on the other side of the stream, farther up, and stopped.

A long, low, familiar whistle came through the dark. She waited to be sure. It came again. She whistled back, leaped down, and splashed across the stream, glad, shouting. "Mr. Sherlock Garrison! Imagine meeting you here!" She felt utterly and sublimely silly. "Had you much trouble crossing the ice? Where are the hounds?"

Chris walked toward her, saying in a sober, startled voice, "It didn't take the devil out of you." Then he laughed. "I've been everyplace else and finally I had sense enough to come here. I was up at the dunes where we used to picnic and skate. Did you hear me whistling upstream?"

"No. I *must* have been thinking hard." She was serious. "I was making some plans."

He put an arm around her with concern. "Mainly, are you all right?"

"I'm all together."

Robin waded into the stream and led Chris over the smooth, wet stones. They climbed to the dry sand and sat down. He looked around at the shadowed hills, at the rosette of lights on the plain. "Were you afraid?"

"No, I felt safe."

"You didn't really say how you are, Rob." Chris leaned near to see her face.

"I began to feel a lot better today. I ate plums and greens and seeds. I slept a lot."

Chris waited. She would not go on. It seemed to her now that in the first hours she had been like a furious, desperate, disconnected world. Being here had related her again. It was over, *that other*, put away, locked up.

A coyote yapped.

"Hear him?" she asked.

"How else do you feel?"

"I don't feel."

"I should think," Chris said with calculated indifferent warmth, "that friends have a few rights—to something more than a casual answer."

237

"Oh, all right!" she said, angrily ashamed. "I hated Papa! I hated myself! I felt as if I'd burst with hating everything, and I didn't enjoy hating; I couldn't keep it up. But"—she stopped and drew her breath—"Papa meant to kill me—"

"Stevie told me that."

"The terrible way he felt seemed so unfair. To tell you the truth, I was so miserable about Blackie that once or twice I didn't care if Papa did kill me. Also, I thought, 'I've broken off with Blackie, I've exerted my precious will, and what happens?' But, Chris"— she began to speak low and slowly—"I must have a big cold space in me, too."

"Why?"

"In the midst of that awful night, when I felt the most like a frantic animal ready to do anything to save myself, I had wonderful flashes of understanding, as fast as a dream. Once I even thought that it wasn't fair to Papa to let him kill me and suffer and get into trouble, because he wasn't just furious with me; it was everything that has happened to him lately and—maybe all his life. I grew about ten years in that hour. And I wanted to live and be what I am! To show him, too!" When tears ran down her cheeks, she struck them away with the back of her hand, and sat in a long defiant silence.

Chris had not meant to hurt her but he guessed that lifting the cover a little would create a needed vent. He pressed her arm in sympathy.

Robin leaned forward and gathered up a handful of sand and let it run through her fingers. He waited. She drew her knees up and covered her feet with sand. "Chris, are you ever afraid?"

"Not in Apache, but—"

"Chris, I found out what it's like to be afraid. I didn't really know before."

"Well, we both know now," he said.

They sat thinking of this.

Finally Robin said, "What about Stevie?"

"She's in bed. She says she's going to stay in bed a year," he said sadly.

"How odd to set a time." Her voice was strained, wondering.

"There's talk," Chris said mildly. She sat up straight and waited for him to go on. "Rumors about the shooting. No one knows anything for certain, but there's gossip. Lord, the gossip!"

"Did you"—she hesitated—"did you hear anything about Papa?"

238

"I heard he had been to the sheriff to explain things."

"They're old cronies."

She did not care that people were talking about her; she would not be inundated by these aimless and petty vulgarities. She sighed and was about to speak, but there was such an agreement of affection and sympathy between them that she let it be felt in silence.

Chris stood up. "Come on, Rob, you're going back with me." He pulled her to her feet.

"I've no place to go until I find a room, unless—"

"That's what I mean."

"Oh, may I? Chris!" she said gratefully. "But your mother might not want me and I don't blame her. It would worry her."

"Mom worries about trouble. She's had enough of it. But she knew I was trying to find you and she probably knows I'm bringing you back."

"Are you sure?"

"Sure."

They went across the field in the darkness. As the sight of the lighted town forced a reminder of its curiosity, Chris thought reluctantly of the prudence of his decision. He was angry with himself at the flare of apprehension that would not be dissolved in his reasoning mind. He had never been in trouble. His father had been "hot-headed" much like Robin. Chris knew there was little wisdom in that. He was aware that he was neither bold nor daring, but he knew that he had an enduring, everyday courage, and he clung to that. Only today he had had to listen to Charter tell him he'd put him up in front if he weren't colored, and from the way the man had said it Chris knew he expected him to be grateful. Instead he was seething, but he needed the job, and in some ways Charter was better than the others, so he just nodded and went on with his work. Damned if he'd thank him.

"Chris, are you worried about going in town? You're so quiet. *Are you?*"

"It's impossible to be a Negro and not be," he said curtly.

"I'm not the whole white race!" she said.

They walked without speaking, a void of sadness and antagonism between them.

When they came to Dirty Spoon they took the narrow road on its dark edge. Sounds blew to them like a part of the tangy air. An evening hymn, the voices rich and fervid, streamed from the open church; in a silence a woman's laughter; a mother calling, "Jane-ee, Jane-ee"; someone playing a saxophone, hot and sad, all alone, "Somebody Stole My Gal."

They cut over and passed near an arc light at a street's end. Under the lamp, among the darting miller moths, little boys still played. One of them turned his black face up in an innocent evil grin and shouted, "Hot damn!"

When they were past, Robin and Chris looked at each other and smiled.

They walked a block below the park, avoiding Burkett Street, reaching the Garrison house from the west. Robin placed her cold hand in Chris's dry, warm palm and he led her through the darkness to the kitchen door, from which the only light shone. The Tannehill house was dark.

Cleanliness lay like a carved pattern on the silent room. Chris went to speak to his mother in the bedroom off the kitchen. When he came back he was smiling. "Mom says we might want something to eat. Buttermilk and hot cornbread."

"She expected me," Robin said with pleased surprise.

"I think she did." Chris made sure that the shades were drawn and they sat down to eat the good supper. When they had finished, Chris looked at Robin's bruised face and said, "You'll be all right in a day or two more." He shook his head, and almost said something against Des, but thought better of it since Robin had not. On the way to his room he said, "I'll be home tomorrow noon, and if your dad isn't around I'll go over and tell Stevie, and your mother can bring you some clothes."

Mrs. Garrison came in, wearing an old-fashioned white cotton nightgown, carrying another one over her arm. Robin saw her eyes note the fading bruises. They greeted each other hesitantly.

The nightgown fell voluminously about Robin's slender body, and the woman smiled, but when her lips closed on her smile, a moment of suspicion made her eyes stern; then the equivocal expression returned. Robin stood still, feeling painfully uncertain.

"Come on, chile. I reckon you're tired."

A vivid blush spread over Robin's face and neck. "You're welcome enough," Mrs. Garrison said with gentle dignity. "It's the talk and uneasiness. No fault of yours. I'm just thinking of Son."

"I know," Robin whispered. "I don't want to mix you up in our troubles."

"We just be careful." Mrs. Garrison thought a moment and went on sharply, dropping into her everyday speech. "I don't want Marie hearin' *nothin'* 'bout this! You hear? She and Son savin' every penny they make to go up to the university next year or two. They goin' to get married."

"I know that."

"Well, now, boys and girls can't seldom ever be friends. There's always some feelin' kinda hangin' around. 'S natural. But seems like you and Chris more like kin, but nobody is goin' to want to believe that. Marie knows, but she hadn't ought to be embarrassed by talk."

They went into the small room and she waited for Robin to get into bed, then turned the light out and lay down carefully, keeping well to her own side.

Robin lay stiffly, tears of shame wetting her face. Mrs. Garrison breathed in a quiet, unnatural rhythm. They did not move to settle themselves for sleep. Robin wiped the tears with the hem of the sheet, which smelled of fresh ironing. She wanted to whisper good night, but only a long shuddering sigh came with the end of her crying.

"Now, now," Mrs. Garrison said. "Ain't nothin' wrong can't be fixed somehow." She turned on her back and, resting her arm along the pillows, she began to smooth Robin's hair.

"My hair's full of sand," Robin said in an unsteady voice.

"That's no mind now."

Robin flung herself close to Mrs. Garrison and hugged her.

"You go to sleep," the woman said low and tenderly.

"I'll get a room tomorrow," Robin said more calmly.

"Sh-h-h now," Mrs. Garrison whispered. Then she added aloud with a very small laugh, and with irony, "All of us together, the Tannehills and the Garrisons, got enough trouble to set up in the grief business. I swear, we all goin' around actin' happy as larks with all this stuff cooped up in us. Beats all how we do it! But we better go to sleep now and mend ourselves. I'll hol' you awhile."

TWENTY-SEVEN

CHARTER was a good fellow. Des kept saying this over and over in his mind. They had gambled many a night together. Charter wouldn't want his wife and all of Apache to know that, and it ought to make him understand this whole situation. Des slid down in the lobby chair, hoping no one would say a word to him. It was late; he had sat in the Royal all night, thinking, looking out the window into the empty street. Jim Charter was an Irisher like himself, or half anyway, and he was a swell fellow. He had been poor all his life until he made plenty of money in the automobile business; he'd remember how it goes when you don't have money to back you up if you get in a scrape. Des closed his eyes; the one that had hurt so much had quit hurting; he couldn't see out of it, so what the hell, he was half blind. That goddamn Blackie — just when he needed him, he took off for parts unknown; all that crap about wanting to be a gambler just like him! If Bowman hadn't heard from a porter in a cheap little hotel that Robin had a room there, he'd think Blackie had even taken her away. He never wanted to see either one of them again. He repeated this in his thoughts as if to convince himself. The night he threw Robin out, by God, he had meant to go to the hotel and beat the hell out of Blackie. But Stevie's fainting dead away frightened him so much that he stayed home. Finally they had all gone to sleep in miserable exhaustion, and slept until noon. He got up and went straight to the Bella Brock. The clerk said that Mr. Collier had left on the five-o'clock morning train. No, there was no message.

The question began again. Had Blackie been decent enough to go away and leave Robin alone for *his* sake? He almost fell into the trap of believing this. Hell no, gamblers are floaters, and Blackie was just like the rest of them, only worse. He had no honor. Probably Robin had warned him and he had run away. He had no honor at all. Des's thoughts stood still. He was shocked to feel no anger against Blackie, only the hard pain of betrayal, the humiliation, the loss. He opened his eyes and they stung with tears, even the blind eye. A hell of a note, a blind eye could cry but it couldn't see. No tears, anyway, his eyes were just wet. By God, I'm still a man, he said to himself. But there was no solace in it. A great bleak despair spread out in him.

"Hey, Mistah Desmond!" Bowman was saying in a low voice and shaking him. "Mistah O'Tannehill! Man, yu done slep' in this back-breakin' chair half the night."

Des sat up.

"Worry gonna poison yu right down to yu shoelaces, man."

"I don't worry about anything, Bowman, you know that."

Bowman looked out into the desolate morning street. "It's gonna blow today. See the sand already kickin' up out there?" He studied Des. "Say, how 'bout yu comin' down home with me and havin' a Dirty Spoon fulla whiskey and git hol' of yuself?"

"Thanks, not now, Bowman. I got something on my mind, something I have to do today."

"Ain' nothin' with more trouble in, is it?"

"No, this is something else."

"Well, ah'm gonna go on home then."

"See you tonight," Des said and stood up. "I've got to wash my face and wake up."

"Come on back here, Tannehill," Jim Charter said. "We'll sit in one of these new cars where we can talk."

Charter slid behind the steering wheel and Des sat beside him. The high-ceilinged garage was gloomy and cool, and quiet, save for the sounds the mechanics made at work. From his seat Charter could see the street door of the show room up front.

"Jim," Des said, "I want you to do me a favor."

For an instant Charter's eyes gleamed warily; then he smiled, his loose, friendly mouth warming the words, "Sure thing."

"I don't want to borrow any money."

Relieved, Charter said, "Well, you could sure have it. You know that."

"Thanks," Des looked down upon the short, powerfully built man and tried to take courage from his own height. "I hear you've fired that Garrison kid because" — he could not bring himself to mention the reason, and, realizing in his discomfort that Charter knew the reason well, he hurried on — "and, by God, Jim, that puts me in a kind of a bad light, my daughter too, and the whole family. I don't want you to think I'm trying to horn in on your business, but maybe you didn't get the straight of it, with all this goddamn talk going around."

243

Charter stepped on the clutch and absently moved the gear shift from neutral to low, to second, to high, and back to neutral. His eyes assumed a confidential, listening expression; he forced a direct gaze, but the muscles of his face were strained.

"*I've* got nothing against the Garrison boy," Des said. "I'm just trying to protect my name. As long as I've been here — and I don't need to tell *you* my profession, Charter — you've never heard a word against me and my wife and kids. I'll challenge anybody on that score."

Charter nodded agreement.

"But that story going around is a goddamn lie!" Des said.

Charter wet his lips. "That oldest girl of yours is kinda wild, more willful maybe than wild, but —"

Des bristled.

Charter smiled and said, "The boys spoil all our pretty girls."

"My girls may be good-looking all right, but they've got brains too! Robin —"

"It's the gods' truth, Tannehill, I've never heard anything out of the way."

"Then, by God, why did you fire that nigger boy? That makes it look like the truth to the whole town!"

"Before that, I mean," Charter said.

"Hell, there's nothing to it."

"Well, a fellow I wouldn't exactly want to call a liar was out turning the water off his lawn that night and saw them go by. His wife saw them too from the doorway. They both swore it was Robin and Chris."

"In the dark," Des said with disgust. "How do they know who it was?"

"Well, that's the story, and some of the business people don't want anything like that to get out about Apache, and the only way to stop it is to punish them, make them see it's wrong. We've already given Chris a warning — he'll understand that. No rough stuff here, but if he wants to work — of course, if he feels biggety, he can always go someplace else."

"Warning? Hell's fire! A lot of these old farts are as crooked as a barrel of snakes. And some of these 'respectable' women—" Des stopped and began again. "Apache's a good clean town. I'd say the majority of the people are good people, but in my line I see the seamy side of towns, and it isn't always what you read in the society column. Things are like that — open and hidden. People are, too. I'll bet my last dollar that some of the best people in this town, the *best*, I mean, not the hypocrites, didn't have anything to do with this holier-than-thou stuff. They'd probably just forget it and give the kids a chance. I respect those people. I've got no use for—" Des was flushed; he sat forward in the seat, his eyes hot and accusing. "Why, I cover up for you fellows — you damn hypocrites — all the time. I'm not even asking you to cover up for me."

"I've daughters of my own growing up." Charter's voice was appealing. "And as my wife said, what would I say if this happened to one of them?"

Des leaned back and tried again. "Listen here, Charter, I'm concerned about my own daughters, especially the younger one." His voice smoothed out in confidence. "You can't do anything with some of these modern boys and girls. They're a fright. They don't have the respect for their parents that they had when I was a boy. That oldest girl of mine *is* hard to handle, but Christ almighty, she's decent. She knew the Garrison boy at school, but there's no fooling around there. He's a smart boy, reads a lot, and they're friendly and that's all."

"I'd say that's more than enough."

"If I thought there was anything wrong, I'd give her a good beating."

Charter looked at him closely. "There's a rumor around to that effect," he said boldly, with a slow smile.

"That just goes to show," Des said, his gaze clear and honest, "how they can stretch things. I boxed her ears one night for getting home late with Drake Bishop. By God, Jim, I set an hour for her to get in and I had to keep my hand up."

"I appreciate that, but Jesus Christ, look here, man, the story *is* around, the damage is done, and I had to let Chris go. Though I'm damned sorry I did. He was a good worker, he has a head on him, and I was thinking of promoting him, but I couldn't very well put him over anybody in the office."

Des's face lighted. "Say, Jim, you carry a lot of weight in this town. Why in hell don't you just take him back and say it's all been a mistake, or say nothing? It'll help you and it'll keep me from going around with my tail tucked. Why, I may have to leave, but I don't want something like that following me, or left behind."

Charter sighed. "Jesus, I never thought it would get into all this. I'm sure sorry. I don't see what in Christ's name I can do now. I can't go against all the other fellows. I'm in business, man. I've got to keep my nose clean."

Des realized at last that it was useless, and he was sorry he had come here and humiliated himself. The one foot that he had kept in respectability was slipping. Before he knew it he would just be known as a crooked gambler with a whore for a daughter. But Charter would keep one foot in corruption and end up a city father!

"Well, I'm sure sorry," Charter said with genuine sympathy. "It's too bad Hauser fired Robin. Good old O'Brien wouldn't have done that. He would have braved it out; he thought a lot of her, said she was destined to go places. This trouble may be hard on her, Tannehill."

"Hell," Des said, concealing the jolting shock he felt on hearing that Robin had lost her job, "you can't get her down. She's just like me. That little job won't mean a thing to her. Why, she's too proud to let this scandal worry her. That's why I'm around here talking like a woman. She's got a lot to learn, but she'll get along all right."

"I just hope this blows over. It's pretty serious, you know that."

Des looked worried again.

"I hear that young daughter of yours won a gold medal in some state music contest this week. My wife belongs to some culture club and she was telling me last night how Mrs. Lafe Sutton was telling yesterday that she sent this in without your daughter knowing it, and wanted to bring her to the club to play it but said she was too shy."

Des was amazed that Stevie had done anything like that, and he thought sadly how she wouldn't even touch the piano any more. He said, "If it's gold, we'd better melt it."

Charter laughed. "Don't be modest, man. You know that's kind of unusual for Apache. By God, Tannehill, you disgrace us on the one hand and honor us on the other!"

"Well," Des said, giving Charter a proud and knowing look, "that's the kind of fellow I am. Variety is the spice of life."

"Why don't you go into business?" Charter asked him seriously. "You'd make money and everything would be all right."

"I am in business. What would you fellows do for a little secret sin? You're safe with me."

It was Charter's turn to feel embarrassed that he had not returned the security, but he revealed no sign of this. Instead he said critically,

"You should have come to me right away, Tannehill, before all this got out in the open."

"If it's just a below-the-belt pipe dream of some old worn-out boys and girls, how the hell could I get in here first?"

"I guess you're right," Charter said.

Des opened the car door and stepped out.

Charter had an idea. "Say, Tannehill." he spoke almost in a whisper. "How about me and some of the fellows having a little game over at the Royal tonight?"

Des had no protection with his pay-offs lagging, but his urge was strong to keep a respectable light on things as long as he could. He would rent his old room at the Royal and take a chance. Bowman would look out for him. The law wouldn't touch these men if they did arrest him. "I'll be there tonight," he said. "I'll tell Winston to let you in the back door and you can go right to my room." He nodded to Charter and left. "I'll give the bastards a good trimming," he said to himself, "eye or no eye," and went home to take a nap so that he would be in the prime of his powers.

He'd be up and gone before Belle got home from work. He had something else on his mind now, too.

TWENTY-EIGHT

STEVIE shifted weakly in bed, pushing the books away, and lay on her side "just thinking." She spent most of her time this way. As she turned she heard the envelopes crackle under the pillow. The dry, hot wind blew in the window, lifting the curtain in a limp greeting.

A sense of doom as implacable as the mythological destinies hung over her mind, and more palpably over her bed and at night in the corners of the room, whispering that she would never be allowed to finish anything begun. This pitiless doom, whose shape pursued her hours, mumbled of unforgiveness. For what? For what? She retreated from the sounds of Apache and rummaged, critical and despairing, through the innocence of her past and the list of her imperfections and failures; through the now appalling history of "betrayals" by friends, by Des and Belle and Robin. They blindly had no idea of their defaults, but she could see "clearly." This superior but cruel gift, sometimes a solace, was best unrevealed. And they were all more fortunate than she; they went about their lives in spite of everything. She was filled with admiration or jealousy, depending on her mood of tenderness or melancholy.

She had not seen her father for days, and Robin only once. If no one came it hardly mattered, although there were moments of fierce, concentrated wishing not to be alone, especially in the evenings when the mourning doves began their plaint. Belle would be ironing or sewing or cleaning the house after the day's work, separated from her; there would be nothing to prevent listening to the unvaried cooing lament of the doves. Noon perhaps was best; Belle came home to eat and prepare a lunch for her. Floss had sent word that she would come by for an afternoon. The first day alone she had thought of a composition Mrs. Sutton had wanted her to memorize, but the music was demoniacal; the mean little black notes spun at her accusingly.

Quick steps sounded on the porch, the door flew open, and Robin came in as if she were dancing, but really staggering with library books, a movie magazine that Des used to bring home from trips for Stevie, a bag of peaches, a malted milk, and a tiny table that fitted over Stevie's chest and held a book on its adjustable top. This last was a wonder. Robin set it up at once, raised the top at an angle, and stood back, exclaiming.

Stevie touched it with sly pleasure and smiled more to herself than at Robin. This addition to her comfort made the bed seem even more like an island home. She knew that Robin, so taken up with the present, had no idea of the profound future meaning of this little table. Afraid that she might reveal herself, Stevie picked up one of the books, a naturalist's notebook, deliberately chosen by Robin with the hope that it might encourage Stevie to go outdoors, if only to watch for a lizard.

"The librarian said that French writers are an immoral lot!" Robin said. "So we'll have to put them off. When she dries up and blows away from absolute airy purity, you should study to get the job of librarian, Stevie! Nothing but hypocrisy gets past her eagle eye. Oh, I really shouldn't say that about her, but wouldn't you like the job?"

Ignoring this suggestion, Stevie reached under her pillow, saying, "Here are two letters from Las Vegas I hid. They must be from your great love Blackie. I'm glad *he's* gone. We'll have some peace in *that* department."

Robin felt herself trembling. She placed the letters in her purse, turning away from Stevie's sardonic gaze, and said casually, "They'll keep." She turned back and said, "Drink your malted, Stevie. See, I brought straws for you."

As on Robin's other visit, Stevie searched her sister's face for the faded bruises. Had she gone out like that? To the library? To work? But then, she had lost her job. Mama had said so. "Where did you get the money for all these things?" she asked suspiciously.

"From my last salary check."

"What will you do when it's gone?"

"Get another job. Now, don't worry. I'm on the trail of something right now — something temporary. There'll also be a few little checks coming here for news I'm sending to other papers. Watch out for my mail, will you, Stevie?"

Stevie began to drink the malted milk, feeling more assured. When Robin came the atmosphere in the room sang with a sense of life. The premonitions of doom and the hesitant longings for death faded like a night lamp still burning but ineffective in the loom of day.

"Thanks for everything," Stevie said, uncomfortably aware of the difficulty of a simple thanks, of any free expression among the four of them, except of their differences. It seemed to her that she and Robin and Des excelled in spontaneous and even clever expressions of their enmity. Belle excelled in saying exactly the wrong thing to Des when he was most ready to explode. Stevie knew just how far she could go in her insults to Des. Robin knew too. She and Des had quarreled like two master quarrelers competing. Now that the terrible violence has ended their furious word games, Stevie thought, I'll bet they'll miss each other. But, she added, still to herself, I'm sick of all this — of them — even Robin. She withdrew a little from including Robin, but only because this last was more complex, for she admired and scorned her sister, envied and criticized her, and, because she had begun to feel utterly dependent, resented her. She gulped down a mouthful of malted milk and blurted out, "I'm supposed to like them just because we're related, and we're not related at all!"

"I thought you were Papa's baby no matter what."

"Families should be *related!*" Stevie said in a desperate voice squeaky with strain.

"Why?"

"Because!"

"Why not unrelated?" Robin asked, and meant it. She felt no resentment that they were unrelated in the deepest ways to their parents and at times to each other.

"You don't even care?" Stevie said in a shocked, stern way.

"No." Robin's voice was quiet, without even her good humor or defiance.

The intimacy between them was acute, but they were not accustomed to exploring or sharing their bond by familiar confidences, and now they maintained an aching dignity in the midst of their exchange.

"Maybe," Robin said, "they feel bad that *we're* not related to them?"

"I'll bet!" Stevie said with bitterness.

"They have their side of it, too."

"Well, it doesn't bother them!"

"We don't know that. You sound so superior and snobbish."

"Well, you sound like a hypocrite! You know you don't love them."

"Yes I do — in my own way." Robin expected relatedness only in romantic love and in friendship; she would be rather uncompromising in her search for it.

"You don't love them! Say it!" Stevie demanded.

"Yes I do and you do too — only more!"

250

Stevie sat up in bed, knocking the little table over. "I do not! You love them more!" she said.

"Oh, what's the difference."

"Don't you dare say I love them more!" Stevie yelped as if she had been kicked.

When Robin saw the nervous mottled flush spreading over Stevie's face and neck, she said lightly, "Methinks ..."

Stevie lay back on her pillows and stiffened her face against the rising emotion. Then her expression cracked and broke like ice shattered by a subterranean current. Tears rolled down her cheeks, and she kept her eyes closed tight as if to deny them. "Oh," she wailed. "All my life I wanted a family!" Then she added with the same desolate emphasis, "And a house with a fence and a gate, and—Papa to be—" She held the movie magazine over her face and sobbed. The dream of spending her life with Papa was over. She was free, at last, of the dream, but not yet free of the pain.

Robin stood by the bed and smoothed Stevie's hair, saying over and over, "Poor baby, poor baby." Then she went to the kitchen and wet a cloth, and was bathing Stevie's swollen face when she saw Des coming across the vacant lot. "Here comes Papa!" she said. "Just be quiet, pretend you're napping."

Robin rushed out the front door.

The back screen banged and Stevie heard her father's quick footsteps coming straight to her room. She turned on her side, facing the wall, and held her quivering eyelids down, pretending sleep, pretending death. He waited a moment, turned, and went with quiet steps away.

TWENTY-NINE

THE NEXT EVENING, as soon as it was dark, Des went home, cutting across vacant lots, head up, feet familiar with the paths, walking as if destined, urged beyond all pride, his pride bending down like the weeds he stepped on. He did not know where this feeling had come from after these terrible weeks and months, yes, months. But here it was, an omen, a sign, his luck changed at last. Maybe it was the Boneless Woman or maybe it was just that in some ways he could see he had been wrong.

There were two oblongs of light in the house—Stevie's window and the kitchen door. He had not seen Belle for some time; they had avoided each other by the hours they kept. He went up to the screen and knocked lightly. Belle was drying dishes; she put the towel down and came to the door. Her face was in shadow. He watched her surprise and then he smiled with a kind of formal courtesy and took off his hat. "I'd like to come in, Belle," he said, still smiling.

She reached up and dropped the hook into place. "No," she said without expression.

"I won a little money last night."

She said nothing.

The glow in Stevie's window went out.

"If you'd let me come in and talk—" He felt framed in a hostile slab of light.

"You can come here when I'm not here," she said.

"I won't bother you, Belle—" He hated himself for having gotten in the position of begging; then the earlier mood returned and he said with a strange sense of satisfaction, "I guess I didn't always do right." He stood up straight. Nobody had any use for you if you whined; if you wanted to tell your troubles, you had to talk about them as if they were something to laugh about in the past, even though you were right in the middle of them. You had to have pride. But he didn't give a damn about his pride just now. It was in the way. "I'll try to do right."

"You're saying that now but you won't change. It'll be the same all over again, Des. It took me a coon's age to make up my mind, but it's made up." Her words sounded innocent, quiet.

"Why, you're as stubborn as a mule," he said in a tone of flattery.

Belle stepped back.

"Wait!"

She came nearer the screen and he looked at her through the dark mesh, wondering what he could say that would move her. It was an odd truth that no clever blarney came to his tongue. She was pretty; he hadn't noticed for a long time. She wasn't standing gracefully, he could see this; it had been a source of annoyance for years. Now he felt only compassion for a girlish awkwardness she had never quite lost. She was strong, but so small and timid, so lacking in artifice, so affectionate and agreeable, so ready to take a back seat. She would never be able to take care of herself! She needed him! A piece of her short, straight hair fell down over one eye, and the way she poked it back over her ear with one finger was so touching that he impulsively reached for the door handle, to go in, to take her in his arms, to protect her.

Alarm showed in her eyes; her whole face became afraid.

He withdrew his hand and looked away, toward Mrs. Polk's house. The eerie glimmer that every night showed in all the windows like a sickness went out. The back yard was now dark. In this privacy his enormous feelings assailed his control; the anguish, the loneliness, the heartbreaking, unendurable loneliness, the need, struck him with the awesome force of a brute. He began to sob. He stumbled forward and leaned against the screen, hearing the rusty, metallic rip as it gave. He looked up at Belle, clearly seeing her shocked expression, and he said in his voice of terrible humility, "I never loved anyone but you, it's the God's truth, I never—"

"A funny kind of love—lately," she said without malice.

"Don't—" He looked at her again. She was backing into the middle of the kitchen, as frightened as if he were threatening her.

"Go away, Des," she said in a shaking, obstinate voice.

"Is that all you have to say?"

"I can't turn back, I guess. I've got started going my own way and I can't turn back."

"I want to take care of you."

"I can take care of myself, Des," she said tiredly. "Please go away now. I've got to get up early in the morning."

He looked at her without belief. She went into the middle room, came back, and handed him one of his handkerchiefs through the broken screen.

"All these years," she said with dull resentment.

As he put on his hat and walked toward the alley, he heard a long hissing sigh behind him in the darkness of Mrs. Polk's doorway. He could not make out whether it was satisfaction or sympathy. He looked back at Belle. She had turned off the light.

He went straight to the Royal. It was not late and several men were sitting in the leather chairs, talking. Des paid no attention to them; he gave Winston the high sign and walked to the rear. On the way he glanced into the cage at Farquarson, and the clerk gave him a sullen look, bolder than he had ever dared when Des had money. Farquarson was still sore over the cut of last night's small winnings; he had told Bowman he thought Des was lying about the amount. The truth was that he hadn't used the marked cards and had played a hard game against Jim Charter and his business cronies. He had needed Blackie last night; his head was too hot; but he had beaten them and won a little money. The stingy sons-of-bitches had kept him up all night to use his room, just to gamble off a few dollars. But they knew they were beaten fair and square, that he was the better man.

Des pushed the door open into the big hotel kitchen. The night was warm and the cook and the dishwasher were out in the alley. Winston came in and smiled at him.

"You?" the porter asked, surprised.

"Yes, me."

Winston went over to a dark corner behind some food cases and brought out a pint of bonded bourbon. Des paid him and Winston went back into the lobby. Des sat down on a lard can and opened the bottle and took two quick drinks.

Bowman came in and sat down on a box. "Got thim blues, uh?"

Des couldn't answer. He handed Bowman the bottle.

"Bettah not on the job."

"That's right, Bowman." Des sat looking down at the floor,

"I hate to see yu so beat, man."

"Sometimes it's pretty hard to keep up your bluff, Bowman."

"My own bluff all wore out, Tannehill, right down to my ee-ssentials. You know," he said in calm judgment, "that damn bluff is a awful load on a man's back. Hard enough t' stan' upright without that. Yu lissen t' me yu'll git plum rid of it. Plenty o' man left, reckon yu know that."

"Thanks." Des let the old man's affection warm him for a moment and then he said, "Bowman, I'm all through."

Bowman laughed softly. "Yu ain't. Yu a young man. A year 'r two from now yu be—" He broke off and said, "It'll pass."

Des took a small drink and said, "I feel so bad I don't even want a drink."

"Well, yu got the miseries, man, they gonna stick with yu awhile yet."

"Say, Bowman, what do you think of a fellow sitting here moaning like a woman?"

"Think he jus' settin' heah moanin' like a man. Ain't nothin' t' be ashamed of."

"You know, Bowman—"

The kitchen door opened slowly and a strange man walked over and flashed his badge. Des and Bowman were startled and Bowman stood up. Des sat where he was and upended the bottle; the whiskey ran out on the floor, some of it sinking into the old wood, its fragrance thick in the warm air. He was cold sober.

"Is that some of the stuff you sold to your guests last night?"

"I had this in my pocket when I came in here tonight," Des said casually. "I came back here where I could have a quiet drink." He stood up with an easy expression on his face.

"It's against the law," the stranger said with mock patience. "I suppose I don't have to tell you that."

"I'm no bootlegger," Des said. "And you've got no evidence, unless you can use the smell." He decided to stall. "You can't find a man in this town ever bought any liquor from me. That's a serious offense; I wouldn't want to take that chance."

"Where'd you get it?" the man said, pointing to the aromatic stain on the floor.

"Over the state line."

"That's what they all say."

"Well, I'm no bootlegger and I'm no stool pigeon." His temper was rising. "You can track down your own game."

The door opened again and another stranger stood there without closing it. Des saw Farquarson leap off his stool and lock himself in the cage. Everything was clear.

"I'll have to arrest you," the stranger said, and the second one remained in the doorway as a witness.

Des turned suddenly and made for the open back door. The two men caught his arms. He twisted free of one and raised his doubled fist.

"Don't hit the law!" Bowman shouted.

There was a lull in the scuffle.

"Don't insult the law, Mister Tannehill," Bowman said formally and calmly.

The reason for Bowman's calm flashed in Des's mind, but Bowman hadn't seen what he had seen in the cage.

"No," Des said savagely. "Just bribe 'em!" He clipped one of the men neatly under the chin and flung the other one off, his powerful strength ready for action. "You won't ever put me in jail *here!*" he said, wanting to fight. "Or anyplace else!" He saw Bowman behind the one man waving his long arms impatiently. Des backed through the door, colliding with the cook and the dishwasher, and ran swiftly down the alley.

The wan light in the street at the alley's end was like a blaze to reveal him. He slowed, stepped out on the sidewalk, and turned in the direction of Jail Park and home. He couldn't go home! The realization nearly stopped him. Keep your head, he said to himself, and crossed over into the continuing alley, walking fast in this strange place, avoiding the dim shapes of empty kegs and boxes stacked behind the stores. An alley cat slithered past, pursued by another. His foot caught in a circle of wire and he nearly fell. He swore.

The angling side street was deserted except for a boy and girl dancing together on the shadowed walk while a portable phonograph at their feet softly played "Sweet Sue." Des passed them, ignoring and ignored, and, part way along the block, entered a narrow passageway and climbed a steep flight of stairs. The elderly hotel clerk was at the window watching the dancers, and Des went down the hall as if he were a resident. He could see the iron fire escape through the open door at the end of the passage, but he could hardly see the numbers on the doors. When he came to 21 he knocked delicately, urgently. There was no answer. He knocked again.

"Who is it?"

"Queenie!" he whispered, close to the door. "It's me!"

"What do you want?"

"Let me in!"

256

"Leave me alone, will you? Go away!"

"Queenie, I'm in trouble!"

"So am I!"

"Real trouble!" he whispered.

The key was turned, the door jerked open, and he went in quickly. She closed the door and stood back looking at him, her eyes like flares.

"The law's after me," he said in a low, confiding voice. "I queered myself with Jim Charter, and I think the bastard gave Farquarson a few dollars to tip off the law the first chance he got. I was having a drink tonight and Farquarson had his chance, a frame-up for bootlegging."

"Well, what next?" Robin said, more in anger than despair.

"By God, I don't know." He pushed his hat back. His hair was damp. She looked at his hands. "I suppose you hit somebody."

"I wouldn't have, but two of them jumped me. I didn't hurt him."

"That won't make much difference if they catch you."

"I don't care any more," he said forlornly.

"Well, why are you running, then?" she asked coolly.

He ignored that and said, "Queenie, I've got to hide out till I can get away."

She locked the door. "Sit down. You see what I've got here. A bed, a chair, and a table."

He was embarrassed. He thought he ought to tell her he was sorry about the beating but he could not. Better not to mention it.

"Somehow I never thought you'd leave," she said. "I want to get away myself—my reporter job is gone."

Des looked at her with suspicion and then he said, "I *have* to leave, Queenie, you know that."

"Who's going to take care of Stevie?" she asked, looking directly into his eyes. "All her life, maybe?"

"I guess you'll have to look out for her."

"Papa, you shouldn't do this to me! I haven't even got started."

"That's the way things happen."

"I want to help Stevie. It isn't that. But Stevie—"

"Poor old Stevie. Life's too tough for her."

"She's decided to be an invalid. She's that afraid! I want her to live her life, but *she doesn't want to.*" Robin walked over to the window and looked out, speaking softly, speaking with love, "I *want* to live my life!

I read it somewhere, and I didn't know what it meant"—her voice changed and burned with rebellion— "'the tyranny of the invalid.'"

"You mustn't talk like that. She'll come out of it someday. You can't keep the Tannehills down," he said with shaky pride.

"That's all right for you to say; you're leaving. And Mama knows that Stevie is a papa's girl. Stevie just wanted you, and if it isn't you, it's me. Maybe she doesn't even love me, I don't know; she needs me. And right now I don't want to be needed." Robin kept looking out the window, speaking toward the street below, seeing the dancers and feeling hypnotized by the slow identical rhythm of their enfolded bodies. "Stevie loved you, and when that stopped, she stopped in her tracks. She'll have to learn all over again." Robin felt the strain of meeting Des after the violence, as if she had only now realized his presence.

"If I make any money I'll send it to you for Stevie."

"You know you won't, Papa," she said without accusation.

"Well, you can't ever tell," he said dreamily.

They felt drugged with the shock and the sorrow of the days just past. They did not speak, and in the stillness they listened to the staccato footsteps of someone walking by on the street below.

"As soon as this blows over," Des went on then, "you can get some kind of job here."

"I don't intend to stay here."

"Where the hell are you going?" he said, forgetting himself, and added in his thoughts, where the hell is that Blackie? "Where are you going?" he repeated with his own natural courtesy.

In spite of her unwavering resolve against him, this admission of his respect—for that is what it was—nearly undid her. She dared not look at him, but she felt her strength and in it her compassion rising like a stream of clear water rushing over the dry, stony bed of her anger.

"I'm going away, Papa." She was speaking tenderly. "I'm going away and work on newspapers, and I'm—"

"What about Stevie?" he said.

"I'll take her along. If I have to take care of Stevie, I will, but it won't stop me."

"We both can't leave now, and, by God, I've got to!"

"You can go first. We'll stay with Mama until she's all set."

"See that you do."

Robin swung away from the window and faced him. Her old anger slyly rose up again. "I like your orders!"

"I said, see that you do," he spoke evenly.

"It's odd how responsible you are when you're free!"

"All right! All right! I've got nothing to say to you any more about what you do!"

"You certainly have not!" she said, and sat down in the chair at the table. "And how did you know where I am, even the room?"

"I can find out a few things," he said arrogantly.

The clear, sharp talk cut through the tortured air between them.

She folded a letter she had written to Blackie and placed it in her purse with the letters she had received from him. Then she moved again to the window and stood looking down into the placid, empty street. The boy and the girl had gone. Long night shadows reached across the pavement and lapped over the shop fronts on the other side. A fork of distant lightning flashed on the metal towers of wheat elevators along the railroad tracks. She thought of Blackie. The calliope music still seemed to drift across the plain. It added to the sense of unbearable isolation she had felt in all the little towns for as long as she could remember.

From his seat on the bed Des studied Robin at the window with her back to him. She appeared fragile. But she was out of the nest. She couldn't wait to get out. That was nature. Stevie had all her pinfeathers but she was dragging her wings. "I wonder *why?*" he said, half aloud.

"What?" Robin asked.

"Nothing." Now, by God, that was against nature. Even the Boneless Woman, that poor lonesome lump, had got out into the world, had turned her trouble into something she could take pride in. What would ever happen to Stevie? She had no bluff, no epidermis, no protective coloring. This made him think with renewed fright of jail, and he began to walk around in the small room.

After a while he called Robin to listen, speaking very low. "This is the night that Bowman gets off at two o'clock. I'll tell you what I want you to do."

She nodded; she had been waiting for him to form a plan.

"You go down to Dirty Spoon to Bowman's house." He told her how to find it. "You wait there till he comes home to be sure you'll see him tonight. Just sit on the porch; you won't have to wait long."

"What shall I tell him?"

"Ask him to come uptown a little early tomorrow and see if he can get me a night ride on a truck going west."

"How?"

"Don't worry about that. He knows where the long-haul truckers hang out. Some of them like to have riders; they get lonesome going across the desert. It might take him a day or two, or he might get me a ride tomorrow night. He can let me know here."

"Am I to be the messenger?"

"No, by God, they'll catch me sure. You go about your business as if nothing had happened while I hide out here. You just bring me something to eat, a loaf of bread, some cheese, and a sack of apples."

"How will he let you know?" she asked.

"That's none of your business. We have ways."

"Good."

"Tell Bowman just to send me word of which night, nothing else. But he's to tell the trucker where to pick me up. I can't show myself here in the main part of town. I'll wait at the house, from dark on. I want to see Stevie once more. Have you got everything straight?"

"Yes."

"Now don't say anything to anybody!"

"Do you think I'm an idiot?"

"I'll sleep while you're out," he said. "You can sleep tomorrow. You'd better tell your mother to pack my clothes and gambling stuff."

A sense of secret excitement hung over their thoughts, crowding out the reality of events. No matter what he might feel when alone, she was sure now that he was finding pleasure in being pursued and outwitting his pursuers. He was afraid only of being caught. Some of his mood became a part of her own.

"Now, listen here, Queenie, you'd better go get that Garrison boy to go down there with you. You'll be out late."

"I've been out late before," she said with an edge on her voice.

Des walked back and forth without saying anything.

"Besides," she went on, "Chris has troubles enough from trying to be a good friend to me."

"You could catch Bowman as he leaves the hotel, but I'm afraid someone will see you and that damn law will be up here after me."

"Listen, Papa, being out in the dark in Apache is the least of my worries."

"I guess you get that from me," he said.

She smiled at him for the first time; he hesitated and smiled back. She opened the door very quietly and went out.

THIRTY

A SPENT STORM was passing over and a tangy wind was blowing off the plain. Low clouds moved swiftly, their violence broken, revealing a thin moon's luster in high serenity above the storm. Between the night horizon and the somber sky a pearl-white radiance waited for the shimmer of distant lightning.

Robin walked on the country road just beyond the town. The wind blew hard against her, seizing her breath, whipping her hair and her clothes, leaving her spirits turbulent with the residue of the crucial years in Apache. She tried to separate and understand the events, but they were indivisible, especially those connected with Des and Blackie. After so much anguish pressed into so brief a time in which she had observed herself surviving and learned to conceal the pain, she thought she had grown old. But last night and tonight her youth had come back, changed; her young heart quivered again with uncertain answers and grand longings, with reckless confidence and wild pain. She had thought herself dead and resigned, but she was alive and aching in every nerve of grief for the two men she had loved. No matter how much she wished them gone and out of her life, she could not relinquish them until their meaning was clear. Would that be never, or tomorrow?

Belle and Stevie, wounded deeply, had their brief hate to protect them at this acute time; their hate, which had wounded Des in return; their hate, which would dissolve in time, adding its own scars. Belle had her new place in Apache, and her hope. Stevie, with her inordinate need of love, fearfully rejecting its very promise, had only her despair, already limiting her life by a demand for perfection in place of the illusion of it she had lost. She, Robin, was hurt less, far less, because Des had not been able to reach her, not even with blows; they had met in savage equality and laid down their arms. They had fury between them, but no hate; under the pretended indifference flowed some recognition, intuitive and sure. Blackie had been like the word *love* of their silence, not to be spoken. They had centered on him, and poor Blackie, she thought, in innocence of their combat, had loved them both and been driven away.

She pushed Blackie out of her thoughts and went over again last night's talk with Bowman as they sat together on his neat porch in Dirty

Spoon. He was silent a long time after she had asked him about the truck ride for Des; she could hear his solemnity through the dark.

"I been expectin' it, I been knowin' it in my bones." He said he would arrange with a trucker; and then he told her about Des's eye. He knew all about it—that the sight was gone. Had Des told him? No. He knew.

She drew in her breath, and he, thinking she was going to cry, said sharply, "But it ain't jes' his eye!"

"I know that," she said in a low, awed voice, and Bowman's tone softened.

"O' cos, he can't see the marks and he need to see 'em, 'cause he ain' no fella with a weakness for gamblin'. Gamblin' his business, I reckon."

"Both," she said. "He started when he was a little boy. Another little boy would have delivered groceries, but Papa gambled."

"He *did?*" Bowman exclaimed with admiration. "Now, that little scamp was already lookin' for somepen more outa life than groceries!"

"But all this couldn't happen from his eye alone," she said, as if she were dreaming back.

"Only if it's our own eye," Bowman said, shaming her.

"But the way he's changed! It's a lot, Bowman. Maybe you don't know all that."

"I knowed."

"Then, what do you think?"

"Oh, it's more'n you and me'll ever think."

"Yes, but I wish I knew."

"Well, one trouble is, Mistah Tannehill a clean man in a dirty business."

She said nothing.

"An' seems like for some time now, it got to eatin' into his self-respeck. Somepen eatin' into it, anyway."

"Why didn't he give it up, then?"

"His self-respeck clean et up before he knowed it." Bowman studied a bit. "No. He got a *little* left. Tanny ain' gonna *never* have *none.*"

"I hope not!"

"Oh, man," Bowman said in deep sadness, "Us humans is confoundin' to one another!"

When she left Bowman last night, she tried to convince herself that she had the rest of her life to figure out what had really happened to them all, the Tannehills who had wandered around from town to town in four states, keeping close together and apart, unrelated to their neighbors and finally to themselves

But here tonight she was walking on this country road because there was no place else where she could be sure of being alone; and because she felt "at home" outdoors in the night and the wind. Yet she had a sense of waiting. She looked at her watch but could not see the time. Her watch would not reveal it properly anyway. A watch, no matter how fine, with even one small defective part, might cease to run. And again, there were watches of poorer quality that ran on and on, losing or gaining, yet keeping time.

But a man was more than a watch.

Two seed-full puffballs flew by on the wind, scattering their seeds—each seed so complex, so finally unknown, containing in some destined form the image of its maturity; dependent on and effected by the soil, the air, the sun, the rain, the warmth and cold; endangered by the chance hoof, the eyeless foot, the grasping hand, the worldly wheel that could crush or cripple it before its cycle was complete. Here was the new seed in multiple possibility persuaded by the very wind on which it flew, the heads-or-tails of earth on which it fell.

But a man was more than a weed.

And yet, how exceptional was a weed! How then, was she to know herself, her father, Blackie, her mother, her sister? She felt stranded. Wouldn't a sensible person forget it all? No! If you forgot it in your thoughts, you remembered it in your bones. Forgetting or remembering didn't matter; you had to go on in your fashion, as they were all about to do, were already doing.

Once, on the eastern slope of the Rockies, she had seen a cedar tree that a man had slashed with an ax and left standing. The cedar had formed an ugly, knotty scab of bark, and sent out a branch—for balance, perhaps, or survival, and its symmetry was changed. But *this* was the tree she had looked at, admired, and understood. As ancient, as new as tonight's wind, it spoke to her now from that other time, and she listened knowingly, one with the tree. Stevie heard many things others could not, but such a voice signaled her in vain. Belle obeyed without hearing. Blackie heard in his own way, she felt sure. But Des?

He had lost half his sight; had he lost half his hearing? Where and in what time of his years had he lost them? Once or gradually? And why?

Why? It was the way Bowman had said—no one could know the whole truth of himself or another.

And suddenly this was more like a stimulant than a sorrowful fact. One accepted the wind one could not see—and never expected to see—but men explored endlessly the winds of the world. They gave them names and studied their ways. The purpose was necessary to the pursuit, but only the search was living.

The burdensome wrath against Des began to seep out of her; the vibrating fever against him abated. Understanding might be years away, but the process had begun. A clarity loomed in her that was not indifference, or even forgiveness, but a peaceful removal from that night and all its now lucid meaning.

She felt clear of him, and related to him at last.

But never, never, would any man place an angry hand upon her; she'd see to that in some subtle feminine way yet to be known, already sensed. This was no resolution of revenge (there was no revenge in her), but an unwavering elation of what she was and what she was free to be.

The urging whistle of the 10:22 came through the night. She began to walk fast toward the station, which was not far away, closed and dark. She passed its brick platform and climbed the embankment to the tracks, and went along the ties toward the distant beckoning of the train—this train that more than any other, as she and Chris agreed, linked them with the outside world.

She held her hand against her pocket, where she had placed the money and the letter from Blackie, a fine letter which she would keep and reread, a love letter for which she would never have to make excuses. She would never tell Blackie that Des had beaten her in rage against the two of them together—and himself. Des was his luminary.

The postscript said, "I'll wire Tanny after I hear from you." Did that mean he expected her refusal, or that he would tell Des the truth if she came? It did not matter. She was not going. She closed her eyes and thought of Blackie with such passionate longing that the low vibration droning through the rails was like a part of her emotion.

"Blackie!" she called into the wind, softly, intensely. "Blackie, I love you! Please, please hear me!" It seemed to her in this moment of avowal that he would hear.

She was glad to give way to this love, to say to herself aloud, without shame, that, gambler and cheat, she loved him truly. She wanted him to know. She was glad at last to acknowledge her will for what it was, under her quivering love—sly, cool, dangerous, and shattering, her will that strengthened and broke her heart.

"Blackie!" she called, "Blackie, I love you! You asked me to say it—I'm saying it now!" Her words blew away on the wind.

The low, mourning voice of the train came again. The rails sang. Robin walked back on the ties, turning to wait, her loneliness as searching as the call of the train. She thought that no music, no song would ever speak for her spirit as truly as the wind, and the beckoning and farewelling call of a train going through lonely places.

She had come here with her secret, to tell it to no one. "It's a mean, low trick, but I'll do it. I'll take the money Blackie sent me to join him, and go where I want to go—and work. I've got to! I can take Stevie too. I'll write Blackie tonight and explain it all, and he'll forgive me because he loves me." She felt ashamed.

The beam of the locomotive burst through the dark. She saw herself leaving—free, free!—in a fantasy that would soon come true . . .

She set fire to a twisted newspaper and swung it back and forth like a lantern to flag the through train. The signal came in answer, brief and tolerant. She dropped the burning paper, covering it swiftly with gravel, and stamped out the flames.

The rails gleamed in the long headlight, their humming lost in the big, intense life of the train. Robin went down the embankment and stood clear.

She picked up her bag and stepped off the track, going along near the roadbed to watch for a door that would open like a flash in the stately pause.

The train was long and powerful, headed for far places.

She was shaking with joy, wonderful joy! The engine was rushing toward her, breathing its great breath, braking its speed, slowing. A chain of plaintive sounds traveled through the machinery from one car to the next, protesting and lamenting at this unscheduled halt, and ended with a strained singing resonance of steel against steel. She heard the metal door open, the tense wait, a porter's voice calling into the dark; she saw herself stepping up, the door slammed shut, heard the wheels turning, gathering speed, resuming rhythm.

The swift cars thundered over the plain like a stampede of night-black horses, their shining coats and wild manes flying by. Not this train, she said in her mind, not this night, and, with impenitent desire and grief, not this love *ever!*

She started walking gravely back. Around her she felt the vast, hard land like a solitary and longing presence possessed by the wind that was always going away.

Something she thought of made her hurry, a feeling of something unresolved. She began to run. She reached the sidewalk and kept running, her swift steps making a cadence on the stone.

Des sat on the low porch, waiting. His traveling bag was just, inside the door. Bowman had said when he brought the message about the ride, "That ol' hotel gonna be plum dead when you gone." They hadn't said much; they both felt too bad.

Des peered through the night at the silent bundle that was Stevie sitting in the rocking chair on the lawn. He had wrapped her in a quilt and brought her out here. She hadn't even asked him where he would go. Maybe she felt bad too. Maybe not.

He had only a little money in his pocket—the least he had ever had for a trip. He needed to beat somebody out of enough to get a good suit and go to Nevada to work in a gambling house till spring. He might save a nubbin and search for a place to run a game. Or he might have to keep on working till he ended up in some little joint as a shill—as low as a gambler could get, by God. But he could still deal blackjack with one clear eye, or work at the wheel; nothing smaller any more. He might get into a good place if he could get dressed up. He was still a handsome man with a winning way—so they said. But, hell, that was no life for a real gambler. The routine was tiresome, dealing long hours for a daily wage with no cuts in the game. The weekly average never came near what a man could win gambling on his own in regular times. It was a *job*. He knew he'd never stay with it. He'd end up a drifter. He couldn't bear to look beyond that. And there wasn't a damn soul in the world to give a good goddamn. That Boneless Woman must have been a Jonah.

"What're you thinking about, Steve?"

"I was watching the leaves when it lightnings. But it's too dark now. I can only hear them. The first ones are falling. Like me."

"That's only the wind blowing them off!" He was irritated by her self-pity, glad that he had felt no such unattractive emotion. Or had he? "It's a long time till winter. But, Stevie, you've got to stay out of that damn bed. I won't be here next winter to keep the fire going. The Queen and the Princess will be out to work."

Stevie said nothing. He felt her antagonism, and he could not understand it.

Belle was still behaving as if she were afraid of him; she had run off down the alley to her friend Penny, the Christian recruiter, who didn't know God from Santa Claus. Right in the middle of packing his bag. He was cleaning and oiling the revolver; that was all he was doing. Belle began to tremble and cry and she ran out the back door without even saying good-bye after all these years. He had a notion to fire through the ceiling or over her head just for the hell of it, but he remembered just in time that he was a fugitive; and he didn't want to be caught with a gun. He'd pawn it someplace and never reclaim it. Or maybe he'd keep it. Who knows?

"Maybe I'll turn into a desperado," he said aloud, but Stevie made no comment. Hell, I'm no highjacker, he said to himself. I'm a gambler, a tinhorn gambler on the skids. But a gambler just the same. Belle wanted a businessman. He had gone to the door to call her back and explain about the gun, but it was pleasant to see her frightened after the other night and the stubborn way she had repeated "No" through the screen. When he had finished packing his clothes he had tossed the gun into the bag. From now on, he had thought, what the hell.

He could not distinguish Stevie's expression in the thin dark, but he recalled the look she gave him when he came to pick up his belongings and wait for the trucker. Her mouth had trembled and turned down and her eyebrows were askew in a nervous frown. Both he and Belle came of good strong stock; he wondered why his girls were so delicate and high-strung.

"Whatdoyousay, Stevie?"

There was no answer.

The wind whirled dust against his shoes. He listened to the grains tick on the leather. He thought of this country he had known so long, and he was leaving it forever. He liked the wind and this wide gray land, open as far as the eye could see, like a barrierless world. It would be the mountains now instead of the high, free plains. He would have to get used to them, although he would feel shut in, the way he had felt when he went to the Rockies.

He took a rapid stock of his life, as he had heard that a drowning man does before he goes down. "Hell's fire!" he said aloud.

Stevie's voice came out of the gloom. "Don't start that again!"

"I was just thinking."

This was a year to remember. Perhaps he would buy a little notebook in which to write the dates of important happenings in his life. His father and grandfathers had kept such books, filled with storms, panics, crops and failures, all such events that did not fit properly into the record sheets of the Bible. He would have to list winnings and losses, the piano, the divorce, Stevie's odd sickness, and Robin's leaving home. And the date of his own departure. The gunshot nick in his hand, healed now but tender. Not so good for a notebook. He thought of the generations behind him and how, in the last few, they had come steadily down in the world, even when they were good men and women. Down in money. He had tried to live in their world and his own, because he could never live completely in one or the other. Now he would be the first of his people to break off, to slip into that shadowy society of wasted men.

He lowered his face into the cup of his hands, and Stevie thought he was crying.

"Has the world turned against you?" she asked with desolate mockery.

"To hell with the world!" he said in a low voice. "It don't give a damn about people!"

"Aren't we part of the world? Although I doubt if I am."

"Well, you mustn't talk like that," he said, ignoring her question.

Running steps sounded on the walk. That must be Robin. She was always running and almost a woman. He would have to tell her to be a little more ladylike. No, he wouldn't tell her anything. His thoughts warmed at memories of the little girl Robin, who liked wandering around in the night so that they had to search for her, who had cried when he scolded her and fought when he punished her; and of Stevie, who had adored him and been frightened of anything that threatened to separate her from him. He smiled at her dependence. Well, Robin would take his place with Stevie now. He felt jealous and relieved. He was glad there would be no one but himself to look out for.

Robin came out of the darkness of the trees, up the walk, and lightly onto the splintered porch.

"Hello, Stevie," she said, panting. "Hello, Papa."

He thought her voice concealed a sign of grief. He looked at her but he could see her face only as if through a veil. She had a strange, luminous beauty sometimes. Even if she was his daughter he had to think it; she was proud but she wasn't vain.

"You should have been a man," he said uneasily.

"No. I like being a woman."

"You'll get in trouble."

"Of course, but I'll get out."

Stevie sighed. Were they going to start arguing again, even at the very last?

Robin sat down on the grass. They were all quiet, listening to the night sounds. A boy's voice carried from a long way off. Dogs barked. Motors started and throbbed on other streets. Their own street was dark and still. A door slammed. Mrs. Garrison's steps went out on her porch, then back inside. Maybe she was lonely or troubled. Chris had got a temporary night job with an enemy of Jim Charter's. The wind had gone down and a sudden gust brushed through the trees.

My clothes are in bad shape, Des thought. Aloud, he said gaily to Stevie, "Pard, the next time you see your old dad he'll be dressed up like a million dollars. I want to see you educated by then. I want to be proud of you!"

"Uh-huh," Stevie replied in irony.

He wondered if he would ever see them again.

"Remember these things," he said, and he gave them like a parting gift old warnings of insurmountable obstacles. It seemed to him clear for a moment that he was leaving behind him on their lives the scars of his own thrashing about in the fury of his enormous energy defeated. But they're young, he thought; they'll get over it.

Stevie leaned her head wearily against the back of the chair and gazed into the utter darkness of the tree. Why did he live his own life with such gusto and try to frighten them?

"Remember these things!" Des repeated.

"Why?" Robin asked. "They may never happen."

"I'll be long gone by then."

"It won't be all bad," Robin said. "It's wonderful to be alive!"

"That's the truth, Stevie!" Des began to feel more cheerful. "That bed will get the best of you and you'll never have any future."

"I don't want any future. I'd rather be—"

"Don't you let me hear you talking about being dead!"

"Isn't it too late for that? You've—"

"By God," he interrupted her, stunned by the accusation and determined not to hear it spoken. "By God!" He was angry now. "You can't get out of living by blaming it all on me!"

"That's where you're wrong," Stevie said satirically. A vast, cold waste of loneliness, and obligation without meaning, was all she could envision. Her body and mind ached with the pain and fear of it. "Maybe I can't get out of existing, but I *can* get out of living! Tell me some more about *life,* Papa. It's your last chance."

He sat in dazed silence, receiving her blows. They seemed to him unjust; he could not accept them, but he knew they would rankle in him the rest of his days. If he had injured them—his beloved Stevie most of all—he was also setting them free. And he was injured too. He was destroyed. This final, ominous knowledge staggered him. Was it true? And why? How had it happened? He didn't give a damn. The desperate silence spread in him until it was immense, a single feeling: *to hell with everything.*

The big lights of the truck swung round the corner a block away and lashed into the dark street. Des rose and brought his traveling bag from the living room. He stepped onto the lawn. Robin stood beside him. She wanted to tell him that perhaps she understood him a little, that their trouble was over and done with, that ...

The truck driver slowed, looking for the house number.

Des looked at Robin as if he were going to speak.

The truck stopped, vibrating and shaking. The driver sounded the impersonal horn. Des hesitated, then went over to Stevie, bent down, kissed her cheek. She turned her face away. He bent a second time, as if to make sure of remembrance.

"Good-by," she said, as if to force him away.

"Be a good girl," he said, and his face crumpled up; the tears came and he wiped them away with the back of his hand. He sobbed once, stood erect, and drew a long breath.

Robin had divided the money and placed half in the envelope from Blackie on which, under a street light, she had written his name and address and a quick note to Des.

She would give Blackie back to Papa and Papa back to Blackie. She had that power.

Des's voice came sure again. "Tell your mother I won't bother her any more. She needn't worry."

"Here," Robin said, very low.

"What's that?"

"A message for you."

"How'd you get it?"

"Oh," she said as he had said last night to her, "we have our ways."

"The devil you say."

"Open it later."

They said no more, estranged by their separate and sudden griefs.

He turned away, blinded by hot tears, and walked fast along the broken walk. He stumbled once and swore. When he reached the curb he looked back, past Robin to the dark shape on the lawn, whose edges now blended into the night. He got into the truck. The driver shifted to low gear and stepped on the gas, creating a rush of harsh sound. Des leaned from the cab and shouted above the mounting roar of the powerful motor, in his old spirited voice that shook only a little.

"Good-by, Sprouts. Here goes my bottom card!"

The truck pulled away, rumbling along slowly at first, gathering speed in the second block. Robin ran to the curb. Her eyes held to the small red tail light jolting in the dark. It was all she could see on the night street, that lonely and angry eye; then it too was gone as the truck turned into the highway going west.

She went back and lifted Stevie with an effort almost beyond her strength and carried her into the house. The whole of Stevie's misery was not fully known to her; and her self was partly hidden from Stevie; but they were bound together by their common experience and by Des's default. She was aware of a hesitant fear at the first long, weighted flight, but this so mingled with her sense of living that she had no need to resist it. Beyond the thicket of tonight's emotions there was an irresistible little clearing of happiness at the thought of the prospective journey. Stevie would get out of bed in order to leave. Further than that, except for the knowledge of her own resilience, Robin could only guess. A few months' work here of any kind would add the needed money. She knew she must go. She was impelled like the seed to fly and fall and burst its shell; to free the image of her small and changing destiny, as fixed and unfixed as that of every living thing.

"He didn't kiss *you*," Stevie said as Robin dropped her onto the bed. The wistful triumph in her tone was childish and clear.

Robin had no reply. She wanted to go back to her room for one more night, to be alone to write Blackie of what she had done.

"Good night," she said. "Sleep tight."

They heard Belle come in the back and lock the door that had always been open for Des.

CPSIA information can be obtained
at www.ICGtesting.com
Printed in the USA
BVHW081215090620
581035BV00003B/284